SANTA CLAUS REBOOTED & REVAMPED

JEFF MALPHURS

Table of Contents

For Zoe & Jillian...
Forever my Moonlight Lady and Sweet Baby Mine

SANTA CLAUS REBOOTED & REVAMPED

SANTA CLAUS
REBOOTED

BOOK 1

Prologue

The world in solemn stillness lay...

As snow falls on a medieval village in what is now known as Türkiye. An old man, well into his 90s, is the sole person out on the dark and narrow cobblestone street. The rhythmic plunk of his cane and the shuffle of his leather shoes are the only sounds in the otherwise silent night. He protects his thin frame, emaciated by age, with a black, hooded overcoat, but he shivers still. His beard, as white as the new fallen snow around him, cascades down the front of his coat to the middle of his chest. His long, red stocking cap, with its end that drapes down next to his beard, adds the only color to the otherwise black and white landscape.

Not all cities of the Middle Ages were as big as Rome or Constantinople, so not all houses of worship were large, elaborate temples like the Pantheon and the Hagia Sophia. Some towns were tiny, such as this particular village. Some houses of worship were small and humble because they were for a relatively new religion called Christianity. Such is the chapel where the old man stops. Beside the chapel is a courtyard, enclosed by an iron fence. In the courtyard is a Nativity scene. It is the village's only decoration to signify the Christmas season.

Even compared to modern displays, the Nativity scene is intricate, especially in contrast to the chapel and the village. There is a modest stable constructed from scrap wood, but that is nearly invisible against the ornate four and a half feet tall white marble statues of Mary, Joseph, and the three Wise Men. A smaller statue of the Baby Jesus, also marble, is in a kindling cradle and is the real star of the scene. It is so expertly carved and realistic that it seems as though it were created by a Renaissance Master, though the Renaissance would not arrive for nearly a thousand years. The Baby Jesus's arms are outstretched toward the heavens, like an infant just learning to reach up for his mother. Or, perhaps, his Father. Real goats and sheep meander through the display. During the rest of the year, the courtyard is their home. In this season, however, they are bit players in the drama the statues are telling.

The old man shuffles up to the fence around the courtyard and opens the creaky gate. He's breathless with the exertion it took to get this far, but he moves on, eager to get to the statues. A sheep trots to him and rubs against his leg. He stumbles, but steadies himself against the fence. The old man chuckles in spite of himself.

He struggles into the midst of the Nativity scene, his tall frame towering over the statues. He stops in front of the smallest of them, the Baby Jesus. He opens his coat to reveal a gray wool tunic. From a pocket of the tunic, he removes a cloth and stoops to brush the new fallen snow from the baby's angelic face, revealing eyes so realistic, they look as though life burns within them.

The old man speaks in a frail, raspy voice. "Hello again. Has it been a year already? Time has certainly been kinder to you, my holy infant so tender and mild."

He kneels beside the statue of the baby as best he can. His movements are slow and laborious. A sheep wanders too close and bumps him again. The old man chuckles once more as he pets the sheep on the head. He reaches into his coat and retrieves a small leather satchel. From it, he withdraws a handful of quarter-sized lemon cakes, which are baked hard like cookies.

"There you go, fellow. A biscuit for you and a few for your friends." He tosses a handful of sweets a few feet away. The other sheep and goats run to them.

"Now, dash away. Dash away." He shoos the sheep beside him with a gentle wave of his hand. When the sheep sees the other animals swarming the treats, it runs to join.

The old man turns his attention back to the statue.

"A lean year for the children, unfortunately. The coffers are bare and getting around to their homes is not as easy as it used to be." The old man pauses to catch his breath. Finally, when he has his wind, he sighs with deep resignation. "For the first time ever, I hired someone to help with the distribution of what little I had to give. I paid him as well as

I could, but he took the gifts he was meant to deliver and disappeared. 'Twas a shame actually. He was a good boy as a tot."

The Baby Jesus statue, its face of heavenly peace directed skyward into the gloomy night, collects more snow. The old man brushes it away. As he does, there is a brief slip of a shadow among the other statues. The old man looks up to a space between Joseph and Mary. He watches for a moment, but there isn't anything there.

A goat ambles beside the old man. It brushes him too hard in its zealous search for more snacks and forces him off balance. He falls to his side and his hip gives a sickening crack. It's loud enough to scare the goat away. The old man grunts, the great pain in his hip turning his easy smile into an agonizing grimace.

He rolls to his back, hoping to ease the searing pain. His anguish seems to fade as he looks to the Baby Jesus again. Shaking, he reaches toward the baby's hand to hold the little marble fingers.

"Our last meeting, I'm afraid." His easy smile returns. "It is sufficient to meet my fate by your side."

There is a sudden patter of feet on the cobblestone outside the courtyard. The old man turns his head to look. A young girl no more than seven years old runs to the gate and peers in. She sees the old man sprawled in the snow, his hand still reaching up to hold the statue's finger. Like the old man, she wears a long, dark overcoat. Her hood is up to protect her from the deepening freeze, but her face beams with a sweet innocence known only to children.

She turns to someone behind her. "Father! Do you see what I see?" She spins back to the old man. "I'll help you! I'm coming!"

She pushes the gate open, a mere twenty feet away. From behind her, a man comes into view. "Stop! Don't go in there!" It is her father's deep voice and she stops abruptly. He walks up beside her, reaches around her, and closes the gate.

"He's hurt! We have to help him!" she pleads with her father, her large brown eyes welling with tears.

"He is too far gone. Besides, there is no reward in it. Come along." The girl's father ushers her away from the gate.

"But he has helped us before and now he needs us!" She spins from under her father's hand and runs back to the gate. The old man, his face collecting snowflakes like the statue of Baby Jesus, sees the concerned stare of the young girl.

The father grabs her by the arm, a little too roughly. "He is a peasant and a waste of his years! He should be a rich man but has squandered his money!"

"He gave it all to others! To us and people like us!"

"Not tonight, he didn't. Now we can't afford a Christmas goose and we shall be without. Come. Nature must do its work and it isn't for a child to witness."

The father shepherds the girl away, but she looks back with a sympathetic glance. The old man manages to smile at her. His own sweet expression, one as innocent and compassionate as the child's, says many things at once.

Listen to your father. I'll be okay. Merry Christmas.

His eyes relay the message and hers say she understands. She turns and follows her father down the cobblestone street, away from the church and its courtyard. The old man watches her go, then turns back to Baby Jesus.

"The ground is cold, dear infant. I am ready if you'll allow it." His voice fades as the strength saps away from his body with his remaining heat.

From behind one of the marble Wise Men, there is a shadow again. Then, a small man emerges. He is the same size as the figures. Though smaller than a normal man, he is perfectly proportioned. He steps in front of the old man, as if from thin air. He wears a Highwayman-style overcoat. Its raised high collar covers his face and reaches nearly to the edges of his tricorn hat.

The small man kneels before the old man. With a gentle touch, he helps the old man sit up. The old man winces as the broken bones in his hip grind against each other.

"Thank you for your kindness," rasps the old man. The small man steps back, merely a black silhouette in the grayness of the night.

He drops his collar to reveal his youthful face. He has a dark complexion and sharp features. When he speaks, his voice is high-pitched, but strong, like that of an early teenager. His accent is unlike any the old man has heard before. "The thanks should go to you."

The old man squints through the thin layer of snow on his face, trying to get a better look at the person before him. "Do I know you?"

"No, but I know you. You are the Wonderworker, the Christmas Eve Saint. On the twenty-fourth of December, for countless years, you have slipped a silver coin in the sock of every child who leaves one pinned to their front door."

The old man huffs with defeat. "I did not have enough for all of them tonight. They will be so disappointed." "Most likely it is the parents who are disappointed, as I'm sure many of them stole your gift to their children." The small man motions in the direction that the father and his daughter went. "That much is obvious, I'd say."

"Wherever the money ended up, it served the children in some way."

"Your charity has left you penniless."

"The Christmas Eve silver I passed to children, and their families perhaps, was not charity. It was never mine to clench in my fist." The old man turns to the statue of Baby Jesus again. "It was His."

"You revere Him as if you knew Him."

"I do." The old man touches his coat in the spot just over his gigantic heart. "He steers my heart and guides my actions. I don't worship this beautiful statue. It is simply a stand-in for the real man who came here to show us all how to live."

He gazes at the figure again. "But I must admit, I have to remind myself that this child is not alive. It's so majestic, I feel that sometimes I can see its chest rise in breath." The old man peers at the small man. "It is a miraculous piece of art, given to this village anonymously by its sculptor. I would guess something as beauteous as this comes from glorious Athens, perhaps even ancient Babylon before it, were it not for its subject matter. It was placed here on Christmas Eve many years ago and never explained."

"It was a gift to you, given as a reward for all you do and have done. Not the Christmas Eve errands but the meaningful missions you did the rest of the year."

"Did you know the sculptor?" The old man perks up with new interest.

The small man smirks. "What if I told you, it took me less than a day. Not just the baby." He motions toward the other sculptures. "All of them."

"That can't be." The old man shakes his head.

The small man replies, "I'm very efficient with my hands."

"Maybe," the old man chuckles with doubt. "But it couldn't have been you because it was left here nearly four decades ago. You are barely an adult. Besides, you can't know so much about me. We've never even met."

"Perhaps not. But I've been watching you from afar."

The old man turns back to the Baby Jesus and swipes new snow from the statue's face. "I don't understand."

"You are a physician who has given away your time and services to the less fortunate. For more than sixty years, you've been a fierce defender of children exploited by evil-minded adults and child-slave traders."

"Yes. I lived selfishly for my first thirty years. Imagine those I could have helped had I started sooner."

"Even so, you've fought for those who cannot fight for themselves for three score. Not a bad body of work."

"It was never work." The old man grabs the statue's marble fingers again, as if for comfort. "Now, my beneficent acquaintance, if you don't mind..."

The small man takes another step toward him. "You can continue."

The old man smiles with peace. "I've reached the end of my days, I'm afraid."

The small man is undeterred. "I am from a line of beings who have lived since the Enchanted Age before the Crystal Comet. My people, my Saints, live in the land of Eno and are much like the children you have given your life to defend. Come with me and you and I will protect the innocents for years to come."

The old man is stunned by the small man's words. He regards him with an amiable, but concerned, smile. "Benevolent sir. I know not of this age or land of which you speak."

"I can teach you about both."

"There is no time for me to learn such things."

"To me and my kind, time is not a concern."

"But I am old."

"I will make you young."

The old man holds up his frail, shaky hand. "Look. I am weak."

The small man holds out his hand and clenches it into a fist. "I will make you strong."

The old man shakes his head. "I am dying."

"I will make you immortal."

The old man looks to the Baby Jesus statue. With his other hand, he releases the baby's fingers and reaches up to brush more of the new fallen snow from its face. The gloom of the late evening dissipates and the baby's face seems to illuminate from within.

"Honor him further by joining me." The small man's fist opens. He extends it closer to the old man. The old man follows the statue's gaze to the heavens. Even there, in the dark clouds overhead, there seems a new flush of light. It is the moon behind the thinning clouds perhaps, the old man thinks. Or it is something else entirely. The old man cannot be sure, but the message is clear. He turns to the small man and reaches out his hand. The small man takes it without a second's hesitation.

And so begins the story of the real Santa Claus.

Part One

Strings of street lights, even stop lights, blink a bright red and green... In the biggest metropolis imaginable on the American West Coast. Skyscrapers crowd the skyline, but none are more magnificent than the collection of eight buildings known as The Spires. The staggered heights of The Spires reach higher than any of the other buildings around them and they mark the hub of the city's action. The Spires are awash in multi-colored lights as the festive Christmas season reaches a fever-pitch.

Christmas isn't Christmas without a shopping mall and this particular city has plenty of them within the infinite miles of zigzagging pavement in the canyons of the high-rises. There isn't, however, a bigger mall than the one at the center of The Spires. And within that mall, suitable to the splendor of the city and its buildings and their responsibility of being the grandest of everything, is the biggest and the best Santa's Village the holiday has ever known. There are candy cane columns, hills of snow, strobing lights, a forest of beautifully decorated trees, and presents. Infinite presents. Wherever there is an empty spot, there are perfectly wrapped presents of all different sizes. Name it and this Santa's Village has it to excess.

The Village teems with frenetic activity as happy children and their doting parents rush toward it from the far corners of the mall as "Santa Claus is Coming to Town" blasts from gigantic speakers. In the middle of the Village is the most amazing gingerbread workshop the mind can envisage. The workshop looks as though it were magically and mystically conjured from gigantic jellybeans, candy canes, icing, and sugar drops. And in front of the workshop sits the most grandiose, and most delicious-looking, gingerbread throne ever fashioned.

A team of elves, dressed in North Polian standard-issue green and red uniforms, run about to the converging children in the crowd. The team directs the rush of children into the line that surrounds the workshop like a maze. Within minutes, the line is filled to capacity. At the elves prompting, the children begin chanting.

"Santa! Santa! Santa!" they yell. "Santa! Santa! Santa!" Their yells turn to screams of anticipation. "Santa! Santa! Santa!" Their screams turn to ecstatic pleas that seem loud enough to topple the gingerbread workshop and send the banks of snow on its roof careening down in an avalanche.

But the snow isn't snow. It's blankets of cotton peppered with just enough silver glitter to give it that Christmassy glisten. The wrapped presents are just empty boxes and the elves aren't real elves. They are young, enthusiastic people with pointy latex ears hoping to send even younger people into the conniptions of Christmas cheer. The throne isn't gingerbread, either. It's wood, paint, and papier mâché. And the workshop isn't candy or magically conjured, is it? Of course not. It's more wood, planks and beams and boards that have been painted to look like every sweet treat in the known universe. Step through the golden door into the workshop and it becomes all the more evident that nothing in this village is as it seems.

The inside is just exposed plywood and 2x4s. It smells fresh, but without that crisp evergreen pine needle fragrance that tips off the nose that it's Christmas. The smell is good, but it's one that's more like a lumber yard than a forest. Despite all the fakery, though, it's still the grandest workshop in the center of the most spectacular "Santa's Village" in the middle of the biggest mall in the tallest of buildings at the hub of the most vibrant city in America. And it is there, inside that pretend workshop, that the real action of Christmas is unfolding.

A man named Chris, appearing about 60 years old and dressed in a traditional red Santa Claus suit with white fur trim, sits on a stool. He can hear the children chanting outside the walls of the workshop and it makes him smile. He's been waiting all year for this.

His full white beard is real and he has a thick, powerful build. He bends over and laces up a shiny black boot, taking his time. He stamps it on the floor before he does the same with the other one. When he finally stands, he is a perfect Santa Claus, in the perfect workshop, in the perfect Santa's village in the midst of the perfect holiday season.

Chris adjusts a small, nearly invisible microphone on the white lapel of his thick red coat. "I'm leaving the workshop." He walks toward the door. "Let me know if you read me."

A faint voice, with a heavy British accent, comes across an earpiece Chris has tucked in his left ear. It's no bigger than a corn kernel and is nearly impossible to see. "We read you."

"Is the computer working? We can't flub this," Chris says.

The voice responds quickly, "We're fine now. We just rebooted."

Outside, the loud music fades, but the children's chanting only intensifies. After several moments, Chris steps out of the workshop. If there was a single word that encompassed the rapturous feeling gushed forth - the delirious, over-the-top, heart-pounding feeling that comes once a year when a ravenous mob of children finally see the one person they've been out-of-the-way good for (even when their parents weren't watching) - this would be a good place for it. Suffice it to say, they utterly lose their collective minds with an uproarious cheer that echoes through all eight buildings of The Spires.

The elves leap around, urging the children on, as Chris hams it up like a professional wrestler in fast forward. He steps to the throne and bellows for all to hear, "Ho, ho, ho! Kringle in the house!"

It takes a bit for the kids to calm down, but the hysteria slowly fades in the crowd as a new feeling settles over them. They begin to realize that in a short matter of time they will, one by one, have to confront the big man and, with one shot at glory that offers no do-overs, tell him all their hearts desires. Their overt elation gradually devolves to quiet anguish and hand-wringing.

Chris sits on the throne and waves for the first child in line, a shy girl. A photographer stands behind a tripod nearby. An eager Elf brings the child forth.

"This is Ashley, Santa," the Elf says, feeding Chris the child's name. "Remember Ashley?"

Chris's voice is deep and booming. "Why, of course I remember Ashley! So good to see you again, child!" Chris helps Ashley onto his lap as he chuckles a low "Ho, ho, ho".

"Well, Ashley, have you been a good girl this year?" She nods as the Elf walks back to the line to queue the next child. "What would you like for Christmas, little miss?" As Chris speaks, he scans the massive audience and spies a man and woman, both in their early 30s, gleaming with joy and waving at their little princess on Santa's lap. Expensive jewelry adorns the woman's neck and a gold watch is on the man's wrist.

Ashley shrugs at Santa's question.

"Is that your Mommy and Daddy?" Chris points at the pair and waves. They wave back and clap. Ashley nods. Chris gets close to her ear and whispers so no one else could possibly hear. "Let's see if I remember correctly. You live in a big house with lots of nice things, right?"

Ashley nods again.

"Do you know your address?" he prods.

She nods.

"My memory isn't as good as it used to be," Chris continues. "Why don't you whisper your address to me? That way I'm sure to hit your house and bring you lots of wonderful toys again."

Ashley leans close to Chris's ear and begins to whisper. Chris angles himself just right so that his coat's lapel is by her mouth. Chris can't help but smile.

CHAPTER 2

Moments earlier, in a highway rest area far across the city...

Randall Zack, a skinny Englishman about 45 years old, sits behind the wheel of a white utility van. He's a pointy man with pointy features who wears a worn-out tuxedo, a top hat, grungy gloves, and a monocle over each eye. He must constantly squint to hold in both lenses. His voice is the one Chris heard over his earpiece.

In the seat next to him sits his brother Fred, who is a tall, well-muscled 40-year-old man. He is heavily scarred and has dark circles under his tired eyes and an iPad in his lap. He yawns as big as a hippo.

Mosh Pit is a heavy, powerful black man no more than twenty-five years old. He wears a white headband with a red sun and a Japanese inscription. He sits on a bench in the cargo bay of the van, but leans forward between the front seats. He watches as Randall straightens his collar.

"Why do you bother with that suit?" he asks, earnestly.

"I've told you before, Mosh Pit. If you want to be rich, you have to look rich." Randall rubs his hand down the breast of his coat. Dust and soot fly up from the fabric, causing him to cough. One of his monocles pops out and dangles by a thin cord. Randall is quick to return it and he squints harder to hold it in place.

"It's not even clean. Just flat! You ain't fooling nobody!"

"I'd rather have a pressed, dirty suit than a clean, wrinkled one."

Mosh Pit retorts quickly, as he's been waiting for the right moment to say, "I'd rather have ten pounds of sushi!" He turns to Fred. "How you think about it, Fred?" Fred yawns again. Mosh Pit rolls his eyes, then whines, "We're wasting our time. I don't think this is gonna work."

Randall shakes his head, causing another lens to pop from his eye's squinty grip. "Au contraire, Moshy m'boy," he says as he readjusts the monocle. "We have concussion grenades, shackles and chains, and a multitude of advanced weaponry for anyone who tries to stop us. My plan can't fail."

"Well, it ain't very fair. I wanted to be Santy Claus. I woulda made a better one than that jailbird Chris. No kid is gonna believe him to be the jolly ol' elf!"

"Oh, Mosh-o, how many times do we have to go over this? The mall was hiring older gents with real beards and he was the only chap we knew with a white one. You can do it next year."

"But Sumo warriors can't grow beards!" Mosh Pit howls as he slumps on the bench. Fred looks back at him, then yawns again. Just then, the radio receiver on the dashboard bleats.

Randall quickly adjusts the volume. "Quiet! We have something!"

Chris's voice comes across with some static. "Why don't you whisper it to me? That way I'm sure to hit your house and bring you lots of wonderful toys."

Mosh Pit giggles with glee. "Hit your house! You guys hear that? Ol' Jailbird Chris actually said he was gonna hit the kid's house right to her face!"

"Shut it, knucklehead!" Randall barks.

Over the radio, little Ashley's voice is soft, but clear. "Four forty South Glenlake Circle."

Randall excitedly snaps his fingers at Fred, "Four-four-zero South Glenlake! Got it?"

Fred finally perks up and punches the screen on the tablet. After a few seconds, he turns the screen so Randall can see. A map is pulled up and a red dot blips in the center of it.

Randall claps once and starts to sing. "'Tis the season for some stealin'!"

He starts the van, throws it in gear, and guns the gas pedal. The van veers from the highway rest area and rockets up the dark road.

CHAPTER 3

Back at the best and grandest Santa's Village...

Chris, still full of Christmas cheer and "Ho ho hos", waves another child toward him. A sad-faced boy steps forward at the Elf's nudging. He is pitifully underdressed for the occasion. His clothes are shabby and threadbare. The boy's mother is also dressed in old, worn clothes. She waves as he sits on Chris's lap.

"Remember Aiden, Santa?" the Elf asks.

"Of course, I do. What can I get you for Christmas this year, young man?" Chris says. His tone is suddenly a little flat, as if the job has lost its zest. The boy's response is somber.

"Can you get my dad a job? He hasn't been able to find work since..."

Chris hurries him off his lap and nudges him toward the exit. No time for conversation. No time for a picture.

"Yeah, sure, kid. No problem. One job for Daddy on the way."

Aiden's sadness lifts from his face as he looks back at Chris. His smile is one of pure relief. "You mean it, Santa? You really mean it?"

Chris motions him away with a dismissive wave. Another Elf ushers him off from Santa's throne as Chris looks for the next child in line. Aiden joins his mom, overjoyed, and gives her a thumbs up. They hug each other tightly.

"He said he would. He promised!" Aiden can hardly contain his happiness.

Chris glances after them once more and shakes his head. The next child is obviously from a family that is much more fortunate in life than Aiden. Chris is eager to talk to him.

As the next child moves up, a diminutive man named Ooby, appearing about 40 and only 4'6" (though perfectly proportioned), stands outside the line. He is smaller than the actors playing the elves and about the height of most of the children. Ooby is neatly dressed in slacks and a suave leather jacket and has distinctive features, like a Native American. He lifts a hand to his ear and taps a small hearing aid device. As clear as if he were standing right next to him, Ooby can hear everything Chris says.

"Tell me where you live, young man, so I'm sure to bring you lots of presents. Just whisper your address in my ear." Chris is full of cheer again.

Ooby glares at him. He pulls a gold watch from his pocket and checks the time.

"Where is he?" Ooby's accent is distinctive and unlike any other accent in the world. It is the same as the small man who helped the old man over fifteen hundred years earlier in the European chapel's courtyard.

Ooby is that small man.

ay across the city at 440 South Glenlake Circle...

In the immaculate home's foyer, a few hushed clicks emanate from just outside the front door. Suddenly, the door swings wide open. Randall, Fred, and Mosh Pit file into the foyer and close the door. Randall twirls a walking cane and carries his bag of gear and an empty duffel over his shoulder as he stashes a lock pick kit in his pocket. He uses the cane to point at a control panel inside the door.

"Alarm. Alarm."

Fred goes to the panel with his iPad. Mosh Pit disappears inside the house. Within seconds, Fred has the alarm disabled. From deep inside the house, Mosh Pit exclaims, "Jackpot, boys! Little Ashley and her folks are loaded!"

Randall walks into the living room where there is a 70" TV, a fireplace, and a Christmas tree. It's a Hallmark movie worthy setting. Randall hurries to the pile of presents under the tree and tears into the first one he grabs. He uncovers a diamond necklace. He opens another, revealing an expensive electronic gizmo. Under his smile, he says, "Spoiled blokes."

Randall stops when he hears a faint thud and looks around, unsure of its source. After a moment of silence, he shrugs and starts back at the presents. Another thud, louder this time, draws his attention to the ceiling. He squints his eyes tighter around his monocles, as if it helps his hearing. Something is up there, he thinks. That's when it becomes undeniable. Randall hears what can only be described as steps over him. They are barely discernible, but Randall knows he isn't mistaken. Someone is on the roof.

He turns to call out to Fred and Mosh Pit, but stops when he notices sooty ashes drifting down the chimney. With a wily grin, he looks up again. "Up on the rooftop. Click, click, click…" he sings lowly.

He approaches the fireplace, cane gripped tightly in his hand. He hears something ping-ponging from brick to brick, all the way down the length of the chimney. Randall rears back the cane, ready to strike. A small crystal bounces out onto the floor. Randall glares at it. He kicks it out of the way, squats to look up the chimney's shaft, and sees nothing but a black void. He chuckles to himself. "Get a hold of yourself, mate. It's just a bit of ice from the roof tinkling around."

Randall pulls his head out of the fireplace and immediately notices a man by the tree. The man is tall and lean, dressed in a black, long-sleeved shirt, dark pants, a black beanie cap and black leather work boots. He has a moustache and a short, Spartan-style beard. The man appears to be in his early 30s and has a handsome, angular face, as if he were chiseled from stone. His eyes are friendly, though, and he's strangely reminiscent of the old Christmas Eve Wonderworker that Ooby helped so long ago.

His name is Nicholas and he is that man.

Nicholas nods to Randall and smiles, without a hint of malice or smugness. "Randall Zack. You should be using your considerable intelligence to make an honest living." He motions around the room. "You're better than this, my friend."

Randall rears his cane back like a bat again. "You picked the wrong house to wander into and give life lessons, ol' chap!" He charges, swinging the cane.

Nicholas sidesteps him, blocks the swing, and easily takes the cane from him.

"Help!" Randall hollers so the others can hear. Nicholas leaps and kicks Randall in the chest, sending him reeling against a far wall. His monocles pop out and his top hat flies in the other direction. Mosh Pit and Fred arrive simultaneously and are surprised to see Nicholas standing over Randall. The two thugs have their hands full of stolen goods, but they drop everything and rush him. Fred goes first.

With a spinning back kick, Nicholas dispatches Fred, then turns toward Mosh Pit, who charges like a bull.

"Bonsai!" he yells as he moves in on Nicholas, who swiftly uppercuts him. Mosh Pit drops into a heap.

Nicholas pauses over the two groaning, incapacitated men, but the click of a gun spins him around. Randall has a revolver aimed at him and is staring at him as if he is familiar.

"You obviously know me. Do I know you?" Randall asks.

Nicholas freezes in place and slowly raises his arms in surrender. "I don't think so."

Randall narrows his eyes, thinking deeply. Then, he snaps his fingers in realization. "Yes! Yes, I know who you are!"

Nicholas gives a slight grin. "I seriously doubt that you do."

"The guys in prison tell stories about a mysterious child protector. A hero for the innocent. A real champion of wholesomeness and a boogey man for bad guys. I thought you were just a myth, but here you are." Randall begins to squeeze the trigger, then adds with a sneer, "Your legend ends tonight."

Nicholas holds out a hand. "Wait! Answer me one question first."

"Shoot," Randall replies, then snickers at his own pun.

Nicholas asks his question quietly. Earnestly. "How did you end up this way?"

Randall shrugs. His answer comes too easily for Nicholas's comfort. "I watched a busy body like you destroy my father thirty-five years ago. I guess it embittered me."

Nicholas looks at him sadly, sympathetically. His shoulders slump just a bit under some new weight.

"But I shan't be defeated as easily as he," Randall continues after a moment. As he pulls the trigger, Nicholas touches his wrist. Randall fires the pistol three times in rapid succession, but Nicholas moves so fast that he is a blur, then gone.

"What the...?" Randall looks at the empty space where Nicholas had been. The three smoking holes in the wall show that his aim was true.

Randall looks frantically for his disappearing target and finds Nicholas beside him.

Nicholas punches Randall, who flies into the tree and topples it with a crash of lights and ornaments.

CHAPTER 5

Back at Santa's Village...

Chris is waiting on his throne because the next boy in line is crying. Chris uses the spare moment to whisper into the microphone on his lapel.

"Guys? You get those last few addresses? We hit the motherlode. Tell me you got 'em." He waits, but there is no response. "Guys? Randall?" He taps his microphone.

Ooby has moved closer. He checks his timepiece again and speaks in a near whisper, as if to himself. "C'mon. Where are you?" He huffs impatiently. "That's it! I'm taking this ol' Frog down myself."

Chris points at the next child behind the one who can't stop crying. The girl, a 6-year-old, sees him motioning for her and she runs to him and jumps in his lap. Chris looks past her to search for her parents. Instead, he sees Ooby. He eyes Ooby's nice clothes and smirks.

"I like how you got all dressed up for the occasion, kid, but you still gotta wait your turn to see Santa Claus," he says as he motions for an Elf to remove Ooby.

Ooby points an accusing finger at Chris. "I am not a kid, and you, sir, are not Santa Claus."

The little girl in Chris's lap gasps. "What? You're not Santa Claus?"

"Beat it," Chris says as he glares at Ooby.

"I know you're only doing this to feed rich families' addresses to your ring of thieves. What a despicable betrayal of trust you're committing with that suit. Even worse, you just made a promise to Aiden that you have no way of delivering."

Chris leans toward him and speaks through clenched teeth. "I don't intend to make no deliverances on no promises."

Ooby widens his stance and balls his fists. "Well, it's game over, you rat-fink. Come easy and I won't be forced to take you down the hard way."

The little girl's mouth falls open. "Is that true, Santa Claus? You're a thief and a fake?"

"He's not the real Santa, Trudy. Not even close to a passable one. The real Santa doesn't have to ask what you want for Christmas." Ooby narrows his eyes at Chris, whose mouth cracks into a wide macaroni smile.

Chris puts Trudy down beside the throne. "You've leveled your accusatives and made your threatenations, Short Stack. Now let's see if you can back it up." Chris pushes himself up from the seat. He towers over the much smaller Ooby.

Chris catches sight of three Security Guards, who happen to be walking up the mall's crowded corridor in his direction. They are there by chance, drinking milkshakes and enjoying the festive scenery like everyone else, but Chris immediately surmises they are coming after him.

"You're with the cops, eh?" he says, looking back at Ooby. "Figures a little scamp like you would call for back-up."

Ooby looks over his shoulder to see the guards approaching the Village. He's as surprised as Chris. "I don't need back-up for the likes of you, Bub."

While Ooby is distracted, Chris pounces. He lifts Ooby easily over his head as the crowd gives out a collective gasp.

"Be seeing you, Squirt!" Chris barks as he pitches Ooby into the cotton snowbank by the workshop. He tears off his hat and white wig and tosses them on top of Ooby to another cacophony of shocked exclamations from the crowd.

Chris sprints to the side of the Village, leaps the rope boundary around it, and runs down the main corridor of the mall. Though his full white beard is real, his head is bald and covered with mottled prison tattoos. He's in good shape and very fast for a man of his age. As he runs, he strips off his red Santa jacket. Beneath he is wearing a white tank top, revealing more body graffiti.

Ooby pops his head out of the fake snow and throws the Santa hat to the side. His face is red with anger. "Oh, now you get the fury, Bub!" Ooby sprints after Chris.

The security guards, who have no idea what's happening, drop their milkshakes and run after Ooby.

CHAPTER 6

Back at the mansion on Glenlake Circle...

Nicholas puts the finishing touches on the Christmas tree, which is upright and lit and decorated even better than before. The presents are re-wrapped and everything is back in its place. Behind him, Randall, Fred, and Mosh Pit are seated in a circle with their backs to each other. A red ribbon binds them together.

"C'mon, man, let us go. We won't do this no more," Mosh Pit pleads.

"I'm sorry, but this is the only way you can get back on the right path," Nicholas says with genuine sympathy. "The police are already on their way."

Just then, there is a loud clatter in the chimney. Ashes blast down in a plume as a small person drops into the fireplace. He is Ooby's size and very similar in appearance, but he seems to be only in his teens. The three crooks look at him with surprise.

His name is Doodle.

Like Ooby, his voice is high pitched and his accent is unique. "Nicholas!" he says excitedly.

Nicholas turns to him and speaks in a calming tone. "Doodle, I believe I asked you to stay outside until I was done."

Doddle doesn't take the queue from Nicholas and chatters on without breathing. "I stayed in the sleigh as long as I could!" Nicholas throws up a hand to motion for Doodle to zip his lips about the sleigh. Doodle takes notice. "Um, I meant I stayed in the truck plane as long as I could!" Doodle winks as he points toward the ceiling.

Nicholas chuckles under his breath at Doodle's effort to cover his mistake. Doodle is animated and loud as he continues. "Ooby took on Chris by himself and now he's in trouble and he needs your help and we have to go save him!"

Nicholas looks at the three crooks, then he listens for sirens. They wail in the distance outside the house. "Okay, Doodle. If you'd be so kind as to watch these fellows until the police arrive, I'll go see how I can assist Ooby. Can you do that for me?"

"Sure!" Doodle proclaims. He turns to them and furrows his brow in an attempt to look intimidating. "Want me to scuff them up a little?"

"No, of course not," Nicholas returns. "Just watch them. Help will be here in a minute or less." Nicholas starts for the front door. "After the police have finished here, wait outside for me. I'll be back in as soon as I can."

Doodle gives a dutiful salute as Nicholas darts out the front door. When he's gone, Doodle looks right at Randall. "What's with the two monocles, Mister?" he asks.

Randall shrugs. "Well, when my vision went bad in one eye, I got the first. When the other went bad, I naturally got a second."

"Why didn't you just get glasses?" Doodle replies.

Mosh Pit chips in, "That's what I always ask him!"

"Forget my monocles," Randall says to Doodle. "How 'bout you release us from our binds? We'll be good from now on."

Doodle stands in front of him and crosses his arms. "Oh, I plan on releasing you, but I don't want you to be good. In fact, I want you to be very, very bad."

Randall raises his eye-brows and his monocles fall out and hang around his neck by their thin cords. Mosh Pit is speechless. Fred just yawns.

Doodle cracks a sly smile. "How would you fellas like to make a world of money?"

Randall licks his lips and nods eagerly, bouncing his monocles up and down.

Outside, as two police cars pull into the driveway with their lights and sirens going full blast, a dark sleigh, pulled by a pair of small deer, takes to flight from the roof. Four Policemen jump out of the cars and run to the open front door without noticing the silent object that disappears into the night sky.

CHAPTER 7

Back at the mall...

Chris runs up the crowded corridor. The wide hallway splits and then opens in the middle, overlooking the first level down below. Chris pushes by people, trying to stay ahead of Ooby and the guards. He runs into a sign in the corridor that reads "Ride the Iceberg Express - Level 1". Chris looks over the railing.

The crowded first floor is twenty feet below. The Iceberg Express is driving by beneath him. It's a free driving, brightly-colored mini-train that doesn't need tracks. The engine pulls eight boxcars filled with happy children and parents who are enjoying the ride. Each box car is big enough for a family of five and is only six feet tall. The entire train is fifty feet long. It clangs and whistles as it makes its way through the crowd at five miles an hour. Chris heaves himself over the railing.

The train's Engineer, an overly cheerful woman in her 50s, clearly loves her job. She pulls the whistle and sings over a microphone in the little train's engine. "All aboard the Choo Choo train. All aboard! All aboard! Rolling down Santa Claus Lane! All aboard! All aboard!"

The crowd parts for her train and kids clamor to get on at every stop she makes.

Chris lands on top of the train's caboose with a heavy thud. The family in the car beneath him notice, but quickly continue with their festivities. Chris sees Ooby sprint along the level above. Ooby leaps over the side and lands on the car ahead of Chris.

The train rolls on and passes a sign-spinning Elf, who waves two flags, hooked on long, plastic candy canes. The Elf holds one in each hand. One reads "Ride the North Polescalator". The other reads "To Santa's Village".

Ooby snags one as they go by. Chris squats down and takes the other. The costumed Elf looks at his empty hands, befuddled. Ooby rips the flag off of his candy cane and grabs it by the hook, brandishing it like a fencing sword.

"So, it's like that, eh?" Chris scoffs. Chris rips the flag off of his cane and presents it as a sword, too.

"En Garde," Ooby replies. The two square off atop the moving train.

"Eat candy cane, Munchkin!" Chris yells as he attacks with broad and high arcing swings like a raged Viking. Ooby defends with skillful precision. Their canes clash and a fierce battle ensues.

The train's riders are oblivious, as is the Engineer who continues singing and blowing the whistle with glee. Bystanders in the mall's corridor, though, watch with delight, thinking they are getting a choreographed show while they shop.

Chris rampages and Ooby retreats to the front of the train, leaping from the roof of one car to the next, defending himself with his cane the whole time. On the car behind the engine, Chris plows into Ooby and sends him flying from the train. In mid-air, Ooby reaches out with the crook of his cane and hooks a pole atop a cell phone kiosk. He spins on the end of the candy cane, 360 degrees around the pole, and ends up over the train again. He kicks Chris with both feet, sending him to his back. Chris leaps up and attacks with his cane once more. Ooby, back on the train, is invigorated and starts to beat Chris with his superior swordsmanship.

"Of the eighty-six most utilized moves in swordplay, I invented forty-seven," he says as he suddenly disarms Chris by sending his cane sailing into the air and off the side of the train.

Ooby draws back the candy cane and thrusts the tip of it into Chris's belly. The plastic candy cane breaks to pieces. Chris initially reacts as if he's been stabbed, but when he sees the cane blast apart on impact with his stomach, he gives a hearty laugh. "Enough of your speechifying!"

He kicks Ooby in the chest so hard it sends him bumping and rolling off the end of the train. Ooby grabs the edge of the last car. He hangs there, feet dangling precariously, and holds on for dear life as the train moves forward. Two of the security guards from Santa's Village arrive behind the train on a pair of Segways.

"Stop in the name of mall law!" one of the guards says as he reaches out for Ooby, bearing down on him with the Segway. Overhead, Chris tries to stomp on Ooby's fingers, but Ooby moves them just in time.

In the caboose's back window, a small boy, Jeffy, lollipop in his mouth that bulges out one cheek, looks at Ooby in wonder. The boy's mom, dad, and sister stare in total shock. Finally, Jeffy smiles, pulls the lollipop from his mouth, and offers it to Ooby.

Ooby can't help but smile. That is, until Chris tries to stomp his fingers again. Ooby shuffles his hands on the edge of the train as Chris stamps his feet in pursuit of them.

As the security guards close in on him, Ooby makes an exasperated plea. "Please, guys, call the real cops! That man is a dastardly criminal!"

One security guard is insulted. "Real cops, eh?" He steers in extra close to Ooby and tries to grab him. "You'll wish for real cops when we slap you in mall jail and give you hot cocoa without marshmallows!"

Inside the caboose, Jeffy's face drops and his hands slap the sides of his head. "No!" he wails.

Ooby sees Jeffy's horror and is quick to reassure him. "He's only joking, Jeffy! There's no such thing as cocoa without marshmallows! Not even in mall jail!"

Jeffy looks relieved as Ooby keeps moving his hands away from Chris's stomping feet. Jeffy's mom protectively pulls Jeffy away from the window. "How'd you know his name?" she exclaims.

Ooby ignores the question and pushes himself off the caboose and onto the security guard's Segway. He climbs fluidly from the front of the Segway, around the guard and up his back, and onto his shoulders. From there, Ooby leaps back onto the caboose and front kicks Chris, who stumbles onto the car ahead.

Chris drops to his chest on the roof, reaches between the cars, and pulls a clasp that releases the caboose from the train. The caboose separates and drifts behind. Ooby runs the length of the caboose and jumps to the train again as Chris retreats to the next car up the line.

Ooby looks back and sees Jeffy's face in the window of the caboose. The drifting car causes the security guards to veer their Segways off course and slow down. Chris releases the next car and Ooby must leap to stay with the moving train. Another car drifts behind.

The Engineer drives on, oblivious to what's going on behind her. She's too happy driving the train and singing into her microphone to notice a thing. "All aboard the Train Choo-choo! Rocking Tinsel Town with you!"

The train passes under an area draped with low hanging garland crisscrossing the corridor. On his leap to the next car, Ooby front kicks Chris, but Chris's stance is wide and Ooby just bounces off his chest.

"Let's get down to business, shall we?" Chris snarls with clenched fists. Ooby squats low and bounds forward, right between Chris's legs. He spins, staying low in a tripod position. Chris turns toward him.

Ooby smirks. "I'd rather just get down." The low hanging garland clothes-lines Chris across the chest, pulls tight as the train moves forward, and rockets him backwards. He falls off the back of the train and screams in terror all the way down, arms waving, feet flailing in dramatic fashion, as if he's fallen off the edge of the Grand Canyon. In reality, it's only a few feet. When Chris hits the floor, it's a non-event. He rolls into a reverse somersault and leaps to his feet, not missing a beat.

Ooby jumps off the train and sprints after Chris, who rushes toward the mall's exit by the Food Court. Chris is moving fast, but Ooby is quicker. He flies at him with a jumping side kick that lands square in the middle of Chris's back. The blow knocks Chris into a table as bewildered patrons flee the sudden chaos. Ooby strikes a fighting stance as Chris stands and brushes himself off.

"Put up your dukes, you putrid woebegone weasel!" Ooby rushes at Chris, fists swinging. Chris puts his hand on Ooby's forehead and extends his arm. The much shorter Ooby swings at the air between him and Chris. Chris lifts Ooby high and slams him head first into a trash can so that only his legs are sticking out. Chris laughs again and dashes out the exit as Ooby's feet helplessly kick the air.

Outside, on the sidewalk in front of the stupendous mall's grand entrance, Chris stops and looks for a hasty escape. From the high roof behind him, an ice-like object falls. It is the same crystal from the chimney at the house on Glenlake Circle.

The crystal smacks the sidewalk and bounces into some nearby hedges. The sidewalk is crowded with shoppers entering and leaving the mall. Chris stops by a convertible parked nearby. A man unloads a stroller from the car as his wife places a babbling baby in it.

Chris pushes the unsuspecting man to the ground and opens the door to the convertible despite the screams of the wife. Two uniformed police officers run up the sidewalk, draw their guns, and aim them at Chris.

"Halt!" the first one commands. Chris pulls a metal canister from his thick red pants. He yanks a pin from the object and holds it up for the baby's father and mother and the police officers to see. He grabs the stroller with his other hand and pulls it and the baby close to him.

"This is a grenade and this situation just got serious!" Chris exclaims as he holds the grenade over the stroller.

The baby looks at the peculiar object and giggles at it. The watching crowd gasps and the officers drop their guns immediately.

"Okay, pal! Take it easy! Take it easy!" An officer barks back in a panic, not at all taking it easy.

During the commotion, Nicholas steps out onto the sidewalk from the hedges. Ooby, covered in disposed food, runs out just in time to see Nicholas step between the police officers and Chris.

Nicholas holds up his hands as he smiles sympathetically at Chris. "You've been a very naughty boy, Chris."

Chris glares at the new player intruding on his game. "Stranger, you don't know the half of it." Chris drops the grenade in the baby stroller and kicks the stroller down the open sidewalk. He jumps in the convertible and peels out into the parking lot. "Have fun with that, losers!" he yells over his shoulder as he tears away.

Without a second's hesitation, Nicholas sprints after the stroller as the baby's parents scream in terror. He catches up to the speeding stroller, stops it, and shoots his hand in to retrieve the grenade from the baby's side. He turns and hurls the grenade fifty feet into a dumpster against the wall of the building. Then he covers the stroller with his body to protect the baby inside.

The grenade explodes, but the blast is directed up the side of the building. No one is hurt. Nicholas reaches down and calmly withdraws the baby from the stroller. The baby jabbers at him and he coos back in a comforting tone. He walks the baby's stroller back to the waiting mother and father, who takes the baby from his arms, ever so grateful for his actions. Ooby runs up to Nicholas as the mother hugs him and the father shakes his hand.

"Nice throw," Ooby says in reference to the grenade. Nicholas smiles at him and steps away from the gushing parents.

"Poor Chris. Will he ever see the error of his ways?" Nicholas says with a disappointed shake of his head.

A police officer points off in the far distance of the parking lot as Chris drives the convertible at an increasing rate of speed. "That guy is getting away! Once he's on the freeway, we'll never find him!"

Nicholas's response is soothing and calm. "Not to worry, Officer Mike. My friend's aim is true." Nicholas tosses the crystal to Ooby, who removes his scarf from around his neck under his jacket. "Do what you do best, buddy."

Ooby grins as Nicholas takes off in a sprint into the parking lot. Far away, Chris drives the roaring convertible through the crowded parking lot toward the highway.

Ooby holds the scarf like a sling and puts the crystal in the fold. He whips it around several times and releases it. The crystal line drives all the way across the parking lot and lands in the backseat of the car.

Nicholas, still running, dives between two parked cars out of view of the crowd. As he does, he touches his chest and vanishes.

In the convertible, Chris is laughing aloud and steering the wheel like a maniac. "I like to leave a place with a bang!" he harps proudly to himself. "I sure know how to make a lasting impact!" His own jokes make him laugh harder. "If storks deliver babies from the sky, then I just sent that baby back to the stork!" He adjusts the rearview mirror to try and see the mall's entrance far behind him. Instead, he sees Nicholas in the backseat. "Hey! What gives?"

Nicholas, his face now darkened with deep, somewhat carnal, but well-controlled fury, wraps his arm around Chris's neck in a sleeper hold. Chris's eyes go wide, then roll until his lids fall shut. It happens in seconds.

"Your willingness to hurt a baby greatly offends me," Nicholas whispers harshly as Chris slumps in his grasp. Nicholas releases him and smoothly takes control of the car.

Moments later, Nicholas pulls the car to the curb by the mall's entrance. Chris is unconscious in the passenger's seat. As Nicholas gets out, a young girl runs up to him.

"Wow, you're fast!" she chirps. Nicholas rumples the girl's hair.

"Well, Rosie, that's because I ate my leafy greens when I was your age," Nicholas replies. The crowd cheers as do the police officers. Nicholas finds Ooby and walks toward him. Ooby is standing with his arms crossed.

"You were supposed to wait for me," Nicholas says lowly so no one else can hear. "For somebody who has all the time in the world, you sure are impatient."

Ooby's retort is fast. "He was a horrible Santa Claus. I couldn't allow any more children to be exposed to him and his toxic ways."

Nicholas nods. "Well, now that you put it that way…"

Behind them, the police officers cuff the still unconscious Chris. One of the officers identifies him.

"This is Chris Boopingsly!" she exclaims. "He runs with a pretty tough crew. Back to jail for you, Boopingsly!"

Nicholas and Ooby walk to the mall's entrance, separating themselves from the adulating crowd.

"You used the 'naughty boy' trope again," Ooby complains.

"Not the 'catchphrase' argument," Nicholas returns with an eye roll.

"Why don't you ever tell them that they're going on the bad list? That's all I'm asking. How many perfect situations are you going to let pass by? At least try it. Say it with me." Ooby deepens his voice. "'You're going on the bad list.'"

Nicholas shakes his head. "I'm not saying that." The automatic doors open and they go into the Food Court. "Let's just find the elevator to the roof and go pick up Doodle."

Ooby stops in the corridor. "What? Where did you leave him?"

"With the others. Someone had to stand watch until the police arrived."

"Oh, no, Nicholas, he isn't ready to be left alone with people of Randall Zack's ilk."

"Come on, Ooby, how else is he going to learn the ropes?"

Ooby is indignant. "The last time you trusted him and left him alone, he went missing for five days and turned up in Holland with that group of deviants."

"That wasn't his fault. He said–"

"He did as he always does and said whatever it took to get himself out of trouble! Don't be so gullible, Nicholas!"

"Oh, Ooby, always fearing the worst," Nicholas says. They continue past the Food Court and up the mall's crowded corridor. Nicholas picks a piece of old food off the shoulder of Ooby's jacket. It's leftover from his brief confinement in the trash can. "At least your pessimism comes with snacks." He sniffs the morsel. "Mmm. General Tso's chicken. My favorite."

Ooby storms away. "You're wracking my nerves!"

Nicholas can't help but laugh as he drops the food in the nearest garbage can.

CHAPTER 8

Back at the house on Glenlake Circle...

The four police officers enter through the front door with weapons drawn. They see Doodle standing in the great room alone. He looks sweet and innocent and has tears pooling in his big eyes. The officers are immediately sympathetic.

An officer squats down in front of him. "You okay, little Buckaroo?"

Doodle wipes away the tears. "I called on accident." The police officers holster their guns.

"Well, that's all right," one of the others replies. "We're just glad you're okay and nothing is–"

From the side, Mosh Pit charges in. "Bonsai!" he caterwauls as he belly-blasts all four officers at once. Randall appears from another room, monocles and top hat in place. He's twirling his cane. Mosh Pit repeatedly sumo slams the policemen until they fall in succession.

"My turn, gents," Randall says as Mosh Pit steps back. The police officers are all on their hands and knees, trying to get back to their feet. Randall rears back the cane like a golf club. "Fore!" He whacks each officer in turn, knocking the lot of them out cold. Randall begins twirling the cane again.

Fred, yawning, appears from the living room and retrieves a set of car keys from one of the fallen officers. Randall turns his attention to Mosh Pit.

"How many times must I tell you, 'Bonsai' is a little tree? If you insist on preempting a sneak attack with a battle cry, then please say 'Banzai' correctly."

"Okay, okay. I just get confused when I get excited," Mosh Pit moans.

Randall faces Doodle. "You're the boss. Where to now?"

Doodle is flattered. "Really? I'm the boss?" He pulls up his pants, puffs out his chest, and leads the way to the door. "Somewhere rough and tough. We need a mean hideout to discuss mean business."

Randall nudges Mosh Pit and mocks Doodle behind his back. Mosh Pit laughs and plays along. "Sure thing, Mister Big Boss Man."

CHAPTER 9

Back at the mall...

Nicholas and Ooby are standing by an elevator in a less trafficked area. A nearby security door blasts open and Mr. Jingleheimer, the mall's harried manager, rushes out. He is an extremely anxious man in a three-piece suit.

"Where's my Santa? Where's my Santa? Oh dear, this is tragic! This is horribly, awfully tragic!" he cries as he hurries up the hall. Nicholas and Ooby watch him go by.

"What's the problem, Bub?" Ooby asks.

Mr. Jingleheimer doesn't even look up. "I've lost my Santa Claus! It's tragic, I say!"

"Why don't you call the agency for a replacement?" Nicholas interjects.

"I did! I did!" Mr. Jingleheimer wails. "It will take at least an hour! If only I could find someone to fill-in until the replacement gets here!"

Ooby and Nicholas look at each other and shrug with shared indifference. The elevator door opens and they step on. As Nicholas hits the button inside, Mr. Jingleheimer can still be heard.

"There are hundreds of children waiting to see a Santa who isn't there! They'll be so disappointed. All of the children will be terribly disappointed!"

The elevator doors are sliding closed when Nicholas's hand swipes between them, triggering a hidden sensor. The doors reopen. He looks out with a concerned expression and sees Mr. Jingleheimer rounding the corner into the crowded part of the mall.

"I'll do it!" he calls. Mr. Jingleheimer stops in his tracks and turns toward him.

"Nicholas!" Ooby protests. "Tomorrow is Christmas Eve and we're much too busy for that! Not to mention Doodle! We have to go get him before he does something irresponsible!"

Mr. Jingleheimer is walking back as fast as he had walked away. "Splendid! Splendid! I believe we have a spare suit in the back that will fit you perfectly!"

Nicholas steps off the elevator as Mr. Jingleheimer walks to him and sizes him up.

"Yes. Yes! This will work! We'll just fatten you up with some padding and give you a fake cotton beard! This will work!"

Nicholas, with his hand still between the elevator doors, looks back at Ooby. "Aren't you coming?"

"To watch you trifle away valuable time in a ridiculous costume? No way!" Ooby punches the elevator button repeatedly.

Nicholas turns to Mr. Jingleheimer, who now has him by the wrist and is tugging him toward the back office.

"You know, I could use a helper Elf," he says.

Ooby stops pressing the button and glares at Nicholas. He shakes his head. "Don't you dare," Ooby whispers under his breath.

"Of course!" Mr. Jingleheimer harps, suddenly happy and relieved. "You can never have too many Elves." He looks in on Ooby. "Come along, little fellow. I have a suit that will fit you perfectly!"

Ooby rants and fusses as Nicholas smiles and reaches into the elevator to pull him out.

CHAPTER 10

On the sketchy side of the city...

The police car, stolen from the downed officers at the house on Glenlake Circle, takes an exit off the highway. It pulls into the parking lot of a dive bar and finds a parking spot amid a sea of motorcycles. Doodle, Mosh Pit, Randall, and Fred get out.

"This place looks nefarious enough," Doodle says with a wide smile. He leads the way into the dark and grungy pub with the other three following. The tough, leather-clad patrons immediately glare at him over their mugs. "Yeah," Doodle spouts excitedly as he takes in the prickly surroundings. "This is my kind of place."

The Barkeep stares as Doodle walks closer to the long bar. Doodle gives a nod before asking, "Not a very cheery bunch, are they?"

The Bikers give a collective, disapproving grunt to his loud question. Randall, Mosh Pit, and Fred hang back toward the door with caution, seemingly ready to flee if Doodle starts too much of a stir with the regulars.

"Why should they be?" the Barkeep barks back. "Everyone spent their last bits on the music box." The Barkeep nods toward a 50s style jukebox on a far wall. "All this quiet makes them ill-tempered."

"I have a few coins," Doodle says with a shrug. He looks back at his trio of new friends. Randall motions for him to feed the box as he and the other two take another step back toward the door.

"You'll play number fourteen if you know what's good for you!" someone squawks from the moody crowd. Doodle trots to the jukebox, digs in his pocket, and puts in the money. More angry patrons yell for "Number fourteen!"

Doodle looks back at Randall, Mosh Pit, and Fred with a hopeful grin as he punches the number. "Probably a good villain's anthem. A mad and mean tune, I'd bet. Some George Thorogood or Johnny Rotten would be my guess."

After a moment, Burl Ives's version of "Holly Jolly Christmas" begins. The demeanor of the crowd changes instantly. They all hold up their mugs, swing them back and forth, and sing along. Doodle is stunned. "You've got to be kidding me," he murmurs.

The Barkeep smiles wide and chimes in over the singing crowd, "Gets you in the holiday spirit just in time for the jolly fat man, doesn't it?" He holds up his own mug. "To the jolly fat man!"

The Bikers all cheer and repeat his toast in unison. "To the jolly fat man!"

Randall, Mosh Pit, and Fred are relieved and walk over to an overtly dejected Doodle. "Jolly fat man. Yeah, right," Doodle mopes under a furrowed brow.

"Your kind of place, eh?" Randall teases.

"I sure do like it!" Mosh Pit raves, genuinely enjoying himself as he jigs to the music.

"In the spirit of the season, your first round is on me, young fella!" the Barkeep chuckles to Doodle. "What can I get for you and your friends?"

"Something rough. Something tough. Something strong. A round of fall down juice!" Doodle snaps, his mood darkening.

The Barkeep waves him off. "It's Christmas! Only eggnog will do!"

Doodle drops his head, exasperated. Behind him, the patrons are singing and forming a conga line. "At least give it the good stuff," Doodle pouts.

The Barkeep leans over the bar to get a better look at Doodle. "Are you of age?"

"Of age plus a few hundred!" Doodle fusses. The Barkeep raises an eyebrow at him, as does Randall.

"Likely story, friend," the Barkeep chuckles. "Not that it matters. We don't serve the hard stuff here. I'll get you some hot apple cider. Another good Christmas beverage!" He sweeps his arm over the room toward the crowd. "It's what they're all having!"

Doodle storms off to a dark table in a back corner of the room. Randall and Fred follow, but Mosh Pit is reluctant because he obviously wants to join the conga line. Randall tugs him by the coat sleeve.

"Business first," he whispers. "Once we hear what the little goofball has to say, you can dance." Mosh Pit slumps and gives in.

At the table, Doodle gets right to it. "You guys think you know Santa Claus? You only know the image put forth by some ancient English poem and a sugary cola's old marketing campaign! You don't know the real Santa Claus at all!"

Randall finds a seat across from Doodle and Fred and Mosh Pit sit on either side of him. "Tell us then, where do we have it so wrong?"

CHAPTER 11

At the mall in Santa's Village...

Nicholas sits on the gingerbread throne, appearing a bit uncomfortable in the traditional red suit and hat. He wears a big fluffy white beard that is obviously fake. Ooby, dressed in a green and red elf suit, is grouchy as he walks a 9-year-old girl up to Nicholas, who beams at the sight of the child.

"Well, hello, Betty. My, how you've grown in a year! How are you tonight?"

Betty stops short of Nicholas and puts her hands on her hips. "You're not the real Santa Claus!"

"What makes you say that?" Nicholas says softly.

"You don't fit the profile! Your beard is fake, you're way too skinny, and you haven't even asked me if I've been a good girl! The real Santa always asks that first!"

Nicholas can't help but smile. "But I already know the answer."

Betty isn't willing to listen. "I'm not wasting my time talking to a phony! What's the point?" She rears back and kicks Nicholas in the shin. He winces as she rushes by Ooby, who is shocked into silence. She stops and points at him. "And you're the worst elf ever!" She storms over to her waiting parents.

Ooby walks up to Nicholas, incensed. "Another blown chance for my catchphrase. If anyone should be on the bad list, it's her."

Nicholas is serene in his response. "You know better than that. She may be high-spirited, but she's not bad."

"You never put anyone on the bad list," Ooby objects. "If I didn't keep one, there probably wouldn't even be a bad list!"

"No child is all bad. Just as no child is all good. But all are deserving of what we can give them," Nicholas says lowly, so the waiting children can't hear. "Now, please, bring up Deon. He looks a little worried."

Ooby waves for the next child in line, who approaches the throne tentatively. He is a sheepish 6-year-old. Nicholas lifts him to his lap.

"Hello, Deon," Nicholas says.

Tears well in his big, brown eyes. "I heard that girl say you weren't the real Santa Claus."

"Oh, but I am," Nicholas replies. "Children expect me to look a certain way, so I wear a disguise sometimes to meet those expectations. Like this big fluffy beard." Nicholas removes the fake beard to reveal his own. "This is real though. Try it."

Deon tugs on Nicholas's short beard. He nods. "That's real. But you aren't very fat. Santa Claus is supposed to be fat."

"That's because I've been eating my fruits and vegetables like I'm supposed to. A healthy diet will help you grow big and strong. Do you eat your fruits and vegetables?"

"Most times. I don't like some things though," Deon says as the anxiety drains from his face and he begins to warm up to Nicholas.

"Is that why you hide your broccoli in the plant next to the table?" The boy nods. "And your Brussels sprouts and peas?"

Deon nods again. "Yeah, but I do everything else I'm supposed to! I clean my room and make my bed sometimes!"

"I know," Nicholas smiles. "Which is why I'm going to bring you that remote-control airplane you want so much."

"You are?" Deon is overjoyed.

"Sure. You've been a very good boy." Deon hugs Nicholas. Then, Nicholas points straight ahead. "Okay, now. Smile for the camera." A flashbulb goes off, capturing the tender moment between Santa Claus and child.

CHAPTER 12

At the biker bar...

Randall, Mosh Pit, and Fred are sitting with Doodle, sipping mugs of apple cider as the crowd of bikers sing along to another Christmas standard playing on the jukebox.

"So, my pea-sized chum. Tell me your insights into Santa Claus and how it ties into your profitable proposition," Randall rattles.

Doodle looks down into his hot apple cider. Steam from the liquid rises from the mug. "Eighty-five percent of the gold in Fort Knox and the New York Federal Reserve is owned by other countries besides America. Those countries have elected to move it all to a new repository in Kuala Lumpur in the biggest and most top-secret bank transfer in history."

Doodle blows gently on the steam from his mug. The steam rolls to the middle of the table and swirls into a circle of dense fog. The story Doodle tells plays out in the mist like a magical hologram. Randall, Mosh Pit, and Fred lean back in their seats, amazed at the vision coalescing on the tabletop.

From the fog, a loading dock at an American harbor emerges. A dozen forklifts crawl up a gangplank in a line to an enormous Nimitz-class Aircraft Carrier. Each one carries a pallet of stacked gold bricks.

"Five days ago, a gigantic Aircraft Carrier left the United States for Malaysia," Doodle continues. The foggy vision changes to show the Carrier sailing in the open sea. Sailors, stationed at anti-aircraft guns, watch the sky. Several American fighter jets patrol overhead. "At this moment, it is still en route."

The foggy hologram dissipates from the center of the table. Randall leans back in toward Doodle. "Impressive trick with the steam. Is that magic?"

"I don't know. What you consider magic is commonplace to other kinds in this world," Doodle says. "My people, a few of us anyway, have an innate ability to manipulate mists."

"Wow!" Mosh Pit bellows. "Can you conjure storms and turn water into weapons?"

Doodle shakes his head. "We're not mutants from the movies or..." he looks hard at Mosh Pit and his Sumo headband. "Or Japanese anime characters. What I just did is about the extent of it."

Mosh Pit stares at Doodle in amazement. "I was thinking of anime! How'd you know? Can you read minds, too?"

Randall raps the table with his knuckles. "Forget all that! Please, Doodle m'boy, tell us how you know about the ship and the gold!"

Doodle gives a sly grin. "I have access to one of the most advanced intelligence networks on the planet. We monitor every plane in the sky and every ship on the sea. We know about all crime and military maneuvers as they happen and sometimes before. Governments can keep secrets from each other, and criminals can hide from the police, but neither can keep secrets or hide from us."

"And who exactly is 'us'?" Randall pries.

"I thought that was clear by now! I work for those who you might call Santa Claus," Doodle retorts.

Mosh Pit jumps into the conversation with child-like joy. "Santy Claus! He's the best!"

Doodle turns to him. "Like I said, you only know the fictionalized, commercial version of Santa Claus. Nicholas and Ooby don't even use that name for themselves."

Randall draws Doodle's eyes back to him with a wave of his hand. "Allow me to make a prognostication. If we were able to somehow know a little about the real version of your boss, or bosses, then I'm supposing we'd be able to find that Carrier and get that gold. Is that right?"

Doodle nods. "If you know everything about the so-called Santa Claus, which I do, neither will be a problem."

"What's not to know about Santy?" Mosh Pit queries in a rhetorical fashion. "He lives in the North Pole with a bunch of elves who make super-awesome toys. On Christmas Eve, he flies around the world and delivers presents to all the good girls and boys. Easy peasy lemon-squeezy."

Doodle rubs a hand over his face, again frustrated. "That's hogwash. Firstly, who you call Santa Claus lives in Antarctica. At least that's what you northerners have named it. Secondly, we're not elves and we certainly don't make toys. We're artisans of some of the finest textiles, pottery, watches, clocks, and handmade ceramic pieces in history. Our work commands the highest prices in the most prestigious markets across the globe. We've also created a line of premium chocolates and confections that have single-handedly changed the gourmet candy landscape. We aren't mere toymakers!"

Mosh Pit is downtrodden by the news that goes against everything he grew up believing. "This is all too much. You're telling me Santy lives in the South Pole?"

"Of course!" Doodle trumpets. "The confusion comes in that the South used to be North and vice versa. The poles reversed at the end of the Enchanted Age. I thought everybody knew that!"

Mosh Pit shakes his head in confusion. Randall rubs his gloved hands together, releasing a new puff of dust. "Tell us about this Enchanted Age, if you will."

Doodle talks fast as if he is reiterating facts that everybody should know. "It was the time of the unified continents and magical beasts, and my kind, the Eno Saints. The crystal comet crashed and brought forth the world we know today." Randall and the other two look at Doodle dumbly. "When the crystal comet struck the unified continent, the poles reversed, the land masses separated, and the New Age was born. The humans rose up and took over the world and my kind were forced to move to the one place where humans couldn't live."

"By that, you mean the South Pole or, more precisely, the old North Pole?" Randall surmises.

"Exactly!"

"You and the other elves and Santa?"

Doodle is indignant. "We're not elves! And Nicholas came way later. Don't bother asking your questions. I already know them. How does he get down the chimney? How does he make it all the way around the world in one night and carry all those presents? How does he know so much about people and live so long?" Mosh Pit and Randall nod. Even Fred perks up and takes an interest.

"The secret to Santa Claus lies in the crystals from the core of the comet."

Randall slaps his hands together. Sooty dust flies anew. "So that man tonight was Santa Claus? The real Santa Claus?"

Doodle cocks his head at him. "That was Nicholas. You didn't meet Ooby. They're a team. And again, they don't use that name. Anyway, the fact that it was him shouldn't surprise you. His legacy has always been more about helping children than delivering presents."

Randall grits his teeth, a realization dawning on him. "About those crystals. Tell me everything you know."

Doodle blows more steam from his mug into the center of the table. The hologram reappears, this time showing the earlier scene from the mall's parking lot where Ooby swung the scarf like a sling. Doodle jeers as he points in the mist, "That's Ooby."

"Forget him. Get to the crystals," implores Randall.

The misty hologram focuses on the small crystal.

Doodle continues. "When the crystal comet struck the Earth, the core split into several pieces. Now, wormholes open between its broken parts. When used correctly, one can access the wormholes and teleport between the pieces of the crystals," Doodle says. "Ooby calls them space-time conduits, but everybody knows they're wormholes."

In the cloudy hologram, Nicholas vanishes from the parking lot, reappears behind Chris in the convertible, and puts him in a chokehold.

Mosh Pit points at the image. "Told you ol' Jailbird wasn't a good Santa!"

Randall is beside himself with excitement at the prospect of the crystals.

"There are four crystals in total," Doodle goes on. "Nicholas has the two smallest pieces. One, he keeps on a necklace. The other he drops down the chimney or through a window or what not. When he touches the crystal on his neck, he is instantly teleported to wherever the other crystal may be. Those are the ones he uses while he's fighting crime day to day and on Christmas Eve when he has to get in a house to deliver presents."

Randall rubs the bruise on the side of his face, remembering the fight he had with Nicholas in the Glenlake Circle home. "He moved so fast," he mumbles. "It makes sense now."

"No. That's not how he beat you so easily. We'll get to that," Doodle interjects. "First, I gotta tell you about the big crystals. The two big crystals do the heavy lifting. Those are the money crystals. The ones we have to get for my plan to work."

This time, Randall blows steam from his mug toward the center of the table. Doodle reaches out with his hand and swirls the steam around until it's dense enough for another vision. Now, a football-sized crystal appears. It breaks into two perfect pieces. One piece falls into an open-faced case that is just big enough to hold it. The other falls into another case in what looks like the bed of a small truck.

"One of the big halves is in Eno. That's what we call our town in Antarctica." Doodle points at the second crystal in the fading hologram. "The other half of the crystal is bolted in the back of the sleigh that Nicholas and Ooby use to fly around the world. This is how they manage to carry all those presents on Christmas Eve."

Doodle waves his hand through the dissipating steam cloud. It grows in density at his command and the hologram returns, this time showing a small man like Ooby standing with a present over the crystal in the case. He drops the present toward the crystal. It disappears. The hologram then shifts to the back of the sleigh. The present reappears over the second crystal.

Mosh Pit reaches for the present with a wide, toothy grin. His fingers grasp for it but pass completely through the hologram. It fades for good.

"Mosh Pit!" Randall chastises.

"I'm sorry," he moans and slumps in his chair. "I thought that present was for me."

Doodle resumes. "We transport presents from our staging facility in Eno to the sleigh, wherever in the world it may be. The presents pile up over the crystal in the sleigh and are categorized for the children Nicholas happens to be visiting. It's very coordinated and efficient. This keeps the sleigh from having to be too big and our deer don't get overworked pulling a heavy load."

"Yay! He has reindeer! At least that part of the story is true!" Mosh Pit perks up again.

"Yeah, mostly. Sure. Whatever," Doodle grumbles dismissively. "Somehow that old poem got the names of the deer right, but that's about all."

Mosh Pit claps. "There's Dasher and Dancer and Prancer and..."

Randall nudges Mosh Pit. He wants to keep Doodle talking without interruption. "Okay. We know how he carries all the presents. Now tell us how it's possible that he can get about the whole big wide world to deliver all those presents in one night."

Doodle points at Randall's bruised cheek. "This is the part that relates to his speed, as you learned about so well earlier tonight."

Randall rubs the sore spot again.

"The crystal back in Eno is in its case, which sits at the base of a very ancient Grandfather Clock. The crystal is attached by a network of wires to the Clock. I don't claim to fully understand it since Ooby won't let me reverse engineer it, but..."

"Reverse engineer?" Mosh Pit asks. "What's driving a train backwards got to do with the clock?"

Doodle's mouth drops open and he stares at Mosh Pit in utter disbelief. Randall laughs as if it's no rare occurrence for Mosh Pit to make such a goofy statement. "He means that Ooby won't let him take the clock apart to see how it works." Mosh Pit nods, fully on board now.

Doodle rolls his eyes. "Anyway, as I was saying, the crystal in Eno is connected to a clock that Ooby built. Everything within a certain distance of the crystals assumes the nature of the clock. If Ooby sets the Grandfather Clock to a super-fast speed, it impacts everything within its power. We call the process the Time Bender. Nicholas has a wristwatch that is linked to the crystal clock. When he presses a button on the watch, he activates the Time Bender. Time for Nicholas and everything a few feet around him moves super-slow."

Randall thinks back to earlier in the evening at the house on Glenlake Circle. Randall remembers aiming the gun at Nicholas, who then touched his watch. Time around Nicholas slowed as he continued moving in real time. The bullets came at him in succession, but they were going in super-slow motion. Nicholas dodged them and stepped by Randall.

"Nicholas feels as though he is moving at normal speed," Doodle continues. "But to someone outside the Time Bender's influence and in regular time, he's moving mega-fast. Like light speed fast. That's why Santa Claus is nearly impossible to see on Christmas Eve." Randall's anger suddenly mounts. Doodle can't miss his overt annoyance. "Everything alright?"

Randall responds through clenched teeth. "I'm fine. Just starting to put some pieces together. Continue."

Doodle cracks a wry smile, as if he senses that Randall is vexed by something in his past that involves Nicholas. "He has that effect on people like you, you know?" Randall shoots a stabbing glare at him, so Doodle backs off. "Back to the clock. Ooby adjusts it on Christmas Eve so that it encompasses our whole town, the sleigh and the deer, and Nicholas. By Christmas morning, we've worked for an extremely long time. For the rest of the world, it's just been one night."

Mosh Pit gushes with gleeful approval. "That's smart! And awesome! And awesomely smart! You guys are rocking it!"

"Who is this Ooby?" Randall asks, ignoring Mosh Pit's fanboy outburst.

Doodle's eyes darken with a sudden shift in his mood. "Only the most oppressive despot in history. He's the oldest of our kind. Thinks he's the smartest, too. That's not saying much because our kind isn't known for being too intelligent."

"Let me guess. He isn't nearly as smart as you," Randall gibes as he sips his cider. Doodle doesn't catch the obvious sarcasm.

"Right! You're right! I am smarter! But he thinks I'm naive because I'm young."

"What are you? Fourteen? Fifteen?" Mosh Pit asks with true curiosity.

"Three hundred!" chimes Doodle.

"Of course. You're immortal. We must have forgotten," Randall simpers.

"Ooby has hidden us away in the coldest place in the world so he can control us. My people used to own this planet until Ooby imprisoned us under an ice shelf!" Doodle is getting louder and louder as he speaks. He pulls a vacation pamphlet from his shirt and hands it to Randall, who quickly glances at it.

"Bora Bora?"

"It's warm there. That's where we'll go when we're free," asserts Doodle.

Randall folds the pamphlet and pockets it. "So, we'll take over the sleigh, then fly you to Bora Bora. The other oppressed Saints will transport through the crystals. Is that right?"

"Precisely. Once we're there, I'll tell you where the boat is. You can use the sleigh and the Time Bender to steal the gold."

Mosh Pit spouts more unintentional adulation for Santa Claus. "But Santy knows everything. Won't he know what we're planning?"

"He only knows what his handheld computer tells him," Doodle says as he sips from his mug. "We have access to global databases. That's where we get our information. Without his handheld, he's as clueless as you guys."

Randall winces at the insult but presses on. "And what of his immortality? Don't you think that might complicate our situation somewhat?"

"My kind have exceedingly long lives, but we're not immortal," Doodle explains. "As far as I can tell, neither is Nicholas. He's not invincible either. He's tougher than most men, but only because he's trained himself over a long period of time. He's spent time in the Shaolin Temple studying Kung Fu. He went to Brazil to learn Jiu Jitsu from its earliest practitioners, and he practically invented Krav Maga."

"Awesome!" Mosh Pit pipes in, eager and happy. "I wonder if he knows Sumo?"

Randall backhands him across the arm. "Easy on the geek-outs," he murmurs through clenched teeth. "We're not here to sign up for the Nicholas fan-club."

Mosh Pit slumps back in his seat. Randall turns to Doodle again. "He's a real tough guy. I think we know that already. How do we beat him?"

"Just because he's super-skilled, ages slowly, and heals faster than normal doesn't mean he can't feel pain or be defeated in a battle." Doodle drains his mug of cider in one sip and begins looking for the Barkeep for a refill. "Unlikely, maybe, but not impossible. Especially if you know his tricks and can level the playing field, so to speak."

"That's what I want to hear, my bantam-weight amigo," Randall says, grinning again. "How do we do that?"

Doodle waves at the Barkeep, who is still dancing with the rest of the crowd and doesn't see him. He gives up. "Who cares anyways? Our beef is with Ooby."

"Yours maybe," Randall retorts lowly, almost to himself. "Mine is with Nicholas." He nudges Fred, who is in the middle of a monstrous yawn. "Right, Fred?"

Fred gives a listless nod.

"So where does Nicholas begin delivering presents tomorrow night?" Randall asks as he pushes his mug of cider in front of Doodle.

Doodle takes Randall's mug with a nod of appreciation. "At midnight in the Land of the Rising Sun. Where else?"

"Oh dandy. Just dandy." Randall rubs his hands together in devilish fashion. Then, he smacks Mosh Pit's back.

"Hey! What'd you do that for?" Mosh Pit grumps.

"Looks like you'll get your chance to fight like a Sumo warrior after all, Moshy! I believe we're going to Japan!"

CHAPTER 13

At the magnificent mall...

Nicholas and Ooby, now back in their original clothes, walk across the roof of the sprawling building to a gray sleigh. It's just a bit bigger than a two-man bobsled and is attached by leather harnesses to two small white-tail deer standing side by side. Their antlers are full and wide, but they aren't much bigger than German Shepherds. The glorious city, all lit and pulsing with life and excitement, stretches out into the night as far as the eye can see.

"Longest hour of my life! Imagine me, a mere Christmas Elf!" Ooby rants.

Nicholas chuckles with a slight shake of his head. "Imagine." Nicholas pets the deer. They lap up his affection. He takes two cookies from his pocket and feeds one to each.

Ooby gets in the sleigh. "You never said how things went with the rest of the gang."

"Well, for starters," Nicholas sighs. "Randall shot at me."

Ooby gives an expression of shock. "What? Randall? Little Randy Zack?" He leans back into the seat and shakes his head with reservation. "I guess I can't say that I'm surprised. He was always quite a stinker. Was Fred there, too?"

Nicholas pats the deer. "Yes, but more subdued than I remember."

"A subdued Fred is a far better Fred if you ask me."

"True. With his history, he could be very dangerous if he wanted to be." Nicholas looks at the lights of the city, lost in thought. Ooby senses Nicholas has more to say, but needs prompting.

"You seem disturbed by something besides Randall shooting at you. What is it?"

Nicholas turns to him. The deer scamper behind him, perhaps wondering why the petting stopped. "I sent their father to jail exactly thirty-five years ago tonight."

Ooby throws up his hands. "Oh, Nicholas, not again! You've got to stop beating yourself up over lost causes. In the time we've been doing this, there have been plenty of instances of us busting succeeding generations of the same family. Sins of the father, repeated by the son. Blather, blather, blather!"

"I'm serious, Ooby. Randy and Fred were there that night, remember? Kids should never witness their father's fall from grace. What if I'm the reason they've turned to a life of crime?"

"Gerard Zack robbed half the banks in London with his kids in tow! What were we supposed to do?"

Nicholas turns his attention back to the deer. He gives each a few more cookies, which they gobble with gratitude. "I just hope I didn't fail them in my attempt to do good."

"You never failed them, Nicholas. We did what was necessary. Gerard's actions were financially crippling untold numbers of families in all of Britain. He was stealing their life savings. He was stripping away college funds from children."

"Randall also called me by the term they use for me in jail."

"Uh huh. The ol' boogey man for bad guys thing again."

"Right. Ooby, what if he makes the connection? What if he realizes I'm the guy who did that to his dad?"

"He was ten at the time. He won't. Besides, you brought them extra nice presents the next night."

"People aren't as easy to appease as you'd like to think."

"They don't appreciate what you do for them on Christmas Eve like you'd like to think."

"The children do, Ooby. The children are appreciative."

Ooby crosses his arms defiantly. "Those appreciative children grow up to be unappreciative adults."

Nicholas chuckles lowly. "Here we go. The same argument every December."

"Come on, Nicholas. You know this whole thing has gotten out of hand. A hundred years ago, it wasn't so bad. Now, there are just too many children and they all expect too much. Their image of us is a parody of what it used to be. The commercialized Santa Claus has no resemblance to who we are or why we do what we do."

Nicholas leaves the deer and walks to the side of the sleigh. "I know you'd rather just scrap the whole Christmas Eve agenda and go on some real life-saving missions like every other night of the year, but I've told you a thousand times, we're not doing that."

"Christmas Eve takes our energies from where we should be focusing them. That's all I'm saying."

Nicholas slides into the sleigh's narrow bench seat beside Ooby. He flicks the reins. The two deer lift off, pulling the sleigh behind them. They fold their legs beneath their bodies and bob their heads in unison. Within seconds, they are high over the city. The flight is fast, quiet, soft.

"I couldn't disagree more," Nicholas replies. "It might be our most important endeavor."

CHAPTER 14

At the stately house on Glenlake Circle...

The sleigh carrying Nicholas and Ooby lands softly and silently on the roof of the home. Doodle is leaning beside the chimney, waiting. As soon as the deer and sleigh touch down, he leaps into the back. Nicholas flicks the reins. The deer lift off again.

"I was getting worried that you two forgot me!" Doodle exclaims.

Ooby turns in his seat to look at him. "We had an unexpected delay. Any problem here?"

"Nope," Doodle chirps proudly. "The police came right after Nicholas left. Those three are on the way to getting what they deserve."

Nicholas grins. "You're very enthusiastic about this work, aren't you?"

"It's fun to punish bullies!" Doodle says with a wide smile as his eyes drift to Ooby.

"Ooby has to check on things at home, but I'm going to shut down a sweatshop in Mumbai." Nicholas seems genuinely happy that Doodle has taken such a sudden interest in their mission. "Want to tag along?"

"Sure!" Doodle replies without the slightest hint that he is betraying his mentors.

Ooby objects. "No. No. We have too much to do before tomorrow. I need Doodle's help with the others."

"Oh, come on! You never let me have any fun with Nicholas!" Doodle gripes.

Ooby keeps a calm demeanor. "There will be other sweatshops. Tonight, I need your help."

"But I'll watch from a window! I'll even stay in the sleigh!"

"Doodle, I said 'no'. Head home and I'll be right behind you." Ooby motions to the large half of the crystal beside Doodle. It looks exactly as Doodle described to Randall and his crew.

"No fair!" Doodle pouts. "This is just like every time any of us want to go somewhere! You put us all away in that far off land to oppress us!"

"It's to protect you! I hope you haven't been talking that gibberish in front of the others again!" Ooby returns heatedly.

"Scared they might hear the truth for once?"

Nicholas holds up a hand. "Okay, gentlemen. That's enough. Let's calm down."

"I'll calm down when Doodle does as I ask without fighting every word." Ooby points a rigid finger toward the crystal. "Hop through that crystal this very minute before you get yourself in trouble!"

Doodle folds his arms in another display of outward defiance.

"Now, young Saint!" Ooby barks. It is loud and sudden enough to startle Doodle. He flings his arms about in a quick tantrum, then he touches the crystal and vanishes. Exasperated, Ooby says, "That boy! He thinks he's so smart!"

"He is smart," Nicholas responds in a soothing voice, trying to calm Ooby's nerves.

"Bah! He's only three hundred and barely got his wits about him! Why, I was a bumbling stooge at his age!"

Nicholas nods. "Perhaps you were, but I doubt it." He flicks the reins again. "It's a mistake to assume you're the only one of your kind whose intelligence will progress beyond that of a human eight-year-old. Doodle is advancing much quicker than a normal Saint. He even shares your ability to manipulate the mists. If nothing else, you must allow him some leeway just because of that. Learn to trust him. Who knows? He may be the leader of Eno one day."

Ooby is indignant. "Not anytime soon. I have a few millennia left in me."

Nicholas can't help but smile. "I stand corrected."

"You bet your baboon bippy you do!" Ooby crawls over the seat into the back of the sleigh. "But I understand what you're saying, Nicholas. He's a smart kid. I took care of his mother while she was carrying him and I delivered him at birth. I was the first to hold him. Even then, I sensed the electricity coursing through him. That's a great thing and highly unusual to my kind. But potential like that comes with pitfalls. His intelligence can be used for things in the light or things in the dark. I'm trying to steer him correctly through discipline and tough love. I'm not sure your unconditional forgiveness is the right approach with him. He's making a habit of taking advantage of you."

"Perhaps," Nicholas nods. He looks back at Ooby with a wry smile. "I'll try to be more surly, churlish, and obstinate in the future."

Ooby cracks a smile back as the serious conversation turns light-hearted and easy in a moment. "Your inability to be any of those is exactly why I sought you out so long ago. Besides, I hear I have that side of the personality spectrum covered enough for the both of us." He claps Nicholas on the shoulder as a sign of a truce. "Are you sure you won't need my help?"

Nicholas shakes his head. "It's a simple stopover. I'll be fine."

"Very well then." Ooby touches the crystal in the sleigh's bed and disappears. Nicholas clicks at the deer as they fly on, high and fast.

CHAPTER 15

In the backstreets of Mumbai, India…

The warehouse is large, open, and poorly lit. It is filled with the sound of rattling sewing machines as over a hundred children construct purses with fake designer labels. The children, from 5 to 12 in age, are sweaty and overtly distressed.

Six cruel taskmasters pace a long center aisle between the rows of tables. They yell mercilessly at the children. Three of the men have whips. Three have clubs.

Nicholas steps from the shadows. The six men have yet to notice him, but the children look up as he stops at the end of the center aisle. He speaks loudly for all in the building to hear.

"Children, you may stop!"

The six men notice him all at once. They glance quickly at each other as if confirming that they are truly seeing such a brazen challenge to their authority, which is something completely foreign to them. In unison, they ready their weapons and move in Nicholas's direction.

"What did you say?" one taskmaster barks.

"I said," Nicholas growls between clenched teeth, suddenly exhibiting something exactly opposite of the unconditional forgiveness Ooby had mentioned earlier. It is the dark expression that overcame him in the convertible with Chris. "These children are free to go."

Another taskmaster can't help but belch out a guffaw. "That so?" He turns to the hall full of children. "Back to work, you vermin! Every one of you!" He turns to Nicholas as he pats his club in his open palm several times.

A third taskmaster hastens his approach toward Nicholas. "I don't know who you work for, but you stumbled into the wrong warehouse!"

Nicholas gives a mischievous grin. "Work? None of this is ever work."

Amid the distraction, all the children flee the warehouse.

The first taskmaster sprints at Nicholas. "Get him!"

All six men charge, their weapons poised for attack. As they come, Nicholas widens his stance and balls his fists.

What follows is not an easy thing for anyone involved, but after ten minutes...

All is calm. All is bright.

Part Two

So led by light of a star sweetly gleaming…

An airplane flies high over the Pacific Ocean. Randall, Mosh Pit, and Fred sit together in a row of seats. Mosh Pit is in the middle and his substantial bulk crowds the other two.

"I can't believe we're gonna steal all the gold in the world!" Mosh Pit blurts with an excited clap of his hands.

"Don't talk about that here, you idiot!" Randall chastises in a hushed tone.

Mosh Pit drops his head. "Sorry."

Fred offers nothing but a yawn.

Mosh Pit sees and gives Fred an approving nod. "Say, Fred, maybe you'll be able to get some sleep while we're flying."

Randall elbows Mosh Pit in the arm, trying to nudge him more into his own seat. "He can't sleep. He's an insomniac."

Mosh Pit laughs aloud. "Ha! An in-zombie-act!" He points a finger at Fred, who could care less. "At least he only calls me an idiot!"

CHAPTER 17

High in the sky over the massive continent called Antarctica...

The gray sleigh contrasts with the white-out below. While the Northern Hemisphere is enjoying a wonderful winter wonderland, it's the middle of the summer for Antarctica. Despite this, the landscape is still freezing cold and covered in ice and snow. The only difference between summer and winter in this part of the Southern Hemisphere is that the land is drenched in perpetual daylight in its summer months.

Seated at the reins of the sleigh, Nicholas presses a button on the dashboard. A sliding door opens in a glacier and he steers the sleigh into it. The sleigh zips down a winding, three-mile-long tunnel bored into the ice shelf. At the end of it, there is a huge cavern, which creates a dome in the ice over exposed black rock. The dome is as big as any modern football stadium and at least one and a half times as high.

Within the giant dome is the beautifully quaint, secluded town of Eno. Neon lights cross the ceiling of the dome and illuminate it in a soft blue glow. Because the dome was carved from the ice shelf in a valley between black granite mountains, there is a huge rocky outcrop jutting inward on the edge of the dome. The town's colorful buildings are on the sides and atop the rocky protuberance. They are simple, colorful dwellings stacked tightly on and above each other, like those along the coast of Positano, Italy or the favelas of Rio De Janeiro, Brazil. Oddly enough, there are no noticeable Christmas decorations.

At the center of the city is a large common area with gardens of unique plant-life in the middle. Small, open golf cart-like vehicles traverse the roads cut in the gardens. The inhabitants all resemble Ooby and Doodle in that they are perfectly proportioned to humans, only smaller by nearly half.

Six small deer, like the two pulling the sleigh, fly freely beneath the dome over the city, frolicking happily. Two Unicorns roam the streets below. They match the deer in size and are nearly identical in appearance to ibexes, except their coats are pure white and they each have a single, straight horn extending from their foreheads instead of two backwards sloping ones.

When the sleigh emerges over the city from the tunnel, there is an eruption of cheers from the small people, the Saints of Eno, well below. The six deer fly in close to greet the sleigh and two deer pulling it. Together, the sleigh and its six deer escorts fly to a landing area on top of the biggest Mega-Building in Eno, which is a large industrial structure that looks like an old factory. It isn't nearly as aesthetic as the radiant residences surrounding it.

The sleigh hovers over the pad for a moment, more like a descending helicopter than a plane. With an expert handling of the reins, Nicholas lands the sleigh, ever so softly. Ooby is standing nearby.

"How did it go?" he asks as Nicholas hops from the sleigh.

"The taskmasters were a lively crew, but the children are safe now. That's all that matters." Nicholas pets Dasher and Dancer. Then, he releases them from their harnesses to fly off with the other deer, who are hovering overhead, eager to reunite with their friends. "How are things progressing here?"

Ooby starts in a huff as they cross the sleigh pad toward an entryway to the building. "Thankfully, I was able to get here before Doodle talked too much of that rubbish to the rest–"

"Ooby," Nicholas interrupts as he holds up a hand. "I meant with the Christmas Eve preparations."

"Oh, right. Of course." Ooby is clearly still perturbed. "Sometimes, that boy…"

Nicholas raises an eyebrow. "Let it go, my friend. The preparations, if you please."

Ooby shakes his head as if to clear it. "We're as ready as we've ever been. Every stop has been planned to the last detail and our timetable is set. We just have to prepare the sleigh. Why don't you go get some rest?"

"Sure. After the run-through," Nicholas says as he opens the door for Ooby to enter first.

They walk into a complex resembling NASA's mission control center. The large room is lined with multiple rows of computer consoles. The computers are vaguely familiar, as if precursors to modern desktops, but they are different, too. The idea is the same, perhaps, but the technology that got them where they are was developed in a totally separate way. There are numerous Saints working at the multitude of keyboards. At the front of the room are large monitors with digital maps of the world. The Saints are all humming a pleasant tune in perfect unison.

"The final census report is in," Ooby begins. "The routes have changed in some areas of Europe and China due to population consolidation. I've made the appropriate adjustments to the Time Bender to allot for the increased volume."

"And the U.S. Aircraft Carrier?" Nicholas queries.

"Way out at sea. We won't interfere with their airspace at all. However, you should be aware of an illegal rocket launch out of Tokyo."

"Ah, Saki Crocodile again, I presume."

"Who else?" Ooby says with a shrug. "He's launching after four A.M. Japan Standard Time, so we should be long gone by then."

Nicholas shakes his head with bemusement. "Poor Saki. Such intelligence and potential, but so misguided."

"Yeah, we seem to see a lot of that this time of year," Ooby sighs.

As they pass through the building, the Saints wave at Nicholas with unfettered excitement. He speaks to those who are near and greets them with pats on the back.

"Excellent work Tug, Kooble, Noot," he touts with heartfelt praise. "Glad to see you Jubby and Gok." He follows Ooby into an adjacent room.

The new room is much bigger than the computer center. In fact, it's immense. This room is where all the main work in Eno is performed. Another hundred Saints construct wooden clocks as they hum a melodic tune. They all look up and cheerfully wave as Nicholas passes by. He high-fives some and greets still more by name.

"Hello Wibble, Ishy, and Drib! You're all doing great work, friends." He waves to all in the room. "Thank you, Saints, one and all!"

Nicholas's impact on the peaceful little beings is hard to miss. The Saints are thoroughly enamored with him and it shows. They blush, nod, or gesticulate emphatically. When he touches or recognizes them individually, they light up and smile like children at a parade where the guest of honor is tossing out candy.

Ooby smiles at Nicholas's instant boosting effect on the crowd of Saints. "They would follow you into battle, if they knew of such a concept."

"They're working so hard. A well-deserved break is coming soon."

"This year's work has been done for weeks, but they insist on coming in at their own volition. They're simply too delighted to get a head start on next year's inventory of outgoing stock. Our 'Wee Ones' line of clocks, ceramic figurines, and glass collectibles are commanding higher prices around the world as they become renowned for their quality and craftsmanship."

Nicholas holds his index finger up to interrupt. "You're pitching me, Ooby. This isn't a sales meeting."

"Of course. Sorry. I'm so used to giving that speech to the trade officers that it has become automatic," Ooby says in defense of himself. They walk to a pair of poles that descend through a hole in the floor to a lower level. They get on and slide down, side by side.

The floor below is the staging area for the factory building. A huge open space that is as large as the factory area and computer center above, it's where the multitudes of presents are processed for distribution throughout the world. Convoluted conveyor belts zip the presents in from other, unseen parts of the facility. The presents are categorized into massive stacks near a tall, ornate Grandfather Clock on one end.

At the base of the giant Clock is the other half of the football-sized crystal, just as Doodle described it to Randall. A conveyor belt goes up the center of the room and dead ends at the Clock. A hundred more Saints are working in the huge room, humming in unison like the Saints in the other areas. As Nicholas walks by with Ooby, he waves to all and speaks to a few.

"Hey Goomy, Faddle, Kipper," he smiles. "Good work Hooble and Pook."

Ooby continues with his well-rehearsed speech. "In exchange for our 'Wee Ones' products, we received the Mitacom Nine game system from Bass Industries for all kids eight and over. From Rankin's Department Stores, we have the Annabelle and Andy Fantasy Set or the Flammable Fists of Fire action gloves for those aged four to seven."

"Excellent. What do we have for the toddlers this year?" Nicholas asks.

Ooby answers quickly and with glee. "You'll love this! We have Mr. Goose's Tickle Drill!"

Nicholas nods with happy approval. "Bravo, Ooby! That's fantastic! The children will be so pleased."

"We also have the usual model trains, dolls, and sports gear for children who already have the aforementioned," Ooby resumes as Nicholas beams. "Plus, one remote control airplane I had to scramble to find at the last minute because you promised one to Deon. I thought we agreed you wouldn't guarantee specific toys to children within a week of Christmas."

"Consider that a one-time offense," Nicholas muses.

Ooby scoffs, "One time. Yeah, right." He's obviously heard it before. They continue through the staging area. "Speaking of making promises, Chris Boopingsly did exactly that on Santa Claus's behalf tonight. It is a bit more difficult to follow through on than a plane."

"What might that be?" Nicholas asks as he continues surveying the staging area.

"Aiden asked Santa to bring his unemployed father a job."

Nicholas shakes his head. "Ouch. That's a tuffy. Especially since we're so short on time. Any ideas on what we can do?"

"I've reached out to some folks I know. There are a couple of options that fit his skill-set I can pursue while you rest," Ooby says.

Nicholas gives a confident nod. As their conversation pauses, Nicholas looks down at Ooby with a gaze of admiration. He knows Ooby cares deeply for human children. After all, saving the children was Ooby's mission before it was Nicholas's. Though he puts more emphasis on their physical well-being, Ooby hates to see them suffer disappointment of any kind. In that way, he is not at all different than Nicholas. Though Ooby hardly ever admits it, he is pleased with their Christmas Eve efforts and the joy they spread on this one night is paramount. Nicholas is confident that Ooby will come through because, when it comes to the children, Ooby always does.

Ooby catches Nicholas's expression. "Oh, for goodness sakes, what?"

Nicholas smiles. "I was just thinking that you have procured some very expensive toys this year. Did we build enough units to receive all of this in trade?"

"We have half a billion gifts to give. Enough for every child who observes Christmas," Ooby says proudly.

"But our export demands must have been outrageous. How did we build enough clocks, figurines, and collectibles?"

"We didn't. This year's new project made up the difference. By utilizing the personnel in the candy district and mass producing our own line of gourmet chocolates, we had enough."

Nicholas stops. Ooby keeps walking, but turns and looks back. "That's a good thing, Nicholas."

"Oh, I know it's a good thing. It's a great thing, actually," Nicholas says. "Remind me again, who came up with that idea?"

Ooby turns away with a fling of his arms. "Oh, for crying out loud! You know who!"

Nicholas follows. "Yes, but it wouldn't hurt for you to say it."

"Doodle, okay!" Ooby barks. "It was Doodle's plan! I see what you're doing! Good for Doodle!"

Nicholas follows him. "Good for you for recognizing Doodle's brilliant idea. That's exactly what an effective leader does. Together, you two have assured that it will be a great Christmas for all the children."

"Bah! It's a waste of a day when we should be doing our real work!" barks Ooby, who seems to be making a conscious effort to project cantankerousness.

Nicholas recognizes Ooby's outburst isn't from genuine anger and chooses to playfully antagonize him further. "Uh oh. Someone isn't in the holiday spirit. I think Ooby needs a big, Christmassy smile on his face." Nicholas picks up one present, then another, as they go by on the conveyor belt toward the staging area. He shakes each of the gifts by his ear. "Where oh where is the Tickle Drill?"

"Again, I say Bah!" Ooby says as he continues off in a huff. Nicholas laughs and follows him.

After they go, a green sleigh, bigger than the gray two-man sleigh and perched on the main conveyor belt, zips toward the crystal at the belt's end. The gray sleigh comes in on another belt and stops when the two sleighs are side by side.

Several Saints, all business and working fast, swarm the two sleighs. The crystal is unbolted and placed into the green one, and the Saints secure it.

CHAPTER 18

On the airplane...

Mosh Pit, in the aisle seat now, is sound asleep and covered by a ridiculously small blanket, which, on his massive chest, appears more like a bib on a baby. His snores are so loud and comical that a case could be made that he is faking. He isn't. Mosh Pit is deep in the Land of Nod.

Beside him in the center seat, Randall nudges Mosh Pit's encroaching girth back into the direction from which it had come. Fred, heavy-eyed, stares out the window beside Randall.

"Our time is near, Bruvva," Randall says lowly, as if talking to himself as much as he is to his overtired brother. "After all these years, we will avenge our Fadda." His thoughts are coalescing as he speaks. From deep in the caverns of his mind, ideas emerge and he gives them words. Perhaps he had never even thought them before, but now he has a new hatred blooming in his heart. Now, he has someone to hold responsible for all his life's missteps and misfortunes. Now, finally, he has someone to blame.

"He took everything from me. From us," Randall continues. "He put our Fadda away and left us alone. Soon, he will pay."

Fred looks at Randall and raises his eyebrows. Randall pauses, ready to hear a profound response to his words. Instead, Fred yawns.

The plane's Captain makes an announcement over the intercom. "Ladies and Gentlemen, we are starting our final descent into Tokyo. Welcome to the land where the sun rises to give birth to every new day, which, today, happens to be Christmas Eve!"

"And where the sun sets on Santa Claus," Randall quips with an expecting glance at Fred. Fred doesn't laugh. Randall makes a sour face at his non-response.

Outside the plane, the sun is rising behind Mt. Fuji.

CHAPTER 19

On the sleigh pad atop the mega-building in Eno...
Nicholas emerges from a doorway wearing a heavy, deep red leather jacket. He also has a thicker, warmer beanie cap, black pants, and his familiar workman's boots.

All eight deer are attached to the large green sleigh and most of the Saints have circled around it, creating a huge crowd on top of the building. Everyone cheers as Nicholas walks out. He sweeps his hand way over his head in a wave and turns all the way around to be sure to see and acknowledge them all. Around the sleigh pad, a single strand of traditional multi-colored Christmas lights hangs to celebrate the occasion. Nicholas sees the lights and gives a hearty laugh.

"Nice touch! Very good!" he says as he finds Ooby in front of the crowd.

Ooby gives a slight shrug. "It wasn't my idea. It was theirs," he remarks as he motions to the mob of Saints.

Nicholas gives appreciative waves in a circle again. "I love the lights! Thank you all very much."

The Saints continue to cheer as Nicholas walks by the sleigh to a small, cleared area. The marble figure of Baby Jesus from so long ago is in the empty space. Nicholas approaches it and removes his cap. The figure's lifelike eyes, as before, gaze heavenward and his little hands are upturned toward the town's overhead dome. A respectful hush falls over the Saints as they allow Nicholas his annual moment with the statue.

"Hello again, my young friend. Has it been a year already?" Nicholas drops to one knee before the figure. "If it is your will, let us be a blessing to the children tonight."

He bows his head in silent prayer for a prolonged moment. The Saints bow their heads along with him. The sleigh pad is completely silent except for the faintest scamper of deer hooves. Ooby doesn't bow his head, but he watches over the scene with an approving grin.

Nicholas mutters a quiet "Amen", then stands and leaps aboard the sleigh. "Thank you everyone for the hard work you will do throughout our long shift tonight! Merry Christmas!"

With that, he flicks the reins and the deer launch into the airspace under the ice dome. He waves as the crowd of Saints on the sleigh pad give an uproarious cheer. The sleigh whirls over the town a few times, then jets for the ice tunnel's entrance and disappears within it.

Outside, over the ice fields of Antarctica, the sleigh emerges from the glacier and rockets skyward into the season's perpetual daylight.

Moments later, at a computer terminal within the Mission Control Complex, Ooby punches some buttons on a keyboard. He is surrounded by Saints at other terminals. "Establish up-link. We are tracking. Time Bender at the ready."

Other Saints furiously rattle the keys on their own keyboards.

"Let's get this silly night over with so we can resume our purposeful business, shall we?"

A few of the nearby Saints give barely audible grunts of disapproval at Ooby's comment, but they don't stop working. He raises an eyebrow at their nearly imperceptible responses. None of the Saints look at him.

"Perhaps 'silly' is a poor choice of words," he says. The Saints give no indication that they've heard him. "Well, it's not like we're saving lives tonight," he continues defensively. Still, no reaction from the group. He sighs in resignation. "But we will make so many children happy and I guess that's something."

The Saints finally stop typing on their keyboards and look at Ooby in unison. Their collective smiles reveal the absolute joy that they take in the night's work. Ooby glances around at them and returns their smiles, but only for a moment.

"Very well," he says, suddenly business-like again. "Let's get back to it." The Saints resume their work but keep their smiles.

CHAPTER 20

At the stroke of midnight, on the rooftop of a house in Japan…

The sleigh is parked and the eight deer scamper eagerly as they wait. The small crystal flies up from the chimney and lands on the roof by the sleigh. Nicholas appears over the crystal with an empty sack in one hand and cookies and a carrot in the other. He steps softly to the deer.

"They left cookies for me and a carrot for all of you," he says with a chuckle. "If they only knew." He sticks the carrot in his mouth, then feeds the cookies to each of the eight deer in turn. They eat in greedy chomps and gulps. "We're making record time, team. Stupendous job."

He gets in the sleigh and they lift off silently and effortlessly in flight. On the next rooftop over, the deer drift to a stop. Nicholas, moving extremely fast thanks to the Time Bender, gets out with his sack, which is already refilled with presents. He approaches a metal smoke stack, drops the small crystal down, touches his chest, and disappears.

In the home's living room, Nicholas appears beside the wood burning stove. He opens the gift bag, but pauses when he hears muffled groans. The sounds are protracted, as if they are happening in slow motion. Nicholas sees the Takeda family, a father, mother, and two children, girls of 4 and 6 years of age, tied up and gagged with handkerchief muzzles. They are panic-stricken.

Nicholas reaches for his wrist watch and deactivates the Time Bender and time returns to normal around him. When he speaks to the father, it is in perfect Japanese. "What happened?"

From behind him, Nicholas hears a loud battle cry.

"Bonsai!" It's Mosh Pit and he's charging fast. Nicholas reacts with a stiff sidekick to Mosh Pit's stomach. Mosh Pit doubles over, but a concussion grenade rolls in from the other side and explodes. The blast pitches Nicholas against a wall.

Mosh Pit recovers and charges again. He sumo slams Nicholas from behind, burying him deeper in the wall. Nicholas reaches for his wrist watch, but Randall is there with his cane.

"Fore!" he cries as he swings and wallops Nicholas in the ribs. Mosh Pit attacks and crushes Nicholas against another wall. Randall swings again with such force that one of his monocles pops out. Nicholas drops to one knee under the onslaught. Randall tries to swing a third time, but Nicholas catches the cane, rips it away, and swings it at Randall's legs. Randall goes down.

Mosh Pit leaps into the air and lands his huge body on top of Nicholas, who finally topples to the ground. Fred moves in and swipes the watch from Nicholas's wrist as he and Mosh Pit wrestle.

Nicholas rolls from under Mosh Pit and elbows him in the head. Randall, up now, retrieves the cane and swings it once more. Nicholas dodges it as Mosh Pit bear hugs him from behind. Randall takes another swing and pounds Nicholas in the chest. Mosh Pit rams him into the wall repeatedly. Nicholas shrugs from under Mosh Pit's vice-like grip and elbows him. Mosh Pit stumbles back from the blow.

Randall swings yet again, but Nicholas blocks the cane with his forearm and kicks Randall in the chest. Mosh Pit rushes in for more. Nicholas dodges his attack and floors him with a spinning back kick.

Fred activates the Time Bender and tosses it to Randall. Nicholas can barely react as Randall charges toward him, suddenly with super-speed. Even at an obvious speed disadvantage, Nicholas has the where-withal to use the tools available to him. He tosses the small crystal and vanishes, only to reappear several feet away.

Randall stops for a second to look for him, but Nicholas is behind him. He kicks Randall in the back. The watch tumbles from Randall's grasp and slides over to Mosh Pit's feet. Nicholas tosses the crystal again toward the watch. Mosh Pit is within the radius of the Time Bender's effect. He picks it up and punches Nicholas as soon as Nicholas reappears in front of him.

Mosh Pit moves at superspeed as he begins ramming Nicholas with great force. The furious attack plows Nicholas deeper and deeper into the wooden wall until he is nearly plowed through it. Finally, Nicholas drops to his knees and Mosh Pit jumps on him, crushing him flat to the ground. Nicholas is buried beneath Mosh Pit's substantial girth so that only his arms are visible.

When he sees that Nicholas's hands aren't moving, Mosh Pit rolls off of him, out of breath and tired. Randall moves in quickly and delivers another blow with the cane to Nicholas's unconscious body. As Fred snatches the handheld computer and the small crystal from Nicholas, Mosh Pit stands. Once Fred is clear, he leaps, smashing Nicholas under his weight once more. Beneath Mosh Pit, Nicholas gives out a faint groan.

"There should be a second crystal!" Randall barks. "We must have both crystals to make the wormhole!"

Mosh Pit and Randall continue to pummel Nicholas in rapid, unrelenting fashion. Fred frisks Nicholas between blows. He finds the second crystal on a chain around Nicholas's neck and swipes it, just as Mosh Pit drops on Nicholas again for no good reason.

"Strong work, lads! Let's go!" Randall pants.

The trio stops the attack and hurry past the restrained family. At the door, Randall gathers his bag of chains, grenades, and other gear. He looks back at Nicholas, who is already stirring from unconsciousness, but still down.

"You've just been Ran-Zacked," he boasts. "Farewell, Santa Claus!"

The door slams as Nicholas strains to roll over with an exasperated moan. Once fully conscious, his immediate worry is for the Takeda family. He crawls to them and breaks the father's restraints with his bare hands. He then frees the children as the father unties the mother. The adults and two children assist Nicholas to his feet.

The father, Kuni, gives his report of events in a harried and anxious blurt of Japanese.

"They attacked us several hours ago right before we had dinner! They've been waiting for you ever since!" He points to the dining room table piled high with empty dishes. "They passed time by eating! A lot! Especially the big guy! He didn't even leave any corn for popping!"

Nicholas is not so much ignoring Kuni as he is focusing his attention on the children. Their welfare is his real concern.

"Is it really you?" the 6-year-old daughter, Noriko, asks.

"It is. Are you okay?" he says, looking at both of the girls. They nod in unison. "I'm so sorry this happened."

By now, the last few hours' trauma has been replaced with adoration and disbelief that the legend of all legends, the real, honest and true Santa Claus, is indeed standing before them, in the flesh.

"I hope you'll enjoy what I brought you this year," he smiles. He turns to Kuni. "Outside, please. Help me outside."

Kuni helps Nicholas to the door. The children walk beside them, assisting as much as they can. They are too small to offer much in the way of physical support, but their willingness to help does wonders for Nicholas's spirit. He can only smile at them as he shuffles his way to the home's exit.

Outside the house, in the front yard, Nicholas holds his ribs while leaning on Kuni. He looks up to the roof and sees that the sleigh is gone. He searches the sky, but sees nothing.

"They took it. They took the sleigh," he laments.

"How will you catch them?" asks Kuni.

Nicholas looks to the front door. The children are there with their mother between them. They gaze at him hopefully. He is careful to lower his voice when he answers. "I can't. They're working in a different time parameter. They're far away from here by now."

"Where will they go?" Kuni continues.

Answering in English, Nicholas replies, "To my home."

Kuni also begins speaking in English. "What must we do? How can I help?"

"Do you still have your motorcycle?" Nicholas asks.

Kuni shakes his head. "I sold it when I got the one-horse sleigh."

Nicholas chuckles, but winces with the pain in his ribs. "You have a one-horse sleigh?"

"Yes!" Kuni exults, suddenly happy. "An open one! I give rides in the city during the holidays! It has jingle bells and everything!" He can't contain his passion for his new job. "People love going on it and I love taking them!"

Nicholas forces a smile. In this instance, he'd prefer a motorcycle. "I'll send a crew to repair and clean up your home as soon as I'm able. Now, about that one-horse open-sleigh…"

CHAPTER 21

High in the night sky, somewhere over Asia...

Randall, Fred, and Mosh Pit sit three abreast in the sleigh. Fred sits in the middle this time. He is pushed into Randall's side by Mosh Pit's girth. Mosh Pit watches the world below, oblivious to how badly he's crowding out his seatmates. Randall slaps the reins on the deer over and over again, much too harshly.

"Look-it that long snaky thing down there!" Mosh Pit whoops, like an over-excited child.

"That's the Great Wall of China, m'boy," Randall says. "We've been flying for less than five minutes and we're already over China. Amazing! Simply amazing!"

Mosh Pit is suddenly stumped. He strokes his chin in thought, then points his finger in the air. He moves his finger around, thinking deeply. "But if we're going to Bory Bory like we told that little fella at the pub we were gonna do, shouldn't we have gone the other way?"

"If the crystal clock thing works like I've surmised, Fred has plenty of time to take the scenic route," Randall returns, again unnecessarily slapping the reins against the backs of the deer.

Fred perks at the mention of his name, but only for a second. Then he yawns and rests his head on Mosh Pit's shoulder.

"Where are you and me going?" Mosh Pit asks as he adjusts his shoulder to better accommodate Fred.

"We're trying out the space-time conduit. The wormhole," Randall says with a motion toward the crystal in the back of the sleigh.

Mosh Pit shakes his head. "I don't think I'll fit through no wormhole." He pats his substantial belly. "I had a pretty big dinner."

"We'll soon find out. First, we have to get a few items we need for our trip," Randall says as he scans the landscape far below. He spies a team of six Mongolian Mercenaries, traveling a rural mountain road in an old military Jeep.

"And there is item number one." He turns the sleigh and descends toward the caravan of slow-moving mercenaries, which really aren't moving that slowly. Instead, the sleigh is in a different time scheme and therefore moving much, much faster.

"But they weren't part of the little guy's plan!" Mosh Pit chimes in, suddenly indignant. "None of this is!"

Randall yawps, "We're changing the plan, old chum. As a general rule, I don't take orders from fairies, imps, or elves." Randall holds up Nicholas's handheld computer. "Soon, we'll know everything that little pinhead knows and we won't need him anymore."

CHAPTER 22

Inside Eno's Mission Control Center...

Ooby is staring at the large computer screens with profound worry. Several Saints are watching him, taking cues from his reactions as to whether or not they should be worried too.

"He's way off course! Why is he so far off course?" Ooby exclaims. The Saints around him look befuddled. "He should have made seven thousand and forty-one stops between where he was and where he is now! Why isn't he stopping?" None of the Saints can offer an explanation. "Link me to him! Something isn't right!"

In the staging area of the building below the control room, the conveyor belt is moving toward the Grandfather Clock with the crystal at its base, but no presents are on it. The Saints are waiting for word to proceed supplying them again. An ominous silence, except the whirring of the moving belt, hangs over the big room. Doodle watches anxiously from the back.

Suddenly, Mosh Pit appears over the crystal. He looks around for a moment as all the Saints are paralyzed by the shock of his unexpected arrival.

"Aren't you all a bunch of cute little nose nuggets?" he says with genuine sincerity. "Too bad Randall says I got to slam you!" He charges the Saints with playful growls, as if he is chasing children in a game of 'Tag'. The Saints scatter, not at all seeing the fun in Mosh Pit's antics.

Randall appears over the crystal next. He turns and gazes at the elaborate Grandfather Clock and touches it with awe.

"Amazing," he whispers. Then, he yells out to Mosh Pit. "Mosh Pit! Outside!"

Mosh Pit continues to chase the fleeing Saints out of the building's exit as the six Mongolian mercenaries appear over the crystal, one by one. Each mercenary has a machete in a sheath on his hip and carries an oversized weapon of some sort, whether it is a machine-gun, rocket-propelled grenade launcher, or high-powered crossbow. They are all on high alert and ready for battle.

All six of the mercenaries look around, thoroughly confused as to where they are. Since there is obviously no imminent threat to them, they begin to relax their defensive stances. Each man lowers his weapon. They seem lost as to what they are supposed to do or why they are there.

Randall follows Mosh Pit's path out of the building, but before he leaves, he turns and motions toward the befuddled mercenaries. "No rest for ye merry gentlemen. You have your orders. Crack on, mates!"

The mercenaries look back and forth at one another. Finally, one of them gives a shrug and saunters away. The others follow suit and disperse from beneath the Grandfather Clock.

CHAPTER 23

In the courtyard...

Mosh Pit is chasing the Saints this way and that. Because he is laughing so hard, it is impossible for him to discern the trauma he is causing his poor, unsuspecting victims. He is genuinely having a blast, but the Saints run from him as if he is brandishing a rattling noise maker in a theme park's haunted house. Their shrieks of terror bounce off the ice walls and the overhead dome in heart-wrenching echoes.

Randall steps out of the large factory building's door and gazes at the surreal town and the colorful villas and beautiful gardens within the dome. He nods his approval.

"This will work just fine," he says.

Doodle walks up behind him, hands in his pockets and cheesing a big-time grin as Mosh Pit terrorizes the Saints. He appears a little too proud of himself and his betrayal of his sweet people. "Work for what?" he asks Randall.

"I'll need a secure place to hide my gold. This will soon be Randall Zack's New World Bank. By the morning, I'll control the value of every currency on the globe." Randall quite literally rubs his gloved hands together, the defining action of a scheming villain.

"Do whatever you wish. Just get me and my people to Bora Bora," Doodle replies. "I get that Mosh Pit is having some fun, but maybe he could tone it down a bit. My poor friends are genuinely scared. When they're scared, they hide. Once they're hidden, we'll have a heck of a time getting them to come out for our trip."

"As long as the gold is where you say it is, and as plentiful, we'll do as we agreed." Randall scopes out the surrounding buildings. As he surveys the town, he is already thinking about how he'll use the resources available to him.

"You were supposed to take us first!" Doodle gripes. He withdraws his hands from his pockets and places one on his hip. The other hand wags an accusing finger at Randall. "That was the plan!"

Randall looks down at Doodle and smirks at his ornery stance. "The plan has been modified, my cheeky chap."

An alarm, similar to an air raid siren, blares to life throughout Eno. The mercenaries file out of the factory building, in awe of their surroundings. Their weapons are still lowered about their waists in a casual, non-threatening fashion.

"And them? Are they more modifications?" Doodle snips.

"In the art of war, one must be willing to adapt," Randall states as he walks on to the center of the courtyard.

"Art of war?" Doodle questions in a low whisper. The severity of the situation he has invited into his homeland suddenly dawns on him.

Randall watches Mosh Pit, now chasing the Saints well off in the distance, still giggling loud enough to be heard through the whole town. The Saints are retreating to the security of their homes.

"Well, I guess there are no heroes among this bunch," he mocks. "Just in case though..." Randall motions for the lead mercenary to step up, who happens to be holding an RPG-7 rocket-propelled grenade launcher. The mercenary stops next to Randall, who points at a far building. To Doodle, he says, "That structure there. What is it?"

"It's our recreation center," he grumps, then adds sarcastically, "Why? Do you and your new friend feel like playing some ping-pong?"

"Is it safe to assume it's empty since it is an all-hands-on deck kind of day in Christmas-Land?" Randall asks.

"Our town is called Eno and that particular building is indeed empty today. So what?" Doodle says, now with arms folded in defiance.

To the lead mercenary, Randall says, "That one will make a suitable statement for now."

The lead mercenary lifts the RPG-7 to his shoulder. He side-eyes Randall, as if to make sure his command is serious and final. Randall gives a slow nod. The mercenary fires the weapon and a small missile zips across the courtyard like a comet. It bombards the building in the lower levels with a fiery explosion. The Saints scream out from their hiding spots at the loud blast. The building is engulfed in smoke, but other than some blown out windows on the floor of impact, there doesn't appear to be too much damage.

Randall glares at the mercenary. "Load up another and do it again! I'm trying to make a bold statement here!" The mercenary holds a finger to his lips in a 'shush' motion. Randall is indignant. "Why you... how dare...!"

The mercenary uses his shushing finger to redirect Randall's eyes back to the building. Right on cue, numerous support beams break at the level of damage and the entire building topples in on itself in a smoking heap. Even though Randall wanted that exact result, he is still surprised by it. He looks back at the mercenary and grins with approval.

The mercenary winks and ambles back to his position in front of the others. Doodle, still nearby, watches the building collapse with his mouth dropped wide open.

The two unicorns, Enlitas and Excitas, sprint by and disappear into a group of buildings.

Randall, by now starting to expect the unexpected in this strange new world, gushes happily when he sees them. "Oh, my! Unicorns? Am I really seeing living, breathing unicorns?" He turns to Doodle, who only frowns in response. "This land is full of wonders! Simply unbelievable, isn't it?" He seems sentimental for all of two seconds. As quickly as it came, Randall's childlike wonder is gone and his face bends into a stern grimace at Doodle. "Take me to the main computer terminal and the Ooby fellow you never shut up about. Now!"

Inside the control center, Ooby is watching the events outside unfold via a closed-circuit video feed on the monitor. He is fighting back tears over the destruction of the recreation building and the trauma being suffered by his poor Saints. A door behind him swings open and Randall and Doodle march in. Ooby gasps when he sees Doodle by Randall's side. All six mercenaries follow, guns at the ready.

"Hello, laddies," Randall chirps. "Follow my instructions and no one shall get hurt. Where, pray tell, is Ooby?"

Without hesitation, Ooby leaps to his feet. "Of the thirty-five most used moves in the major martial arts systems, I invented twenty-one!" He rushes Randall and leaps into a series of kicks and punches.

Randall weathers the barrage with surprisingly deft defensive maneuvers. At the first lull in action, he thrusts his hand on to Ooby's forehead and extends his arm. Ooby, held back at Randall's arm's full length, swings at the empty space between them.

"Yet you never thought of a defense for this?" Randall trills.

Ooby finally gives up on his punches, but remains in a fighting stance. "Let all the others go and I'll give you whatever you want!"

"Fair enough." Randall looks around the room and signals for the rest of the Saints to leave, which they do, without question and shockingly fast. Randall shakes his head, again in disbelief. "Boy, there really are no heroes here." He looks back down at Ooby as the mercenaries circle around them both in a threatening show of force meant to demonstrate the hopelessness of resisting.

Ooby relaxes his fists and slumps somewhat. Randall lets him go. With a defeated sigh, Ooby looks at Doodle. "How could you do this?"

"The Eno Saints aren't your servants!" he retorts, as if this is a moment he has planned for a long time. "We deserve to be free in the world, but you keep us imprisoned here against our will to do your meaningless work for an ungrateful population of humans!" Doodle seems finished with his prepared speech, but then a sinister grin crosses his face as he adds, "We're blowing this popsicle stand!"

"Popsicle stand!" Randall guffaws. "Jolly good, kid! And apropos." Randall turns to Ooby, again switching easily to his ominous demeanor. "Now, Ooby, where is the ship with the gold?"

Ooby glares at him. "That's what this is about? You're going after the aircraft carrier from America?" Ooby can't help but smile at the preposterousness of the proposition. "Well, that will be impossible for a lifelong petty thief such as yourself, Randall. The gold transfer is the most heavily militarized operation happening in the world right now."

"Impossible perhaps for me on my own, but not if I have the power of Santa Claus," Randall crows.

Ooby shakes his head. "You can't even begin to understand such power."

Randall pulls Nicholas's handheld computer from his pocket. "I've had a good teacher." He motions toward Doodle. "We know all we need to know, from the crystal comet and the Enchanted Age, to the time warping device on the clock, to the wormholes."

Ooby shakes his head slightly and whispers an exasperated retort. "They're space-time conduits."

Randall shrugs. "Whatever." He turns to Doodle with the handheld outstretched. "Find the carrier for me, my dear fellow. Upload its real-time location to this."

Doodle snatches the handheld from him and hurries to the main computer terminal. He plugs in the device and starts typing. Images flash across the monitors as Doodle manipulates the keyboard with lightning-fast fingers.

Randall sneers at Ooby. "Fred is the computer whiz of this crew, but Doodle seems quite capable himself."

Doodle chimes in as he's rapping the keys and causing a barrage of new windows to pop up across the huge screen. "Our computers predate the advent of human ones, so they evolved totally differently. Ours are much superior, I must say. There's no way Fred could do what I'm doing."

Randall nods in agreement. "Besides, he's far less eager to please."

Doodle finishes with the computer as the monitors settle on a map of the Indian Ocean. A small red blip flashes on the screen East of Madagascar. He unplugs the handheld console and tosses it over his shoulder to Randall. The incoming console catches Randall by surprise. He snares it, fumbles it a few times, then finally secures it in his grasp. The effort causes both of his monocles to pop from over his eyes.

"I transferred everything to Nicholas's handheld," Doodle brags. "It's totally independent from the mainframe now."

Ooby takes the opportunity to appeal to Doodle. "He will destroy us, Doodle. Can you live with yourself knowing you were part of this?"

"He's freeing us," Doodle smirks. "We're going to Bora Bora and you're not invited." He gets up from the computer and goes to Randall's side. "Don't worry, Ooby. Once we're gone, you and Nicholas can carry on as you wish. I'm sure Randall will rent you a little corner of this frosty cavern." He turns to Randall. "I'd recommend you let them stay in the recreation center."

Randall pockets the small console and laughs heartily. "Indeed!" He squints at Ooby as he motions toward Doodle. "You raised a chippy one there, didn't you?"

"Give me a few minutes to go downstairs and gather up my people, then get us out of here." Doodle starts for the door that leads to the stairwell.

"Just to be clear," Randall questions. "Everything I need is on this?" He brandishes the handheld console.

"Yes. I already told you that." Doodle throws open the door and holds it open, presumably for Randall to follow.

With a nod to the mercenaries, Randall says, "Merry Gentlemen, if you would please." Randall steps away from the main computer. The mercenaries fire their weapons in a consolidated burst at the monitors and all the equipment. Sparks fly and fire erupts.

"No!" Ooby yells.

Randall walks to Doodle and waves for the mercenaries. "Grab Master Ooby and meet me outside."

"Master Ooby?" Doodle huffs. "He likes to think so maybe."

Randall answers lowly. "Ooby will take it as a respectful honorific, but between you and me, I meant it sarcastically." Randall leans toward

Doodle and gives him a wink, but it's probably sarcastic too. "Now, m'boy, pray tell. Do you have any weapons here in Eno?"

Doodle gives a single shake of his head. "We don't have any defense systems here. Ooby and Nicholas practice Kung Fu and Judo and whatever other martial arts, but they don't use weapons."

Randall rubs his chest, remembering his fight with Nicholas. "Yes, I'm aware of the martial arts. 'Twas the Kung Fu he most likely used on me."

Doodle smirks. "Ooby isn't very good at that, but he's a real expert when it comes to–"

"Swinging at the air? Ha!" Randall interrupts, then he's back to business. "Does this place have any contact with the outside world?"

"You just destroyed it," Doodle says.

"Indeed, I did." Randall gives Doodle another wink. "Or shall I say, we did. Come along, Lord Doodle." He leads the way down the stairs to the staging area.

Doodle pauses, still holding the door, as Randall struts away. "Lord Doodle? Another sarcastic honorific?" Doodle says, suddenly questioning Randall's snide intentions.

Over his shoulder, Randall gives his curt reply. "I wouldn't disrespect you like that! You're the smartest fellow I know. Besides, we have a rock-solid, iron-clad, written-in-stone contract of a deal."

Doodle furrows his brow for a beat, but shakes off the moment of doubt, puts on a confident smile, and follows Randall downstairs. From there, they exit the building.

In the courtyard, Mosh Pit is bent over and gasping. He sees Randall approaching and turns to him with a joyful grin.

"These little crumb-snatchers are fast and hard to catch," he says between labored breaths. "But the ones I did get seem to bounce really good!"

"Wonderful. Glad you had such fun," Randall drones with a dismissive wave of his hand. "Time to go. Seems our ship is coming in." He holds up the handheld computer without explaining why. Mosh Pit tilts his head dumbly.

"He means the aircraft carrier with all the gold," Doodle pipes helpfully from Randall's side. Mosh Pit nods with realization, finally getting Randall's reference.

"He knows what I mean," Randall snaps at Doodle. "That's a hilarious and self-explanatory pun! Our ship is coming in! Jolly good joke!"

Mosh Pit looks at Doodle and raises an eyebrow. They both shrug.

Behind them, the mercenaries prod Ooby forward with their guns. Randall looks around, but sees none of Eno's inhabitants out and about. "So, all of the little ones are hiding?" he says.

"I told you," Doodle replies. "They're easily frightened. Believe me, they're gone for hours. Now I have to figure how to convince them to come out since they don't trust you."

"Us, Lord Doodle," Randall says as he motions between himself and Doodle. "They don't trust us. Perhaps it's for good reason." He turns to one mercenary and nods. "Time for the ice breaker."

The mercenary pulls a crossbow off his shoulder. He has an arrow loaded and ready. Attached to the arrow is a concussion grenade and a timer. The mercenary sets the timer for 1:30:00. It begins counting down 1:29:59... 1:29:58...

The mercenary aims the crossbow straight up and fires. With the timer counting down the seconds, the arrow soars up to and sticks in the ice ceiling way overhead. The grenade and timer dangle just below it.

"What's that?" Ooby asks nervously from behind him.

"A concussion grenade. Don't worry, Master Ooby. It won't cause a very big explosion," Randall states matter-of-factly.

"Then what's the point?" Doodle retorts.

"Well," Randall answers. "It'll shatter the ice in the ceiling of the dome, which will fall and crush the buildings, the gardens, everything but the gold once it's here. After that, I'll bulldoze the debris to the side and burn it. The heat from the flames will melt more of the dome, making it wider and higher. My world bank will have skyscrapers and skylights and dirigibles floating delicately through the wisps. It will be a global marvel worthy of its status as the monetary capital of the world."

"Hey!" Doodle protests. "We only have an hour and a half?"

"Don't worry, Lord Doodle. You and your kind will be safe in Bora Bora," Randall smiles as he points at Ooby. "Except for him, of course. He'll be tied to a pole when the ice falls."

Doodle doesn't miss a beat as he glares at Ooby. "Bet that will hurt like hail!"

"Hurt like hail!" Randall throws his head back with a laugh. "Jolly good!" He ruffles Doodle's hair. "Let's crack on then, m'lord. We've a few more details to attend to." He turns to the mercenaries guarding Ooby and motions for them to follow. He struts back to the large factory building with Doodle by his side. Mosh Pit hurries to catch up.

Inside the staging facility, Randall walks toward the Grandfather Clock. The group follows.

"Mosh Pit and Doodle with me!" To the mercenaries, he bellows, "You guard the Clock and the crystal." Then, he motions to Ooby, still held at gunpoint near the door to the outside. "Be alert and keep an eye on him." Randall continues toward the crystal, steps on it, and vanishes.

Once he's gone, Mosh Pit stops by the stalled conveyor belt full of presents. He takes one at random and flips the tag to read it. Slowly, he sounds it out. "To De-on." With a carefree shrug, he says, "Sorry Deon. It's mine now."

He walks to the Clock, steps on the crystal, and instantly disappears. Doodle starts for it, too. Ooby is restrained by three of the mercenaries when he makes an attempt to rush at Doodle.

"Doodle! Wait!" Ooby calls.

Doodle stops over the crystal. "What?" he asks sharply.

"Randall won't take the Saints to Bora Bora or anywhere else," Ooby pleads. "He'll betray you after he gets the gold. But you can still stop this before it goes too far. Your life will last for the better part of forever. That's a long time to regret what you're doing right now. Please. We're your family. Stop listening to those dastardly men and help us."

Doodle stares at the crystal for a long moment, then he shakes his head. "Those sound like the words of a sore loser."

He glowers at Ooby, then dramatically stomps his foot on the crystal and vanishes.

Far over Asia...

The sleigh hurtles through the night sky at an astonishing rate of speed. Fred yawns as he handles the reins. Randall appears over the crystal behind him. He moves up front and nudges Fred with his elbow.

"So far, so good, Fred. We found the perfect place to store our gold. Where are we?" he asks as he looks over the side. Fred points out the dark blot beneath the bright stars that is the Himalayas. "Is that Everest? Already?" Randall whistles in amazement. "Unbelievable!"

Mosh Pit appears over the crystal with an exasperated huff. He's a bit off balance and catches the side of the sleigh to steady himself. "Whew! Wormholes are crazy!"

He steps off the crystal and moments later, Doodle appears. The disparaging smile that he gave Ooby is still plastered across his face. Mosh Pit and Doodle sit down behind Fred and Randall, as Fred proudly hands Randall a cardboard box. Randall is more than eager to take it.

"You got it? Very good! Very good indeed! It couldn't have been easy at this time on this night." He opens the lid and is immediately disappointed. "Oh, for goodness sakes, it's green! Why on Earth would you get a green one?"

Fred glares at him. Randall sees the seriousness of Fred's icy stare and quickly backpedals.

"It's fine," Randall says with a fake grin. "It's fine. Probably better than a red one." Randall withdraws Nicholas's handheld computer from his pocket to avoid Fred's peevish gaze. With an awkward clearing of his throat, Randall says, "Kindly set a course for the middle of the Indian Ocean, Bruvva." He points to the left. "We are drawing ever closer to unimaginable fortune."

Fred doesn't move. Randall motions left again.

"Two clicks to the left, m'boy." Fred gives him nothing. *At least he's looking forward and no longer shooting daggers at me*, Randall thinks. "You know what, I'll do it," he chuckles. "Might as well share the workload."

Randall holds his hand out for the reins. Fred looks down at his hand and looks away again. A long moment passes. Just when Randall is about to withdraw his hand, Fred slaps the reins in his palm. Randall smiles.

"Thank you, dear Bruvva. I really do like the color you picked out."

Fred rolls his eyes and folds his arms. Randall takes the reins and snaps them sharply against the deer. They turn and grimace at him, as sternly as Fred did a moment earlier. He pops them again. They angle toward the left.

"Now fly away, little scoundrels! Fly away all! Let's see how fast you can go!" Randall lashes the reins against their backs over and over again.

Behind him, Mosh Pit opens Deon's present with the excitement of a small child. He tosses the ravaged wrapping paper to the bottom of the sleigh and looks at the remote-control plane intended for Deon. He glances at the sleigh around him, then back at the toy. He nudges Doodle and holds up the plane. "A toy aero-plane?" he asks with genuine confusion. "I'm on a flying sled! Why would I want a stupid toy plane for Christmas?"

Doodle's riposte comes heavy with a contemptuous tone. "You grabbed a random present off of the staging line. The sticker even said 'To Deon.' Why would you think it would be something you wanted?"

Mosh Pit's face glazes over. Doodle's fiery rebuttal is not computing somewhere behind Mosh Pit's eyes. "Oh well," he says with a shrug and tosses the plane over his shoulder. It arcs toward the crystal, then disappears over it as it transports through the wormhole.

Doodle leans in between Randall and Fred. "This guy is shaving points off my I.Q. just because I'm sitting too close to him. Can I come up there with you?"

Mosh Pit finally takes offense at Doodle's condescending attitude. "Hey! Everybody deserves to get what they want for Christmas! A toy plane isn't what I want!"

Doodle looks up at Randall. "All I want for Christmas is a closet full of swim trunks."

Randall smiles at Doodle and musses his hair. "Well, little chap, I hope you have a big closet." He grabs the box that Fred had given him and hands it back to Mosh Pit. "Put this on, Moshy. It's almost show-time."

Mosh Pit takes the box as Randall turns back to Fred. "Let's make room for our pocket-sized pal up here, shall we?" He motions toward the crystal behind them. "If you'd go watch things in the South Pole, I'll send for you when we're ready."

Fred slowly, sleepily climbs into the backseat as Doodle hurries into his place.

"Enough with the stuff about me being small. I'm a right good size for my kind, you know?" he says.

Randall leans into Doodle as he settles in Fred's seat. "Very well, but I must remind you that you're one of our kind now." He winks at Doodle. "Big fella."

The deer look back in unison and give Doodle a leer of betrayal through squinty eyes. Randall laughs as he lashes the reins on them.

"Eyes forward, varmints!" He snaps the reins on their backs again for no good reason.

CHAPTER 25

On a narrow road on a mountainside...

Nicholas, huddling against the cold, drives a horse drawn sleigh through the blustery, wind-driven snow. He passes a sign that reads 'Summit of Mount Fuji - 3 Kilometers'. The horse pulling the sleigh is trudging as hard as he can through the inclement conditions and going surprisingly fast, pushing every one of his muscles to the limit.

"Thank you, dear friend," Nicholas says from the sleigh. "You are doing wonderfully and going much faster than I could have on my own."

The horse hears Nicholas's encouragement and lowers his head with determination, tugging even harder as he goes up the road's steep incline.

At the same time, in the courtyard in Eno, three mercenaries tie Ooby to a lamp post and walk back toward the entrance to the staging facility and Clock Room. Ooby scowls at them.

"Bagziin. Khoorloogiin. Damdin," he says urgently.

The three mercenaries look back at Ooby in amazement that he knows their names. When he speaks again, it is in perfect Khalkha Mongolian, the native language of the men's homes.

"Yes. I know who you are." Ooby says. Concern crosses the three men's faces. "I also know that times have been tough in the villages where you all grew up. Money is hard to come by. But surely you know you are not doing honorable work. What would your sweet mothers say about this?"

Damdin steps forward. He is the tallest of the three and his face is the grimmest. He is the one armed with the RPG-7 and has stood out as the leader of Randall's team of Merry Gentlemen. When he speaks, it's in perfect English.

"They would thank us for providing them food for their tables."

"What has Randall promised you? Gold?" Ooby asks. "He could steal every ounce of gold in the world and it won't be enough for him to part with a flake of it. He won't pay you. His words are no good."

"Whatever he pays, it's better than your promises of one night of benefit for spoiled children. Do you know what I went through as a child in the gold mines of my homeland? You brought me trinkets at Christmas but abandoned me." He motions to the two men behind him. "You abandoned us for the rest of the year."

Ooby looks at him pitifully. "But Damdin, you were saved from the mines. You all were."

Damdin's reproach is swift. "Not by you. Not by the fantastical toy deliverer known as Santa Claus. Our deliverer was a mighty man and I will never forget his face. He was tall and strong and looked nothing like you or the fat man in the red suit that you work for." He turns and joins the other two as they start away.

"You boys will be so embarrassed if you ever meet Nicholas," Ooby whispers lowly.

The door to the staging facility and Clock Room slams shut as the three men go back inside. Ooby looks around the courtyard and realizes it is completely empty. Not a creature is stirring.

"Someone free me please," he calls out. "Come and help." He searches in every direction. Nothing. He calls out again, this time with more desperation in his voice. "Please Saints! This is not a time to be frozen by fear! I need you!" He continues searching the courtyard and the surrounding buildings. Finally, he sees the slightest movement in the window of a residence. In it, a little hand reaches up to pull down the blinds. Ooby sighs with resignation and eases his back against the pole. "My poor frightened Saints," he mutters.

Just then, one of the unicorns, Enlitas, steps from the recess of a nearby building, looking for danger in every direction. She is understandably skittish. Behind her, Excitas emerges sheepishly. Ooby smiles at the two unicorns and clicks his tongue softly. They take a few tentative steps in his direction, but pause once they are out of the shadows.

"Enlitas. Excitas. Please. Come to me," Ooby says gently. The unicorns look at each other, then dash to Ooby. They nestle up close to him as if his presence could protect them from any danger. "I know you can't free me, but that's not important right now," Ooby says as calmly as possible. "I must go into the ether. I know it's arduous and it's been a long time for both of you, but it's our only chance to find Nicholas. Please, dig deep into your sweet spirits and take me there."

The unicorns rear up on their hind legs and twist their heads from side to side. They grunt at one another, as if communicating. At first, Ooby is afraid they are refuting his request. When they set their legs, as if preparing for a strenuous feat, he knows they are encouraging each other.

"Thank you for exerting the effort this will require," Ooby says as he squats low against the pole. "I can't navigate the higher realms as well as you, but if you can get me to him, I'll handle the mists."

The unicorns buck a final time and give determined snorts. Ooby closes his eyes as the unicorns touch the top of his head with their horns.

"The ether," Ooby whispers. "Take me to the realm of the ether."

The unicorns' horns begin to glow.

On the summit of Mt. Fuji, Nicholas waits by the sleigh in the driving wind on the edge of a deep volcanic crater. The horse is exhausted by the long, punishing journey from the bottom. Nicholas scrubs the horse's neck with his fingers as it exhales in explosive blasts of frost.

"Good boy," Nicholas coos. "Thank you. I'm sorry for waking you up in the middle of the night and asking so much of you. You did an amazing job."

While praising the horse, Nicholas looks to the stars, seeking solace in their twinkling flickers of light. A rapidly drifting mist bank moves across the sky. It dances high over Nicholas, as if caught in a crosswind, then descends and stops on the mountainside beside him.

The mist fights to stay together in the wind as it shrinks and condenses into a small humanoid shape. Within seconds, Ooby coalesces into form, standing before Nicholas as a misty apparition.

Ooby opens his eyes as if he is coming out of a trance. He sees Nicholas and nods. "You remembered the contingency plan. Highest nearby location." His voice is otherworldly, dream-like.

"It has been centuries since it was necessary," Nicholas says. "Enlitas and Excitas are okay?"

"So far," Ooby answers. "I don't know how long they can maintain it."

Nicholas speaks quickly. "Then we must hurry. Randall and his team came to Eno, didn't they? Is everyone all right?"

Ooby's foggy figure fights to stay together in the wind. "Everyone's fine. Scared but fine."

"How much damage did they do?"

"They blew up the recreation complex and destroyed all of the computers."

Nicholas slumps at the news.

Ooby continues. "They're after the American aircraft carrier with the gold. They have a complete understanding of the crystals and the Time Bender."

Nicholas shakes his head. "Impossible. How could they learn our secrets?"

"It was Doodle."

Ooby's words strike Nicholas like a bolt of lightning. "Doodle? No! He isn't capable of betraying us like this! He wouldn't even if he could!"

"He can and he did. He left with them."

"But why?" Nicholas is clearly hurt.

"He's always viewed our protection of the human children and Eno Saints as acts of oppression. He convinced himself that he's a hero fighting for the freedom of his kind, but I think we both know the truth. He is wicked and malevolent."

Nicholas resists Ooby's revelation. "No, Ooby, don't say such a thing! Doodle isn't evil-minded and he wouldn't be doing this if he was aware of the havoc he's causing us and the Saints! He's just being a bit short-sighted right now." Nicholas sighs, still fighting to resist that Ooby may be right. "We'll bring him back to us. He'll see his error."

"I hope so," Ooby says, but not because he believes it. Out of respect for Nicholas, he is trying to soften the truth that has become undeniably evident to him. "We'll worry about that later. For now, go to the base of the mountain. As soon as I can set up communications, I'll arrange to get you home. You'll be here by tomorrow. Hopefully, no later than mid-morning."

"It's Christmas Eve, Ooby," Nicholas says. "Mid-morning tomorrow is out of the question. We have to resolve this tonight and deliver all the presents before the children wake up."

Ooby's image sputters and falters in the wind like static from a bad television signal. Snow blows through his weakening mirage. "First, we have to regroup and get everything back together and find Doodle. We'll then call for help in beating Randall Zack and his crew."

"And Christmas?" Nicholas asks.

"It will have to wait until next year. There's nothing more we can do."

"Christmas can't wait!" Nicholas turns on his heels and looks out at the lights of the sprawling Prefecture below him. "It just can't!"

"There are more important things right now!" implores Ooby. "Randall planted a bomb in the ceiling of our dome. Without the deer, we can't get to it. In a short time, it will explode and demolish Eno with falling ice. That's my concern, Nicholas. Not Christmas."

"All the more reason to get the sleigh back in a hurry. I'll catch up to Randall and crew, stop them, retrieve Doodle, and return with the deer in time to dispose of the bomb. Then, we'll only be an hour behind on our route."

"We're already an hour behind! It took you that long to get to the top of Mount Fuji and now you have to get back down. That's another hour before you can even do anything about finding them. Even if we get everything back to normal, that kind of time deficit will be too much to overcome."

"No excuses, Ooby! We have to do this!"

"Be rational. We don't know where in the world Randall is with the sleigh. You're grounded in Japan and I'm grounded here in Eno. We can fix this, but it won't be tonight. We have a perfect record with Christmas up until now and missing one due to circumstances beyond our control isn't the end of the world."

Nicholas shakes his head. "It might as well be for the waiting children."

"We have to save Eno!" Ooby rebukes him forcefully. "We can't do that and save Christmas, too! For once, we have to think about our own survival and the survival of our kind! The rest of the world will have to wait! We can't do it all!"

"That's why Christmas is so important," Nicholas returns in an impassioned tone. "On this night, we must. Christmas is the last thread that connects us back to the enchanted time in which you once lived. For humans, it's a return to something cherished. We are born into the Garden of Eden of childhood, but we are gradually coerced out of its gates as we begin to grow older. Christmas offers us a reprieve from the cold cynicism of the outside world. For a short stretch of the year, we let go of the selfishness we have nurtured within ourselves. We let a light shine within us that we have been taught to cover up and shut away. Grown-ups get a glimpse of something we once had as children and children get to hold on to something that they will soon be forced to let go. Christmas is a reboot of our souls to the good and pure default settings that the Creator placed in us. Without it every year, we will languish. You and the Saints have an inherent innocence that humans forget way too soon. We require that annual recharge or we will lose ourselves to darkness."

Ooby's wavering image gives a noticeable slump of resignation. The fight in him is gone, but he gives one last argument as a whisper. "Eno could be lost."

Nicholas reaches out to the wavering specter of his dearest friend. "Eno and all the Saints are lost anyway if we fail to deliver whatever enchantment we can to the world. That is our purpose. That is our gift. That is the magic of Christmas."

Ooby pauses and finally nods. "In all of our centuries, you've never expressed yourself so clearly or succinctly."

"Christmas and all that we stand for has never been so threatened," Nicholas replies with a soothing smile.

"Very well, Nicholas. We'll fight as hard as we can to make this happen, but out there, you're on your own. I won't be able to help you much from here."

Nicholas breathes in the frosty air, rolls his shoulders, and flexes his chest in a gesture of renewed confidence. "Just tell me where the carrier was when you last checked. I know how to get there."

On a United States Nimitz-class Aircraft Carrier, somewhere in the Indian Ocean...

The sleigh lands gently on the bow of the fight deck. Mosh Pit is at the reins, dressed in a Santa Claus suit. He has a white beard, gloves, hat, everything that makes him look the part, except the suit is green.

Randall adjusts his monocles and rubs his hands over the lapels of his coat, as if to tidy up. Doodle watches, then runs his hands down his sleeves as if to smooth them out like Randall. Randall sees Doodle mimicking him and smiles. "That's right. Get spiffy." He turns to Mosh Pit. "Showtime, mate. Remember your lines?"

Mosh Pit nods and gives him a wink.

There are four F-22 Raptors on the opposite end of the expansive deck, well away from the sleigh. The jets are presumably ready to go airborne at the slightest indication of a threat to the ship.

As Randall, Doodle, and Mosh Pit disembark from the sleigh, five American sailors run toward them, brandishing rifles. The sailors surround them and the sleigh. Randall and Doodle hold their hands up as flashlights click on them.

The first sailor's voice is booming when she bellows, "Halt! Do not move!" She moves her light to shine on Mosh Pit. "Wait. Santa Claus?"

"That's a double H-O with an extra ho," Mosh Pit says in an artificially deep voice. Under the fluffy white beard, he's very proud of himself.

The sailors surrounding them look quizzically at each other. The first sailor steadies her aim on the trio. Doodle recognizes the group's apprehension. "He means Ho Ho Ho," he chuckles with apprehension of his own. "You know how it is, right? He says it so much, he's always looking to put a new spin on it."

The first sailor thinks deep as she draws the letters in the air in front of her face.

"Double H-O..." she mutters. "With an extra ho." Finally, she gives a big grin. "Yeah! It's Ho Ho Ho all right." She nods to her partners. "Yeah. I like it!" The other sailors lower their weapons and bob their heads in agreement.

"It's a fresh update on an old thing. Like Ho cubed!" another sailor echoes.

A third sailor chimes in, "I have a sweater that says Ho cubed!" He laughs at his own comment. "It's all together awesome."

"Maybe someone should make a sweater that says 'Double H-O with an...'" the first sailor starts but an impatient Randall sharply interrupts her.

"Excuse me, but this vessel is under threat of impending invasion! We're here to prevent the loss of the gold!"

"Who are you?" the first sailor demands with a sudden loss of good cheer. The other sailors turn their weapons and flashlights abruptly toward Randall. Randall thrusts his raised hands even higher in a sudden panicked reaction to the full attention of the guns.

"I am Heimlich von Chokin of the Malaysian Gold Repository. I must speak to whoever is in charge."

The fourth sailor steps closer to Randall, zeroing the beam of the flashlight on his face. "That'd be Admiral Chucklenut." He narrows his eyes at Randall as he leans in even closer. "Why are you wearing two monocles?"

"He says when his first eye went fuzzy, he got a monocle. When his other eye did too, he naturally got a second," Mosh Pit chortles.

The sailor shrugs. "Why don't you just get glasses?"

"That's what I've been saying!" Mosh Pit laughs.

Randall glares at Mosh Pit. "Let's stay focused, shall we? Imminent threat, Admiral. Now!" Behind him, the deer scamper and jump, as if preparing to fly away. "Please tie the deer down," Randall adds. "They sense the extreme danger."

At the helm of the Super Carrier, a gruff, stout man about 60 years of age stands at the ship's controls. He is Admiral Chucklenut and he is not happy when the five sailors lead in Randall, Mosh Pit, and Doodle.

"What is the meaning of this!" he demands. He turns from the view of the open ocean through the large window before him and eyes the group. His gaze is harsh as he quickly moves from Randall to Doodle. Then, he stops on Mosh Pit, dressed as Santa Claus. His steely glare softens and his lips curve into a slight smile.

The first sailor takes the lead. "Mister von Chokin claims to have information on an attempt to steal our cargo," she says.

The steely glare returns as he looks back at Randall. "What's this nonsense?"

"An attack is coming, I assure you," Randall says. "Mister Claus is here to assist in preventing the theft of the gold before you can reach the Malaysian Repository."

The Admiral, his eyes shifting to soft and gentle again, turns back to Mosh Pit. "Mister Claus, I'm honored to meet you. No offense, but you're not exactly as I imagined you to be."

"I know what you're getting at. Trust me, I get that a lot." Mosh Pit winks as he rubs a hand down the front of his green suit. "The red one is at the cleaners."

Admiral Chucklenut nods and grins. "Ah, I see. Again, no offense, but we're the most heavily armed ship in the entire United States Navy. Surely, you can't do anything we can't do for ourselves should we fall under attack."

"You know my pror, priotit, er, ah, main thing is to the children of the world tonight," Mosh Pit stumbles over what seems to be a premeditated script. "So, you can imagine the importancy, er, um, the meaningness of this situation for me to be here." He finishes with a glance at Randall, who nods his approval at the muddled recitation.

"Yes sir. I know you're busy," Admiral Chucklenut replies. "But I haven't received any word from my nation's command about this attack."

"That's because the United States is stealing this gold!" Randall erupts.

"What?" The Admiral explodes with great indignation. "Never!"

"As you know, this gold belongs to many other nations besides the United States. They have no intention of letting you get to Kuala Lumpur," Randall says.

The Admiral is stricken. "Impossible, I say! Again, I say impossible!"

"I say not at all impossible, good sir!" barks Randall. "American banks have very little gold of their own and their greed overtakes them on this night in what can only be described as a financial coup!"

"This is an American vessel," the Admiral argues. "They could simply direct me to take it elsewhere and I would. They wouldn't steal from their own ship."

"But they must make it look like it was stolen or the whole world will take up arms against them!" Randall sees the Admiral's stern expression palliate as he begins to see the plausibility of the fictional scenario. "They will stage an attack soon. It will be very large scale and it will easily overwhelm all of your defenses. That's why we've come." Randall places an assuring hand on the Admiral's shoulder. "Santa Claus will get this gold to Malaysia before the Americans can take it!"

The Admiral hangs his head in disbelief. "How will you do it, Santa?"

Mosh Pit is slow to answer, so Randall nudges him. "Oh, right! The same way I transport presents from the North, um, South, er, ah, North Pole to my sleigh."

The Admiral looks at him. "There is a lot of gold and it's extremely heavy. There's no way your sleigh can carry it all."

Mosh Pit doesn't have a preplanned answer ready for the Admiral's question so he shoots a panicked glance at Randall.

"It won't have to," Randall cuts in without much delay. "Take a ride with us and we'll tell you all of Santa's secrets."

Admiral Chucklenut pauses in deep consideration.

"Please," Randall implores him. "We haven't much time!"

"Very well," Admiral Chucklenut finally says. "Let's go." He turns and jogs from the helm. Randall, Mosh Pit, and Doodle hustle to catch up.

In the dark sky over the Super Carrier, the deer and sleigh zip through the air with Randall, Mosh Pit, Doodle, and the Admiral on board. The Admiral laughs as if he is having a great time.

"Whee!" he crows with undeniable glee as he throws his hands over his head like he's on a rollercoaster and having the time of his life.

Back on the flight deck of the Super Carrier, the Admiral, serious again, looks at the crystal in the bed of the sleigh. Several sailors are tying the corners of the sleigh down to the deck again so the deer cannot fly off.

"You say this crystal transports stuff from one place to another through a space-time conduit?" he asks Mosh Pit.

Doodle is quick to correct the Admiral. "Just call them wormholes. That's what everyone else calls them. At least the people who matter."

"That's right," Mosh Pit responds with a vivacious nod. "Wormholes. The big stuff goes through the wormhole between the big crystals, presents and what-not."

"The other crystal is already in the vault in Kuala Lumpur?" the Admiral presses.

"Sure is," Mosh Pit assures him.

"And the chimney scenario. How does that work?" the Admiral prods.

Randall jumps in. "Two smaller crystals. They work just like the big ones." He nudges Mosh Pit. "Show him."

Mosh Pit takes one small crystal from his pocket and tosses it across the deck. It skitters to a stop between two Sailors standing a foot apart.

Mosh Pit touches the other crystal on the chain around his neck. He disappears and reappears directly between the two Sailors. He's too big for the space between them and his sudden girth jars both several feet in opposite directions. Mosh Pit smiles at his trick.

The Admiral scratches his chin as he thinks hard for a long moment. When he speaks again, it is in a low, thoughtful tone, as if one of the great mysteries of his life has finally been revealed. "So that's how you do it? That's how you move all the presents around the world in one night?"

Mosh Pit nods again, understanding the Admiral's awe, for he had come to understand it only the day before.

Randall intercedes. "We just have to feed the gold into the crystal and your mission is complete. Simple as that. May we proceed?"

The Admiral looks at Mosh Pit one more time. His expression is one of complete sincerity and it begs Mosh Pit to be honest.

"If any of this story is false, many people could suffer. Tell me, is this on the up and up?"

Even Mosh Pit can't miss the plea for the truth burning in the Admiral's eyes. He smiles wide to answer, but has a moment of reservation. His face falls and his voice falters. "You know, Admiral, sir…"

Randall sees that Mosh Pit is vacillating and perhaps about to reveal the ruse. He jumps in again. "Of course, it's on the up and up!" he bleats with desperation as he elbows Mosh Pit in the chest. He turns to him so that Admiral Chucklenut can't see and mouths the words *Think of the gold!*

Just like that, Mosh Pit's internal conflict between honor and greed proves fleeting. He looks at the Admiral and adds, "I wouldn't be here if it was, er um, I mean, weren't."

Mosh Pit's assurances, or that of Santa Claus from the Admiral's perspective, is enough. The Admiral gives a single, final nod on the subject and turns to the sailors behind him.

"Get this crystal to the vault. All hands report to help transfer the gold." He turns back to Mosh Pit and Randall and shrugs. "If you can't trust Santa Claus on Christmas Eve, who can you trust?"

On the snowy summit of Mt. Fuji...

Nicholas and Ooby break communication. Ooby's image disperses in the wind. Nicholas hurries back to the sleigh and rubs the horse's face.

"I know the journey up the mountain has tired you out, but time is of the essence. Do you think you can push your limits and get me back down post haste?"

The horse whinnies, perhaps indicating that he can, but his weary voice can't hide his fatigue. His legs are weak and his body is failing him. Nicholas, knowing the poor horse has nothing left to give, smiles and puts his forehead to the horse's nose.

"You would try with all of your might, but I think this time I ask too much." Nicholas scrubs the horse's cheeks with his fingers. The horse whimpers. A moment later, the horse gives a sad whinny. An apology, perhaps? Whatever it is, Nicholas nods with understanding.

"I know I just said Christmas is in peril and we must be willing to sacrifice everything to save it, but that was when Ooby and I were the ones at risk. We know what we signed on for. You didn't. I couldn't live with myself if you got hurt in any way for something I asked you to do." Nicholas wraps his arms around the horse's neck, as the weary beast leans heavily into him. "The light of the Creator goes before us, my friend. If He wills it, His torch will lead us through the darkness. Christmas is in His hands now." Nicholas clicks at the horse with sincere affection. "Let's relieve you of some weight, shall we?"

Nicholas releases the horse from the tack and harnesses connecting him to the sleigh. He walks shoulder to shoulder with the horse as they start down the mountain. It will be a long trip to the bottom.

The horse neighs. Nicholas chuckles. "Thank you, but no. I won't abandon you up here in the cold. Your well-being is of the utmost importance. If it means Christmas must wait, then it must wait." He winks at the horse as he gives it a knowing smile. "But if I've learned anything in all my years, it's that Christmas always finds a way."

As they round a downward sloping corner, a campfire comes into view. Its flames dance in the wind much like Ooby's apparition did. Nicholas pats the horse's neck. "You see? Light in the darkness."

The horse nickers with renewed life and bucks his head as if nodding. Nicholas pulls his scarf up around his mouth and nose and approaches the campfire. A lone woman sits beside it on a log, roasting a wire rack of chestnuts. She is an elderly woman, at least 80 years old, covered in layers of heavy coats to shield herself from the blustery wind. Behind her is a one-person tent, made of heavy canvas, struggling to stay pitched in the gale. The flap is closed, but the tips of a pair of skis stick out of the tent a few inches. Beside the tent is a high-powered telescope aimed heavenward.

The woman looks up as Nicholas and the horse step into the radius of the fire's light. A smile brighter than the fire crosses her face as she waves the two in closer.

"Merry Christmas, fellow wayfarers," she says with bottomless cheer and a slight Austrian accent. "Please come close and warm yourselves." She holds up the rack of nuts by a handle and thrusts it toward Nicholas. "Help yourself to a snack."

Nicholas steps closer and pulls the scarf a little more snugly around his face.

"Thank you, ma'am," he says as he takes a chestnut and tosses it from hand to hand until it cools.

The woman stands from the log, her movements smooth and brisk, not at all reflective of her advanced age. She motions Nicholas toward it, offering her seat. "Please, sit. Rest a bit."

He waves her off, preferring to stand. "You're a long way from Tokyo. What brings you way up here on Christmas Eve?"

The woman places the rack of chestnuts back over the fire.

"Christmas Eve brings me up here," she says. "Wherever I am in the world on Christmas Eve, I go out to the darkest spot I can find so I can watch the night sky."

"Why?" Nicholas asks.

"To see Santa Claus. Or at least to try and get a glimpse of him." She pauses and grins widely. "You're thinking it's silly for an old woman to do such a thing, aren't you?"

Nicholas shakes his head. "Not at all. I'm sure Santa Claus would be thrilled to know he has such a committed fan."

The woman laughs in a joyful burst. She thrusts her hand at Nicholas. "It's nice to meet you, mountain stranger. I'm..." As she says her name, Nicholas says it with her. "Holly Siltoe." She pauses, surprised. "How do you know my name?"

Nicholas takes her hand and shakes it. "Sorry. Synchronous speaking. It's a trick I learned a long time ago. It takes a while to perfect and pops out involuntarily sometimes."

"You say things at the same time someone else says them, eh?" She chuckles. "That must make you so popular at parties." She says it with good-natured sarcasm.

Nicholas laughs. "Do you ever see Santa Claus?"

Holly sits back down on the log. "No. Not for many, many years. He moves too fast. Oh, but I'll keep trying. One day maybe I'll catch his eye."

"What will you do if that happens?"

Holly grins through a sigh, as she loses herself in deep thought. "I don't know. Maybe just give him a wave or a smile to let him know I'm thankful for what he did for me so long ago." She stares into the fire.

A memory recurs. A bad memory softened by a good one. "I was raised under some rough conditions," she continues. "Not the worst thing imaginable, but bad enough, I guess. Santa Claus intervened when he didn't have to. Put me on a different course. He was so kind and had the gentlest eyes and most serene smile. I'll never forget the goodwill that emanated from him." She rubs her hands together as she pulls herself back to the present. "I've lived a good life since I last saw him. One full of adventure and purpose. I've had incredible experiences and seen some beautiful places. I try to help other people, especially children, the way he helped me." She finally looks back at Nicholas. "I've always hoped to see him again, just to let him know I appreciate what he did for me."

The horse whinnies, as if to interject something important to the conversation. Holly looks at the horse and laughs. "Well, I guess he has something to say on the subject!"

Nicholas holds his hands out to the fire, turns them to warm both sides. "I think he's saying that if Santa Claus knows when kids are sleeping and awake and all that stuff, then he probably already knows you appreciate what he did for you."

The horse nods in agreement.

"Maybe he does," Holly concedes. "Maybe I know that deep down. Maybe, after this long, I just like looking for him, even though I know I will probably never see him again. It takes me to some pretty pristine places." She indicates the beautiful view from the mountain. "It's just kind of my own personal Christmas tradition, I suppose."

"Traditions are important," Nicholas says.

The horse whinnies again, making his agreement known.

"I told you what I'm doing up here, but you never shared what brings you two out on this cold, cold night."

"I'm in need of a favor," Nicholas says.

"Sure. How can I help?"

"My horse friend here..." Nicholas turns to the horse, realizing he doesn't know his name. The horse neighs with pride. Nicholas nods. "Skippy." He looks back at Holly with a smile. "His name is Skippy."

"Not your horse, I gather," Holly jests.

"No ma'am, he isn't, but he did a great service by getting me up here in record time." Skippy chatters loudly, again with great pride and satisfaction. "He's exhausted now and needs a break. However, I need to get down this mountain as fast as I can."

"Do you always scurry about so frantically on Christmas Eve?" Holly gives him a wry, playful smile. Under his face covering, Nicholas can't help but return it.

"This year more than most," he says.

"I'll gladly take Skippy down the mountain. I promise you, the pace I keep will not tire him out. Is there somewhere specific he needs to be returned?"

"His family lives just outside the city. He knows the way. If you can take him back there, I would be forever in your debt. Oh, and his sleigh is at the summit. Would it be possible to return that as well?"

Holly nods. "No problem. In fact, it will make my trip down the mountain easier. It's you who are doing me the favor."

"Well, that's good to hear because there's more. I need your tent and skis."

Holly raises an eyebrow. "Why would you need those?"

"As I mentioned, I need to go down this mountain in a hurry. Faster than I can run."

Holly shrugs. "Of course. No point in me staying up here all night anyway." She checks her watch. "Santa Claus has surely passed by."

"Thank you," Nicholas says as he steps past Holly and the fire, removes the skis from the open flap of the tent, and begins dismantling the tent poles.

Holly watches him with bemused curiosity. "I get needing to borrow my skis, but would you care to tell me how my tent will help you get down the mountain any faster?"

His hands move rapidly as he refashions the tent into something else. "I need to go even faster than skis can take me. I'll only need one anyway."

"At my age, two skis aren't of much use to me, much less one. I only brought them to pull my gear," she says as Nicholas stretches the tent's tie-down ropes out into several long lengths.

"I'm glad you did." Very quickly, he finishes with the ropes. "To show you my gratitude, let me give you what you came to see."

Holly laughs, her amusement at Nicholas becoming difficult to hide. "You're going to show me Santa Claus, eh? Sure. Okay." She shakes the rack of chestnuts as the cracking of their shells makes loud pops. "You're either very deluded or very comical, stranger, I'll tell you that much." She sets the rack back in the fire and turns to Nicholas, who is now right behind her. She is slightly startled. He sticks out his hand.

"Thank you, Miss Siltoe." She takes his hand and he lifts it to his scarf-covered face and kisses the back of it with the wool in between. "It was an absolute pleasure."

Holly looks hard at him, as if finally seeing his eyes for the first time. Something stirs in her, a spark of recognition from her distant past.

"The pleasure was mine," she stutters, suddenly nervous around the stranger she had been so comfortable with a moment ago.

He turns from her, grabs a single ski and the contraption he made from the tent, and hurries to the steep declining road.

"Count to ten, then look through the telescope." He looks back at Skippy. "Thank you, friend." The horse neighs and bucks up with excitement.

Holly looks at the telescope, which is no longer pointed into the sky, but now aiming down the edge of the mountain. When she looks back at Nicholas, he is holding out the reconfigured tent like one might do when folding a sheet in half. He stands on the solitary ski with one boot jammed in the binding and the other directly behind it, like a slalom water skier.

The wind catches the tent, which is now just a canvas drape with pieces of rope tied to each corner. The powerful gust fills the drape with air and jolts several feet out in front of Nicholas. He holds fast to the ropes. When they stretch tight, the canvas reveals itself to be a rudimentary parafoil kite. Harnessing the force of the wind, Nicholas launches off the mountain into the tempest. Holly gasps as he disappears into the night. She sprints to the telescope, counting under her breath.

Nicholas rockets through the air, thirty feet above the surface of the mountain. When he touches down, he zips across the snow on the ski at phenomenal speeds, steering the kite by pulling one side of the ropes or the other. He moves like a skate blade on ice. The wind gusts again and lifts him skyward. He lands after a few hundred feet in the air and cuts back and forth across the face of the steep mountain, shredding the new fallen snow.

Holly reaches the count of nine as she peers into the telescope. All she sees is a tree, way down the mountain, well out of view of her naked eye.

"Ten," she whispers.

In the scope, Nicholas hurtles into view in front of the tree. He turns and looks directly at her. His scarf is off his face and his smile is effervescent. It only lasts a split second, but Holly recognizes him right away. She inhales in disbelief with such a sharpness that the cold air hurts her nose and throat. It is the man from her ancient memory. The man she came up the mountain to see.

She smiles. "It is so good to see you again, Nicholas." Then, with a contentment that reaches the very core of her soul, she says, "I want to wish you a Merry Christmas from the bottom of my heart."

Part Three

Above thy deep and dreamless sleep, the silent stars go by...

While a high-rise skyscraper looms tall over the Tokyo cityscape. Inside of it, way in the upper floors, Nicholas strides up to the large desk of a Japanese mobster, Saki Crocodile. Saki is 40 years old and, like his last name, bears a striking resemblance to a gigantic Australian reptile. His eyes are cold and dark and his features are long and angular. Even his teeth are sharper than what would be considered normal.

Saki glares up at Nicholas from his laptop. He is not used to being disturbed, especially late in the night, by a stranger who is standing like he is waiting to be called upon. Nicholas just nods and smiles. Saki looks behind Nicholas, as if searching for the means by which he entered, even though an open door is behind him.

Finally, Saki sighs, "Who are you and how did you get in here?"

Nicholas points at three humongous henchmen, who hurry through the open door. One holds an ice pack to the top of his head. Another cradles one arm with the other. The third has a ridiculously large number of tissues wadded into each nostril, as if to stop a nosebleed. All three give sheepish waves. Saki erupts from his seat and barks furiously at them in Japanese.

"Go easy on them," Nicholas intervenes. "They tried very hard to keep me out. Didn't you, fellas?" The three nod their heads in unison. "They're very good at their jobs, too. It was no walk in the park to get up here." The henchmens' expressions of shame are gradually replaced by returning confidence as their heads slowly lift with pride. "I could immediately tell they were very serious about not letting me in." Nicholas smiles and regards each man in succession.

"Yet, they failed to do exactly that," Saki gnashes. "Three of my best men couldn't keep out one of..." He pauses to look behind Nicholas and the henchmen. "You are alone, I presume." Nicholas nods as do the henchmen behind him. "One of you," continues Saki with a disappointed roll of his eyes. The henchmen hang their heads again. "How did you know where to find me?"

"It is my business to know a lot of things. For example, I know that you are Saki Crocodile, Asia's most powerful crime kingpin," Nicholas states.

Saki shrugs. "That's no secret."

"I also know you are launching an Epsilon-class rocket in four hours. It's carrying an unauthorized satellite into low orbit."

This gets Saki's attention, but he does a good job of keeping his surprise contained by merely raising his eyebrows. "Who are you?"

"My name is Nicholas. Pleased to meet you." Nicholas offers his hand, but Saki only glances at it with overt disdain. He doesn't shake.

"Are you some kind of super-spy? Who do you work for, Nicholas?"

"Let's just say it behooves my organization to know what is trafficking the world's skies. On this night in particular."

Saki sighs heavily and slumps back down into his chair. "So let me guess. You don't want me to launch the rocket or you will report me to whatever government agency you work for, correct?"

Nicholas leans into the desk. "No. You can launch your satellite, but I want you to launch it now. And I want to be on it."

With that being said, Saki is not at all good at hiding his shock.

Out in the ocean, aboard the Super Carrier, a hundred Sailors form a cramped line in the ship's gold vault. Like a bucket brigade, they pass gold bricks up the line to the crystal. The final sailor in the line tosses them, one by one, on the crystal. They immediately disappear.

On a ledge above the sailors, Admiral Chucklenut, Randall, Mosh Pit, and Doodle watch.

"Step lively, sailors! Let's go! Put your backs into it, all of you!" Admiral Chucklenut commands.

Randall stands beside him, rubbing his hands together, again looking like an archetypal scheming villain. "Faster," he says as he licks his lips with greed and leans into the Admiral. "Make them go even faster."

On the roof of the Tokyo skyscraper, Saki stands next to Nicholas as Nicholas stares upward. He points up at a barely visible star in the light-polluted sky, then tracks a line over to the only other star that can be seen through the smoky fog. Saki watches, puzzled.

"When you asked to come up here, you said we were under a serious time crunch and you needed to chart a course," Saki says. "Yet you are star-gazing in the smog."

Deep in thought, Nicholas removes a miniature, pocket-sized abacus from his coat and makes a series of quick calculations by moving the tiny beads around with his thumb.

"An abacus?" Saki smirks. "Really?"

"I lost my handheld computer," Nicholas states with a shrug, as if the abacus was the next logical thing to use. "The abacus makes the math easier."

"Of course. Sure it does." Saki is clearly patronizing Nicholas and does not believe anything that he says.

When Nicholas writes on a small slip of paper and hands it to him, Saki can't help but look at it as if it were anything but the scribblings of a crazed mind. "What are these...?" Saki squints down at the numbers on the paper. "Random digits?"

"Coordinates and a time. Send the rocket over that spot at that precise moment, then you can send it into orbit wherever you want."

Saki looks at the paper again. "Ah, yes. Clearly." He can't help piling on the sarcasm. "Shall my launch coordinators use their compass and slide rule to plot these out?"

"If that's how they best function, yes." Nicholas doesn't seem to catch Saki's mocking tone. "Sometimes the old ways are the best."

In a white room in the basement of the Tokyo skyscraper, Nicholas stands beside a tall, skinny rocket. He is wearing a silver jumpsuit and holding a helmet under his arm. Multiple Technicians in hazmat suits stand on platforms around the rocket and make final preparations.

Several stories up, a round aperture slides open in the ceiling above the rocket. The space is no bigger than an inflatable swimming pool, just barely bigger around than the rocket's circumference.

An aperture in the next floor above the first opens a second later and the one above that opens in succession. All the way up the height of the building, the floors separate into a perfectly round chute for the rocket.

"I built the building five years ago." Saki is in a small blast proof room next to the rocket. He peers in through a thick window and talks into a microphone that broadcasts through speakers in the room. "The launch silo was placed next to the main elevator shaft in the center with thick concrete walls. It was barely visible on the blueprints."

Nicholas nods. "Once it was built and the walls erected, no one even knew it was there. Smart."

Saki nods with pride behind the glass. "I thought so. That's why we launch at night. By the time this rocket is skyward, we can seal the floors and deny ever knowing anything about any rumors of a launch from my building. Usually, the reports are few and far between and easily dismissed."

"You've established quite an operation here, Saki. I can only imagine the impact you would have if you allowed yourself to engage in legitimate business practices. You could illuminate a lot of lives." Nicholas gives Saki an endearing smile.

Saki leans back from the microphone and narrows his eyes at Nicholas. "You never asked what kind of payload this rocket is carrying."

"I already know," Nicholas says. "You're a tough man, Saki, but you have a softness for the people in this community and for your entire homeland. The divide between a bad man and a good one is sometimes smaller than one might think." Nicholas puts the helmet on his head and jams it down. "It just comes down to the decisions the man makes."

Saki smirks. "You don't know me very well if you think I'm even a little bit good."

Nicholas raps the body of the rocket with the back of his hand. "Let your light shine before others, that they may see your good deeds."

With that single remark, Saki realizes Nicholas knows exactly what the rocket is carrying, but that, as is so often said, is a story for another time.

CHAPTER 29

Faraway from Tokyo, in Eno...

Three mercenaries pile the gold bricks on the conveyor belt as the bricks appear over the crystal beneath the Grandfather Clock. The conveyor belt is moving in the opposite direction from normal. Instead of moving presents from the staging area to the clock, the belt is now carrying the gold bricks from the Clock, where they are transported through the space-time conduit from the Super Carrier, to the back of the room.

At the other end of the conveyor, Bagziin, Khoorloogiin, and Damdin are removing the bricks and stacking them in tight, neat piles on top of wooden pallets. Bagziin begins singing "Silver and Gold" from the TV classic "Rudolph the Red-Nosed Reindeer".

"Silver and gold," he sings, in a surprisingly sweet voice. "Silver and Gold. Everyone wishes for silver and gold. How do you measure its worth? Just by the pleasure it gives here on Earth."

Khoorloogiin and Damdin shake their heads at him, but they don't stop passing the gold bricks.

"You're no Burl Ives, Bagziin. Besides, it's just gold. No silver," Khoorloogiin snipes.

"Yeah," Damdin adds. "We wouldn't waste our time on silver. Gold is where it's at!"

"Well, the song is about decorating a Christmas tree, not accumulating wealth," Bagziin retorts in a huff. "How would a Christmas tree look without both?"

Khoorloogiin and Damdin lose themselves in deep thought, so they stop working. Bagziin has to hurry to keep up with the gold bricks as they keep coming down the conveyor belt. He must do triple the labor to keep them from falling off the end in a clumsy pile.

Bagziin yelps. "C'mon guys! I can't do it all by myself!"

The distracted pair resume working. "I guess you're right," Damdin concedes. "A Christmas tree with just gold doesn't seem right."

"It's a dismal thing without silver," agrees Khoorloogiin.

"Silver and gold," Bagziin begins singing again. "Silver and gold. Mean so much more when I see..."

Khoorloogiin and Damdin join in for the next verse. "Silver and gold decorations on every Christmas tree!"

Meanwhile, in the bright white basement of Saki's building, a technician stands on a ladder and restrains Nicholas to the fuselage of the rocket. Metal chains go around his torso and legs, but his arms are free. He is wearing a backpack and the silver helmet with its mirrored visor up. On the side of his chest, beneath his left arm, a small canister is strapped to his suit. A rubber hose runs from the tank to his helmet.

Saki Crocodile stands beside a scientist, still behind the glass.

"There is no way this will work." His voice echoes through the speakers in the cavernous basement clean room.

"Why not?" Nicholas starts. "I have my parachute." He pats his backpack. "My oxygen." He pats the small tank. "Oh, and my clock and key." He holds out his hand.

The technician finishes securing the chain around him and gives him a stopwatch and the key to the padlock holding the chains. Both are together on a lanyard. Nicholas puts the key and the watch over his helmet and around his neck.

"You won't survive a jump from that altitude," Saki's voice chimes from the speakers.

The scientist's voice, in a hushed tone, as if he doesn't mean to be heard, immediately follows Saki's voice. "Forget the jump. He won't survive the G-forces of the launch."

Nicholas hears the scientist and gives the technician a nervous shrug. The technician shakes his head in a way that says he doesn't care if Nicholas makes it or not. "At least then, we won't have to worry about him spilling the beans on our launch complex," the technician says loud enough for Saki to hear.

"If that's the case, maybe we should change the settings and put him over Antarctica," Saki gibes, like Nicholas isn't right there listening.

"I told you I wouldn't reveal the secret payload of this rocket and I am a man of my word," Nicholas says as he swipes down the visor on his helmet. "I don't approve of your tactics, Saki, but I know you to be a man of honor as well."

Behind the glass, Saki looks at Nicholas with a blank face that does little to reveal he's flattered. "If you make it and ever need a freelance job..."

"I know where to find you," Nicholas says from under the helmet.

"Listen for the alarm on the watch," Saki says.

The technician climbs down the ladder from Nicholas's side. He hurries out through a side door. From behind the glass, Saki gives Nicholas a 'thumbs up'. Nicholas responds likewise, then looks up past the top of the rocket and the narrow chute that leads through the hundred or more floors of the building.

Through the speakers, Nicholas hears Saki's voice for the final time. "Skip the countdown, boys. Let's do this so I get home to my mother before Santa passes through."

The rocket's engines begin to rumble loudly and Nicholas hits a button on the stop watch. There is a fire from the engines, then the rocket takes off like a flare. In a second, it's gone.

In the night sky over Tokyo, the rocket jettisons from the top of the building, leaving only a flaming trail behind it. Nicholas grimaces against the extreme G-forces as the rocket roars into the cloudy, smoggy night. The rocket arcs westward in its trajectory, high over the city.

A lower stage of the rocket, just below Nicholas's feet, drops. The smaller engines by his heels ignite. Though quieter, the rocket is still moving at supersonic speed. Beneath the helmet and visor, Nicholas clenches his eyes tight. Ice forms on his helmet, his suit, and the rocket.

Within a minute, the lights of cities in Asia are pinpoints. The planet's curve becomes visible on the rapidly dropping horizon. Half a minute after that, a huge area of the world below the rocket is blanketed in conspicuous blackness.

The Himalayas, Nicholas thinks as he steals a glance downward. *In the middle of that, Everest.* Nicholas's thoughts are correct. Everest is indeed far below him as the rocket is taking a similar course to the one the sleigh followed earlier. The rocket is still speeding into the high atmosphere around the Earth, but the G-forces have relaxed. Nicholas's arms begin to float. With his frozen, gloved hands, Nicholas fumbles with the key around his neck.

The stopwatch alarms as Nicholas works the key in the icy lock. The chains fall away and Nicholas drifts from the rocket. For a moment, he is weightless and floating, like the chains nearby. The horizon stalls beneath his feet. Finally, gravity catches him and his sight-lines reverse course. With great and terrible speed, Nicholas free-falls back toward Earth.

The ice on his helmet melts away as the visor begins to glow red with heat until it finally cracks. The suit shreds to tatters to reveal his clothes underneath. The ocean appears out of the darkness far below him. Nicholas reaches for his backpack and pulls the ripcord. A high-altitude parachute unfurls and fully opens within seconds. He pulls off the helmet, lets it fall, and begins searching the ocean far below for the Super Carrier.

He is still very high up when the lights of the Carrier come into view. He pulls on the control lines to make minor adjustments to his descending path. At the rate he's drifting down and the Carrier is advancing through the water, he appears on course to intersect with it perfectly.

He is watching the Carrier intently when a patrolling F-22 Raptor flies up from behind him and hurtles by in a blink. For a split second, the Pilot sees Nicholas out of his window and locks on him, his head turning like an owl's as he zooms away. It's just an instant, but Nicholas thinks he sees the Pilot's mouth drop open.

"Uh oh," Nicholas mutters to himself.

Way out in front of Nicholas, the jet makes a wide turn and darts back. Nicholas is a sitting duck, still too high to release himself from the parachute and moving much too slowly to evade the jet. He can only watch as the jet zooms toward him again.

When it's within range, it fires a series of rotary cannon blasts. The bullets miss Nicholas, but hit the parachute and some of the suspension lines connecting him to it. The chute loses its open canopy and folds up like a crumpled, discarded napkin.

Nicholas dangles helplessly from the flapping parachute. His descent becomes a near free fall again. The jet makes another wide circle and zips back. The pilot misses when he fires the jet's machine gun again, but the parachute catches on the wing as it goes by.

Nicholas is jerked hard as the jet races off again, this time with him attached. The pilot is unaware that Nicholas is caught on the wing as he starts another circle. Nicholas bounces against the bottom of the jet as it turns.

Nicholas looks down and sees that they are passing over the Carrier, but it is still too high for him to drop off. He grabs on to the bottom of the jet's fuselage and rips the parachute pack off his back. He holds on to the front of the wings with his hands and hooks his feet on the back. He is sprawled across the belly of the plane like an 'X'. Fighting to find a hand-hold in the wind, Nicholas crawls to the left wing. The wind is unbearable. He huddles up next to the cockpit and knocks on the glass enclosure.

The pilot turns and looks, startled to see Nicholas there. He tries to shake him off with spinning maneuvers and deep rolls. The jet goes into a dive toward the water and accelerates. It is only fifty feet off the ocean's surface when it flattens out and rotates through three more rolls. Through the cockpit's glass, the pilot waves just before Nicholas falls.

Nicholas splashes down into the water, but skips across the surface several times before he submerges. He comes back up, breathless and disoriented, and sees the Carrier way ahead of him. The jet lands on it.

With fierce determination, Nicholas swims after it. The ship continues away and, despite his extreme effort, he can't gain on it. A sleek seagull swoops in low over Nicholas, as if to investigate this strange, new thing in its domain. Nicholas glimpses it overhead and points at the Carrier ahead of him. Then, he buries his head in the water and continues swimming. The gull squawks loudly and climbs back up into the air.

Back in the courtyard in Eno, whatever mystical connection Ooby had with the unicorns has been broken. The magical beasts lay at his feet, panting and exhausted. Ooby squats against the pole, his hands still restrained behind him.

Enlitas perks up her head and gives it a troubled shake. She snorts anxiously.

"What is it, Enlitas?" Ooby asks. "What are you sensing?" She bounds to her feet and rears up on her back legs. Excitas jumps up as well and stands close to her side, as if to calm her.

"A distress call? From whom? The sea beasts or the air animals?" Enlitas gives a vivacious nod and drops back to her front hooves and paws at the ground rapidly.

"A seagull near the ship, eh? Okay. It must be about Nicholas then." Ooby turns to Excitas. "One more time, friends. Please. Take me there and let's get him some help."

Excitas spins several times, then braces next to Enlitas. They touch horns as before.

In the ocean, trailing the Super Carrier, Nicholas still swims with all his might, but the ship is even further away. Well behind him, a small, fast-moving fog bank, like the one on Mt. Fuji, materializes. It glides swiftly over the surface in a fluttering back and forth path, like a searching spotlight. It finds Nicholas and moves over him, hovers for a moment, then darts beyond him toward the ship. Nicholas doesn't notice as he swims. He looks up at the Carrier, which is now barely visible in the distance.

In Eno, Ooby is still tied to the pole and squatting low against it. The unicorns are over him, their glowing horns touching Ooby's forehead. All three are entranced. Ooby whispers in a calm, soothing voice. "Let's help him. Let's find him some help."

In the ocean, well ahead of Nicholas, the misty apparition dives into the black depths and disappears. All is quiet except for the sound of Nicholas's rhythmic breathing and his arms cutting through the water.

The Carrier is so far ahead that it no longer offers any light. The only illumination comes from the bright stars in the heavens. Nicholas is all alone in the ocean, but shows no sign of slowing or giving up.

Then, behind him, two dolphins breach the surface, swimming side by side toward Nicholas. He hears them coming. As they pass, one on each side, he reaches out and grabs their dorsal fins. They continue swimming with Nicholas between them, holding on tight. They propel themselves forward with fast, powerful thrusts of their tails. Between them, Nicholas plows through the water, creating a foamy wake. He streamlines his body with theirs to decrease the drag and the trio speeds up.

After several minutes of swimming at breakneck speed, they catch up to the Carrier. The ship is like a huge mountain jutting up from the surface of the ocean and its deck is over five stories high. The dolphins veer Nicholas to the side of the Carrier, but there is no way for him to climb up to the deck.

An Orca breaks the dark water behind them. Nicholas is alerted to its presence by a loud exhale from its blowhole as it jumps from the surface in a high arc. He looks over his shoulder and sees the Orca's rapid approach, its dorsal fin cutting through the water so fast that it creates its own wake within that of the mighty Carrier's. Nicholas doesn't question the whale's intent. Instead, he tightens his grip on the dolphins' fins and takes several deep, rapid breaths.

The Orca dives into the depths and accelerates until he is well below the two dolphins and Nicholas. As if the whole dance was timed and choreographed by an outside force invisible to them all, the dolphins follow the Orca's lead and dive deep beneath the surface in tandem. Nicholas holds fast between them.

With the Orca in a deep dive far below, the dolphins take Nicholas twenty feet under. First, the Orca reverses course and launches himself straight up toward the surface, directly beneath the trio. Then, in perfect unison, the dolphins turn upward.

Nicholas braces his legs as the Orca catches up and places its nose on his feet. The whale, making huge sweeping thrusts with his tail, is speeding faster than the dolphins can go. They careen off to each side just as the Orca pushes Nicholas above the surface with such power that it sends Nicholas rocketing skyward. The Orca leaps out of the water, exposing the entire length of its body, before splashing back down on its side. It is enough to catapult Nicholas high enough to clear the side of the Carrier. He slingshots ten feet above the side in a high arch and lands gingerly on its deck.

Nicholas looks back and salutes the dolphins and the Orca as they tread water and click and squeal, giving calls of encouragement. Ooby's fog bank forms over them for a moment before it dissipates.

Nicholas, on the Carrier's stern, sees the deer and sleigh far ahead on the bow. In between the bow and the stern, the Super Carrier stretches the length of three football fields. A little beyond mid-deck, the F-22 is parked with its cockpit canopy swung open. Watching the full deck intently, Nicholas removes his wet and tattered jumpsuit. The ship is suspiciously quiet. The deck is deserted and there are no alarms or sirens to indicate any kind of danger.

Nicholas decides to take advantage of the Carrier's empty deck and starts toward the bow in a low crouch. Then, near the front of the deck, a door bangs open and a line of Sailors emerges. Nicholas stops, looks around quickly, and hides behind a nearby bulkhead.

Toward the front of the Carrier, near the jet, the Pilot leads the crowd of Sailors. Admiral Chucklenut, Mosh Pit, Doodle, and Randall follow. Behind them, another line of Sailors pours out onto the deck.

The Pilot is hyper-aware and he's talking fast and a little too loud. "I'm telling you, sir," he calls back to the Admiral. "There was a paratrooper! He was coming right for the ship when I accidentally snagged him with my wing!"

The Admiral strides up beside him as the Sailors fan out and take defensive positions. "Were there others?"

"Not that I saw," the Pilot replies.

The Admiral turns to Randall and Mosh Pit. "Is this the attack you warned us about?"

Randall, slightly confounded, just goes with it. "Yessir. This is it."

"One man? Our attackers sent a one-man army?" The Admiral is unconvinced.

"It's just the beginning. I promise you, there will be more. Many, many more." Randall's tone is almost pleading.

The Admiral directs himself to Mosh Pit. "Now what, Santa Claus?"

Mosh Pit is tongue-tied in the moment and doesn't answer. All he can manage is a slow "Uuuhhh."

Randall interrupts. "All the gold is moved, so there isn't much else we need to do." Randall is thinking hard as he talks, making it up as he goes. "The best course of action now is to form a line along the side of the ship." He talks louder and directs the Sailors with dramatic hand gestures. "Everybody to the side! Quickly now!"

The Sailors stand still as the Admiral glares at Randall. "Why in the wide world of sports would we do that?"

"To surrender!" Randall chimes as if it makes complete and total sense. "It's the only way. Next, there will be schools of submarines, flocks of helicopters, and herds of warships!"

The Admiral looks out at the dark ocean and sees nothing. "I don't think..."

Randall persists. "Hurry! To the edge! They might have mercy if we don't resist them!"

Still, the Admiral doesn't move. He turns to Mosh Pit, who finds himself in the uncomfortable position of having to address an issue for which he isn't prepared.

"Well, it is, um, pretty important that I, uh, get away and not become involved in a lengthy sea battle," he stammers. "On this night, we must think of the children after all." His semi-erudite advice hits the Admiral just right.

"Of course. If you were delayed here, the world's children would suffer and we can't have that." The Admiral shrugs. "Very well." He barks out his orders so all can hear. "Sailors, you heard Santa Claus! To the side of the ship!"

The hundred or so Sailors run to the edge of the ship at the Admiral's command.

"Brilliant," Randall whispers as he leans close to Mosh Pit. "Sometimes you are nothing short of a genius."

Mosh Pit beams with pride at the praise. "The suit demands a sharp wit," he whispers back as he gives the collar of his coat a tug. "And these mucous maggots demand a nice dip in the briny deep."

"Perhaps they should put their hands up in case our adversaries are looking through binoculars," Doodle suggests to the Admiral. "Lest they torpedo us from afar."

Randall turns to Doodle and raises an eyebrow, as if he forgot he was there.

The Admiral nods, now in total deference mode. "Sure. Why not?" Loud again, the Admiral barks. "Hands up, Sailors." He walks to the side and puts his hands up, too.

Randall whispers to Mosh Pit again. "Okay, Moshy m'boy. It's your time to shine."

Mosh Pit grins widely as he rips off the fake beard and his green Santa hat. "Better yet, my time to slam!" He activates the Time Bender wrist watch.

At the stern of the Carrier, Nicholas watches as Mosh Pit, moving at superspeed, sumo slams the Sailors from behind in rapid succession. One by one, they fly off the side into the sea like falling dominoes, including the Admiral.

Toward the bow, Randall and Doodle start toward the sleigh further ahead. They are laughing at Mosh Pit, who is giggling while he smashes the Sailors. Because he is moving at superspeed, his giggling sounds like a hyena on fast forward. Mosh Pit is finished in seconds. He speeds next to Randall and Doodle in a flash before he turns off the Time Bender.

"Good work," Randall says to the still chuckling Mosh Pit.

"My best slamming yet," Mosh Pit replies, breathlessly.

Together, they arrive at the sleigh. The deer tug at their harnesses. They leap, but the sleigh is still tied to the deck. Every few seconds, they try again.

Doodle's eagerness is hard to miss. "Thank goodness that's all done. Are we off to Bora Bora now?"

"Uh, yeah. Sure," Randall claims, half-heartedly. "As soon as we retrieve Fred and the mercenaries from Eno."

"And the rest of the Saints, minus Ooby," Doodle persists, somewhat suspicious that Randall left them out. "Right?"

"Er, sure, yes. Of course. That's what I meant." Randall gives Doodle a sly grin. Then, he turns his attention to the deer, as if to divert the conversation. "The deer look hungry." To Mosh Pit, he says, "Go to the galley and find them some food."

"Like what?" Mosh Pit asks.

Randall shrugs. "I don't know. Apples. I think deer like apples." He looks at Doodle, who also shrugs. "Get yourself something, too, Moshy. I'm sure you've worked up quite an appetite."

Mosh Pit walks back to the entrance to the interior of the ship. "Okay. Apples it is." Then, he adds, almost giddy. "And maybe a little sashimi for me."

"We better get the crystal from the vault where they kept the gold," Doodle says with a glance into the empty back of the sleigh.

"Indeed, we shall, Master Doodle." Then, with a wink, Randall says, "After that, it's Bora Bora or bust."

Randall and Doodle follow Mosh Pit toward the door.

At the Carrier's stern, Nicholas watches Mosh Pit leave, trailed by Randall and Doodle. When they're all gone, he runs to a bulkhead and punches a red button that drops all the lifeboats on that side of the ship into the water.

He looks over at the closely grouped Sailors, who are floating by the back of the ship. They swim toward the lifeboats. A few wave their appreciation. Nicholas gives a quick salute, then sprints toward the sleigh at the front of the ship.

At the bow, Nicholas is almost to the sleigh when he hears the door open behind him. He dives behind another bulkhead as Mosh Pit exits the door with a handful of apple slices and an armload of covered dishes. Fred is with him now, having just been transported from Eno to the ship through the crystal.

"You shoulda seen me, Fred! Slam, slam, slam! Bingo, bango, bongo! They were screaming the whole way down to the water!" Mosh Pit bloviates. "It was the most fun ever! I wish you coulda seen me!"

Fred can only manage a subtle shrug, which is quickly followed by a huge yawn.

Mosh Pit nudges Fred with the covered dishes. "They didn't have any Japanese cuisine, but they had something even better." Fred takes the dishes, but doesn't bother to look beneath the covers. Even food doesn't seem to interest him.

"Okay, you overgrown gerbils. I got dinner for you," Mosh Pit says as he holds an apple slice to Dasher, who turns up his nose. Dancer does the same when Mosh Pit offers one to him. "C'mon, you dumb beasts. Eat so you can do a lot more flyin'." He holds a slice to Vixen's mouth, but he also turns his head.

The rest of the deer scamper and stomp. Vixen rears up on his hind legs and punches at Mosh Pit with his front hooves. Mosh Pit pulls back just in time, but Fred is so startled that he drops the covered plates, which are full of holiday sugar cookies. They scatter across the deck. The deer yank against their reins in an attempt to get to the sweets. Mosh Pit gawks at the fallen cookies.

"That was my dinner!" He draws back his fist at Vixen, as if to retaliate.

Before he can swing at the deer, Nicholas darts from behind the bulkhead and plows Mosh Pit to the deck. Fred sees and swings at Nicholas, but Nicholas blocks Fred's punch and kicks him in the chest. Mosh Pit rebounds and charges. He and Nicholas trade blows with the deer watching and scampering. Mosh Pit tries to activate the Time Bender, but Nicholas swipes it off his wrist, sending it spinning across the deck. Nicholas dives for it, but Mosh Pit tackles him. They throw punches, each landing powerful blasts.

Fred goes after the Time Bender, but Nicholas fends off Mosh Pit and punches Fred, who flies into the back of the sleigh. The blow knocks him completely unconscious. Mosh Pit rushes Nicholas from the side, but Nicholas kicks him. He falls, rolls up, and tosses the small crystal behind Nicholas. He touches his chest and disappears.

Mosh Pit reappears right behind Nicholas, but Nicholas turns and catches him with an uppercut. Mosh Pit sails backwards. He throws the crystal near Nicholas again, but Nicholas back kicks him in the stomach. Mosh Pit doubles over, holding his gut, breathless. Nicholas punches him, flattening him on the deck.

Nicholas dives toward Mosh Pit, but Mosh Pit tosses the crystal. He disappears and reappears, though still on his back, fifty feet away.

Nicholas goes there, but Mosh Pit retreats with the crystal several times. Each time he reappears somewhere else on the deck in a more advanced stage of recovery. In one spot, he's sitting up. In another, he's on one knee. In a third, he's standing up again. Finally, he throws the crystal near Nicholas, appears before him, and re-engages him with sumo slams.

Nicholas endures the attack, countering with punches and kicks. He starts to get the upper hand again when Mosh Pit throws the crystal twenty feet away. Nicholas dives for it. Mosh Pit disappears. Sliding across the deck on his chest, Nicholas punches the crystal toward the open door where a set of metal stairs lead down to the lower levels of the ship. It settles on the top step.

Mosh Pit reappears there. Nicholas slides to his feet and tears open Mosh Pit's green Santa coat. He rips the crystal necklace from his chest and head-butts him, sending him bumping and rolling down the long staircase. Nicholas picks up the other crystal and sees the Time Bender watch by the sleigh. He starts toward it, catching his breath and clicking to the deer.

Two feet behind him, a grenade rolls to a stop. He sees it in barely enough time to pitch the crystal ten feet away and disappear. He reappears in mid-air. The grenade explodes, sending him flying further still. He is flattened by the blast's near-miss, but he gets up, only to see Randall and Doodle and five of the Mongolian mercenaries, including Bagziin, Khoorloogiin, and Damdin, in the doorway. Doodle rushes toward the Time Bender as the five mercenaries lock their weapons on Nicholas.

Randall, carrying the bigger sleigh crystal, laughs.

"Everything you've done to catch up to us has been for naught," Randall crows. He walks to the sleigh and sees Fred is still knocked out cold in the back. Randall sighs and puts the crystal next to him.

Doodle brings Randall the Time Bender watch as he turns to Nicholas with a ridiculing curl of his lip.

Nicholas's voice is low and remorseful when he says, "Doodle? How could you do this?"

"I know, I know. My family. Long time to live knowing what I've done. Blather, blather, blather," Doodle chatters. "You and Ooby sound the same."

Nicholas shakes his head with an expression of deep concern. "I was going to say, how could you do this and think you'll escape punishment?"

Right after he says it, Nicholas's eyes flare with an intensity that Doodle has surely never seen before. The concern is gone and an unfamiliar shadow of fury darkens his face. It makes Doodle wince as if he were punched in the stomach.

"He doesn't fear you because you're irrelevant, Father Santa Nicholas Christmas Claus, or whatever you call yourself," Randall breaks in. "This ship will be sinking in five minutes. You'll be on it. We will not."

"Mosh Pit is in the stairwell. At least save him before you do anything rash," Nicholas says.

"He bumped to the bottom of the stairs as we were starting up them. I already sent him back to my giant frozen gold vault in Antarctica via the crystal," Randall says as he unties the sleigh's ropes from the eyebolts in the deck. "Against my better judgment I might add." Randall climbs into the sleigh. Doodle follows, still unable to look at Nicholas. "Since I don't feel like putting forth the effort it would undoubtedly require to try and retrieve the little crystals from you, you can keep them. Though I doubt they'll be of much use to you five thousand feet below the sea. Adieu."

Randall turns to the mercenaries. "Finish him and this boat. We'll hover overhead until you're done." He leans in close to Doodle and whispers, "Not."

Doodle giggles as the five mercenaries all nod, not hearing the last comment. They aim their guns and RPG-7s at Nicholas as Randall slaps the reins on the deer and the sleigh takes off with the four tie-down ropes trailing behind it.

Nicholas tosses the small crystal into the sleigh as it starts away from the deck. Doodle anticipates Nicholas's move and swats the crystal with his hand as it arcs over the side. The crystal flies toward the edge of the ship. Doodle snickers with a small sense of triumph.

Nicholas sees the trajectory of the crystal after being batted away. Simultaneously, all five mercenaries unload their weapons at him. Without any other options, he touches his chest and disappears before the bullets and grenades can hit him. He reappears as he's going over the side of the ship and grabs the edge as a series of explosions rock the deck above.

Two of the mercenaries wait for the fiery blasts to clear, then rush to the edge. Nicholas pulls up and slides the crystal between them. He reappears right behind them and scissors kicks them into the water far below. Then, he spins and pushes a lever to release a lifeboat.

Bagziin, Khoorloogiin, and Damdin open fire again. Nicholas sprints along the edge of the deck. At a full run, he pitches his crystal at a 3-inch pipe curving up out of the deck fifty feet away. The crystal goes in. "Please don't be a potty vent," Nicholas says as he touches his chest and disappears.

In an internal hallway, below the deck of the Carrier, Nicholas steps out from behind a door marked 'Mechanical Room'. He looks up and down the long corridor. It's wide and almost as long as the carrier itself. There are doors all along each side and multiple recessed stairwells, too.

At the far end, over a hundred yards away, another metal door has a red hazard sign that reads ORDNANCE ROOM. Another sign on the door declares 'Absolutely No Smoking'. He starts up the hallway, away from that room.

Bagziin leaps out from a nearby stairwell, machine gun rattling. Nicholas dives toward him, rolls, and comes up with a stiff uppercut to his jaw. Bagziin drops.

Damdin comes from a stairwell further down the hallway. He opens fire, but Nicholas leaps to a pipe chase traversing the ceiling. Hand over hand, he moves along the pipes toward the mercenary, avoiding the hail of bullets as he swings.

Nicholas jumps to the other side of the wall, pushes off, and leaps into a side kick that plows Damdin in the chest. Damdin goes hard against the wall and crumples.

At the furthest stairwell, way down the hall, Khoorloogiin emerges with an RPG-7 perched on his shoulder. He takes careful aim at Nicholas.

"No! No! No!" Nicholas yells as he points at the Ordnance Room on the far, opposite end of the hall.

Khoorloogiin grins. Nicholas turns and sprints up the hallway, away from Khoorloogiin and toward the Ordnance Room. He runs past Damdin and Bagziin. Khoorloogiin fires his RPG-7. The small missile streaks up the hall. Nicholas spins and ducks his head just as it goes by, missing him by less than an inch. It hurtles up the hall into the Ordnance Room's door and explodes on impact, blasting the reinforced door inward as a ball of fire shoots out.

Nicholas stops abruptly and watches for a moment. At first, it looks like the initial explosion is all there is going to be. However, when the smoke clears the doorway, Nicholas can see flames erupting within the weapons storage room.

Nicholas turns around and starts running toward Khoorloogiin, who is busy reloading the weapon. Nicholas grabs Bagziin, still unconscious in the hall, by the collar and drags him. He gets to Damdin and grabs him, too. He drags the two mercenaries to a metal door, opens it out into the corridor, and squats behind it with the duo at his feet. Just then, there is a secondary explosion from deep within the room. This explosion is much bigger than the first and it rattles the entire ship.

It sends a wall of dense fire up the corridor. Nicholas and the two mercenaries are safe on the other side of the door as the fire sweeps past in a shockwave of orange. The force pushes against the door. Nicholas has to brace hard against it. The fire passes after several seconds. Nicholas steps from behind the bent and charred door. The entire hall is black and smoking.

The ship gives out a loud, jarring snap. The floor shifts as if cracked by an earthquake. It's enough to force Nicholas off balance. He stumbles a few steps before he catches himself. Something deep within the ship has given away and Nicholas knows it. At the far end, opposite the explosion, Khoorloogiin steps into the hallway again, brandishing the RPG-7 once more and laughing maniacally.

Nicholas turns in time to see him taking careful aim. "Oh, come on," he mutters.

Before he fires, Khoorloogiin's face is stricken by sudden fear. He drops the RPG-7 and bolts up the stairwell. Nicholas turns to where he was looking and sees a wall of water rushing out of the blasted Ordnance Room. Nicholas grabs Damdin and Bagziin, throws one over each shoulder, and dashes up the hallway.

When he reaches the discarded RPG-7, Nicholas drops the two mercenaries to the floor. He pulls the headband from Bagziin's brow and picks up the launcher. Working quickly, he ties his small crystal to the loaded grenade with the headband, aims the launcher up the middle of the tall, spiral staircase, and fires.

Khoorloogiin is scrambling up the stairs as the missile streaks by him. It explodes five stories overhead in the doorway that leads out to the flight deck. Khoorloogiin looks down, thinking the grenade was aimed at him. He sees Nicholas and the other two mercenaries disappear, just as the wall of water fills the spot where they had been at the base of the stairs.

At the top of the charred stairs, Nicholas reappears with the two mercenaries still at his feet. There is a gaping hole in the door from the grenade's explosion. Outside is the expansive flight deck. Nicholas waves Khoorloogiin on.

"Hurry!" he yells, but Khoorloogiin isn't fast enough. The water rushes up the stairs behind him. It overtakes him, lifts him, and thrusts him upward. Nicholas grabs the other two and leaps through the doorway.

On the flight deck, Nicholas and the two mercenaries tumble out of the doorway. A second later, Khoorloogiin shoots out behind them, screaming as the water drives him fifty feet onto the deck in a geyser.

The water continues gushing as the ship starts to rock back at a steep angle. Nicholas drags Damdin and Bagziin to a lifeboat. Khoorloogiin voluntarily dives onto the boat as Nicholas pushes a lever and sends it down to the ocean's surface.

Damdin stirs from unconsciousness just as the lifeboat plunges into the water. He sees Nicholas above them, watching, looking over the side to make sure they make it down safely. For the first time, he gets a good look at his face and recognizes him as the man who saved them so long before.

"He saved us again," Damdin says to Khoorloogiin, who is dropping the oars into the water.

"Who?" Khoorloogiin grunts as he pours all his effort into rowing away from the sinking ship so that they aren't sucked down into the ocean's depths with it.

Damdin points at Nicholas. "The deliverer from our youth." He waves and Nicholas waves back with a forgiving smile.

The bow of the ship begins to lift out of the water as the stern drops below the surface in a tumultuous roar of white water. Nicholas sprints toward the F-22 Raptor. Anything that isn't bolted down to the deck slides into the ocean.

Nicholas climbs aboard the F-22, straps in, and closes the canopy as it begins rolling backwards down the deck.

"How does this go again?" he asks lowly while he flips switches on the complex dashboard. The plane begins to slide backwards even faster. He powers up the engine, gives it full throttle, and begins to crawl up the incline.

After a few seconds, it gains traction and finally launches upward. The Carrier sinks into the ocean just as the plane clears the end of the deck. It dips close to the ocean's surface, but the engine roars and the jet veers heavenward.

CHAPTER 30

Far away from the sunken Carrier...

Randall steers the sleigh. The Time Bender is activated, so they are moving super-fast. Doodle is seated next to him. Fred remains unconscious in the back.

"He's been out a long time. Should we be worried?" Doodle asks with a glance back at Fred.

Randall waves him off. "He's fine. What we should be worried about is how Santa knew where we would be? He was stranded in Japan without his handheld computer."

"Ooby must have used the unicorns' special powers. When they touch horns, they can do all kinds of things. Maybe they opened up some kind of communication through the ether. Since Ooby knew where we were going, he could relay it to Nicholas."

Randall nods, understanding. "Their horns are magic. Of course. Why wouldn't they be?"

"They're the most enchanted beasts of all," Doodle says as he looks over the side of the sleigh. "Hey! Isn't Bora Bora way far west of here?"

Randall laughs. "You only think you want to go there." He steers the sleigh downward toward a dark landmass far below.

Doodle is skeptical. "That so? Where do I really want to go?"

"Madagascar," Randall says. "It's nice and warm, just like you desire."

"What?" Doodle barks, indignant. "That wasn't the arrangement! Besides, the Saints won't like it there! It's humid and full of dangerous animals!"

Randall shakes his head. "It'll just be you, ol' chap. Your people are good workers. I need them to inventory and move my gold as the global economy dictates."

Doodle stands from his seat. "You're going to make them forced servants?"

"Just the ones who survive the hailstorm," Randall says with brutal nonchalance.

"You can't do that!"

"With a magic horn in each hand, I think I'll be able to do a lot of things." Randall glares up at Doodle, who is looming over him as if he could intimidate him by just being taller. In fact, even standing, Doodle is only an inch or two higher than the seated Randall.

Doodle quickly gives up on the attempt of being menacing and instead folds his arms in pouty defiance. "Well, you can land all you want, but I'm not getting off and you can't make me!"

Randall de-activates the Time Bender. The sleigh slows to normal speed as it skirts the tree line. "I'm not gonna make you do anything. And who said I would land?"

Randall grins as his eyes give a glance to the back of the sleigh. Just then, Doodle hears a maniacal snarl behind him. He turns and sees Fred sitting up, rubbing his jaw.

"Who hit me?" Fred hisses.

"My bruvva is always so cranky after a long overdue nap," Randall banters to Doodle. To Fred, he says, "Sleep well?"

"I said, who hit me?" Fred barks.

Randall points at Doodle. "As unlikely as it seems, it was him."

Before Doodle can protest, Fred grabs him, lifts him over his head, and pitches him over the side of the sleigh. Doodle yells all the way down into the jungle below.

Randall looks over and gives a snarky wave. "Ta."

Fred climbs into the seat next to Randall. Fred is angry, clenching his teeth, eyes wide with rage. "You lie. That little creep didn't knock me out. There's no way."

"Of course not," Randall confesses. "It was Santa Claus, but don't worry, he's long gone."

This makes Fred even angrier. "We should've just dropped that nubbin out in the ocean! We're wasting our time way out here!"

Randall motions to the Time Bender watch on his wrist. "We may be a bit off course, but with this baby, there's no such thing as wasting time."

Fred grows red-faced with deepening anger. "You should have left Santa Claus for me!"

"Glad to see you're back, Bruvva. It's been a while." Randall smiles as he activates the Time Bender and the sleigh rockets out of sight.

CHAPTER 31

In the night sky over the dark expanse of the ocean…

The F-22 Raptor streaks toward the South Pole. Though perplexed by the jet's complex controls, Nicholas manages to keep it speeding forward.

Lowly, Nicholas says to himself, "If they used the Time Bender, they might already be there." Suddenly, there is a blip on the jet's radar, moving toward the center of the screen at superspeed. His eyes widen. "That thing is a hundred miles back and moving at Mach Ten. Only my sleigh moves that fast."

Nicholas throttles the jet all the way up. The blip on the screen continues to rapidly close in. He pulls out his pocket abacus and moves a few beads with his thumb. He looks up at the stars through the glass canopy over him and makes a few more moves on the abacus.

"I'll only get one chance at this," he mutters. He pulls the joystick and the jet rolls upside down as the blip nears the center of the screen.

In the sleigh, Randall steers the deer while Fred seethes with fury. Everything around them is a blur as they move at supersonic speeds.

Giddy with a sense of victory, Randall sings, "Fa La La La La! We are so rich!"

Fred doesn't feel Randall's gleeful exhilaration. Instead, he just glares at him. "I gotta wallop something!"

"There are unicorns and dwarfish vermin a' plenty in our new hometown. If you can't find something to punch there, I don't know what to tell you." Randall still grins.

"I need to crush something worthy of my lofty talents," Fred grumbles.

Randall is quick to heap praise on him. "Yes! My bruvva is his old self! He throws cobras like darts and juggles lions like bowling pins! He headlocks nightmares and gives pink-bellies to monsoons!"

"I don't need a carnival barker!" Fred snaps.

"You didn't mind me being your hype-man back in the old days down at the docks," Randall chuckles. "Remember the night when you got in a donnybrook with that entire British Army platoon."

"I whipped all thirty of them without so much as scraping a knuckle or breaking a sweat." Fred doesn't seem at all as though he is exaggerating. "You cheered from a distance."

Randall shrugs. "Far be it from me to get between you and a challenge."

In the cockpit of the inverted F-22 Raptor, Nicholas holds tight to the joystick. He looks toward the top of the canopy, which is now facing down toward the ocean. The blip approaches the center of the radar screen.

"Here we go," he says as he takes a deep breath and punches the eject button. "No parachute this time."

The canopy over the cockpit jettisons away and behind the jet. Nicholas shoots straight down. He drops a thousand feet before the sleigh appears on the horizon, streaking toward him like a bolt of lightning.

The sleigh and Nicholas converge at the same point; Nicholas dropping vertically, the sleigh moving horizontally across the night sky. Nicholas closes his eyes to the impact he fears is coming, but he intercepts the sleigh right over the crystal and disappears. Randall and Fred didn't even know he was there.

In the Clock Room in Eno, Nicholas somersaults from the crystal and onto the conveyor belt. He looks around, briefly disoriented. The conveyor belt is racing toward the huge pile of gold, which the sixth and final mercenary is still busy stacking and arranging.

Mosh Pit is to one side of the belt. He is just starting to stir after being knocked out by Nicholas on the ship and transported to Eno via the crystal by Randall. Mosh Pit sits up slowly. His eyes focus on Nicholas, who draws back his fist as he rides by on the conveyor belt.

"Oh, snot," Mosh Pit moans. Nicholas knocks him out again with a swift right cross. He drops flat on his back.

The mercenary looks up, sees Nicholas on the belt sprinting toward him. He fumbles with his machine gun, but Nicholas jumps and side-kicks the mercenary over the stack of gold. Without slowing, Nicholas runs outside.

In the courtyard, Nicholas sees Ooby tied to the post. Then, he sees the rubble of the recreation building. The Saints are still in hiding and no one moves about the town. Only the unicorns remain by Ooby and they are exhausted and limp at his feet. Nicholas sprints to the post and breaks Ooby's binds with one hand, while constantly surveying the city.

"Is it over?" Ooby asks. He rubs the ache from his wrists.

"Not yet," Nicholas answers.

"You made it to the Carrier, I presume."

"Yes. Thank you." Nicholas looks down at the unicorns. Enlitas opens one eye and gazes up at him. Excitas sleeps soundly. "Thank you," Nicholas says to the unicorn. Enlitas grins and closes her eye again.

Ooby stands. "We have always maintained good relationships with the sea beasts. They were glad to help. Now what?"

"We stop Randall before he gets back here."

"What about Doodle?"

"I only saw the sleigh for a split second. It was just Randall and Fred. No Doodle."

Ooby shakes his head. "They must have double-crossed him."

"It would appear so." Nicholas looks up at the tunnel, high over Eno, then he looks at the bomb that is dangling from the spear in the ice dome overhead. It reads 04:44 and is ticking off the seconds. "They must be getting close by now. We have to hurry. Can you deal with the bomb?"

Ooby looks up at the bomb, too. "Yes. If you can manage without the crystals."

Nicholas takes off the crystal necklace and pulls the other crystal from his pocket. He gives them both to Ooby. Together, they rush to the staging facility and Clock Room.

Inside, Nicholas and Ooby run toward the Grandfather Clock. Ooby sees Mosh Pit and the sixth mercenary knocked out cold on the floor. He looks at Nicholas.

"Did I miss something?" he asks.

"Just a little," Nicholas answers as he continues toward the crystal at the base of the Clock. Ooby grabs the nearby toy plane that had been discarded earlier by Mosh Pit, the gift meant for Deon.

"Be careful," Ooby says as he starts back for the door to the court-yard.

"Keep the Saints safe," Nicholas says as he steps on the crystal and disappears.

CHAPTER 32

In the sky over the ocean...

Nicholas appears in the back of the sleigh. Immediately, Fred turns and sees him.

"Well, well, well," Fred smirks. He dives into the back, fists swinging. Nicholas blocks the punches, but is surprised by Fred's sudden change in demeanor.

"I see the rest did you good," Nicholas comments as he responds with his own flurry of punches and kicks. Fred shows that he is as skilled as Nicholas when he blocks the volley of blows.

"Visions of sugarplums danced in my head! Now it's your turn!" Fred growls. He swings mightily, connecting with Nicholas's body several times. Randall slaps the reins, then he gives them a sharp tug, turning the deer and twisting the sleigh hard to one side. Fred and Nicholas go over the back.

Outside the sleigh, Fred and Nicholas grasp on to separate tie down ropes dragging behind in the ferocious wind. They swing toward each other and attack with fierce punches and kicks every time they are close enough. Since there are four ropes, they jump from one to another, continuing their high-flying fight.

Back in the courtyard in Eno, Ooby operates the console for the remote-control plane. It buzzes loudly over the gardens and buildings. Little faces of the Saints begin appearing in the windows.

One of the small crystals is tied to the nose of the plane. The other crystal is around Ooby's neck. As he steers the little plane, his tongue is out in deep concentration and he is swaying like he just rolled a bowling ball and is guiding it with twisting and leaning body maneuvers.

Beneath and a little bit behind the sleigh, Nicholas and Fred are engaged in a battle full of flipping, rope-to-rope jumps, kicks, and all manner of swash-buckling derring-do. Randall leans over the side of the sleigh and watches when he can.

Now that Nicholas is there in their presence, the two back deer are emboldened. They begin chewing on their leather reins while the sleigh rockets onward at ten times the speed of sound thanks to the effects of the Time-Bender.

Nicholas punches Fred so hard that the momentum swings Fred all the way under the sleigh. Though nearly unconscious, Fred has enough of his wits about him to let go of the rope and grab onto the sleigh's runner. He gives his head a vigorous shake as if to revive himself. Nicholas is hanging on to his rope well behind. He begins working his way hand over hand up the rope, but Fred recovers and climbs into the back of the sleigh.

Fred is there before Nicholas can reach it. Fred immediately whips out a switchblade and saws through the rope. Nicholas leaps to another as the first rope flutters away. Fred slashes hastily at that rope, too. Nicholas leaps to the third. Fred slices it over and over until it finally cuts through and forces Nicholas to jump to the last rope whipping in the wind. He catches it at the very end, knowing he will never make it before Fred can chop through it. Randall looks back with a smug smile.

In Eno's courtyard, the little plane reaches the dangling bomb and circles around it. Ooby steers it so that the crystal tied to the plane's nose touches the bomb, which disappears from the arrow stuck in the ceiling of ice.

The bomb appears at Ooby's feet. He looks down and sees the timer is counting down 01:31... 01:30...

Ooby turns his attention back to the flying plane, directing it into the tunnel in the dome high over the town. Once inside, the plane makes a bumpy landing on the frozen floor. Ooby drops the plane's remote and takes off the necklace. He looks to the sleeping unicorns and begins softly clicking his tongue.

"Enlitas. Excitas. Awake now. Please." Ooby speaks gently, knowing he has already asked so much of the unicorns. Excitas reluctantly opens one eye and peers at him. "I need your services again, my friend. It is most dire."

Excitas opens his other eye and stands on weary feet. The unicorn steps up to him and bows his head to Ooby, who hangs the bomb on his horn. Enlitas, also awake now, comes to Excitas's side.

"Please, Excitas. You must be swift," Ooby says.

Enlitas leans against Excitas and their horns touch. They glow faintly for a moment, then brighten. Excitas's horn grows brighter and brighter while Enlitas's diminishes, as if she is transferring her remaining strength to Excitas. This continues until Enlitas's horn is dull and colorless. She collapses. Excitas, his horn burning brightly now, nods to Ooby. Ooby touches the crystal to the tip of Excitas's horn and he disappears.

In the tunnel, Excitas appears by the plane. He looks up the length of the winding shaft leading to the surface. The timer counts down. 00:55... 00:54...

The unicorn dashes off in a blur. He speeds up the long tunnel, almost as if he were under the influence of the Time Bender, even though he isn't. Within a matter of seconds, he has gone over a mile and is approaching the midway point of the tunnel.

The timer continues. 00:40... 00:39...

Back in the courtyard, Ooby watches the tunnel. He sees a few Saints appear in the windows of the buildings, so he waves them out.

"Come," he calls as he looks around and sees more and more curious faces popping into view. "It's okay. We're okay. It's safe. The bomb is gone." Some of the faces disappear as quickly as they had appeared. He can't help but smile at their childlike innocence. "There are two bad guys by the clock. I need help securing them. Any volunteers?"

Beneath the sleigh, still over the ocean, Nicholas is hanging on for dear life at the end of the last rope. Fred is sawing through it as fast as he can. The wind is roaring, so Nicholas must yell when he addresses Fred.

"Wait! Fred! Don't do it!"

Fred is nearly through the last remaining strands. "Why shouldn't I after what you did to my Fadda?" he asks with deep bitterness.

"Because I can give you a gift greater than revenge," Nicholas returns.

Fred shakes his head. "What's better than revenge?"

"Redemption," Nicholas replies. Fred pauses and looks down at Nicholas, pondering his words for a moment. "I can help you find honest work. You can live with a noble purpose! Fred, your father made the wrong choices, but you don't have to!"

Randall senses his younger brother's moment of apprehension. He is quick to intervene as he lashes the reins against the deer harder than ever.

"Remember how he ruined us! Drop him like a coal filled stocking, Bruvva!"

Fred glances quickly over his shoulder at Randall. Something inside reminds him that Randall is his only family and he can't let him down. He glares back at Nicholas and snips the last bit of rope. "Merry Christmas to all and to all a good night, eh, Santa Claus?"

Nicholas falls from beneath the sleigh and presumably outside the area of the Time Bender's influence. Randall gives a celebratory whoop. Just then, the two back deer finish chewing through the reins, freeing the first six deer ahead of them. The six deer, still connected to each other, veer off to one side, much to Randall's dismay.

"Oh, for crying out loud!" Randall barks as Fred leaps into the front beside him. The sleigh slows substantially because the two remaining deer have trouble pulling its weight. Randall slaps the reins on them.

The deer buck and snort. Fred grabs Randall's wrist and deactivates the Time Bender. Everything around them slows to normal speed.

"What on Earth...?" Randall protests.

"If they can't carry our weight, we'll only fall at superspeed," Fred mutters.

The sleigh is indeed moving in a downward trajectory. Randall nods in agreement.

"Right-o, Bruvva." Randall looks down and sees that they are now over the icy landmass of Antarctica. The night has turned to day as the continent experiences its summer season of perpetual sunlight.

Suddenly, from underneath the sleigh, the six deer fly into view. They cut perpendicular to the sleigh and over it. Nicholas is hanging beneath them, holding on to the chewed through leather straps. He leaps from the free-flying deer and into the back of the sleigh. Fred dives into the back after him and their fight starts anew.

"Hang on Fred!" Randall cackles as he checks his watch. "Almost time for the bomb to explode! With his home destroyed, he won't have anything to fight for!"

On the side of a snowy mountain, Excitas emerges from the tunnel's opening, still carrying the grenade on his horn.

00:15... 00:14... 00:13.

He flings the bomb off his horn into deep snow. Then, he bolts back into the tunnel.

In the Clock Room, Ooby enters, rope in hand. He sees Mosh Pit and the last mercenary are still down and out, but just starting to arouse. Fifteen or so Saints follow Ooby, like timid sheep. Mosh Pit groans as he sits up. The Saints look as if they might turn and run. Ooby senses their anxiety.

"Easy," he says. "Stay with me. We can beat him. It will take all of us, but we can do it." The Saints all frown, nervous and scared. "Follow me, Saints! Charge!"

Ooby, alone, but believing the others are right behind him, runs toward Mosh Pit, who is still dazed and confused. Ooby gives a loud roar as he goes.

"Welcome to Ooby's world of pain, Bub!"

Ooby attacks Mosh Pit, who snaps out of his stupor and holds his hand against Ooby's forehead, extending his arm to its full length. Ooby swings helplessly at the space between them. Mosh Pit snickers, fully enjoying himself again.

In the sleigh over the snowy mountains, Randall tries to control the last two deer, who are struggling to keep the sleigh airborne. Nicholas and Fred slug it out behind him. The other six deer follow closely.

Randall checks his watch, then turns to yell at Nicholas. "The weather reports for Eno just came in. It predicts fire and brimstone on the heads of your saintly hobbits!" He glances at his watch once more. "Right about now!"

Nicholas blocks one of Fred's punches and puts him in an arm-bar to hold him. The fight pauses as Nicholas looks far ahead of the sleigh to the side of a mountain. Just then, the bomb explodes, causing a plume of fire and snow to flower in their path. Behind it, the tunnel remains open.

Randall gives an angry grimace while Nicholas smiles.

"How did they reach my bomb?" Randall bellows.

Nicholas twists Fred's arm and pummels him with a series of blows. Randall furiously slaps the two deer with the reins and aims the sleigh toward the opening.

The sleigh enters the ice tunnel as Nicholas and Fred continue to bash each other. The two deer pulling the sleigh follow the well-known course of the tunnel and the other six deer trail close behind.

Randall leans over the dashboard of the sleigh and stretches to reach the tackle for the reins at the front of it. He pulls a pin that releases the last two deer. They fly up and back, happily rejoining the other six behind the sleigh.

Randall grips the side of the sleigh as it slams against the bottom of the tunnel and rockets downhill on its runners like a luge. Nicholas and Fred bounce high from the impact. Once they catch their balance, they resume slugging it out.

Randall digs in his bag and pulls out a set of chain shackles. He turns in the seat and clips one side of the cuff through a tie down anchor in the side of the sleigh. Then, he waits with the other side until Nicholas steps near him during his slug-fest with Fred. When Nicholas makes a move backwards, Randall cuffs the shackle to Nicholas's ankle without Nicholas realizing it. He then grabs the crystal from under the two combatants' feet.

Randall pitches the crystal over the front of the dash. As it slides down the tunnel a few feet ahead of the sleigh, he climbs over and gives a salute.

"Adieu, suckers," he says as he leaps on the sliding crystal and disappears.

Nicholas and Fred pause their fight as Fred looks to the front of the sleigh where Randall had been. He then looks back at Nicholas.

"Suckers?" Fred is clearly insulted by Randall's inclusion of him in the pejorative.

Nicholas shrugs, then punches Fred with a mighty upper-cut. Fred finally goes cross-eyed. "More sugarplums," he slurs.

Fred falls face first into the bottom of the sleigh. Nicholas leaps into the front seat and looks for the crystal. He sees it sliding down the ice, well ahead of the sleigh. As he starts to climb over the dash, the chain shackled to his ankle pulls taut and he realizes he's trapped on board.

"Uh oh," he whispers.

In the Clock Room, Randall appears over the crystal. He marches to where Mosh Pit is still holding back Ooby.

"Quit horsing around, Mosh Pit!" Randall barks.

He snatches the necklace crystal from Ooby. Mosh Pit grabs Ooby by the wrist and lifts him over his head. The Saints all huddle against the wall in fear. Randall snares one, Lupper, and lifts him off the ground by the collar.

"There is a second small crystal. Where is it?" Randall demands. Lupper, shaking with terror, glances at Ooby, who is high over Mosh Pit's head.

"Don't tell him, Lupper!" Ooby yells. Mosh Pit pitches Ooby halfway across the room. The horrified Saint points toward the ceiling.

"It is in, in the, the tunnel, sir," Lupper stammers.

Randall drops Lupper and kicks him in the rump as he darts off by the others.

"Perfect." Randall turns to Mosh Pit. "Me thinks we have a wall to build." He strides to the pile of gold by the conveyor belt.

"Why?" Mosh Pit asks. "So we can paint a mural?"

"No, you nincompoop," Randall chides. "It's the best way to keep out a pest." With the necklace crystal in his palm, Randall begins touching pieces of gold. They disappear, one by one.

"Like rats and roaches?" Mosh Pit continues, still not understanding what Randall means.

"No!" Randall whines, as he continues slapping the bricks. "The Santa Chap! Nicholas or whoever! He's in the tunnel in the sleigh, plummeting toward us right now! I'm moving the gold up there to block him from getting to us!"

Mosh Pit nods, finally getting it. "At the end of the line, blammo!"

Randall smiles while still transferring the gold. "No Santa Claus means we get lots of servants." He eyes the cowering Saints maliciously.

In the mouth of the tunnel, high over Eno, the gold mounds up over the crystal. Several bricks are added to the growing pile every second. Back in the Clock Room, Randall hands the necklace crystal to Mosh Pit. "Keep sending the gold."

"Where are you going?" Mosh Pit asks as he takes over.

Randall goes to the last mercenary, who is just regaining consciousness. He snatches the mercenary's machete from his sheath.

"I've two horns to claim, the real prizes in this whole caper." He glares at Ooby. To the mercenary, he says, "Finish that twerp."

Randall storms out of the Clock Room. The mercenary cocks his gun and angles its barrel toward Ooby, who can't help but gasp.

In the sleigh in the icy tunnel, Nicholas has tied together pieces of the chewed reins. He is trying to lasso the crystal, sliding far ahead, but the leather strapping is too short. As the sleigh rounds a bend, he recognizes that he is halfway through the tunnel. He knows there is a long drop down to Eno at the end. He expedites his efforts with the lasso. Just then, he sees Excitas ahead, sliding with joy.

"Excitas!" he yells. "Excitas! Help!" Excitas looks back at the approaching sleigh.

Nicholas points at the crystal, which is sliding faster than the unicorn. It passes under him as Excitas leaps into the air and lands in the sleigh next to Nicholas. Like a dog that has performed a new trick, Excitas stands next to Nicholas, tall and proud.

Nicholas rubs Excitas's nose. "I meant I needed help stopping the crystal." Excitas drops his head and mopes, but Nicholas pets his jaws and neck. "You got rid of that bomb, didn't you? Bless your heart, you saved Eno."

Excitas perks back up and nuzzles Nicholas's leg while lapping up his affection. Nicholas turns to look for his team of deer. The eight deer, so happy to be reunited and free of Randall, have lagged way behind the careening sleigh. Nicholas can't even see them. He looks ahead again. Though he can't see the end of the tunnel either, he knows it's coming and the thought of it makes him shiver.

In the Clock Room, the mercenary starts toward Ooby with his gun raised and malice in mind.

"Eno Saints!" Ooby chimes, "It's now or never!"

The group, still cowering by the wall, takes a collective breath. Lupper steps forward to take command of the fearful group. With a simple wave, he leads them forward. This time they follow. They charge the mercenary in a pack.

The mercenary is momentarily distracted by their attack, so Ooby leaps to his feet and roundhouse kicks the mercenary in the chest. He stumbles backwards into the advancing Saints. Together, they overcome him and disarm him. Within seconds, the mercenary is subdued.

"Good work, Saints!" Ooby cheers. Then he looks at Lupper with a proud smile and a nod. Lupper returns the gesture.

Ooby runs to the crystal beneath the Grandfather Clock. He pulls the crystal from its case and takes it toward the group.

"Here!" he says as he slides the crystal on the floor so that it stops in front of the group. "Send him to the tunnel! He won't have anywhere to go up there!"

The group of Saints lifts the mercenary, who begins squawking fervently like an angry duck. In unison, they toss him on the crystal and he disappears.

"One to go, my Mighty Saints!" Ooby calls. He points at Mosh Pit, who is still transporting gold with the necklace crystal. The pile is almost gone. Mosh Pit hears the commotion behind him and smiles over his shoulder.

"Bring it on, you little ankle-biters," he chuckles.

Far over Eno, in the ice tunnel, Nicholas and Excitas stand in the back of the speeding sleigh. Nicholas is worried. He grips the slack chain that is cuffed around his ankle.

"Any chance your horn can cut through metal?" he quips. Excitas just shakes his head, sadly. "Jump out of the back and save yourself," Nicholas continues. "You don't have to stay."

As he speaks, the mercenary appears over the sliding crystal. He is confused by his sudden change in location. With a quick look around, he sees that he is sliding helplessly down an ice chute with no way to stop. He claws at the ice with his hands and feet to slow himself, but it doesn't work.

Nicholas sees him and leans over the dash, positioning himself to help. The sleigh speeds closer to the mercenary. He looks back, sees the sleigh coming and screams. Just before the sleigh runs over him, Nicholas grabs him, pulls hard, and flips him out of the way.

"Use your knife!" Nicholas calls.

Now behind the sleigh, the mercenary pulls out his knife, jams it into the ice and brings himself to a halt. He gives a wave of thanks to Nicholas, who quickly hurtles out of sight down the tunnel.

In the Clock Room, the Saints, empowered and confident, charge Mosh Pit. He effortlessly sumo bounces them in retaliation, two and three at a time. The Saints fly in every direction, like children slinging off a merry-go-round that is going too fast.

Ooby has the big crystal. He slides it at Mosh Pit's feet, who sees it and leaps over it. It hits the wall behind him.

"Ha! Nice try!" he says as he belly bops Ooby and sends him flying.

Just outside, in the courtyard, Randall wanders about, clicking his tongue to call for the unicorns. All the while, he conceals the machete behind his back.

"Come out, you little magical beauties," he says sweetly. He doesn't know that only Enlitas is in the town and she has found a well-hidden place to take refuge.

Overhead, in the tunnel, Nicholas is squatting by Excitas.

"The final bend is right ahead. There's quite a drop-off coming after that. Can you stop yourself?" He points at Fred, still out cold behind him. "And him?"

Excitas nods, then frowns at the shackle and chain restraining Nicholas to the sleigh. Nicholas gives him a reassuring smile. "Don't worry about me."

As they round the final bend, the wall of gold bricks, now completely blocking it, comes into view. Nicholas knows that the impact will be fierce.

"Go Excitas! Go now!"

He pitches the unicorn and Fred over the side as the sleigh speeds toward the wall. He watches as Excitas straddles Fred and digs his horn into the ice, slowing the two dramatically. The sleigh speeds away from them.

In the Clock Room, Mosh Pit is victorious over all the Saints. Ooby bounds back to his feet and desperately charges Mosh Pit again, but Mosh Pit stops him in his tracks with a fearsome gaze. He holds out his fist toward Ooby. The chain of the necklace crystal dangles from his balled-up hand.

"Give me a break, small-fry! You're wasting your time! I'm the greatest Sumo warrior ever!" he brags. "You don't stand a chance against me!"

Ooby glares at him from a few feet away. An idea comes to him.

"I've known many Sumo warriors in my long years," Ooby starts. "When they have vanquished their opponents, they always pound their chests in triumph. You haven't done that, so how do I know you've won?"

Mosh Pit laughs boastfully. "Very well." He rears his head back and raises his arm high over his head. "Bonsai!" With that, Mosh Pit pounds his chest with both fists. When the one holding the crystal touches his chest, he promptly disappears.

In the sleigh, Nicholas braces for impact with the rapidly approaching wall of gold. Suddenly, Mosh Pit appears over the other small crystal. He is in front of the pile, between it and the speeding sleigh. He looks from side to side, terribly disoriented for a moment.

Then, he sees the sleigh barreling toward him with Nicholas behind the dash, waving him out of the way. It's too late.

"Oh, booger," Mosh Pit groans.

Far below, in the courtyard, a loud crash echoes down from the tunnel. Randall sees a few gold bricks fall, followed by some broken bits of the sleigh and a single runner. Then, he turns and sees Ooby standing in the open doorway to the Clock Room. The Saints are converging behind him. He doesn't see Mosh Pit or the mercenary. Or Nicholas, for that matter. He quickly surmises the situation.

"Well, chum, you either overpowered Mosh Pit or, more likely, out-smarted him. My guess is he's in the tunnel with your Santa buddy," Randall says.

Ooby folds his arms. "It's just us now."

"I guess you need a new master and I need a new sidekick." Randall's tone is patronizing and sarcastic.

Ooby gives a fast retort. "The only sidekick you'll get is a flying one to your head."

"Ol' fashioned fisticuffs to the bitter end, eh?" Randall snarks. "Jolly good."

Ooby and Randall start to circle each other as Randall brandishes the machete. Both are obviously stalling, waiting for the other to make a move. They fill the time with insults and tough talk.

"You honestly think you can take me?" Randall taunts.

"With my eyes closed. Who do you think taught Nicholas to fight?" Ooby jabs.

"Who do you think taught Fred?"

"You haven't had a fair fight since elementary school."

Randall grows angry at the remark. "You probably haven't won a fight since the Bronze Age."

"You'll be sorry for that, Bub," Ooby lashes back.

"Says you, Mon chichi."

Before they finally engage with one another, the door to the Clock Room flies open and Nicholas runs out. Ooby sees him and is relieved and thankful he's alive.

While he's distracted, Randall grabs Ooby in a rear choke and holds the blade up in a threatening manner. Nicholas stops in his tracks. The Saints emerge from the building after him, but he motions for them to stay back.

"Easy, Randall. Easy," he soothes.

"How did you survive that impact?" Randall demands.

"Mosh Pit made a great cushion." Nicholas holds up his hands in surrender. "Let Ooby go."

Ooby chokes under Randall's tight grasp.

"Can't do that, I'm afraid," Randall says as he points the machete at Nicholas. "Stay back."

"Take all the gold. Just let him go and leave us." Nicholas speaks in a calming tone, as if lulling a petulant dog.

"It's not about the gold anymore! I want the magic unicorn horns! I want to finish your whole herd of irksome pollywogs!" Randall brandishes the machete at the Saints and grows louder. "I want all the children of the world to know how terrible it is to miss the joy of Christmas morning, and mostly, I want to ruin you like you did my Fadda!"

The Saints retreat as Nicholas takes a step forward.

"Get back! Back, I say!" Randall barks. "You think you're invincible with your immortality and ages of martial arts training! Well, I have your global databases and your secret files! I know everything you know, Santa Claus!"

Nicholas stops. "Maybe, Randall, but here's something you don't know." He gives a sly grin that Randall can't seem to understand. "Ooby invented fourteen of the twenty-three most utilized moves in Judo and he's taught me every one of them. By all standards, I'm an expert of the highest level."

Randall gushes out an insolent laugh. "So what? You're way over there! Your expertise won't help you from this distance!"

"True, but even as good as I am, I would never fight Ooby and let him get as close as he is to you," Nicholas says.

With that, Ooby grips Randall's arm at the wrist, turns hard, twists, and sends Randall flipping in the air. Randall lands sharply on his back. His monocles pop from his eyes and fly off in opposite directions. Ooby jumps on him and straddles his chest.

"You're getting coal for Christmas, Bub, and here's your first lump!" Ooby bellows as he punches Randall with a swift jab and knocks him out. The Saints cheer uproariously. Nicholas comes over as Ooby stands, victorious.

"That was a pretty good line," Nicholas smiles.

"Thanks. I made it up on the fly," Ooby returns.

"I was worried you were gonna say 'you're going on the bad list'."

Ooby shrugs. "What would've been wrong with that?"

They laugh as they join the Saints. A small celebration erupts. The rest of the Saints emerge from their hiding places and join the impromptu festivities. Ooby and Nicholas lead the cheering amongst the growing crowd in the courtyard.

High above, in the tunnel, the eight deer squeeze through a small gap at the top of the pile of gold and fly into the sky under the dome. They gleefully zip through the air.

Excitas and Enlitas are reunited. They touch horns, sending fireworks over the party.

CHAPTER 33

On the sleigh pad...

A crew of Saints have the small gray sleigh prepped and ready since the large green one is a demolished heap in the tunnel. Two other Saints bolt the large crystal in the bed of the sleigh. The eight deer are harnessed and eager. Nicholas feeds them cookies.

"I'm gonna ask a little more from you tonight, team. Three days off and a cookie buffet after this."

The deer all prance and rear back to show they are willing. Nicholas pets them one after another.

In the Clock Room, Ooby supervises another crew of Saints as they re-prep the conveyor belts and presents for distribution.

"Good work, friends. Spectacular," he praises.

Nearby, Fred, Mosh Pit, the last mercenary, and Randall are seated and tied up, back-to-back. Randall glares at Ooby through a blackening eye as Ooby walks to him and stops.

"Ready to tell us where you dumped Doodle?" Ooby asks.

"He went on his own," Randall scoffs. "That's how eager he was to escape your oppression."

"My oppression?" Ooby says.

"Yes. You're evil, Ooby. Look how you keep these poor childlike creatures locked away under a glacier in the most remote recess of the world. Look how you bound us like mere animals. Am I right, Fred? Don't you agree, Mosh Pit?"

Mosh Pit and Fred look at each other. Fred shrugs, his face showing the wounds from his battle with Nicholas.

"I don't know," Mosh Pit starts. "It's not bad here. I like it." He turns to look at the mercenary. "And we really do kind of deserve punishment for all that we did."

The mercenary nods and speaks in a perfect Southern California accent. "For sure, Brah. We totally asked for it." Mosh Pit does a double take, shocked by the mercenary's voice.

Randall is clearly irritated. "Oh, what do you guys know?" He turns back to Ooby. "Doodle will save us, for he knows we are his only friends. Watch and see."

"I really doubt that," Mosh Pit whispers.

Randall nudges Mosh Pit into silence. Ooby turns from them and steps on the re-fitted crystal at the base of the Clock and disappears.

Back on the pad, Ooby appears over the crystal and steps out of the sleigh. He approaches Nicholas, who is kneeling by the figure of Baby Jesus again. He waits. When Nicholas is finished with his silent prayer, he turns to Ooby.

"We don't have our computers up yet," Ooby says.

Nicholas is unconcerned. "We'll do it like we used to, before computers."

"The sun is rising in Japan in two hours," Ooby says. "The Time Bender won't let us create that kind of time."

Nicholas stops him. "Do what you must to find the time. We can't let the children down."

Ooby hangs his head. "But, Nicholas…"

Nicholas turns his head. He can't even consider an alternative to delivering every last present.

Right then, a stressed Saint, Joppy, runs up with a bag. Nicholas greets her with a welcoming smile as if he is happy for the interruption. "Hello there, Joppy. Are all the presents ready to go?"

Joppy nods, but with hopeless dejection. "All but one," she groans.

From the bag, Joppy removes the remote-controlled airplane. It's broken into several pieces. Nicholas's shoulders slump when he sees it.

"Oh no. Deon will be heart broken," Nicholas groans.

Ooby is stunned. His tone is indignant when he says, "We saved the world from a financial coup tonight! Are we really going to fret over one child who may not get the present he wants?"

Nicholas and Joppy turn to him, surprised by either his loud outburst or his thought of letting a child go without the present he most desires.

Nicholas places a hand on Joppy's shoulder and ignores Ooby. "We'll have to make it up to Deon somehow. I hope he'll forgive us."

"Me, too, sir," Joppy says slowly. "Me, too."

Nicholas gets in the sleigh with a noticeable darkness hanging over him. Joppy looks down at the floor, sullen. The mood spreads to the other Saints on the sleigh pad. Ooby just shakes his head. He cannot understand how Nicholas is more worried about a broken plane than the ruined computers and the loss of time that they can't get back.

"I'll go to Malaysia first to transport Randall and the others to the National prison and to notify the Americans about their ship," Nicholas says. "We'll get the gold in the Depository, then we'll finish with Japan and move west, ahead of the sun."

Nicholas flicks the reins and the deer lift off. There is no fanfare as he leaves this time. He steers the sleigh toward the tunnel, his back slouching.

None of the Saints hum. None smile. They go about their business, joyless. The celebration that started after they defeated Randall and his crew is long forgotten. There is too much work to do. Too much to be upset about. A child will be disappointed and that is all that matters. This night will not know victory now. Joppy puts the broken plane in a trash container on the side of the sleigh pad. She sulks away.

Ooby watches her go through the door, followed by the other Saints. None of them share Ooby's pragmatic view of the world. They are too innocent by nature, his Eno Saints. Nicholas, though human by birth, is the perfect likeness of the Saints. Perhaps it was Nicholas who made them what they are now. Aside from Ooby, most of the Saints currently alive have come along after Nicholas did, over a millennia ago. Ooby has trouble remembering what the parents and grandparents of the current Saints were like before Nicholas arrived. Were they so idealistic? Have their children evolved into Nicholas's image under his blessed influence? Ooby knows they are more like Nicholas than they are him, even though they come from his ancient bloodline and share his ancestry. Nicholas is who they all are now.

"And that's a good thing indeed," Ooby whispers to himself. He walks to the trash container, looks in, and sighs.

CHAPTER 34

Inside a Malaysian prison cell...

Randall, Mosh Pit, Fred and the sixth mercenary are tied up in a circle with their backs to each other. There is a big red bow on each man's forehead and a large white envelope stuck to the bars outside the cell.

Several Malaysian guards approach the cell. One takes the envelope and opens it. In the cell's lone window to the outside, Nicholas's shadow looms. As the guard reads the note, his shadow drifts away.

Moments later, in front of the moon, the silhouette of the sleigh slices through the night.

"We were framed by a demented Christmas elf who wanted a free ride to Bora Bora!" Randall protests, as the guards enter and surround them. The guards look at each other with raised eyebrows, indicating their immediate suspicion that Randall is a crazed lunatic.

Mosh Pit looks at the nearest guard. "What time is breakfast? I was thinking, say, Miso soup and some steamed rice to kick things off?"

Fred just yawns.

Out in the Indian Ocean, the Sailors from the sunken Super Carrier are bobbing on the rolling swells in their numerous lifeboats. They are all dejected. Most just stare at the bottoms of their respective boats, listening to the lap of the water against the sides.

The sleigh flits across the moon over the stranded crew. Admiral Chucklenut, sitting at the bow of a lifeboat, sees it and points.

"The green Santa Claus has come to finish us off!" he shouts.

The Sailors all scramble in their boats, looking for cover where there is none. Just then, a loud, booming horn breaks the silence of the night. A large Tanker Ship emerges over the horizon. A powerful searchlight on its bow sweeps the dark expanse in front of it until it settles on the fleet of little boats.

"We're saved," Admiral Chucklenut yells in a sudden change in tone. The Sailors cheer.

On the outside of the circle of boats, the dinghy carrying the five mercenaries drifts alone. Bagziin is the first to alert his friends of their impending rescue. Damdin can't help but pump his fist with relief.

"This is it, boys," he says to the others. "Do your best to blend in and we may get away with it."

He is barely able to get the words out before a small tug boat appears out of the darkness and pulls up silently behind them. On the side of the bow, in bold black letters, are written the words, 'Malaysian Police'. The tug blares a siren and flashes red and blue lights that startles the mercenaries.

Over a loudspeaker, a voice booms from the tug. "Reach for the sky, fellas. You are all under arrest for grand theft, grand robbery, grand larceny, and overall purloining."

The mercenaries reluctantly do as they're told and slowly raise their hands.

In the yard of the Takeda home, Holly Siltoe brings the one-horse open sleigh, pulled by Skippy, to a stop near the house. Its colorful Christmas tree is tall and bright in the front window. In the dawning light of the morning, she sees her tent, neat and folded, and the single ski by the door. Skippy looks back at her with a toothy grin and neighs.

"I see," she says. Just then, the front door opens and Kuni looks out, his children and wife by his side.

"Good morning, Skippy! You found your way back!" he chirps. "Merry Christmas, Miss Siltoe! We were told you were coming. Please, join us! We were just about to open presents!"

"Santa Claus sent elves to fix our house and make our breakfast!" Noriko chimes in from Kuni's side. "There's peppermint cocoa and eggs and smoked Salmon and croissants and every kind of cookie you can imagine!"

Kuni adds, "I believe the cookies are for Skippy, but I'm sure he'll share." The horse prances from foot to foot with a refreshed exuberance. Kuni waves Holly in. "Please, come out of the cold."

She climbs out of the sleigh and pats Skippy's neck as she goes by him toward the waiting family. "I'd be delighted," she replies.

In a small home halfway around the world, Aiden, awake too early, but unable to sleep any longer, rushes into the kitchen. Since the home doesn't have a fireplace or mantel, his stocking is hung on the edge of the small counter by the stove.

He grabs the stocking and pours out the contents on the floor. He sifts through the small toys and assorted candies. What he is looking for isn't immediately there. He peers in the stocking and his eyes light up. He reaches all the way in and pulls out an envelope.

He tears it open and withdraws a letter, which he unfolds with trembling hands. He reads down a few sentences until he gets to the good part.

"Bass Industries would like to extend an offer to your father to act as our regional manager of distribution in..."

Aiden bolts down the short hallway to his parents' room.

"He did it, Dad! He did it! Santa Claus got you a job like he promised!"

CHAPTER 35

Christmas morning dawns…

Across the cityscape of the large American metropolis where The Spires pierce the sky, not far from where Aiden just found his letter. On the roof of a big home, Nicholas leans against the chimney, his arms crossed. He watches the sun's light slowly creeping toward him.

Ooby appears over the crystal in the back of the sleigh. He jumps out and steps next to Nicholas.

"I thought we finished just in time with the Yukon and Alaska, but it seems you've backtracked here," Ooby says. Nicholas only nods. "Let me guess. This is Deon's house and you're not going in without his present."

Nicholas shrugs and looks at his boots as he shuffles them in the fresh dusting of snow. "Maybe you're right about Christmas," he laments. "Maybe we're wasting our time. Is there really a difference between one disappointed child and one billion?"

"Probably not," Ooby starts. "But there is certainly a difference between a billion disappointed children and none."

He holds up the remote-controlled airplane. It is repaired, even better than before, with new paint and flashy stripes down its sides. Nicholas sees it and his face ignites in a huge beaming smile.

"You rebuilt it?" he gushes.

"I built a clock that can contort the passage of time!" Ooby is playfully indignant. "I squeezed that clock for more hours and minutes and seconds than I ever thought possible tonight! I think I can handle a few minor repairs on a toy airplane!"

Nicholas grabs it eagerly and looks it over. "You finally got the Christmas spirit!"

"Well, I couldn't just ignore the way you and the Saints were moping around, tripping over your bottom lips. Somebody had to do something," Ooby says.

Nicholas gives a vigorous guffaw. A real belly laugh. A true "Ho Ho Ho" of the highest order and perhaps the best and most genuine in the illustrious history of all "Ho Ho Hos".

Nicholas tosses the small crystal down the chimney. He waves Ooby over.

"Let's do this last stop together," he says. "Deon's mom always leaves out the freshest spinach." Ooby narrows his eyes at Nicholas and doesn't move. Nicholas grins. "And frosted gingerbread cookies."

"Now you're talking!" Ooby sings. "It's been a long night and I'm famished!"

Behind him, the deer scamper at the mention of the sweet treats. Nicholas puts his hand on Ooby's shoulder and they both disappear.

Across the whole Earth, a blessed Christmas is had by all, for the day brings joy to the world in a way that only Christmas can. Nicholas and Ooby return to Eno at the completion of their work.

The birds of the air and the beasts of the sea rejoice. The deer get all the cookies they can eat. The Saints kick off a celebration that will continue through New Year's Day. Excitas and Enlitas lie down, side by side, for a long winter's nap.

Ooby goes right to work to get the computers back up and running. He even begins making a few necessary upgrades that will help with the nightly missions to save children around the globe. Nicholas kneels before the Baby Jesus statue again to give thanks for the miracle of the day.

And heaven and nature sing.

Epilogue

In Madagascar...

A group of ten menacing Pirates walk up the beach from their small dinghy. They are armed with swords and machine guns. Each carries a shovel on his shoulder.

Well off the beach, beyond the breakwater, a large ship is anchored. The ship is black and has a skull and crossbones flag waving in the wind on its mast. Huge machine guns line the perimeter of the ship's deck. There are also big cannons and anti-aircraft weapons.

The meanest looking of the group, Captain Dagger, a battle-ravaged man in his mid-thirties, points a sword at the edge of the jungle.

"Over there, you treacherous dogs! We buried the treasure over there!"

The other nine Pirates hurry to where the captain directs them.

Just then, Doodle emerges from the thick jungle. He's barefoot, shirtless, wearing a woven palm frond hat, and his pants are cut off at the knees. He strolls out onto the beach, eating a pineapple. He walks right into the middle of the group.

"Morning," he says, crunching as he chews, and with such nonchalance that the Pirates are dumbstruck. He points at the large Pirate ship. "That ship belongs to you guys?"

Captain Dagger steps in front of Doodle, sword at the ready. "Aye! It belongs to me, as a matter of fact." The other nine Pirates encircle Doodle.

Doodle is trapped with no escape, but he doesn't seem the least bit concerned. He just takes a bite of his pineapple, rind and all. "So, I can assume you are a perfidious band of pirates then?"

Captain Dagger looks at the men around him. He laughs, so they laugh too. "Perfidious enough, I'd say." He suddenly glares down at Doodle. "What's it to you if we are?"

Doodle gives him a sly smile. "Perfidious is good. The more perfidious the better."

Captain Dagger points his sword at Doodle's chest. "We grow weary of your small talk, my homunculus little Matey. What do you want? Speak it before we string you up for the gulls and buzzards."

Doodle pushes the tip of Dagger's sword away from his chest, toward the ground. "I don't want anything. Especially from you duplicitous dolts." Captain Dagger is taken aback. The other Pirates gasp at Doodle's insolence. "Lucky for you, I'm generous by nature," Doodle says to Captain Dagger, as if sizing him up. "Bearing gifts, I've traversed afar."

"What could you possibly have that we would want?" Captain Dagger grows impatient.

Doodle takes a bite of his pineapple. A bit of juice escapes his lips as he transforms his mouth into a wily smirk. "I hold great knowledge of great unknowable things." He wipes his mouth with the back of his hand. "Now let me ask you a question."

"Go ahead, my little gift giving Lilliputian of the island forest. Ask away." Captain Dagger sheaths his sword and puts his hands on his hips, waiting.

Doodle's eyes narrow into a glowering scowl as he glances from one Pirate to the next until he is back on Captain Dagger. "How would you fellas like to make a world of money?"

Nicholas, Ooby, the Saints, the unicorns,
& Doodle
will soon return in
SANTA CLAUS REVAMPED

SANTA CLAUS
REVAMPED

BOOK 2

Part One

CHAPTER 1

It's beginning to look a lot like Christmas...

On a ship that sails alone on the Aegean Sea. If Troy was as mighty as legends tell, then as the day stretched out its rosy fingers, the shadows from its towering walls may have reached out into the wine-dark water far enough to touch this lonely Spanish Galleon. It is a large, black vessel, adorned along the upper bow with an array of weapons such as cannons, anti-aircraft guns, and rocket launchers. A Jolly Roger waves at the top of its tall mast. Because Christmas is on its way, the skull on the flag wears a red Santa hat and the mast is encircled by crisscrossing strands of bright LED lights. A bare fir tree is in a stand at the base of it.

On the bridge at the bow of the ship, Captain Dagger, a fearsome Blackbeard-type of Pirate, sits by the helm in a throne made of bright, multi-colored foam water noodles woven together. Below him, on the main deck, the ship's crew of fifty Pirates has assembled around the undecorated tree and the base of the mast. The crew is a rowdy bunch. Many unprompted "Ayes", "Arrghs", "Yo hos", and "Ahoys" emanate from the group. They push and shove each other, as if on the verge of a riot.

"That's enough, ya verminous lot! Settle down," Captain Dagger grumbles from his throne without raising his voice.

The crew doesn't hear him, so they don't quiet down in the least. Captain Dagger huffs, then nods to a monstrous Pirate by his side named Achilles. He wears a Spartan helmet, light armor and sandals, and he wields a sledgehammer, which he pounds against the deck. "Quit yer natterin', ya miserable scalawags!" Immediately, there is silence.

Achilles holds the sledgehammer across his chest as he stands at attention.

Captain Dagger addresses his men in a low growl. "All right, you scurvy curs. As you all know, it's Thanksgiving."

The crew stays quiet. Since they aren't in America, the holiday isn't recognized.

Captain Dagger continues, "Which we've come to know as Black Friday Eve!" The crew spontaneously cheers like a stadium full of rabid soccer fans. "While at port, remember that the buddy system is in effect!" Dagger continues over the roar. "We don't want to be losing anyone in sales stampedes. If you don't get all you're looking for, fear not! Cyber Monday is right around the corner!"

The crew erupts again, with many of the men turning to each other to give hearty high-fives. Captain Dagger lets the uproar carry on for a moment before he motions to Achilles. Achilles pounds the hammer once more. The crew is abruptly silent.

"Now, I know that you're all eager to draw names for our Secret Santa Exchange and to trim our tree, but first we must address an important matter. Our treasure chest is bare and, with shopping in the offing, we need loot! Does anyone have any ideas on how to refill our coffers?"

The crew mutters lowly as they look at one another with befuddled shrugs. Captain Dagger draws his sword and points its tip from one side of the mob of Pirates to the other.

"I need ideas, ye grog swillin' sea maggots! We need coin! Brainstorm. Spitball. Give me something."

The blank-faced crew stares back at him without a word. Captain Dagger sticks his sword tip in the deck and slumps in his throne.

Achilles brandishes the sledgehammer. "The captain said to start spitballing, so start spitballing!"

A frail, old Pirate on the side of the crew raises a straw to his lips. He is about to let a big spitball fly when Achilles looks right at him.

"Except you, Spitball Spalding! For the thousandth time, it's a figure of speech!" The old Pirate lowers his straw in a pout.

Captain Dagger gestures for Achilles to stand down. "Never mind, Achilles. These varmints are a miserable think tank."

A small hand shoots up from the back of the crew. Captain Dagger sees it and rolls his eyes. "Oh boy. This should be good," he jokes under his breath. He motions for the waving hand. "In the back, go ahead."

The Pirates clear a path between Dagger and a small, perfectly proportioned fellow with Native American features. Though he looks like a young man, he is a Saint, descended from an ancient line of beings that existed all the way back in the Enchanted Age. Unfortunately, not all Saints are saintly. In fact, in recent history, there was a Saint who betrayed his kind when he shamelessly schemed with a trio of hoodlums and tried to take over his hometown of Eno. That Saint's name was Doodle.

And this chafed little Pirate is that Saint.

Doodle is not as fresh-faced as he used to be. He's salty with a wisp of chin-hair. His clothes are grimy and ragged. A bandana he wears over his scalp and a short fencing sword he wears in his belt.

"Spill it, Doodle. What've you got?" Captain Dagger says with listless disinterest.

When Doodle speaks, it's with a thick Pirate accent that he didn't have before. "There be a Cruiser five klicks a'here. I be proposin', if the Cap'n be willing, we attack it, guns a'blazin'."

Captain Dagger laughs in a dismissive fashion. "That's a registered orphan transport. It carries nothing of value."

Doodle moves through the parted crowd of men. "With all due respect afforded the Cap'n, sir, it be's registered as an orphan transport because they's knowin' thar be's we feared Pirates in these here unto waters and we wouldn't dare strike an offensive on said orphan vessel."

"Your superfluous piratannical syntax is killing me!" Dagger barks. "Speak normal and proceed!"

Beside the Captain, Achilles points the sledgehammer at Doodle. "He said you may continue in a less piratannical nature!"

"All right," Doodle says in his normal, slightly high-pitched voice. "Ever since I repaired your radio, sir, I've been trolling the airwaves. It would appear that 'orphan' is simply a codeword for 'bank'."

"Are you saying that ship is a bank transport?"

"Aye, sir! Banks use ships to transfer gold all the time. They've figured out Pirates won't bother an orphan transport, so they've taken to calling themselves such. We're guaranteed to find riches aboard her! Gold, jewels, and E-gift-cards galore!"

A cacophony of muttering begins among the crew. More random "Ayes", "Arrghs", and "Mateys" erupt. Achilles pounds the sledgehammer. The din doesn't stop this time.

Doodle yells over the noise. "But there's one thing we won't find! Orphans! It's a farce! A cover! A charade!"

Captain Dagger leaps from his throne. "Shiver me timbers! A sham?"

"A sham indeed, sir! Dare I say, it's a shamalamadingdong!" Doodle retorts.

Dagger slams his fist into his other hand. "That's the most devious kind of sham!"

"Shall we man the battle stations then?" Doodle blurts.

Dagger thrusts his sword high. "Aye! To arms!" The crew cheers.

Achilles is quick to echo Dagger's sentiment. "Battle stations, ye bilge rats!"

A wide, black sail unfurls down the length of the mast below the Jolly Roger with the Santa hat and the ship speeds forward through the inky water toward the horizon.

I t's approaching sunset when the Pirate Ship cuts a wake through the water and veers in close to a white Cruiser. The shorter boat is a small version of a past-its-prime cruise ship, but it isn't displaying any flags - of the Pirate variety or otherwise. Captain Dagger's vessel zips in, parallel to the Cruiser.

Dagger is at the helm, steering his ship with zeal. He raises a brass spyglass and peers into it. On the deck of the white ship, he watches as a single figure, shrouded in a black robe and black hat, ducks into a doorway that leads below deck.

"Well, if that doesn't look like a deceitful banker, I don't know what does," Dagger says as he hands the spyglass to the ever-present Achilles beside him. "Send a warning shot across her bow to let them know where we can hit them if we want to!"

Achilles hurries to the railing over the main deck below. "Fire at will!"

A cannon spits out an orange flame and a basketball-sized orb screams from the barrel. It blasts the Cruiser's bow and splats a gigantic smear of black paint across it.

"Imagine what a real cannon ball would do!" Captain Dagger brays to the other ship. To his crew, he shouts, "That paint bomb should convince them an expeditious surrender is in order!" They cheer as if E-giftcards were mentioned again.

Onboard the Cruiser and below deck, there are a hundred young girls and boys, varying in ages from 5 to 10, huddled in the cargo hold. The robed crew member that Captain Dagger spied up on the main deck runs down the stairs from above. She's not a banker, but a nun named Sister Abby. The kind-eyed woman, in her late 60s, isn't in a robe like Captain Dagger thought, but a black and white habit and head-piece. She's a bundle of frazzled nerves.

"Pirates are upon us! We're under attack! Stay down, children! They're painting our ship as we speak!" Sister Abby calls out frantically to everyone and no one in particular.

The multitude of children get closer, scared and nervous. In a far corner, Nimrod, a pale, skinny boy appearing to be in his middle teens, stands as the other kids cower. Nimrod is tall, but his thin frame swims in his oversized clothes. His face is skeletal. The ridges of every bone in his cheeks and jaws are visible beneath his paper-thin skin. He peers at Sister Abby through dark, sunken eyes.

"Captain Nimrod! Do something! Help us! Those Pirates mean business!" Sister Abby rattles.

Nimrod walks to two women, who are side by side on an inflatable bed. Sister Claire, a woman in her 70s, wears a nun's habit like Sister Abby. Sister Claire is very sick, frail, and comatose. In the bed beside her, Holly Siltoe, a silver-haired woman in her 80s, but so emaciated that she looks even older, is barely awake. Holly isn't a nun. Instead of a habit, she wears cargo pants and a long-sleeved shirt. She watches Nimrod's approach with exhausted eyes.

Sister Abby persists. "What do we do, Captain Nimrod?"

Nimrod leers down at the wounded women on the mattress. "We wait," he growls through clenched teeth as he kneels by Claire.

Holly weakly lifts her hand in protest. "Not her," Holly mutters. "She can't lose anymore."

Nimrod peers over his shoulder at the scared boys and girls. "There's plenty of them. And their merchandise is young and vibrant."

Holly's raspy voice is barely audible when she whispers, "No. Take all you need from me. Just leave the children and Sister Claire alone."

"I'm not one to argue with a lady," Nimrod says. He leaps to her side of the air mattress and opens his mouth wide to reveal two short fangs.

He buries his mouth over her neck where there are two marks already, showing that this isn't the first time.

Holly gives a listless moan. As Nimrod gulps, she gets paler and her wrinkles deepen even more. Nimrod, however, gets a little more color in his skin. Holly is seemingly dead when Nimrod lifts his head, wipes his lips, and sighs with satisfaction.

A brave 8-year-old boy stands from the huddling group of children and points at Nimrod. "You're a meanie face!" he chastises as the sound of another paint bomb blasting the hull echoes through the bay.

Nimrod chuckles, "That's no way to talk to your captain."

"You're not a captain! You tricked Miss Holly and the good Sisters! You stole this boat and tricked all of us!"

Nimrod, appearing a bit stronger than just a few moments earlier, laughs as he starts for the door to the main deck.

Abby squats amongst the children. "We'll all be safe soon. There's a Wonderworker who defends innocents. He'll come." She says it loud enough for Nimrod to hear, as if her words were meant to taunt or scare him.

He turns, his face a vicious contortion, his fangs still revealed. "He'd better!" Nimrod snarls.

CHAPTER 3

The Cruiser has black paint splattered all down the side facing the Pirate Ship. From the helm, Dagger steers the ship within a few feet of the Cruiser and the Pirate Crew drops gangplanks to the Cruiser's deck.

Some of the Pirates board by the planks, while some take a more swashbuckling route and swing over on ropes. All are armed and bellowing strings of "Ahoys", "Yars", and "Avast, mateys". Quickly and completely uncontested, they take control of the top deck of the Cruiser.

"Gird ye-selves against an ambush, me hearties! We'll have a fight 'fore this day is through!" Captain Dagger yells as he struts a plank to the Cruiser.

Doodle is close behind him. He motions Doodle forward and together they spring toward the door that leads to the deck below. Dagger, his sword drawn and ready, opens the door and charges down the stairs with Doodle now by his side. Doodle also has his epee pointed forward and poised for battle. They enter the darkened room of the cargo bay.

"Surrender your treasure smartly and no one need be mangled!" Dagger announces into the darkness. The bay's lights flick on and Dagger sees the crowd of scared girls and boys staring back at him. Sister Abby stands, hands up.

"Please don't hurt the children!" she pleads.

Captain Dagger can't believe what he sees. "Are these...?" He turns to Doodle, who has paused a few stair steps behind him, with an angry grimace. "Orphans?"

"We're from the Youth Center for Wayward Children!" Sister Abby states. "We have no money, but we'll give you what little food we have."

Fear strikes Dagger's face. He doesn't seem to hear Sister Abby, but instead stares at Doodle in a panic. They are standing eye to eye since Doodle is higher on the stairs than Dagger. Dagger loses his Pirate accent and all of his bravado.

"This really is an orphan ship, Doodle! We've threatened children! Do you know what that means? The Wonderworker will find out! He'll come to help them and vanquish us! We have to apologize and clear out immediately!"

Doodle shrugs. Then, he kicks Dagger in the chest and sends him bumping and rolling down the stairs. Dagger crashes to the bottom as Doodle runs up and stands in the doorway, looking down at him. "It also means you'd be on the bad list," Doodle harks. "If there was one!" He slams the door.

Dagger, on his back on the floor, looks at all the pitiful children around him. "I was horribly misinformed." They stare back with unforgiving expressions.

Outside, on the main deck, Doodle sprints back toward the planks to the Pirate Ship. "Run for your lives!" he yawps as he goes.

The crew, loitering in a loose mob and awaiting orders, need a little more convincing. One from the crew pipes in "Run? From who?" They all look around, but there's no one else on the deck and certainly nothing that could be perceived as a threat.

Doodle points heavenward just as a dark, flying object streaks across the sky's fading sunlight. A gray sleigh swoops in low to the bow of the Cruiser, pulled by two tiny reindeer. It slows just enough for its two occupants to leap onto the deck. They land easily and stand back-to-back, each in a dynamic fighting stance.

One man is tall and lean with a physique appearing as if it were forged from fire or chiseled from granite. His ruggedly handsome face is locked in a stern gaze that quickly surveys the Cruiser. Despite his battle-hardened appearance, he has such an amiable aura about him that it nearly betrays his steely eyes and clenched fists. Something about his nature indicates that he would rather have a peaceful resolution to the confrontation than a violent engagement. He projects a deep and heavy concern for the children in the cargo bay below deck.

That man is Nicholas.

Beside him is a shorter, but equally hardened man with distinctive Native American features. Though he stands ready for a fight, like Nicholas, he doesn't crave a skirmish either. Instead, he knows his mission is to make sure the children are safe and secure, and anything or anyone that stands in the way of his doing exactly that deserves whatever punishment he can dole out.

Ooby is that man.

The reindeer and sleigh take off again to the mast of the Pirate Ship nearby, where they hover over the Jolly Roger so they can watch the events from a safe distance. The stunned Pirates look at the new arrivals with a collective of dumbfounded expressions. Nicholas is the first of the pair to speak.

"I expected better than this from you gentlemen," he says with a disappointed shake of his head. "You've never messed with the Wayward Children transport ships before."

Achilles, in the back of the mob of men, speaks up. "Aye, 'tis what we thought at first! Turns out she's a banker vessel, which is out of your jurisdiction, child-protector! Fly away and defend someone worthy of your efforts! Leave us to carry out our Captain's orders!"

The men cheer on Achilles as Doodle ducks behind a metal lock box, hiding from Nicholas and Ooby. A wide smile crosses his lips. It's becoming increasingly obvious that Doodle is in the middle of executing a long-planned scheme.

"They favor the bankers!" Doodle yells out in a deep tone, hoping that Nicholas and Ooby don't recognize his voice. "Now we fight! Captain Dagger says *Charge*!"

The attempt at disguising his voice doesn't work. Ooby looks over the crew before him. "Doodle?" he says, a glint of hope lighting his eyes. "Is that you?"

The crew hears the shouted orders and none question where they come from or if they're advisable. Instead, like mindless robots, they rush toward Nicholas and Ooby in a mob. Ooby turns to Nicholas and gives an 'after you' wave with his hand.

Nicholas pitches a small crystal into the middle of the storming crowd, still fifteen feet away. He leaps straight up, touches his chest, and instantly disappears. He reappears amongst the charging crew. He's already in the middle of a scissor-kick. He takes out several Pirates at once. He lands and starts a clinic on high-flying, acrobatic Kung Fu. Within seconds, he's laid out a quarter of the crew.

Achilles avoids the battle and retreats to the aft deck. He stretches with basic calisthenics.

Ooby joins in with Nicholas, foot sweeping and Judo flipping anyone within his reach. It's a one-sided battle as Nicholas and Ooby work through the group with alarming efficiency. They leave a swath of dropped Pirates wallowing on the deck.

Nimrod emerges from a hatch in the rear of the Cruiser. He wears a black robe with a hood. In the fading light of the sun, his hands are albino white. He spots Doodle behind the lock box. They join up and, without being seen or saying a word to each other, sneak across a plank from the Cruiser to the Pirate Ship.

Nicholas walks to the center of the middle deck, among the vanquished crew of Pirates, and eyes Achilles, who is much taller and broader than Nicholas. Achilles continues his warm-up.

"Head, shoulders, knees and toes, knees and toes!" Achilles sings.

Ooby stands by Nicholas. "He's big," Nicholas whispers.

Ooby waves him off. "You used to fight big, mean Pirates all the time while delivering presents in the Caribbean."

"Caribbean Pirates never stretched before fighting. They often fought cold and pulled a hammy, which shortened the fights considerably. And if memory serves me correctly, Achilles is the most feared Pirate on the high seas. He's undefeated in hand-to-hand combat."

"True. I don't have recent intel on him, aside from the fact that he hasn't removed his helmet in over ten years. He must have a weakness, though. His name is Achilles for a reason, right?" Ooby winks as he grabs a discarded sword from the deck and tosses it to Nicholas.

"His heel?" Nicholas catches the sword and spins it deftly. "I don't remember that being an issue for him, but it's worth a shot. You know, you're closer to his feet. Maybe you should fight him."

"Short jokes," Ooby groans. "Really?"

Nicholas laughs and looks back at Achilles, waiting for him to finish his pre-fight routine.

"Eyes and ears and mouth and nose! Head, shoulders, knees and toes!" Achilles goes through all the corresponding motions to the song. When he finally stops, he picks up his sledgehammer.

"Warm?" Nicholas asks.

Achilles doesn't answer, but instead charges with a deep, frightful roar. In a fluid motion, he drops to his knees, slides across the deck, and comes up swinging his hammer at Nicholas. The head of the hammer barely misses Nicholas's face as he dodges the blow. He counter-attacks with his sword. Achilles defends with his sledgehammer, wielding it as if it were a light rapier. They spar back and forth across the deck and over the fallen crew. Several times, Nicholas somersaults out of the battering sledgehammer's path.

On one occasion, he rolls by Achilles's feet and thwacks his heel with the broad side of the sword. Achilles gives no hint of injury. In fact, the strike just infuriates him. He attacks even more ferociously with the hammer, intent on finishing the fight quickly. Nicholas does all he can to avoid the onslaught by flipping, cart-wheeling, and jumping. Achilles closes in, getting closer with every swing. Nicholas finds Achilles's heel unguarded again and jabs it with his sword, this time piercing it. Achilles's barely notices and his attack shows no sign of slowing.

"Your heel," Nicholas proclaims with exasperation. "Is supposed to be your weakness!"

"That's a shockingly frequent assumption for some reason," Achilles barks back as he swings the hammer, knocking the sword from Nicholas's hand. Nicholas leaps to a mast rope and swings out over the water. Then, like a pendulum, he arcs back.

As he does, Achilles is waiting, hammer drawn back like a baseball bat. When Nicholas is close, he swings. Nicholas lifts his feet high, flips over the swinging hammer, and catches the top of Achilles's helmet. The helmet comes off, revealing Achilles's face and a big, fleshy, pink nose.

Nicholas zeroes in on the giant, bulging thing. Achilles scrambles for his helmet, panicked, but before he can put it on, Nicholas darts at the mast, runs several steps up it, kicks off, and Superman punches Achilles in the snout.

"Shockus to the proboscis!" Ooby cheers from the side with a fist-pump.

Achilles is rocked. His eyes cross and he drops to his knees, then he face-plants. He's out cold. Nicholas turns to Ooby. "Was that Latin?" he grins.

"Partly, I think." Ooby shrugs and waves Nicholas toward the door that leads below deck. "Go check on the kids."

"Where are you going?" Nicholas asks as he steps gingerly over the flattened Pirates.

"I'm going to check around up here. I thought I heard Doodle's voice."

"Doodle! Really? It would be so great to see him again," Nicholas says as he opens the door to the cargo bay down below.

Ooby shakes his head. "If it was him, I doubt he's looking for a joyful reunion."

CHAPTER 4

In the cargo hold, Captain Dagger runs up the stairs and locks the door that leads out to the deck. He presses his ear flat to the door to listen. When he turns to Sister Abby, now glaring at him from the bottom of the stairs, his face is panic-stricken.

"If he comes in here, you have to tell him I didn't know this was an orphan transport!" he pleads. "I thought you were bankers! Nobody cares about bankers!"

Sister Abby folds her arm and stares up at him with a frown. Dagger presses his ear to the door again and hears faint footsteps just outside. The door handle rattles gently. Dagger backs down the stairs a few steps, but not fast enough or far enough. When Nicholas kicks the door from outside, it flies open and smacks Dagger. He bumps and rolls down the stairs yet again.

Nicholas appears briefly in the doorway, just long enough to pitch in the crystal. He disappears and reappears by Dagger at the bottom of the stairs. He wraps Dagger in a chokehold and quickly renders him unconscious as the children behind him gasp in unison. Nicholas stands and holds his hands out to comfort the kids.

"Children. I'm a friend. You are safe."

The boys and girls cheer, but Sister Abby is quick to take his arm. "Thank you, kind sir, but Sister Claire and Madame Holly need immediate help!"

Nicholas follows her through the crowd of kids.

On the top deck, Ooby searches for Doodle and finally spots him with Nimrod, shimmying up the mast of the Pirate Ship. They are climbing, Doodle first and Nimrod following, toward the sleigh, which still hovers there.

"Doodle! I thought I heard you!" Ooby exclaims with a broad smile and a wave.

Doodle climbs into the crow's nest of the Pirate Ship and looks down at Ooby on the deck of the Cruiser. He leers at Ooby from his high perch and blows a sloppy raspberry.

"Oh, that's very immature, young Saint!" Ooby gripes. "You and I will still have a long talk about last Christmas by the way!"

Doodle looks at Nimrod, who can only shake his head.

"He's more pathetic than you said," Nimrod sneers, then he leaps onto the sleigh.

Doodle follows him. To Ooby, he yells, "You should have spent less time worrying about toys for ungrateful humans and more time making a lock and key for the sleigh!" Doodle settles on the bench seat next to Nimrod and takes the reins. He then reaches under the seat and pulls out a bag of cookies. "Alright Dasher and Dancer. You want cookies? Take us home." He slaps the reins and the deer take off, pulling the sleigh away from the mast as Doodle tosses cookies in the air in front of them. They zip forward as they swipe the treats out of mid-air.

Ooby watches in disbelief as the sleigh circles overhead several times, widening its path with each pass. Under his breath, Ooby chuckles, "Maybe there's no lock and key, but there is a global tracking mechanism that–"

Just then, Doodle pitches something from the sleigh. A GPS device clunks on the deck a few feet from Ooby.

"Ta!" Doodle cackles and waves at Ooby as the sleigh rockets out of sight. His valediction is something he learned under Randall Zack's influence the year before.

Ooby runs through the busted door and down the stairs into the cargo bay. He slows down and puts on a good front when he sees the children huddled together. Captain Dagger is unconscious at the bottom of the stairs. Ooby steps over him as a bold boy hurries over.

"Are you a good guy or a bad guy?" the boy barks.

"I'm a good guy," Ooby says, still looking over the crowd of kids.

"You better be because the nice man doesn't go easy on bad guys," a nearby girl says sternly.

Ooby can't help but smile at the two brave children. Right then, Abby runs up, again nervous and panicking.

"Please come! Your friend needs you!" she pleads.

Ooby and Sister Abby high step over and around the children to the back of the cargo bay. Ooby finds Nicholas kneeling beside the inflatable bed with the two elderly women. He's fishing through a first aid kit.

Still a few feet away, Ooby whispers under his breath. "We have a problem outside."

"It can't be any worse than the one in here," Nicholas replies.

Ooby finally notices Holly and Sister Claire, but focuses on Holly, the worse off of the two.

"It's Holly Siltoe," Nicholas says as he nods to the frail, emaciated old woman.

"Who? Her? Are you sure?" Ooby steps closer to get a better look.

"I'm sure."

"That's Miss Siltoe all right," Sister Abby adds.

"Has it been that long? I mean, she looks so–" Ooby starts.

Nicholas stops rummaging through the kit to look at Ooby with indignation. His response is a harsh, urgent whisper. "She's lost a lot of blood! They both have, but Miss Siltoe is close to death."

Ooby kneels down beside the bed by Nicholas and peers down at Holly.

"How'd they'd lose it?" Ooby asks as he recognizes what Nicholas is looking for and rolls up Holly's sleeve to expose her arm.

"It was Nimrod!" Sister Abby chimes, entirely too loudly. The children all shudder at the mention of his name. "We hired him to take us from Egypt to Greece. He was the cheapest captain with the cheapest boat and now I know why! He wasn't a captain at all. He was a–"

Nicholas turns and shushes her. "The children," he mutters.

Sister Abby looks over her shoulder, cognizant of the children again. "He was a vampire," she hisses in a hushed tone.

Ooby shakes his head. "Is it possible?" he asks Nicholas.

"He seemed so meek and mousy. I never would have guessed he's so dangerous," Sister Abby continues.

"It doesn't matter right now," Nicholas returns. "We have to save these two poor souls without scaring the children too much."

Nicholas finds what he's looking for in the kit and pulls out a six feet long plastic tube for delivering oxygen. He tears off the part meant to go in a patient's nose and digs out two syringes with needles attached.

Ooby retrieves an alcohol wipe from the pack and scrubs Holly's arm with it. "A transfusion under these conditions is risky."

"Maybe things aren't ideal, but I'm a universal donor." Nicholas rolls up his own sleeve.

"We're in the middle of the Aegean Sea without any kind of medical support." Ooby tries to keep his voice low, but when he looks over his shoulder at the children, he can tell they have heard every word. He gives them a half-grin. "There's plenty of future doctors and nurses, of course. And architects and scientists. And presidents, for that matter."

The girls and boys all smile, finding some solace in Ooby's reassurance. Ooby turns back to Nicholas and makes sure his voice is nearly inaudible when he says, "But what if this goes sideways?"

Nicholas takes one syringe, removes the needle from the plunger, and squeezes the exposed needle into one end of the tubing. He does the same with the other syringe and pushes its needle into the other end of the tubing.

"Once we were away from shore, Nimrod struck," Sister Abby resumes her testament, whether Nicholas and Ooby want to hear it or not. She puts two fingers, shaped like fangs, to her own neck. "Over and over again, he went back to the well. Poor Sister Claire and Holly kept offering their own necks so that he wouldn't bother the children. He seemed to get stronger each time. And when he wasn't..." She's unsure of her next words. "Feeding, I guess... he was talking to someone on the radio about Pirates. I think he wanted them to attack so you two would show up."

Nicholas ties off his upper arm with a large rubber strap, then rams the needle on one side of the tubing into a vein in his arm. The blood fills the length of the tube. Nicholas grabs the needle on the other side of the tubing.

"Doodle stole the sleigh," Ooby says, still prepping Holly's arm. "All of this was another of his devious tricks. As far as Nimrod..."

Nicholas nudges Ooby with his hand holding the second needle. "Put this one in Holly's arm. It's just like siphoning water from a full barrel to an empty one."

Ooby snatches the needle. "I know that! I've studied medical procedures for two thousand–"

The sight of Nicholas's blood in the tube makes him queasy. His eyes cross and he falls backwards. Abby rushes to help him.

"Oh dear!" she squawks. "Is he okay?"

Nicholas shakes his head and puts the needle in Holly's vein. "He knows the miracle of blood, but he prefers it to be on the inside of his patients," Nicholas sighs. Since the tube is already full of blood, there is no way to tell that it is going into Holly except that a flush of color immediately returns to her face.

Nicholas sits back and relaxes to let the transfusion happen without interruption. Slowly, almost imperceptibly, his skin turns a light gray. And one might be able to say a few wrinkles appear in his face, but such a claim might be met with uncertainty since any appearance of wrinkles was even less noticeable than the slight pallor of his skin.

Holly's change is much more obvious though. Within minutes of receiving Nicholas's blood, she looks twenty years younger. Her skin has a new vibrancy and even her hair is changing, turning from silver to brown. She's still unconscious, but she is growing younger and more beautiful with every passing minute.

Sister Abby places a wet cloth on Nicholas's head. "Thank you, Sister," he says.

She stares down at Holly. "Incredible! She looks so young! Are you sure you aren't giving too much?"

Ooby sits up behind Sister Abby. He is pale and does everything in his power to avoid looking at the blood-filled tube. "He gives too much all the time," Ooby whispers, still getting his wits about him.

Several children huddle around to see if Holly is truly growing younger. They see that she truly is. Even Captain Dagger, also now awake, wanders over. He leans in above the gathered children to watch.

"You can only give a pint," Dagger says.

A 7-year-old girl leans in next to him. "It takes twenty-four hours to replenish the volume loss after donating a pint of blood and four to six weeks to regenerate the red blood cells."

Dagger nods as if she is saying exactly what he was thinking, even though it surely isn't. "And that's if you drink a lot of juice and eat chocolate chip cookies after giving blood."

Ooby goes instantly green and holds his hand to his mouth. "Okay. Enough."

Nicholas's voice is a bit weak when he says, "She needs much more than a pint, but I replenish quicker than most."

Another child, a boy about 8 years old, pipes in, eager to show his knowledge. "Blood is the powerplant of the cell."

The little girl glares at him. "Nuh uh! That's the mitochondria."

The little boy is incensed. "Well, chrysalis is another word for a raccoon!"

"A chrysalis is a cocoon," she fires. "Not a raccoon."

"Well, Pluto isn't really a planet," chimes in an even smaller girl.

"I think you're thinking of Neptune," Dagger retorts.

"Neptune is the King of the Poseidon Ocean!" the little boy quips with confidence.

The children and Captain Dagger begin squabbling loudly. When a small boy yells over the fray, "I like oatmeal cookies better than chocolate chip!" The argument really breaks down into chaos as every child in the cargo hold voices their opinion on what type of cookie is best.

Nicholas gathers his strength and pushes off the wall. He kinks the tube and removes the needle from Holly's arm, but leaves the one in his arm in place. He presses gauze to Holly's needle wound and nods to Sister Abby.

"Could you hold this, please?" he asks as the kids' noise gets too loud. When Sister Abby leans in over him to hold pressure, Nicholas takes a moment to whisper in her ear. Her eyes light up and she nods with vigor.

"Yes! Absolutely! That's a wonderful idea! Count me in!" she says.

Nicholas stands, woozy, and shuffles to Sister Claire's side. As he goes, he looks at Dagger, who is making his point to a little kid about why Lincoln Logs are superior to Legos. The kid isn't having it and grows red-faced with righteous indignation.

"Captain Dagger," Nicholas says softly. "We have much to discuss."

"You bet we do!" Ooby yelps in a sickly manner, but trying to sound serious. "As in major jail time, Bub!"

Captain Dagger abandons his argument with the child to defend himself to Nicholas. "Please, sir. I know who you are. You're the child protector all outlaws fear. I've spent my pirating career doing whatever I could to avoid you. I promise, I didn't know this was an orphan ship."

"Your pirating career is over," Nicholas states flatly as he puts a new, clean needle on the end of the tubing and sterilizes Sister Claire's arm.

"I've been a Pirate for ten years! What else am I supposed to be?" he whines.

"There was a time, Mick Dagger, when you wanted to be a fisherman."

Captain Dagger is surprised at Nicholas's words. Nicholas inserts the needle in Claire's vein and unclamps the tubing. His blood flows into her as it did Holly. Ooby averts his eyes, again instantly queasy.

"I tried, but I wasn't good at it," Dagger bemoans.

"You worked on a fishing vessel and became a Captain very quickly," Nicholas says. "You bought your own ship and assembled a loyal crew. I'd say it was something you did very well."

"Money was hard to come by in that line of work."

"So, you took the easy way and stole from other hardworking seafarers?" Nicholas asks.

Ooby gives Dagger an accusing stare and crosses his arms. "I'll call the authorities!" he asserts. Then, as if following an inspired thought, he pulls out a piece of paper and a short pencil from his pocket. "And you can bet I'm adding his name to the bad list."

"It was a mistake, I tell you! If I had known this was truly an orphan transport..." Dagger starts, then trails off. Finally, he wilts with guilt. "I deserve to be on the bad list. And I'll accept whatever punishment you see fit."

Nicholas reclines heavily against the wall. "There's no bad list and I'm not going to punish you."

Ooby throws up his hands and storms off. "Oh, come on!"

Nicholas peers at Dagger as a father might look at his child who needs correction. "Since your ship is bigger, we're all getting on it and you're taking us to Greece. Sister Claire, Miss Siltoe, and my angry friend and I will get off in Athens."

"And the children?" Captain Dagger asks, sheepishly.

"The children and Sister Abby will stay with you and your crew."

"What? You want me to teach these kids how to be Pirates?" Dagger isn't following Nicholas's line of thought.

"No," Nicholas says with great patience. "I want you to teach them to be fishermen and fisherwomen. At port, you'll trade your weapons for nets. You will take these children and teach them how to reap the bounties of the sea. Not of other people's hard work, but of the sea. Understand?"

"I guess," Dagger shrugs.

"These children need mentors and you and your crew need to set your sails on a noble course again. You will earn an honest living and you will make a positive impact on these youngsters. That's a life of great purpose. I know your heart, Mick. It's a role in which you will excel."

Sister Abby nods in agreement. "Together, we shall make these children into fishers of men and women," she says.

"A life of great purpose," Dagger whispers, as if he has just been given an answer to a question that had forever nagged him. "A noble course." He closes his eyes with contentment and seems to whisper a silent thanks to the heavens. When he looks back at Nicholas, he is inflated with a new reason for being.

"Thank you, sir," he says with genuine gratitude.

"Now, please, inform your loyal crew of their new mission," Nicholas instructs.

"As long as they are my loyal crew, sir, so shall they be yours," Dagger says as he slaps his fist to his chest in a gesture of fealty.

Nicholas then closes his eyes with exhaustion. Ooby is on the far side of the bay, still ranting to himself, barely audible over the loud chatter of the arguing children. "Going easy on a brood of marauders! Beats all I've ever seen!" he grumps with a fling of his arms.

Since everyone is squabbling, they aren't paying attention to Holly. She has de-aged even more by then, and when she turns her face upwards, she is radiant and looks like she is in her early 30s. Sister Abby gasps when she finally notices her.

"Holly! You're so young! And beautiful!"

The children's infighting stops immediately. They all look at Holly, who is just starting to stir from unconsciousness. Unlike Holly, Nicholas now appears as though he has aged ten or fifteen years. As he drifts off to sleep, Holly opens her eyes. She's disoriented, but when she sees Nicholas, her eyes widen and she smiles.

"Nicholas?" she whispers. "I found you again."

The sleigh zips across the sky over Antarctica. The sun hangs low, giving the landscape a dusky appearance as it's locked in the perpetual daylight of the South Pole's summer. Doodle sits at the reins. Every now and then, he tosses a cookie out in front of Dasher and Dancer to keep them flying forward. Nimrod sits beside Doodle, his hood up to conceal his skin from the faint sun. Only his mouth and the pure white skin on his chin and jaws are visible.

"I need more. Find me more," he says with a ravenous hunger. His teeth, normal when he bears them, quickly grow short, but extremely sharp fangs. He looks at Doodle's arm, but Doodle pulls it away.

"Nope. No. Not me, buster! We talked about this on the radio. In short time, you're going to get a buffet, but I'm not on the menu!"

Nimrod's fangs retract and he leans away. Doodle presses a button on the dashboard of the sleigh and a tunnel opens in the side of a snow-covered mountain. He steers the deer toward it.

At the end of the long tunnel, the sleigh emerges in Eno, which is an enchanting village under a dome deep beneath the ice shelf of Antarctica. Colorful condo-style residences and a large industrial factory building line the edges of the dome. In the middle, there is a courtyard with beautiful gardens.

A chirpy alarm sounds as the sleigh enters the dome's airspace. Many of the hundreds of Saints, all about the size of Ooby and Doodle and wonderfully innocent and sweet, rush from their homes to greet the sleigh.

"The alarm is new," Doodle snipes.

As the sleigh darts toward the landing pad atop the factory building, six other reindeer, flying free in the airspace beneath the dome, zoom in close in greeting. Doodle welcomes them with a spiteful jeer. Doodle steers the sleigh to the rooftop pad. A door from the building to the landing area flies open and eager Saints rush out. Doodle leaps out of the sleigh, his arms outstretched in a sarcastic air hug.

"Bring it in, Saints! The prodigal son has returned," Doodle says, knowing full well that the Saints aren't expecting him and certainly won't hug him. The Saints stop in their tracks and give a collective gasp when they see the sleigh isn't occupied by Nicholas and Ooby. The free-flying reindeer pull back too, but then move in to surround Dasher and Dancer in a protective circle.

Lupper, a slightly bolder than typical Saint, steps forward. "Where's Nicholas and Ooby?" he demands.

"I'm fine, Lupper, thanks for asking," Doodle says as he starts toward the door. Lupper follows him closely and Nimrod follows Lupper.

"Excuse me for dispensing with pleasantries, but the last time you were here..." Lupper starts.

"I know, I know. I brought some bad guys," Doodle says with a twirl of his hand. "That won't ever happen again. I promise."

Right then, Nimrod trips Lupper, who falls to the floor. All the Saints gasp again. Nimrod joins Doodle in the open doorway.

"After Ooby's continuous brain-washing since I left, I'm sure you're convinced I'm a deviant and his way is the only one. I won't waste my time trying to convince you otherwise," Doodle says. He and Nimrod exit the landing area and the group of Saints rush to Lupper's side to help him. Doodle pops his head back through the doorway to add to his last comment. "But if a single one of you try to interfere with what I've come to do, you will find out how deviant I can be." He tips an imaginary hat and disappears from the doorway once more.

And with that, Doodle slams the door on the Saints.

Back in the Aegean Sea, the Pirate Ship moves away from the deserted Cruiser. Each Pirate has at least two Children by his side. All look uncertain at this new twist in their fates. Sister Abby moves through the group, supervising the crew and their assigned children as they do their work.

In Captain Dagger's quarters, Nicholas is in a bed, sound asleep. Holly, so much younger now and strikingly beautiful, sits by him. Ooby paces behind her. Sister Claire, now appearing to be in her early 30s also, but not nearly as pretty as Holly, looks into a handheld mirror. She can't help but touch her face.

"I can't believe it," she says, enamored with herself. "It's a miracle." She holds the mirror in front of Holly's face. "Can you believe it?"

Holly is disinterested at first, but when she finally looks at herself, her jaw nearly drops.

"Been a few years since you've seen that face, I'd bet," Sister Claire giggles. She takes the mirror away to look at herself again.

"I've seen blood transfusions before," Holly says. "They don't work like this. They never work like this."

"His veins are a fountain of youth," Sister Claire replies. She saunters off, still looking at herself. She is much too vain for a nun.

Ooby, his mind mired in concern, turns to Holly. "His blood is enchanted. The effects are temporary, I'm afraid. Once your system begins regenerating your own blood, his will process out of your body and you will return to your natural state."

Holly takes Nicholas's hand. "Will he be alright?"

Ooby stops pacing. "With rest, he'll be fine."

Holly caresses Nicholas's face, which is old and wrinkled now. She knows Nicholas, but she doesn't know that Ooby knows. Ooby watches her tender affection with Nicholas.

"He remembers you," Ooby states.

"I'm sure he remembers everyone," she returns.

"He does, but he especially remembers you."

"Probably not too fondly. I practically stalked him." Holly seems embarrassed by something in her past. Something from long, long ago.

"A mere school girl crush," Ooby says with a dismissive wave of his hand.

"That lasted into my twenties." Holly lifts Nicholas's hand to her cheek and holds it there.

Ooby steps behind Holly. He knows her infatuation with Nicholas lasted a very long time. "He gave you the best gift he could."

"Yes, I know. I'll never be able to repay him."

"He wouldn't want you to try."

"I saw him last Christmas Eve. On Mount Fuji." Holly turns and looks at Ooby, her eyes filling with tears. "Any chance he mentioned that?"

Ooby places a hand on her shoulder. "He was elated. He didn't stop talking about it until Easter. Even then, I could tell he thought about you often."

Holly can't help but smile at the idea of Nicholas thinking of her. If the schoolgirl crush ever ended, which Ooby doubted that it actually did, he knew one thing for certain.

It was back big-time.

Deep in the recesses of the factory building in Eno, the Research & Development Department is very lab-like, with different projects in various stages of progress throughout the room's work tables. There are new styled clocks, ceramic pieces, chocolate candies and various other items the Saints are building and testing before putting into mass production.

In the middle of it all, a wide conveyor belt runs in from one end of the room and out of the other. It's a small section of the conveyor system that traverses through many parts of the building. Nimrod and Doodle enter and go to a console by the door. Doodle punches buttons, making the conveyor system come to life. Then, he leads Nimrod to a closet where he opens the door to reveal a large, tarp-covered piece of equipment.

"What's this?" Nimrod says, his hood back on his head now so Doodle can see his elongated, skeletal face.

"This is what I told you about on the radio," Doodle says with a sweeping motion over the item. "This is why we're here. Seventy some years ago, the entire team of reindeer got sick at the same time. Nicholas couldn't make his runs for two nights in a row. He encouraged the Science Division to create a back-up propulsion system for the sleigh in case it ever happened again. Viola!"

Doodle rips back the tarp, revealing a cylindrical device with an array of dismantled wings and propellers. The pieces are on a rolling table. Outside the closet, the new Christmas Eve sleigh, red now and much bigger than the gray sleigh, comes into the room on the conveyor. It stops in the middle.

"And do you know what has two thumbs and was instrumental in getting this bad boy rocking and rolling?" Doodle points his two thumbs back at himself and gives the cheesiest grin ever.

"Uh, okay. Cool. What is it?" Nimrod is unimpressed.

"It's a cold fusion rocket!" Doodle turns to the side and his face sours. In a low, spiteful mumble he says, "Ooby calls it a low energy nuclear propulsion apparatus, but everyone knows it's a cold fusion rocket."

"And how does it help us?" Nimrod presses.

"We attach it to the sleigh. With this thing, we don't need those temperamental, cookie-craving reindeer."

"Does it work?" Nimrod still needs convincing.

"For a long time, it didn't," Doodle pipes. "Ooby built a few prototypes, but he couldn't stop them from blowing up. I suggested a few minor adjustments and he wouldn't even consider them." Doodle's face goes grim again and he turns and mumbles into his shoulder. "He said I was barely out of diapers, but I was well over two hundred by that time! Besides, I skipped my whole diaper stage."

"So anyway," Nimrod says, prodding Doodle to continue the story. He's noticing Doodle's propensity to grumble in bitter asides and he finds it unsettling. Doodle rolls the cold fusion rocket from the closet and pushes it toward the sleigh.

"Ooby just shelved it," Doodle complains. "I snuck into the lab one night and applied my ideas and they worked perfectly. He was mad, of course, but Nicholas wanted to give it a test run. The sleigh never flew better or faster!"

"And yet the reindeer are still used."

Doodle miffs at the mention of the reindeer. "Their feelings were hurt and they sulked for a week because they thought they were going to be replaced. Nicholas couldn't bear their disappointment so he told them this would only be used in the most extreme emergencies. The deer never got sick again and it's been on mothballs ever since."

Doodle begins attaching the machine to the sleigh with surprisingly quick and efficient hands. As he works, he directs Nimrod to a wide side door in the wall.

"How much gas will it need?" Nimrod asks, as he goes to the sliding door and pushes it open. It leads outside into the courtyard of Eno.

"Gas?" Doodle crows. "Haven't you been listening? Perpetual energy, Nimrod! This thing could power New York, Paris, Hong Kong, and Mexico City for the next thousand years without depleting itself!"

Nimrod raises a good point. "Why hasn't Nicholas given this technology to the humans since he loves them so much?"

Doodle jumps into the sleigh, now with short wings sticking out of either side of the back end. The wings have helicopter propellers built into them, like a hovercraft, and the fusion device is on the bottom, right between the wings.

"He wanted to, but the Cold War started."

Nimrod rubs his arms, as if he's suddenly freezing. "It sure did. They fight it here?"

"Not a literal cold war that was fought in the cold!" Doodle snaps. "Don't you know any human history?" Doodle glares at Nimrod and can tell that he does not. "Nicholas didn't trust the humans in power. He was scared they'd turn the rocket technology into a weapon."

"What a boy scout!" Nimrod laughs. "I can't wait to see how he deals with an all-out war between the humans and Pyres."

Doodle motions Nimrod into the sleigh, then leaps onto the bench seat beside him. "He'll try to negotiate peace," Doodle says. "It's up to us to make sure there's no hope for that from the beginning."

"You do your part and, when the time comes, I'll do mine," says Nimrod.

"At this point, this entire plan hinges on your partner," Doodle returns.

"She'll do as she promised," Nimrod assures him. "Guaranteed."

Doodle powers on a remote-control device equipped with a joystick. The fusion cylinder flares to life. He manipulates the RC joystick. The wings roll, pitch, and yaw as the propellers within them start spinning. By the force of the propellers, the sleigh lifts off the ground.

"Well then. Let's go get the Time Bender, shall we?" Doodle pushes the joystick forward. The jet engine blasts and, in an instant, they zip out of the open door to the outside. In a blink, they are gone.

On the Pirate Ship, in the captain's quarters, Nicholas opens his eyes. He's groggy, but happy to see Holly by his side. Ooby and the others are elsewhere in the ship.

"How are you feeling?" Holly asks eagerly.

"Much better, Miss Siltoe," he rasps. She puts a cup of juice to his lips and he sips from it.

"You used to call me Holly. You can again, you know?"

"Okay, Holly," Nicholas smiles. "Looks like the transfusion worked." He sits up, but gets lightheaded.

"It did. Maybe a little too well." She places a damp cloth on his forehead. "You gave way too much."

"I gave what was necessary." Nicholas closes his eyes again. "How is Sister Claire and the children?"

"Everyone is fine. We're on our way to Athens. Should be there soon."

Nicholas is still very weak. "Thank you."

"Last year, it was so good to see you. Before that..." Holly ruminates deeply. "My goodness, it was nearly sixty years."

Nicholas opens his eyes again and looks at her. It takes a moment for his eyes to focus.

"It wasn't that long for me, Miss Siltoe." He corrects himself. "Holly."

She blushes, flattered. "Oh, really. Have you been checking up on me through the years?"

Nicholas gives a listless grin. "It's what I do."

The sun rises over Piraeus Harbor, the main seaport in Athens, Greece. Captain Dagger's black Pirate Ship sails up to the deepwater dock amid the spectacular scenery of the ancient city. The pirates have children next to them. The boys wear their Pirate mentor's hats and the girls wear their bandanas. All seem to be enjoying themselves as they moor the ship.

A long gangplank, only sixteen inches wide, extends from the ship's main deck to the dock. It doesn't have any handrails and the damp air makes the plank slick and slippery. Ooby steps toward it with Nicholas beside him and leaning heavily on him for support. Holly follows, helping Nicholas from behind. Sister Claire is last, the mirror tucked in the belt of her habit. Surprisingly, she's not looking in it at the moment. Instead, she's glancing around to see who might be noticing her and her new youth.

"Walk the plank, you landlubbers!" Captain Dagger says loudly over the chatter of the children and their Pirate partners. Ooby looks at him with a stern expression. Dagger shrugs. "According to our by-laws, I'm required to say that anytime someone actually does it. We haven't rewritten them to reflect our non-Pirate status yet."

Ooby waves him off as he leads Nicholas across the plank. "Pirates and their traditions. Good heavens," he mutters. Nicholas chuckles lowly.

"Focus on your feet, gentlemen," warns Holly from behind them, her hands under Nicholas's arms to steady him. Over her shoulder, she yells to the captain, "And don't forget to notify the rightful owners of the Cruiser and where to find it."

Captain Dagger gives a 'thumbs up'. Several of the children nearby mimic him.

The foursome crosses the gangplank with no trouble and, with Sister Claire the last across, turn to wave. From the deck, Captain Dagger, Sister Abby, the Pirates and all of the children bid them farewell.

The group of four walks the bustling sidewalks along the crowded Athens streets. It's a beautifully bright morning and tourists and locals are out in force. Ooby leads the way, setting a pace that Nicholas, now walking on his own, but panting, has trouble keeping. Holly is close by, ready to catch him if he stumbles.

"Can we possibly bring the record-setting sprint down to a Sunday afternoon stroll?" Holly shouts ahead to Ooby, who is acting quite uncharacteristic in his thoughtlessness toward Nicholas. Ooby acts as though he doesn't hear her.

"He gets like this when he's excited," Nicholas says.

Ooby continues widening the distance between himself and the other three until he stops in front of a non-descript storefront. It's a public health clinic, but a red-cross on the door is the only indicator of that. Ooby bounces where he stands, like a hyper-active child waiting to enter a toy store. He waves for Nicholas to catch up.

"This is it! Hurry! He works nightshift, but hopefully he's still here!" Ooby shouts, a huge smile on his face. When he can't wait anymore, he tugs open the door and darts in. Nicholas and Holly get close, but Sister Claire is now lagging behind them, looking at her reflection in a bakery's window.

"Who is he so eager to see?" Holly asks.

Nicholas replies, "An old friend who may have some answers about Nimrod."

"Must be a great friend to get Ooby so excited."

"Indeed, he is. Nobody gets Ooby as giddy as the fellow in there."

Holly opens the door to the clinic for Nicholas to enter. She is about to follow him in when he turns to her with a strained expression. "I hate to ask, but do you mind giving us a little time? How about we meet you out here in fifteen minutes?" It's clear that Nicholas is uncomfortable asking, but Holly immediately stops and nods as though she understands.

"Sure. Okay. Of course," she says with a smile. Nicholas enters the clinic as Holly steps back out on the sidewalk and looks at Sister Claire. "Well, it's a gorgeous day in Athens. Want to take in some of the sights?" she asks.

Claire never stops staring at her own reflection. "Way ahead of you, Holly."

The inside of the clinic is bisected by a main hallway, which has entrances to several individual, smaller offices on either side. The clinic is a total care facility, meaning a person can go there to see a doctor for just about any ailment short of a life-threatening emergency. Since the hours of operation vary from one office to the next depending on its specialty, and most are not yet open for the day, the clinic is nearly empty. There is one office open to patients though and it is at the far end of the hallway.

That office is darker than the rest since it doesn't have any windows to the outside. A 40-year-old Greek man named Kris seats himself in a chair with a built-in armrest made specifically for blood collection. He is nervous as he glances around the quiet, darkened room.

"Hello," he stammers. "I was told to come here to donate blood." He looks about again, but no one answers and the office appears completely empty. "Anyone here?"

From behind a partition, a tall, thin, very pale and completely bald man with sharp features and glassy eyes, who appears to be about 60, emerges. His name is Sarcastacles and he is wearing something that can only be described as a lab robe instead of a lab coat. It's white like a lab coat, of course, but the bottom of it goes all the way down his long frame and brushes the floor.

When he approaches Kris, it's as if he is gliding instead of walking. And though gliding is often associated with elegance, Sarcastacles's movements can only be equated to a slow creeping, like syrup off a pancake. He stops in front of Kris and towers over him. He smiles down at him in a way that one might say is reptilian in nature. His accent is strong and distinctly Romanian when he speaks. "Please, relax. Relax. I vant to draw your blood."

Kris eyes Sarcastacles up and down with stark concern. Sarcastacles sits in a chair opposite him so that their knees are touching. He opens a blood collection kit as Kris appears ready to jump up and run.

"I've never given blood before," Kris mutters. "What are you going to do? Is it going to hurt?"

With one hand, Sarcastacles gently places Kris' arm across the table between them. With the other, he holds up a large gauge needle. If Kris is looking for reassurance, he certainly isn't going to get it from Sarcastacles.

"I'm going to stick this extremely large needle into the crook of your arm, at a spot where hundreds of nerves criss cross just beneath your skin," Sarcastacles drones in a tone that sounds abrasively sarcastic. "Hopefully, I'll puncture your vein. If I go too deep, I may hit bone. If I miss your vein, I may have to dig around a while until I find it. But, will it hurt? Noooo." He drags out his final word a little too long and much too sardonically. "Not a bit," he adds. Sarcastacles bores into Kris with his cold, dark eyes and smiles. Slightly pointed incisors are barely visible in his mouth.

Kris becomes even more tense. Understandably so. "You've been doing this a while though, right?" he begs.

"Ages," Sarcastacles replies.

"I mean to say, you're good at this, right? That's what I'm asking! Don't you need more light in here? Look, mister, maybe this isn't the right time for me to do this."

Nicholas and Ooby enter the room. They wait by the door beside Kris. Sarcastacles sees them as he disinfects Kris's arm. Kris notices them, too.

"Who are they?" the super-nervous Kris asks Sarcastacles. Before he can answer, Kris says, "Who are you guys? Are you two his supervisors? Shouldn't he have on more lights?"

Sarcastacles gives another listless smile. Ooby is beaming, genuinely excited, and literally bouncing from foot to foot again. "The tall one is a good friend of mine," Sarcastacles states without a hint of emotion. "That sawed-off, abbreviation of a fellow is my cousin. I have not seen either of them for a very long time. As you may be able to tell, I'm very excited that they are here." Sarcastacles nods to both. "Nicholas. Ooby."

Ooby is a little too eager to chime in. "Hello, you white-washed bag o' bones!"

Nicholas places a hand on Ooby's shoulder, meant to calm him. "Good to see you, Sarcastacles."

Kris is as nervous now as Ooby is giddy. He can no longer contain it. "Your name is Sarcastacles?" he spouts.

Sarcastacles points to his badge, which spells out his name. "Indeed, it is."

"That's an odd name! I've never heard of anyone named Sarcastacles before?"

"My mother couldn't spell Sam," Sarcastacles says in an overly dry tone.

Ooby gives a muffled chuckle. "Sam," he says under his breath.

Sarcastacles sniffs the crook of Kris's arm, as if smelling a rose.

"What is that? Why do you do that?" Kris asks loudly.

"Aah, you have B Positive blood. That's my favorite type. It also happens to be my–"

Before Sarcastacles can finish, Ooby interrupts happily. "Motto! It's also his motto!" Ooby laughs uncontrollably. Sarcastacles grins at him. "Be positive is also his motto!" Ooby repeats. He holds on to Nicholas to keep from falling over.

"Hey! Don't distract him! He has to draw my blood here and if he were to miss, he may hit bone! You know what? Why don't you guys reacquaint and I'll just get out of here! Frankly, I don't know why I even came in to begin with!"

Nicholas gives Kris a gentle smile that eases his anxiety in a moment. His voice adds to the soothing effect when he says, "Because blood donation is one of the last pure charities. You can give money, but it can be stolen and used by wrong-minded people for purposes other than what you intended. Blood has no value except to those who need it. By giving blood, you are helping save lives. It's the most noble of causes."

Kris is instantly calm. He, too, smiles. "Yeah. That's it, I guess. I mean, this time of year I try to do what I can to help others. I suppose…"

"Are you two going to talk all day? Both of you are like…" Sarcastacles starts as he gives Ooby a playful wink and continues in a very vampirish tone, "Blah, blah, blah."

Ooby erupts in laughter again. "Blah, blah, blah! Too good!" Ooby leans even more heavily on Nicholas. He seems to be having a hard time catching his breath.

Kris looks at Ooby as if he has lost his mind. "Of course. Right. You concentrate and I'll be quiet."

"The deed is done." Sarcastacles leans away from him. Kris looks down and sees the blood collection bag is full and his arm is already bandaged.

"What? I didn't feel a thing!" Kris gushes.

Sarcastacles steals a sniff of the bag. "Delightful. Have a good day. And remember, be positive."

Kris gets up from the chair. He steps away as Ooby comes close to Sarcastacles, still failing to suppress his uncontrollable laughter. "Be positive! Hilarious! You still got it, Bub!"

As Kris leaves the room, Nicholas shakes his hand. "Thank you for your contribution, sir. Have a merry Christmas season." Kris nods, steals a quick glance at Sarcastacles and Ooby, then looks back at Nicholas, who can only shrug.

"I have juice and a cookie for you," Sarcastacles says as Kris makes for the exit.

"I'm good," he says with a wave over his shoulder. Then, he's gone.

Ooby finally catches his breath and looks up at Sarcastacles. "How's the job?" he asks.

"A pain in the neck," Sarcastacles quips.

"Heard you went to the doctor."

"Had to. I've been a-coffin all day."

Ooby falls against him, laughing. "I'm hungry. Let's get a steak."

Sarcastacles covers his heart with his long, bony fingers, feigning terror. "Stakes give me heartburn."

Ooby is so gleeful that it's hard for him to talk. "How's your family?"

Sarcastacles's emotionless face finally begins to break. "Driving me batty."

Ooby cracks up even more, side-to-side with Sarcastacles. Sarcastacles finally belches out a loud guffaw as he throws a lanky arm over Ooby's shoulders, marking the end of their well-trod routine. It's obvious that it is something they do whenever they see each other. It's even more obvious that they are very good, very close friends.

Nicholas gives them a few moments before he says, "I don't mean to be a party-pooper, but we need to speak to you, Sarcastacles. It's rather important."

"Of course," Sarcastacles says as he wipes the tears of laughter from his eyes. "I need a coffee." He nudges Ooby. "I'll grab my cape."

Ooby howls with laughter. "His cape! This guy with the jokes! You're killing me!"

At a sidewalk café, Nicholas, Ooby, and Sarcastacles sit at a table beneath an umbrella, but Sarcastacles also wears sunglasses and a wide brim hat as extra protection from the sun. He does not, however, have a cape. They drink espresso from small cups.

"You're paler than I am, Nicholas," Sarcastacles muses. "Are the long Antarctic winters getting to you?"

"He just gave a lot of his blood to two women who were in very short supply," Ooby jumps in. "You could say we found them in the Nick of time." Ooby looks at Sarcastacles with a sudden, wide smile and waits for his pun to land. Sarcastacles doesn't laugh. "Huh? Nick of time. Get it?" Ooby persists, trying to get a response out of Sarcastacles, who holds out with a straight face. Even Nicholas groans a bit under his breath.

"Right, okay. Not the time. Got it." Ooby's shoulders droop a bit. "Tough crowd."

"You're trying too hard, Ooby," Sarcastacles says, grinning just enough to show his extended fangs. "Give me a joke I can sink my teeth into."

Nicholas chuckles, his first indication that he is feeling better. "See, Ooby. That's funny."

Ooby folds his arms in a fret. "Ganging up, eh! Fine! You two yuck it up and I'll just sit here and be quiet!"

"I doubt that," Sarcastacles says, then surveys Nicholas from head to toe with true concern. "Do you want a transfusion? We can go back to the blood bank."

Nicholas shakes his head. "Save it for those who really need it. I'm getting stronger every minute. With a little more time, I'll be fine."

Sarcastacles continues. "The women? How did they lose so much blood?"

"It was Nimrod," Ooby replies.

Sarcastacles is not surprised by the news. He receives it with a slow, thoughtful nod. "Ah. Nimrod. So smart and full of potential. But so much like his uncle." He leans back and strokes his chin with his long, milky-white fingers. "With your blood coursing through them, the victims are okay, I presume."

"Yes, but Nimrod is on the loose and he isn't alone," Ooby says. "He's with one of ours. Doodle."

"It seems that they were destined to find each other," Sarcastacles surmises.

Ooby agrees. "They are frightfully like-minded."

"Where did we go wrong?" Sarcastacles sips his espresso as he shakes his head in defeat.

"We didn't," Nicholas interjects. "We just have to find them and help them through this."

Sarcastacles shrugs. "They couldn't have gotten far. With your sleigh, we should be able to catch up to them in no time."

Nicholas shrugs with embarrassment. "They stole the sleigh."

"Oh dear."

"It was a good plan. They really thought it through." Nicholas's tone has a hint of admiration at Doodle's well executed scheme.

Ooby doesn't dwell on the loss of the sleigh, though. As usual, he gets right to the business at hand. "Doodle has long wanted revolution. If Nimrod is of the same thought, then we may have a real problem unfolding before our eyes. We have to get them home before they stray too far."

From the crowd on the sidewalk, Holly runs up to their table. "Nicholas! Sister Claire left me and I can't find her!"

Nicholas is surprised by Holly's sudden appearance. His initial response is to spontaneously smile at her.

Unconcerned, Ooby holds out his hands at the grandeur of the city around him. "Maybe she's sightseeing. It's a beautiful day in Athens, after all."

"No. I'm quite certain she isn't!" She holds up her arm to reveal a handcuff. One side is clipped on her wrist. "She did this!" She turns and points to a bent and broken wrought iron park bench a short way down the sidewalk. "And I did that!" She looks at Nicholas. "I think your blood made me strong!"

Nicholas raises an eyebrow at the demolished bench. The morning crowd is walking around it as if they see it every day. "Indeed, it did," he says.

"But why would Sister Claire handcuff you to a sidewalk bench and run away?" Ooby asks.

Sarcastacles also looks down the way at the bench, then grins up at Holly. "His blood may have given you the strength, but the beauty is all yours."

Holly looks at Sarcastacles for the first time. "No, what little I had of that left me a long time ago."

Nicholas motions between the two. "Holly, meet Sarcastacles. He's helping us track down Nimrod. Sarcastacles, this is Miss Holly Siltoe."

"I'm very pleased to meet you, Miss Siltoe." Sarcastacles stands and offers his hand. His short fangs are just visible enough for Holly to see them. Her raw reaction comes fast and without warning. She slaps his hand away and swipes off his hat and glasses.

"A vampire!" she yells.

Sarcastacles recoils in the sunlight, despite the umbrella over him. "My eyes," he screeches.

Nicholas leaps up to restrain Holly as Ooby retrieves Sarcastacles's sunglasses and hat and helps him put them back on. Patrons of the café look at the foursome, especially at the mention of vampires. Holly doesn't relent in trying to attack Sarcastacles and she nearly overpowers Nicholas.

"It's okay!" Nicholas implores her. "Holly, it's okay! He's a friend!" When she calms a bit, Nicholas puts an arm around her and ushers her away.

They are well down the sidewalk from the café before Holly is pacified enough to talk. "How could you sit there with a vampire after what one did to me and Sister Claire and the children?" she asks Nicholas.

Nicholas holds her tight to him. "He's not like Nimrod. Most of his kind aren't. Sarcastacles is a close and powerful ally. I trust him completely."

Sarcastacles, covered again, and Ooby are quick to follow Nicholas and Holly. Within moments they are right behind them.

"It is my fear that this Sister Claire wasn't as much an unwilling victim as she would appear," Sarcastacles says to Ooby, but Holly hears.

She turns on him, enraged again. "What are you talking about, necksucker? You don't know what happened on that ship or what Nimrod did to us!"

Nicholas pulls her tighter to himself. He's quickly out of breath from the exertion. When she calms down again, Nicholas lets her go and stops by a picturesque fountain to rest for a minute. The Acropolis and Parthenon are behind him. Ooby goes to Nicholas's side as Holly's rage turns to concern for him. Nicholas leans heavily against the fountain. "I'm okay. Just need to slow down," he assures them both.

Ooby turns to Sarcastacles, who is keeping distance between himself and Holly. "You're suggesting Sister Claire is working with Nimrod?" he asks.

"It could be," Sarcastacles answers.

"That's ridiculous!" Holly gripes as she rubs Nicholas's back. "She joined the orphanage a month ago! As a matter of fact, it was her idea to hire a ship and take the kids to Greece." A realization dawns on her. "Oh no. Taking the transport ship was her idea."

"Why? To what end?" Nicholas puffs, still short of breath.

"You gave her your blood, correct? Nicholas, your blood gives great power. As we've seen," Sarcastacles says with a glance at Holly. "It is a wellspring of strength and vitality and would be highly coveted by those with a thirst for anarchy."

Ooby snaps his fingers. "Sister Claire got your blood to give it to Nimrod!"

Just then, a streaming vapor trail arcs across the sky like a comet. Nicholas is the first to see it. It goes to the Acropolis, specifically the Parthenon. As he watches it, the others look up and track it, too. "That's them. No reindeer though," Nicholas says.

"No reindeer. How can that be?" asks Sarcastacles.

Ooby shakes his head rapidly. "No, no, no. Nicholas. They've been to Eno. They don't need the deer because they have the low energy nuclear propulsion apparatus!"

"This may be much worse than we feared," Sarcastacles laments.

"What can we do? Nicholas, tell me what to do and I'll do it!" Holly says, ready to spring into whatever action is deemed necessary.

To Sarcastacles, Nicholas says, "If your suspicions are true, and it makes sense that they are, then Sister Claire will be up there to meet them. I have to get there and stop her." Nicholas starts away quickly, but in ten feet, he slows. He is already out of breath and weak.

"You haven't had a chance to recover, Nicholas! I'll go!" Ooby says, already moving by Nicholas.

Sarcastacles follows Ooby closely. "As will I. Nimrod is my mess. 'Tis time I cleaned him up."

Nicholas looks as though he is about to faint. Holly is close beside him, holding him up. He leans on her as Ooby and Sarcastacles race for the Parthenon. Ooby runs at a full sprint, but Sarcastacles lopes behind, searching the street.

After a hard run, Ooby stops at the top of the large hill just outside the ruins of the Parthenon. He's winded, but he covered the distance from the city's center surprisingly fast. He looks around. No one from his group made it up with him.

"Ha! I'm older than Sarcastacles, but still faster," he chuckles to himself. Just then, a taxi pulls up behind him and Sarcastacles hops out. Ooby glares at him. "You got a taxi while I was running? You could have said something, you know?"

Sarcastacles rolls up his sleeves as he walks up to Ooby, revealing his long, skinny, ultra-pale forearms. "But you were going so fast," he says. "Pumping your arms. Kicking up dust. You were gone in a flash and left nothing more than a smoke trail, by golly. I didn't want to discourage you."

Ooby waves him off with a grumpy, "Bah!"

They walk toward the Parthenon together. Inside of it, they see the red rocket sleigh parked in the middle. Ooby charges through the stone columns without hesitation and stops by the sleigh. He quickly looks it over, then he scans the interior of the empty temple. While he's inside, Sarcastacles skirts the outside perimeter of the columns.

"Doodle! Get out here this instant!" Ooby shouts, but Doodle is nowhere to be seen. Ooby sees a tarp concealing something in the back of the sleigh. "I see you're using the low energy nuclear propulsion apparatus on the sleigh! It's highly unstable when bearing any weight! Even with your fixes, it's a time bomb!"

Doodle's laughter echoes through the structure. Following the sound, Ooby looks to the ceiling. Much of the roof has fallen away, but there are stone cross beams wide enough to hide a person. Ooby can't find Doodle, but talks up into the beams as if he has.

"Enough foolishness, Young Saint! Get down here and let's talk about this past year!"

An open net flies down from the beams and drapes over Ooby. He immediately fights the netting as Doodle stands up from a beam. Doodle pulls a rope that is connected to the net, which is looped over another beam. The rope tightens the net around Ooby. Doodle tugs it again to totally ensnare him.

"That's always been your problem, Ooby," Doodle grouses. "Too much talk. Real change demands action." Doodle leaps from the beam with the rope in his hand. His weight is a counter-balance to Ooby's. As he descends from the beams, Ooby rises off the floor. They pass each other in mid-air. Ooby is twelve feet high when Doodle lands below him. "And, I assure you, real change is coming."

"You're making a huge mistake," Ooby says, helplessly fighting the net.

Doodle secures the end of the rope to a column, leaving Ooby suspended between the floor and the ceiling. "I assess the situation differently," Doodle says with a proud smile.

Sarcastacles creeps around the outside of the temple's columns, looking in on Ooby and Doodle in the middle. He takes a deep breath and is about to charge in to assist his friend when he hears a low moan behind him. Down a rocky decline, ten yards away, Nimrod is squatting beside Sister Claire, his mouth on her neck. He is drawing Nicholas's blood from her body in heaving gulps as she withers and ages back to her original, elderly appearance.

Nimrod, with a hood over his head and dark sunglasses shielding his eyes, breaks from his hold on Sister Claire and sees Sarcastacles staring at him. Nimrod pulls off his hood. His face is broader, his neck more muscular. He isn't nearly as pale as he was before. Nimrod rips off his sunglasses confidently, but since his eyes haven't strengthened like the rest of his body, the flood of sunlight causes him to wince and squint. He quickly returns the glasses.

Sarcastacles gasps at the sudden change in Nimrod and reaches out to him. "Please, Nimrod, don't take the flawed path of your uncle," he says with heart-felt anguish.

Nimrod snarls his response, veins bulging in his neck. "Uncle Vam was the only true Pyre! You should have followed him instead of submitting to Ooby and the humans! You're holding all of the Pyres back! I will show you what our kind can be when we are untethered!"

"Vam was wrong and he eventually admitted as much. His way leads only to pain, Nimrod." Sarcastacles's words are pleading, but not for himself. He truly wants Nimrod to reconsider his actions for his own sake.

"Pain for you," Nimrod screams. He pounces up the rocks like a charging bull, covering the distance in an instant. He backhands Sarcastacles and sends him flying through the columns into the middle of the temple. Sarcastacles is unconscious when he tumbles to a stop beneath the suspended net holding Ooby.

"Sarcastacles!" Ooby cries. He glares at Doodle. "You don't know what you're doing!"

Doodle shakes his head as he steps under the net and points up at Ooby with a rigid finger. "That's what you never understood, Ooby. I know what I'm doing. But more importantly, I know what you're doing. You're predictable to a fault."

Ooby rolls his body, trying to reposition himself in the tight net to be able to see Doodle.

"I knew you would rush to the rescue of an orphan ship! I knew Nicholas would give Nimrod's victims his blood! I knew you'd come to Athens to find your friend who, like you, has given in to the humans' demands and their oppressive ways! And I knew you'd deliver Sister Claire with her enchanted cargo pumping through her veins right to us!" Doodle crosses his arm, as if his claims can't be refuted.

Silently, Nicholas steps up behind Doodle.

"And you know what else I knew?" Doodle asks, seemingly unaware of the approaching threat to his backside. "I knew Nicholas would be right behind me, right now."

Nicholas swipes his arms out to grab Doodle, but Doodle spins from beneath him. He runs halfway across the temple to where Nimrod steps between two columns, his silhouette dark against the morning sun.

Nimrod is seething, a new and mighty power emanating from him. "Well, if it isn't the famous Saint Nicholas. Wonderworker. Child protector."

Nimrod struts toward Nicholas, who is still weak, but tries to hide it. Nimrod continues. "Fierce defender of the innocents and the Eno Saints." He stops in front of Nicholas. Though he is a foot shorter, he gives no hint of being intimidated. "But did you ever protect the Pyres? Did you even care about us?"

Holly appears between two columns at the back of the temple behind Nimrod. She seems ready to charge in, but Nicholas halts her with a slight gesture that Nimrod doesn't notice. "The Pyres are more than capable of taking care of themselves," Nicholas says. "They don't need my protection."

"And yet you brokered the deal between the Pyres and humans, didn't you?" Nimrod accuses as he paces in front of Nicholas. "The treaty that sent my people into obscurity for the last five hundred years is your fault!"

"Your uncle Vam terrorized the humans and caused the Pyres to be targeted by the Slayers Guild. Your kind was nearly hunted to extinction. The treaty saved all of you." Nicholas watches Nimrod's every move. "If that treaty is violated in the slightest–"

Nimrod swings an upper-cut that almost connects, but Nicholas dodges it and drops into a foot sweep that trips Nimrod and puts him on his back. Nimrod leaps back to his feet and lunges at Nicholas, driving him backwards. Nicholas grabs him and flings him across the wide temple.

Again, Nimrod rebounds and leaps at Nicholas. Nicholas sidekicks him, but his strength and speed are lacking. Nimrod takes the blow to the chest and grabs Nicholas's foot. He twists it, sending Nicholas flipping sideways to the floor.

Nimrod leaps on Nicholas's back and wraps his legs around Nicholas's waist. He throws his arms around his throat in a tight chokehold. Nicholas fights to a standing position with Nimrod holding on tightly. Nicholas's face is red and his eyes are wide with the lack of air.

Once on his feet, Nicholas jumps up and backwards. He smacks the ground with Nimrod cushioning him. Nimrod loses his air and his hold. Nicholas spins on him and punches him with all his might. It barely fazes Nimrod, who seems to be gaining power as he gets angrier.

From the net, Ooby calls to Nicholas. "Run, Nicholas! We'll go after them when you've regained your strength!"

Nimrod launches at Nicholas, bowling him over. Nimrod straddles him and starts raining down punches with an incredible fury. Nicholas blocks the best he can.

Doodle leaps into the sleigh. "Yes, Nicholas, run! Run away!" His tone is heartless and mocking. He turns on the cold fusion device. The sleigh lifts off and hovers a few feet above the floor. Holly rushes in, but Doodle sees her coming and turns the back of the sleigh toward her. A flare of rocket fire forces her to retreat.

Nicholas powers himself upward, flinging Nimrod off. Nicholas staggers to his feet as Nimrod rushes in again.

Doodle, hovering the sleigh at Ooby's level, whispers to him. "Now seems like a good spot for the Time Bender."

Below them, Nicholas touches his wristwatch as if on cue, which would usually activate the Time Bender. Nothing happens. Doodle pulls back the tarp in the back of the sleigh so that Ooby can see what is there. It's the large Grandfather Clock and its crystal from Eno. He points his finger at a new metallic watch on his wrist as Nimrod tackles Nicholas below.

Ooby yells out to Nicholas. "He's rerouted the Time Bender to a new watch!"

"To a Wee Ones original, no less!" Doodle hawks. Nicholas fights free from Nimrod and retreats several steps. Whispering again, Doodle says, "And now it's the crystals."

Again on cue, Nicholas produces a small crystal and pitches it to the side, away from Nimrod's charge. He touches his upper chest where his necklace hangs beneath his shirt and disappears, only to reappear several feet away by the pitched crystal.

Nimrod anticipates this and changes course, plowing into Nicholas with his shoulder like a linebacker. Holly, on the other side of the temple now, charges in, but Doodle spins the sleigh and flares the rockets toward her, causing her to retreat once more. He hovers near Ooby again. Nicholas flips the crystal a second time. He disappears from Nimrod's grasp and reappears halfway across the temple. Nimrod charges at him.

Doodle's whisper grows even more ridiculing. "Of course, if it works once, why not do it over and over ad nauseam?" Nicholas tosses the crystal once more. Doodle jams the joystick forward, rocketing the sleigh toward its position.

"No!" Ooby yells.

Nicholas appears over the crystal just as the sleigh reaches it. The front of the sleigh plows into his chest. It pitches Nicholas across the temple. He flies into a column and hits it so hard that the column cracks. Nicholas falls to the ground, instantly unconscious. Doodle hovers the sleigh in the middle of the temple.

"Predictability is your ultimate weakness," Doodle says. "It makes beating you so easy, it's almost sad."

Ooby watches from the net in horror as Nimrod steps up to Nicholas. The small crystal is on the ground beside him. Nimrod kicks the crystal as hard as he can, sending it flying through the columns of the temple and off the side of the Acropolis. Then, he flips Nicholas's hand to his chest.

"No! Please!" Ooby cries, but Nimrod is not feeling merciful.

The crystal arcs high from the rocky outcrop of the large hill, several hundred feet over the city. As it reaches the apex of its trajectory, Nicholas appears in mid-air. He free-falls down to the city below. Nicholas crashes into the tile roof of an old building. The impact creates a crater, but the roof holds strong and he doesn't fall through.

In the Parthenon, Nimrod jumps up to the sleigh, which is now hovering 15 feet high in the middle of the temple. He grabs a bottom runner and flips up and over into the seat next to Doodle. Doodle steers the sleigh over to Ooby again. Nimrod glares at Ooby, then shifts his gaze down to Sarcastacles, still knocked out below the hanging net. Doodle maneuvers the sleigh so that he and Ooby are face to face and only a foot apart.

Ooby is tearful and heartbroken. "How could you do that to Nicholas? He always loved you."

Doodle's retort is quick and full of vitriol. "I always liked Nicholas. He's a fair man. But he allowed you to have a sense of confidence that you don't deserve. Having him around only lets you believe you are better than you are. It's time you realized you aren't all you thought yourself to be."

Doodle turns the sleigh so that the rocket thruster is right next to Ooby in the net. Below, Sarcastacles starts to stir. He sits up, holding his head. Doodle leers at Ooby. "We're on equal footing now. Let's finally see who's smarter."

Beside him, Nimrod starts to laugh, shrill and evil.

Atop the beam where the rope is holding up Ooby's net, Holly runs with a chunk of rock. She slides on her knees and chops the rock down on the rope, severing it, just as Doodle throttles up the rocket.

Ooby, shielding his face in the net, drops out of the rocket's fire just in time. Ooby falls on top of Sarcastacles as the sleigh blasts out of sight. Holly leaps off the support beam and lands next to Ooby's net. She tears it open with her bare hands. Ooby untangles himself and crawls off of Sarcastacles, who is stunned, but conscious. Holly runs to the side of the temple. She looks out over the city where Nicholas fell.

To Sarcastacles, Ooby says, "Are you okay?"

"Brain swelling, massive concussion. I'm just dandy," Sarcastacles replies. "How quickly did Nicholas whip those two brats into shape?"

Holly turns to them, panic in her eyes and voice. "Get moving, you two! We have to find him!"

Sarcastacles shakes his aching head. "Who? Nicholas? Are you saying they won?"

Ooby rushes to Holly's side. "First, we help Sister Claire."

Holly is shocked by the suggestion. "Leave her! Nicholas is somewhere out there and severely hurt!"

"I know," Ooby says. "But he'll be hurt worse if he finds out we didn't help Sister Claire before him."

Eight reindeer fly in a 'V' formation like geese. The lead deer, Comet, carries Lupper on his back. Lupper points toward the roof where Nicholas landed. They descend to him. Below, bystanders have gathered. They are all shocked when the eight reindeer and Lupper glide into view, unconcerned if they are seen or not.

The reindeer land on the roof and solemnly surround Nicholas. Lupper leaps off Comet and gently drapes a web of looped ropes under him. The reindeer put the loops of the ropes over their necks. Lupper leaps on Comet and they all lift off together, but in a circle now. Nicholas is in the woven ropes between them. The Bystanders are amazed when the whole group flies toward the Parthenon on the Acropolis.

In the theatre of Dionysus, the deer and Lupper glide down into the middle of a marble stage where Ooby is standing and guiding them. They ease Nicholas down to the surface with great care. Sarcastacles and Holly are tending Sister Claire, who is supine on a stone bench around the stage. Holly bolts from Claire's side when the deer set Nicholas down. She takes his hand. Ooby goes to Nicholas's other side.

Ooby runs his hands over Nicholas, checking his body for damage. As he does this, he looks up at Lupper. "So good to see you, Lupper. How is everyone in Eno?"

"Safe, sir. Everyone is safe. We didn't know where you were, so I activated Nicholas's necklace tracking device. I hope you don't mind." Lupper is gazing down at Nicholas, near tears.

"Fine job, Young Saint." Ooby continues assessing Nicholas.

"Thank you, sir," Lupper says. "I tried to bring the gray sleigh, but once the deer knew where Nicholas was, I couldn't get them to sit still long enough to hook them up."

Ooby smiles up at each deer and nods his approval. Sarcastacles steps next to Holly as Ooby puts his head over Nicholas's chest to listen to his heart.

"Is he okay?" she asks when Ooby lifts his head.

"We need to get him back to the clinic," Ooby says. "His heart is strong, but he has more broken bones than I can count."

Nicholas regains consciousness, but barely. He looks at Ooby. "Don't move, Nicholas," Ooby advises. "Just rest."

"Miss Siltoe? Okay?" he whispers.

"I'm here," Holly says, trying to smile. "I'm here and I'm not going anywhere."

Nicholas' lips upturn into a weak and listless grin as he looks at her. "And Sister Claire?"

Sarcastacles answers him this time. "We have her. She'll be all right after another blood transfusion."

"Take mine if you need..." Nicholas starts, then fades off.

"Don't worry. We have plenty at the clinic," Sarcastacles says. Nicholas drifts into unconsciousness again.

Back at the health clinic, Nicholas is comatose and hooked to a heart monitor. He's wrapped in bandages and casts. Most of his body is in some sort of supportive splint. Intravenous lines criss cross around him, pumping needed fluids into his veins.

Holly is by his side. Ooby monitors him and Sarcastacles prepares vials of medications. Sister Claire is awake in a stretcher near him, but appears to be her original age of 70. She looks over at him, wracked with guilt.

"They tricked me," she says.

Holly has obviously heard this over and over. "As soon as you're strong enough, I'd advise you to leave!"

Sister Claire shrinks into her bed. Sarcastacles draws close to Ooby, who is now standing watch over Nicholas, but from a distance, giving Holly some space to comfort him.

"Miss Siltoe acts as though she knows him," Sarcastacles whispers.

"She does," Ooby answers. "They met many years ago and have quite a history."

Sarcastacles raises his eyebrows with mild surprise. "I didn't think Nicholas kept close relationships with the humans anymore."

Ooby smiles at a distant memory. "She was a plucky one and didn't give him much of a choice."

CHAPTER 13

The History of Holly Siltoe and Nicholas

Nearly eighty years ago, Nicholas visited the house little Holly Siltoe shared with her mother. He did it the same way he visited nearly every other house that night. The deer pulled the sleigh to a stop on the small, square roof and he used his crystals to gain entry inside.

A crystal dropped out of a pot-bellied wood stove. Nicholas appeared beside it. As usual, he used the Time Bender, so time passed slowly around him. Nicholas was dressed in dark, War World Two era clothes and looked exactly as he always had since Ooby saved him long before.

He looked around to survey the area. It was a modest home with typical late 1940s furnishings. There was a tiny, decorated tree near the stove. He lugged his bag of presents to it. As he unloaded the wrapped presents, a drawn-out noise caught his attention. He stopped to look for the source. Finding nothing out of the ordinary in the room, he went back to work.

On the roof, the crystal flew up through the narrow smokestack and landed in the thin layer of snow covering the wood shingles. Nicholas appeared and started for the sleigh and the deer awaiting him. That's when he noticed something completely out of place by the smokestack. He walked back to it and saw that, beneath an inch or two of snow around the base of the pipe, was a knotted bedsheet. Nicholas kicked away the snow and saw the bedsheet traveled under the snow, off the side, and down to an open window. It wasn't a single sheet, but several that had been tied together to form a rope. Nicholas smiled and pressed his wristwatch to stop the Time Bender.

"Good evening, Holly. You can come out." He turned and walked to his sleigh to peer in the back. Sure enough, little Holly, no more than 7 years old, peeked out from a small pile of presents. She had pigtails and a heavy wool nightgown. Nicholas smiled down at her. Then, he reached in and lifted her out of the back of the sleigh.

She stood barefoot in the snow, grinning up at him. "Santa Claus?"

Nicholas put his hands on his hips, playfully stern. There was no story to offer to explain who he was except the truth. "It was very dangerous to climb up here in these freezing temperatures. And you don't have any shoes on," Nicholas said gently.

Little Holly put her hands on her hips to mimic Nicholas. "Climbing up was easy. Lassoing the chimney with my bed sheet was not so easy," she said with a lisp because her front teeth were missing. She had a very light Austrian accent.

"Your toes will get frostbite," Nicholas said as he picked her up and held her tight to his chest for warmth. With one hand, he rubbed her feet. She rested her head on his shoulder, completely at ease.

"I just wanted to see if you were real. All my friends talk about you, but nobody has ever seen you."

"Ah, so you must see to believe," Nicholas said. "The presents beneath your tree weren't evidence enough, eh?"

"Do you bring presents to all the boys and girls?" Holly asked.

"Certainly," Nicholas nodded. "If their parents allow it."

"Even the bad ones?" Holly persisted.

"You get presents, don't you?" Nicholas grinned.

"Hey!" Holly moaned.

Back inside the small home, little Holly had cocoa at the table and shrank behind her cup as her mom, Mildred, about 30 years old, leaned against the wall. She was of Austrian descent, and was quite attractive, even at such a late hour of the night. She talked to Nicholas, who stood in the doorway, trying to inch his way out. Mildred wore a house robe and the top of it was open enough to reveal a little bit more than it should have.

"Santa Claus, huh? The Santa Claus?" she said, the tone of her distinct accent was overly flirtatious.

Nicholas shrugged and smiled. "Yes, ma'am."

"Well, I hope my little adventurer wasn't any trouble. Ever since the war took Holly's father from us, she's been a daredevil." Mildred looked into the living room and saw the presents under the tree. "It's not many folks who get the chance to thank Santa Claus for bringing so many nice gifts." Mildred smiled seductively and rubbed her chest, revealing even more of what shouldn't have been revealed. "I see the presents and all, but gosh, how do I know you're really him? I mean, you could be a late-night creep who finds his way into homes of lonely, widowed women." She pulled a cigarillo from her robe pocket and put it between her lips. Then, she looked at Nicholas and waited.

He shrugged again. "I'm sorry, I don't have a light."

"Well, gee whiz, a magic gentleman would rub some magic dust between his fingers and make a magic fire," Mildred said.

Little Holly rolled her eyes at her mother's desperate flirtation. Nicholas took the cigarillo from her lips and snapped it in half. Then, he slipped it back in her pocket.

"Smoking is bad for you," he deadpanned. "And for her." He nodded to Little Holly. "Good night and Merry Christmas."

From over her cup, Holly trumpeted, "See you next year!"

He turned and left through the door, as Mildred huffed and pouted.

Christmas rolled around again. Inside the Siltoe house, there was a different tree. Nicholas stopped beside it and eased down his bag of presents. The Time Bender was activated. He saw a wrapped box, about three feet tall, by the wall at the back of the tree. It had a tag that read,

"To Santa", with a bow on top. He stopped the Time Bender and squatted beside it. He couldn't help but smile.

"I wonder what could be in here," he said softly as he lifted the top of the box. Out popped Little Holly with a full set of new teeth.

"Got'cha!" she cheered.

Nicholas mocked surprise and lifted her out of the box. "That's a good one. I didn't see that coming."

"It was my idea, but mom wrapped the box! I'm supposed to wake her when you show up!" Holly was all giggles and grins.

Thinking back to the previous year, Nicholas shook his head. "I think we should let her sleep."

"I made you cookies!" She reached back in the box and pulled out a small brown bag. "All by myself, too. They're called Flour Cookies!"

Nicholas reached in the bag and took out a very white, very lumpy mass of hardened dough. "Do you call them that because they taste like flowers?" He then took an ill-advised big bite.

"'Cuz they're made of flour, silly! And lots of pepper!"

Nicholas coughed into his sleeve as he got his first taste of pepper. Lots and lots of pepper.

"Do you like them?"

"They're delicious," Nicholas nodded and forced himself to swallow. "Delicious. But I still have a long night ahead of me and might need a snack later." He put the cookie back in the bag and squatted in front of Holly. She hugged him tightly the moment he was on her level.

"Go to bed and get as snug as a bug," he said as he returned her hug for a second, then held her out at arm's length.

"What kind of bug? A grasshopper?" Holly smiled.

"Sure. If you like grasshoppers, then you can get as snug–"

"I don't like them, but you must," Holly interrupted. "I put four grasshoppers in the cookies. Among other assorted insects."

On the roof, Nicholas emerged from the smokestack and walked to the sleigh with the deer. He had the brown bag in his hand. The deer scampered in anticipation of cookies. "Not this time, boys. Trust me."

The deer seemed disappointed. Nicholas got in the sleigh and they all lifted off.

Below, the light came on in Little Holly's room. She looked out the window and up at the departing sleigh, a young girl with a huge crush.

Another few years, another few Christmas trees later, Nicholas appeared by the wood stove. On that particular evening, though, he didn't wait. He just turned off the Time Bender and looked around the room, waiting for Little Holly, 11 then, to leap out of hiding. She pounced from behind the curtains. He mocked surprise.

"You got me again!" Nicholas exclaimed in a loud whisper.

Little Holly laughed hard while the sound of a bottle hitting the floor came from the next room. Suddenly hyper-alert, Nicholas turned to the noise.

"That's just Curt," Little Holly said with a frown.

Nicholas carefully stepped to the threshold and looked into the adjoining dining room. A man about 40 was passed out with his head down on the table. His hand hung by his side and a whiskey bottle was on the floor beneath him.

Little Holly stepped behind Nicholas and peered into the dining room around him. "He's keen to eggnog," she said flatly, clearly not wanting to waste her short time with Nicholas talking about Curt.

"Curt? Curt Matthews?" Nicholas asked.

"He's been dating my mom since the summer," she replied.

Nicholas looked down at Little Holly with concern. "Is he treating you alright?"

"He yells a lot, but I just go to my room when he does." She grabbed Nicholas's hand and gripped it close to her face, eager to change the subject. "You know that bike you brought me last year?"

"Yes."

"Well, there was this incident with a ramp and a wood pile."

"Was the wood pile, by any crazy chance, on fire?"

"It wouldn't have been nearly as amazing if it wasn't."

Nicholas rumpled her hair as he stole another worried look at Curt.

Time marched on as time tends to do. The Christmas Eve visits continued for a few more years. Curt married Mildred and Holly grew more and more unhappy with her living arrangements. Nicholas started checking on her throughout the year, but was careful to make sure Holly didn't see him. He knew she had a deepening infatuation with him and he didn't want to encourage it in any way. He just wanted to make sure things were going okay. He also knew Curt Matthews well enough to know that they weren't.

One night, Nicholas was watching Holly's house from a distant rooftop. With the two deer and the small gray sleigh behind him, Nicholas squatted low and peered through the tree line with the hopes of getting a glimpse of Holly. Ooby appeared over the crystal in the back of the sleigh and walked up beside him.

"There are children suffering worse than Holly Siltoe tonight," Ooby said.

Nicholas nodded in agreement. "I know. I just feel bad for her. She used to be such a happy child. So vibrant and full of life. Now, she's sad all the time."

"There's a lot going on in the world right now," Ooby said softly. "I can't think of any child who passes into adulthood without their hurt sticking to them like sandspurs. That's the deal, Nicholas. Some things we just can't help."

Nicholas stood and went to the sleigh. "She never had proper guidance. No father. No grandparents. Her mother didn't offer much and Curt is only poisoning her. With just a nudge in the right direction from someone she trusts, there's no telling what great things she could accomplish."

Ooby got in the sleigh as Nicholas did. They sat side by side. "How many potential Michelangelos and Shakespeares and Einsteins were spun off course in their formative years by circumstances beyond their control? Life is a bitter root more times than not. We can't save them all."

Nicholas flicked the reins and the deer lifted swiftly and silently into the air. He steered the sleigh in tight circles as it climbed higher. Over Holly's house, Nicholas gave another look. "Just the slightest nudge," he whispered.

The Christmas Eve visits happened no more.

Some years later, the outside of Holly's house was sparsely decorated for the Fourth of July. There were a few ragged red, white, and blue banners hanging from the windows. The front porch had patriotic bunting along the length of the rails.

Holly, 17 and quite beautiful, stormed from the front door and darted down the steps. Curt, dressed in a dirty, white T-shirt, followed her. He was angry.

"How dare you talk to me like that in my house?" he barked, slurring his words.

Holly stopped and turned toward him at the bottom of the steps. "This isn't your house!"

Curt whipped his belt from his pants and started down the stairs after her. She spun around and ran away. When he stomped on the bottom step, a hand reached down and nabbed Curt from overhead. Nicholas was lying on his chest on the roof and reaching over the side. He lifted Curt off the ground by his collar. Curt choked and kicked to free himself, but Nicholas held tight.

"Never raise a hand to her again," Nicholas growled. Curt swung the belt wildly overhead, but Nicholas snatched it from him and tossed it over the back of the house. "Do you understand?"

Curt finally nodded and Nicholas released him. Curt dropped to all fours, then rolled to his back to catch his breath. When he looked up at the roof, Nicholas was gone, but a shadow streaked from the roof into the night.

Pulled by two deer, the gray sleigh glided just over the city's skyline. Fireworks exploded in the air in the distance. The city's 4th of July festival was well underway. Many people had gone out in the streets to celebrate the holiday in a raucous, carnival-like setting.

Holly stormed along the sidewalk, furious and unsettled, and completely ignored the holiday festivities around her. She was lost in her own gloomy thoughts as she walked through the crowd of revelers and past the storefronts and booths set-up along the sidewalk. She was bumped by people in the crowd. Every unintentional contact seemed to startle her. She was overwhelmed by the crowd and the noise and the chaos.

From somewhere beside her, a man called to her. "Hey, good-lookin'! Need a ride?"

Holly looked up to see a man in his mid-40s leaning out of the passenger's window of a car stopped in the road. Next to him, in the driver's seat, sat another man of about the same age. Both seemed a little slimy in nature. Holly approached the car.

"Where are you headed, darlin'?" the passenger said.

Holly stopped right next to his window. The passenger reached out to touch her arm. She recoiled. Cars in the road behind them began to honk.

"We're headed to see the fireworks. Hop in."

Holly, overwhelmed again by the stranger's unwelcome touch and the bleating horns and noise of the rowdy crowd, felt disoriented and lightheaded. Just then, she heard a whisper as something moved behind her in a super-fast blur.

"Holly." It was Nicholas's voice. She was sure of it. She turned quickly, but he wasn't there. In a storefront, there was an arrow made from newspaper taped to the window. She hadn't noticed it moments ago, even though she had walked right by there. In an instant, she knew it was for her.

"Hey! You getting in or what?" the stranger persisted.

Holly turned without saying a word and rushed in the direction of the arrow. She pushed her way through the crowd until she came to another arrow that was drawn in chalk on the sidewalk. It pointed down another street at the intersection. She followed it and kept walking until she finally saw a third arrow, also in chalk on the sidewalk, that pointed into a recessed building entrance.

A sign over the entrance read, "YWCA - Center for Runaway Girls". She looked around as the bustling crowd rushed by on the sidewalk.

"Is that you?"

The blur moved past her again and caused her hair to move. She turned in time to see the dark silhouette of the sleigh on the roof of a record store across the street. The sleigh whisked away as fireworks exploded behind it. Holly waved, but it was gone in an instant. She turned back to the YWCA door and went inside.

Perhaps that should have ended Holly's and Nicholas's association with each other for good. If it had been up to Ooby it would have. Nicholas still checked in on Holly though. Frequently at first, then less so as the years went on.

Holly was eager to dip her toe in the world, and so she did. The 1960s were a wild time. Holly grew fiercely independent before women were allowed to be such a thing. She moved to Los Angeles and was one of the first women to study martial arts under Bruce Lee. She took acting classes and tried her hand at modeling. She found the occasional job as a stunt double in some low budget Kung Fu movies, but she still had to keep working at some unsavory places to make ends meet.

When Holly was 23 years old, she waited tables in a smoke-filled bar frequented by business executives and white-collar-types. It was a fairly classy place, but the crowd was as rowdy and chauvinistic as any other to the all-female wait staff.

One of Holly's co-workers was her age and, like Holly, very pretty. Her name was Ellen and she was waiting on a group of four businessmen, who were smoking cigars. She carried a tray of drinks to their table, put down four tumblers in front of the men, but still had a few to deliver elsewhere. As she presented their drinks, she smiled at each man.

The Executive seated closest to her, with slicked back hair and wearing a sharp suit, smacked her hard on the leg once all their drinks were down. "Thanks, doll!" he yelled, overly boisterous.

The smack was hard enough to make Ellen yelp and spill the other drinks. The other men laughed as Holly saw the assault and rushed over to help.

"Hey, you ogre!" she barked. "She has to pay for those other drinks now!"

The Executive rose from his chair. Ellen was quick to try to diffuse the situation. "Holly, it's okay. It was my fault."

The Executive was insulted. "Ogre?"

Ellen whispered to Holly with her back to the man. "Please, Holly, I need this job."

"Then go," Holly whispered back. "I'll handle it."

The Executive squared off with Holly as the other men laughed and made catcalls. Ellen scurried away. The Executive didn't expect a confrontation. He was only hoping to shout Holly into submission and recover from the embarrassment he felt over her lashing out at him in front of his friends.

"I hate a dame who doesn't know her place. How 'bout I turn you over my knee, huh?" he guffawed. The whole bar was watching by then. The mostly male clientele even encouraged him.

"You're welcome to try," Holly said, a little too confident for the Executive's liking.

Since she didn't offer the apology he was hoping for, there was only one thing left for him to do. He charged her, probably hoping she would just retreat and cower. That wasn't how Holly functioned. She sidestepped his charge, gripped his arm, and twisted it in a low circle. The Executive somersaulted forward and landed flat on his back. The crowd fell silent at the sight. The bar's Manager, a portly, bald man, rushed into the fray.

He made a big show of admonishing Holly. "This is the last time you'll sass a customer! You're fired, young lady!"

The Executive stood up, embarrassed and angry. He rushed at her again. She did a perfect jump-spinning-back kick to his chest and sent him flailing to the floor once more. The men at the table with the Executive rushed to their friend's defense and surrounded Holly. The Manager stepped away, quickly excusing himself from the potential melee.

"You're on your own now," he said with his hands held up in surrender to the other men.

"Same as always," Holly smiled as the Executive staggered up and joined the circle around Holly.

"Let's teach this lass some manners!" he roared.

They all moved in at once. Holly started kicking and punching as best she could. She held her ground for an impressive amount of time, but the four men were too strong. They eventually enveloped her like a Venus Flytrap.

A blur streaked around the four men as they tackled Holly. One by one, they flew off of her and landed in the far corners of the room, as if grabbed from behind and flung backwards. The other patrons in the bar were stunned when Holly stood up, victorious. She felt the blur whisk by her as something touched her wrist.

Her eyes followed the blur until it settled at a far table in the corner. She saw Nicholas sitting there. He wore a suit and tie and blended in perfectly with the crowd. He pointed at his wrist, indicating for her to look at hers. A bulky wristwatch was there. He motioned for her to press the side.

By then the four Executives were on their feet. They charged her again. She pressed the watch and everything slowed down around her. The Executives looked as though they were running, but they were moving no faster than a super-slow walk. She looked back at Nicholas. He gave her a wink and a smile. He was moving in time with her.

In real time, the Execs reached Holly all at once and attempted to grab her. Holly was not moving as fast as Nicholas typically did when he used the Time-bender, but she moved three times faster than the Executives. She kicked and spun, punched and foot-swept. The Executives tumbled and staggered from the rapid blows and knocked over tables and chairs. Several times, each man got back up to attack, but each time he was flipped or thrown helplessly to the side.

Soon, Holly had all four beaten into submission. She pressed the watch again and looked around at the fallen bullies, then at the rest of the room. Everyone was staring back at her in absolute shock. She looked at Nicholas, who nodded to the exit. She made a break for it.

In a diner down the street, Chubby Checker played on the jukebox. Nicholas and Holly sat in a booth. Holly was wearing his jacket to keep warm. She lit a cigarette and made flirtatious overtures at Nicholas. He had coffee and she had a glass of beer.

"The tips at that joint were terrible anyway," Holly said.

Nicholas smiled patiently at her. "You want a tip?"

She rolled her eyes and dropped the cigarette in her beer. "That about right?" Nicholas nodded. "Good." She pushed the glass away and reached across the table to take Nicholas's hand. "Is that enough then?"

Nicholas pulled his hand from hers. "For what?"

"For you to finally love me the way I love you." Her words are straight-forward and direct. Nicholas was taken aback.

"Holly, look..." he started, but he didn't know how to finish.

"You don't think that it will ever work because you'll live forever and I won't?" She stared at him, resolute and determined.

"I'm not sure I understand. We're friends. I mean, I've known you since you were little. I don't think of you that way."

"Who is alive today that you haven't known that long? Do you disregard the President and the Pope because you knew them when they were in diapers?" Nicholas looked at the table, unable to meet her eyes. "Nicholas, these little meetings we have every now and then, are they ever going to amount to anything? Do we have a future with each other or not?"

"Holly..." Again, he didn't have an end to the sentence he started.

She knew what was happening and stopped him with a gesture. Tears welled in her eyes. "You may stay young forever, Nicholas, but I won't." She stood from the booth and took off his jacket. He held up a hand to stop her.

"Keep it," he said.

She turned away, but stopped and looked at him once more. "Thanks for your help tonight, but I won't need it anymore. Whatever spying you do on me, you can stop. I'll find someone else to love and love me back, but I can't if you're always looking over my shoulder."

Nicholas was genuinely hurt when Holly left the diner.

It should have ended there, but Holly was never one to leave things unsaid. It took a few more years, but Holly and Nicholas met one more time on Christmas Eve.

Inside a huge, luxurious home, there were elaborate decorations aplenty. Nicholas appeared just outside the big fireplace. He was moving fast, using the Time Bender. He clicked it off, though, when he saw his jacket folded neatly beneath the tree. He looked around and saw Holly leaning against the arched doorway, holding a cup of hot cocoa, wearing a flannel robe.

"Merry Christmas," she purred.

"I wasn't expecting you," Nicholas stuttered. He walked toward her.

"I took a job as a nanny here two days ago. The girl is sweet, but the twins are total brats."

Nicholas stopped in front of her. She offered him her cup. "You're working with kids now? That's good." He sipped the cocoa.

She shrugged. "I'm quitting tomorrow. I'm only here because the job offered me a chance to be around kids on Christmas Eve. Where there are kids on this night, there's you."

"I thought you didn't want to see me anymore," he said.

She swiped the cup from him and put it on a nearby table. "You should know better than that." She threw her arms around him and hugged him tightly. "I love you and I want to be with you, Nicholas, for whatever time I am allowed. If I get old and you find that you can't love me anymore, then so be it. But for now, I can't live without you. You're all I think about." She stood on her tip-toes and kissed him. He pulled away. "Do you feel anything for me? Anything at all?" Tears formed in her eyes as they did during their previous meeting.

"In all my years, I've seen love come in many forms. And I can say, with assurance, you will never find a greater love than what I feel for you."

She smiled and new tears ran. This time though, they were tears of joy. "Then we can be together! Really together, I mean!"

He took off his crystal necklace and put it in her hand. "When my night's work is done, at seven o'clock this morning your time, put this necklace over your head and touch the crystal. It will take you where I want you to go. Where you need to go to be truly happy."

"To you." She embraced him again and Nicholas smiled. She released him, but not before she left a kiss on his cheek. "Until seven o'clock, my love." She left the room with a bounce in her step and he hurriedly put presents under the tree.

Nicholas climbed an ivy-covered trellis to the roof and walked to the sleigh. Ooby stood beside it. "I hope you're not doing something you'll regret," he said. "You gave her the crystal. You're breaking a lot of rules we established many years ago and you–"

Nicholas was uncharacteristically gruff when he interrupted Ooby. "It won't matter. I promise."

Nicholas got in the sleigh and Ooby crawled in beside him. "This isn't like you, Nicholas."

"I know what I'm doing."

"I'm afraid I do, too. You're leaving, aren't you? You're going to go to her and leave the rest of us behind."

Nicholas didn't answer. He just sat in the sleigh without flicking the reins and stared at the dashboard. Ooby watched the stars overhead.

"You're still human, Nicholas. I know the desires of your heart pull at you every day. I know you want, and by all means deserve, someone to love and to love you. This life you have isn't an easy one." He placed a hand on Nicholas's slumped shoulder. "But you know the trappings of an immortal and a mortal trying to have a life together. It will be good for a while, but time passes for one and not the other. The broken heart you would feel now by letting her go will only be amplified by a hundred in the future when the natural process takes her from you."

Nicholas finally looked back at Ooby. "My mind is made up."

"Then I will leave you to your business, my friend," Ooby said. He offered his hand to Nicholas. They shake. There was a feeling of finality as Ooby went to the back and stepped over the large crystal. He gave Nicholas one final glance. Then, he touched the crystal and was gone.

The next morning, in the luxurious home's living room, Holly, dressed and wearing Nicholas's jacket, stared at the clock over the mantle. It struck seven o'clock and chimed with the new hour. It wasn't even through the first chirp before Holly pulled the crystal over her neck and touched it. She disappeared.

Holly reappeared in the beautiful courtyard of a cathedral. Glistening snow blanketed the picturesque setting. There were no footprints marring the new snow cover and the only spot that was cleared was the path to the front of the quiet church. Holly was disoriented. She looked around, then looked at the second crystal on the ground beside her. She picked it up and pocketed it and went up the cleared path. She pushed open the high, wooden door and walked into the cavernous sanctuary. It was a grand medieval church with high ceilings, buttresses, naves, alcoves, and frescoes. It was not an American church. Holly knew that right away. She was somewhere in Europe.

A 65-year-old priest, dressed in ceremonial robes, stood at the front, as if he was waiting for her.

"Merry Christmas," he said with a heavy Austrian accent. "Miss Siltoe, I presume." She looked around, in awe of the church. "Nicholas said you would come," he added. He waved her forward.

She walked up the center aisle of the huge hall, her footfalls echoing. "Is he here?"

"No. There is, however, someone he wants you to meet."

She stepped in front of the Priest, who held out his hand. She correctly assumed he wanted the crystals, so she removed the necklace and handed it and the other crystal to him. He tucked both away inside his robes. He went to an alcove in a dark corner of the sanctuary. She followed, curious.

"Someone he wants me to meet? He was supposed to be here." She felt a flare of anger inside her chest. "Is this some kind of brush-off? I would hope he'd have the courage to do it himself if he isn't interested in me!"

"I assure you, he is very interested in you, Miss Siltoe. In your happiness. In your future."

"Then where is he? I want to speak to him right now!" She grew louder in proportion to her ire.

"He left a message for you." The Priest stepped into the dark alcove. Holly followed. They stood in the darkness, their silhouettes against the sanctuary's light behind them. Holly had her hands on her hips, fuming. "Nicholas is of the belief that the love you feel for him is an expression of the deep love you have inside," the Priest said. "He feels it should be directed to someone who knows how to use it better than he does."

"So, he's playing match-maker?" Holly fumed. "That's a bigger insult than a brush-off!"

A spotlight came on suddenly. In the back of the alcove sat the marble statue of the Baby Jesus that Ooby had made for Nicholas over 1500 years before. It was the same one that Nicholas knelt in front of before every one of his long Christmas Eve nights. The statue's face and arms were lifted to the heavens and his eyes were strikingly lifelike.

Holly gasped when she saw it. Speechless, she stepped into the circle of light. For a long moment, she stared at it. The Priest quietly stepped away and left her alone.

On a balcony overlooking the sanctuary, Nicholas stood in the shadows. He was positioned where he could see into the alcove. The Priest walked up beside him and held out the crystals. Nicholas took them as he watched Holly kneel beside the Baby Jesus statue. She folded her hands in prayer and bowed her head.

"Love at first sight, it would seem," the Priest said.

Nicholas nodded. "Guide her."

"She'll be a mighty one, Nicholas. I can tell that much already." The Priest turned to watch Holly as Nicholas stepped deeper into the shadows. In a moment, he was gone.

Nicholas stood in the bell tower of the cathedral. The sleigh was there. He petted each deer and gave them cookies. Finally, his eyes filled with tears and he leaned heavily against the sleigh, panting as he tried to hold back the flood of anguish that was overtaking him.

Ooby appeared in the back and, seeing the impending breakdown, rushed to Nicholas's side. Without a word, he guided Nicholas's head to his shoulder. Nicholas unloaded his sorrow and Ooby could only hold him as he cried.

In the health clinic, Ooby wipes a single tear from his eye. He has just told the history of Holly and Nicholas to Sarcastacles, who listened intently. They stand behind the couple, out of earshot. Nicholas is still unconscious in the bed. Holly holds vigil by his side.

"Nicholas has experienced great despair over our time together, as you well know," Ooby whispers to Sarcastacles. "He's lost every person he ever knew from his mortal years. He's witnessed generations of humans be born and grow and pass on. He's endured the loss of beloved Saints, who reached the end of their lives with him remaining ever faithful by their side."

"But nothing can hurt the soul like a romantic love which is never allowed to bear its beautiful fruit," Sarcastacles cuts in sadly.

Ooby nods in agreement. "Holly and Nicholas would not see each other for nearly sixty years until they serendipitously met on the summit of Mt. Fuji last Christmas Eve."

Sarcastacles has tears in his eyes now, too. "Destiny has brought them together yet again."

"Another cruel twist of fate, if you ask me," Ooby says. "If Nicholas's body recovers from this reunion, I doubt his heart ever will."

"Humans have a knack for weaving heartbreaking tales with their passions and their fragility and the depths of their love for each other," Sarcastacles says solemnly.

"But that's why they were chosen, my friend," Ooby explains. "It's why the Creator came as one of them and not as one of us. It's why we put their needs ahead of our own."

Sarcastacles sighs. "If only we could make Nimrod and Doodle understand as much."

"So many humans don't even understand it about themselves," Ooby says.

"How can we expect young Saints and Pyres to appreciate something that most humans never will?" Sarcastacles wonders.

"We must learn to trust and have faith in each other when good sense tells us we are irredeemable," Ooby says. "That's what Nicholas does. He reaches out to us until the better angels of our nature reach back."

Part Two

Over New York City, the large, red sleigh rockets across the tops of the skyscrapers, leaving its twisting smoke trail. Then, it slows over Central Park. Nimrod and Doodle, side by side in the sleigh, look down on the city.

"Your smorgasbord awaits," Doodle says with a nudge of his elbow. Nimrod rubs his hands together and licks his lips, like a hungry cowboy who just heard the dinner bell. "Remember what I said. Little bits at a time. Don't fill up on one. We're going for quantity here. It's a numbers game."

"I know, I know! Put me down!" Nimrod replies with urgency.

"Don't turn off the Time Bender. Under no circumstances are you to turn it off." Doodle's tone is stern.

"Quit chastising me for something I haven't even done yet! You're starting to sound like Ooby." Nimrod's eyes are fierce when he glares at Doodle, who is speechless after being equated to Ooby. "I'm starving here!"

Doodle jams the joystick down and rockets the sleigh toward Times Square. There are massive Black Friday crowds in the overly congested area. Cars and buses fill the streets and the city's noises are deafening. The strobing lights and marquees blast the city's hub with a disorienting effect. Seemingly unnoticed in the bustle, a streaking blur works its way through the crowd, in and around unsuspecting people and back again, as if casing the crowd for a perfect victim.

Suddenly, a male street vendor selling hot dogs from his cart, is whisked up for an instant by the blur. He collapses to his back on the sidewalk, two puncture holes in his neck.

Moments later, on the other side of the Square, a woman, prim and proper, gasps out loud and also drops to the ground. Identical puncture marks are on her neck. A third victim, a taxi driver this time, in her cab in the road, slumps after the blur zips around her. She hangs halfway outside her window, wounds on her neck.

The crowds divert around the three victims as if there is a reasonable excuse for their collapse. That is until, finally, the number of victims is so large that their presence can no longer be ignored. A single scream from a bystander rises above the din. It's followed by many more around Times Square.

An elderly, roundish man with white hair, a white beard, and glasses resting on the end of his nose, sits in a recliner by a fireplace. With his plush red robe, he looks more like the traditional Santa Claus than Nicholas ever has. He's resting comfortably with his feet up while he reads a newspaper.

Next to him, in a rocking chair, sits a grandmotherly woman, who, like the man, is in her mid-60s. She's darning an over-sized sock as she rocks forward and back in an easy rhythm. They don't talk. Both seem content to pour their energies into their respective activities. The only sound in the room is the soothing crackle of the fire, the faint creak of the rocking chair, and the rustle of the newspaper.

It's a very Rockwellian scene and an image worthy of the front of a Christmas card. It's disrupted, though, when a young man rushes into the room. The man, named Jordan, is harried and doesn't seem the least bit worried about his rude intrusion.

"President Applebaum, sir," he blurts, which might seem a peculiar thing to say until one realizes that this picturesque little fireside moment is in a living room inside the White House, in Washington D.C., and the sweet, aged man and woman are the President and the First Lady of the United States.

The round man, the President Applebaum, snatches down the newspaper and peers over his reading glasses at Jordan. "Did you call me Applebottom?" he says in a gruff tone.

"No, sir. Why in the wide world would I call you that?" Jordan returns defensively.

President Applebaum stands abruptly. He indeed has a huge apple-shaped bottom. "You came in here for a reason. What is it? Spill it!"

"Your presence is needed in the Situation Room, sir," Jordan stammers.

President Applebaum clenches his fist and looks at Missus Applebaum. "Ahh. An enemy is at the gates."

Missus Applebaum continues knitting and doesn't even look up. "That's good, dear."

"I shall cry havoc and let slip the dogs of war!" the President bellows.

Jordan is immediately concerned. "No, no, sir. I'm not sure that slipping the dogs of war is quite necessary yet."

"War and her ferocious beasts shall parade the ramparts tonight!" the undeterred President barks as he bounds toward the door.

First Lady Applebaum smiles, still knitting. "Go get those ferocious beasts, dear."

The White House's Situation Room is a large conference room with a table in the center and large monitors on all four walls. At the table, eight Advisors, including five Cabinet Members and three Military Officials, are already seated. One of the military men is Admiral Chucklenut, who was in charge of the Aircraft Carrier that implemented the gold transfer from the United States to Malaysia a short year ago. All are twiddling their thumbs, waiting patiently. President Applebaum storms in and the group at the table stands at attention. Jordan follows the President closely.

"Good evening, President Applebaum," the Advisors all say in unison.

President Applebaum stops cold. "Who said that?" The eight look back and forth at each other, confused. "One of you called me Apple-bottom! I heard it! Who was it?" the President accuses. The eight all shake their heads and point at each other, like guilty children. "If I find out who said it, trust me, there will be a reckoning!"

Admiral Chucklenut stands from the far end of the table. "President Applebaum, please. We have a crisis."

Applebaum nods as he goes to the head of the table. "To business then! Who dares threaten this fine nation?" He throws his hand over a big red button on his end of the table and acts as if he'll press it. All eight gasp.

Admiral Chucklenut reaches out with sudden desperation. "Whoa, there, sir! Take it easy!"

"Victorious warriors win first and then go to war, while defeated warriors go to war first and then seek to win," Applebaum screeches into the air. "I'll launch 'em! I'll launch 'em all! Tell me where to send 'em!"

"Hands off the button, sir!" Applebaum says forcefully, like he's chastising a puppy in the throes of chewing a new shoe. "Get your hands off!"

President Applebaum reluctantly pulls his hand away as if disappointed. With an exasperated sigh, Chucklenut turns to a monitor and presses a remote control. The monitor shows a close-up picture of a human neck with two puncture wounds.

The President looks at the large photo and leans back heavily in his chair. "Hmm."

"This unfortunate soul is a victim of an unusual attack an hour ago in New York City." He clicks to another picture of another victim, then another. "Here's a second victim. And a third. There are many more. All on the same block. All are alive, thank goodness, but each victim lost a half pint of blood." He presses the remote rapidly, scanning through a dozen or more photos of bite victims. "Five more in San Francisco. Twelve more in Houston. Here's one from St. Louis. All within the last hour." He flips through more, talking fast. "Ten in Rome. Two in Zaire. Two more in Moscow. Three in Munich. Six in Salzburg. Prague, Vienna, Berlin. All within minutes of the ones here."

Applebaum leans forward in his chair now. He is watching the scrolling photos intently.

"We're not sure what terrorist activity is at play here, sir," Chucklenut continues. "But it's definitely a concerted effort involving multiple perpetrators. And it appears that these attacks are meant to be seen.

They are happening in crowded areas in broad sight of everyone, but no one sees what's causing them."

President Applebaum summons Jordan, who runs to his side in an instant. "Jordan, I must apologize. Earlier when I said, "Let slip the dogs of war..."

Jordan nods with an exasperated grin. "Yes, sir. I was worried for a moment there. I'm glad you've decided to take a more thoughtful approach to–"

President Applebaum points to the sky, suddenly irate. "I should've said, release the Hounds of Hades!"

In the back office of the 'Van Helsing Camping Depot' store, George Van Helsing sits at a small desk. The broad man is about 50 years old, and his office is a sloppy place. He's a large man, dressed like a rough and tumble biker, and he is bored stiff.

When a rotary phone rings, he answers quickly, eager for business. "Van Helsing Camping Depot, how may I assist you?" He listens to the voice on the other end for a moment, then shakes his head. His voice carries a heavy Southern drawl. "Naw. No canteens or cooking gear." He listens some more. "Nope. Not much in the way of portable gas stoves or the like. To be honest, we're pretty specialized in our available camping equipment." More jabber on the other end of the line. He nods. "Well, funny you should ask." He leans to an office window that overlooks the warehouse. There are rows and rows of boxes in the area, each marked *Wooden Stakes*. "Tent stakes. Lots and lots of tent stakes. If you need stakes to hold your tent up, boy oh boy, have you come to the right place." He looks at the receiver after an obvious hang-up. "So close."

He hangs up the phone and pulls a chewed down, unlit cigar from his shirt pocket. He shoves it in his mouth and sighs. Then, he notices a red light blinking on his desk and perks up. He closes the blinds in the window looking out to the warehouse and presses the button. A 1950s video screen pops up from the desk. President Applebaum's face is in close-up.

Van Helsing smiles widely. "Well, well. If it ain't ol' Applebottom! My favorite waterboy!"

On the screen, Applebaum chuckles. "Applebottom at your service! How are you, Mister Van Helsing?"

Van Helsing looks around his small, cluttered office. "Currently questioning my second career choice. Hey! I heard you ran for a public office of some sort."

President Applebaum nods proudly. "Indeed, I did. Commander-in-Chief of the Free World actually. As such, I'm privy to some information you may find very interesting."

"Well, spit it out, Applebottom! What is it? I don't have all day!" Van Helsing looks around his office again, a bit sheepishly. He does, in fact, have all day.

In the Situation Room, President Applebaum is in front of a monitor on the wall. Van Helsing's face is huge upon it. The Advisors are still at the table watching and quite bewildered at how readily the President truckles to a burly ruffian they've never heard of and allows him to utter the forbidden name they are constantly accused of saying.

"Sir, the vampires are active again," Applebaum gushes, a little too eager to spill the latest gossip.

On the screen, Van Helsing pounds the desk with a heavy fist. It appears as though he is mad at first, but then he grins. "Finally."

"They're attacking people all over the world, all at once," Applebaum babbles.

Van Helsing whispers, as if talking to himself. "This is what I've trained for. Me and generations of my family before me for five centuries."

"What do you say, Mister Van Helsing?" President Applebaum leaps from his chair and points to the ceiling again. "Shall we release the Hounds of Hades?"

Van Helsing leans closer to his video monitor so that his glaring face is all that's on screen in the Situation Room.

"Hounds of Hades? We're the Vanhelsingers. Always have been." He smirks at Applebaum. "How many times have I told you, we're not changing it."

"Well, my marketing team feels like that sounds more like a boy band than a team of fierce vampire fighters. I just thought, as we reintroduce ourselves, we could reboot with a new name," Applebaum says, suddenly sheepish. "Rebrands are all the rage, you know? We could use a bit of a revamp, if you will."

"As a matter of fact, I won't," Van Helsing gripes. "You're not on the team, Applebottom! You couldn't pass muster, Mister! You just fetch the water when we're thirsty, remember?"

In the Camping Depot store, Van Helsing punches the button that disconnects him with Applebaum. He leans back in his chair as the video monitor descends back into his desk. "Sweet vindication, at long last." He opens the blinds to the warehouse and looks out over the endless crates of stakes again. "I hope there's a bunch of them vampires," he mutters to himself as he chomps on his cigar. "Because the world is in the market for wooden stakes and the price just went way, way up."

In the health clinic in Athens, Sarcastacles, standing by Ooby and behind Holly, who is still watching dutifully over Nicholas, glimpses a breaking news report on a small, muted TV in the corner of the room. The reporter on the broadcast speaks of the rash of mysterious vampire attacks in big cities all around the world. Sarcastacles turns up the TV as he motions Ooby over.

"What is it?" Ooby asks. He looks at the TV, but he hasn't yet caught what is being reported.

Sarcastacles has true fear in his eyes, though he can't look away from the TV. "It's Nimrod. He's attacking a bunch of people around the world."

Ooby watches the screen as red blips appear on a digital map to show where the attacks have taken place. "He and Doodle are using the Time Bender so it seems like many Pyres are involved," he surmises.

"It will look like a violation of the treaty." Sarcastacles grows even more pale.

"But why would they want that? To what end?" Ooby wonders.

Sarcastacles reaches his hand toward the ceiling and gives a low whistle. "That will have to be determined in conclave. I'll gather the Elders for a meeting." As he talks, a bat flies from the dark corner of the room and lands on his outstretched finger, beckoned by his whistle. He whispers to it and it flies away.

Ooby sees what is happening and nods his understanding.

"Ah. Still using the ancient techniques. That bat will communicate your message with other bats, who will pass it along to the rest of the Elders." Ooby is impressed. "Sometimes, the old ways are the best."

Sarcastacles shoots a perplexed glance his way. "What?" He shakes his head. "You think I'm using a bat as a messenger?" He can't help but laugh heartily. "Heavens, no! Spreading a message like that would take forever! The old ways are terrible!"

Now, Ooby has no idea what is happening. "But the bat?"

Sarcastacles shrugs. "He will use his superior sonar to locate my cell phone. I misplaced it this morning."

The bat returns with a smartphone clutched in its claws. It hovers in front of Sarcastacles and drops it in his hands. "There we go. Thank you, Franklin." He starts scrolling through his contacts list as he chuckles lowly, "A messenger bat. Holy mackerel, Ooby, next you'll be doing complex math on an abacus." Sarcastacles punches a few keys. "Love me some group text."

In Washington D.C., a pack of seven motorcycles roar down Pennsylvania Avenue. They turn into the driveway to the White House and circle around in front of it, revving their engines and tearing up the pristine lawn in huge clumps. Finally, they stop at the front door. President Applebaum opens the door to greet the gang. It's an unsavory group, to say the least. He looks the men over, one by one.

First, there's Big League, a powerhouse slugger-type with a wooden bat in a sheath on his back like a Samurai sword. Then, there's Rip Tide, with long blond hair and a SoCal surfer vibe. Tumbleweed is a round, roly-poly of a man with straw-like hair. Powder Keg is barrel-shaped and wears a demolition hardhat and a bandolier of dynamite sticks across his torso. Tiddlywink is a small framed man in a yellow felt suit. He has a disc dispenser hanging around his waist that looks just like a coin changer that attendants used to wear in the hey-day of video game arcades. Lastly, there's Garlic Scallopini, a monster of a man in a chef's uniform.

Van Helsing leads the group. He stops his motorcycle in front of Applebaum, who can't help but smile, wide and proud.

"So glad you boys could make it," Applebaum says in awe.

"Hello, Applebottom. I present to you the Vanhelsingers," Van Helsing says.

"Looking good, but where's the old gang?" Applebaum asks. "Where's Cow Poke?"

"I sent him out to pasture," Van Helsing says with a dismissive wave of his hand.

"What about Stink Eye?"

"I didn't like how he looked at me."

"Lockjaw?"

"He left one day without saying a word." Van Helsing revs his motorcycle again. "You gonna invite us in or what?"

Applebaum nods and throws open the door as wide as it will go. "Of course! Welcome to my humble abode, team."

Van Helsing drives his motorcycle through the open door. The other six follow on their bikes. They blast through the house at top speed. Within minutes, the barbaric horde is spinning doughnuts and making laps in the formal reception room, known as the Blue Room. Applebaum rushes in, panicked. Van Helsing stops and laughs as his group keeps going.

"Fancy digs, Applebottom," Van Helsing says loudly, trying to be heard over the engine noise. Applebaum can only watch in horror as the gang demolishes the room. "Show him your talents, Vanhelsingers," he commands his marauding crew.

Big League whips his bat from his back and swings it at a vase, smashing it to smithereens as he rides his motorcycle by it. "Home run!" he yells.

At the same moment, Rip Tide leaps on the seat of his still moving bike and rides it like a surfboard while giving the 'Hang Ten' sign. "Shredding the gnar, dude!" he brags.

Tiddlywink is quick and nimble. He leaps off his bike and grabs onto a high chandelier. He clicks out a handful of discs from his dispenser and throws them at Applebaum. They fly in a perfect line and cut off his white beard so that it's squared off just below his chin. The discs stick in the wall beside him. President Applebaum is aghast.

Tumbleweed somersaults off his still-moving bike, which crashes through the wall, and rolls like a giant bowling ball until he comes up in front of Applebaum, scattering tables and shelves in the process. He offers his hand and Applebaum shakes it, his face locked in a surreal expression.

Garlic Scallopini roars up to Applebaum after Tumbleweed rolls off. With the front of his bike inches from Applebaum, Garlic Scallopini draws a deep breath.

"Quarter strength, Garlic," Van Helsing says in warning. "I don't want to put him in a coma."

Garlic Scallopini exhales a small puff of green fog as he says, "Hhh-hello!"

A horrendous stench smacks President Applebaum in the face. His eyes cross and he nearly falls backwards. Van Helsing runs up behind him and keeps him from collapsing. He slaps his cheeks to arouse him.

"Wake up, Applebottom," he says. "You don't want to miss Powder Keg, do you?"

Powder Keg screeches to a stop, strikes a match on his chin, and uses it to ignite a stick of dynamite from his bandolier. He tosses the dynamite to Applebaum who, still not fully awake, quickly becomes so when he catches it. He tosses the dynamite from hand to hand as the fuse burns down.

"I like to make a big impression," Powder Keg chortles. "In the ground!" He laughs as Van Helsing takes the dynamite from Applebaum and lights his cigar with the burning fuse. At the last second, he snuffs the fuse out.

"You get the gist of what he's about, yeah?" Van Helsing asks with a wink at Applebaum. President Applebaum nods, completely exasperated. Then, something outside the window to the front yard catches his eye. He goes to it and looks out. To his horror, he sees another one hundred motorcyclists spinning donuts on the front lawn.

"Who are they?" he stammers.

"New recruits. Trainees. Young and eager," Van Helsing says as he walks over and claps Applebaum on the shoulder. "All hoping to earn a name as a Vanhelsinger. Now let's talk about hunting vampires and how much the government is willing to pay for my wonderful, vampire heart-piercing stakes."

In the health clinic in Athens, Nicholas is still unconscious in bed. Holly puts a damp cloth on his forehead. Ooby approaches her with a cup of coffee. She takes the mug with gratitude.

"Thank you," she says.

"You're welcome. How is he?" Ooby asks.

"He seems comfortable," she says as she takes a sip. "He doesn't seem to be in as much pain."

"You need rest," he says to her. "I can get you a mattress or a cot and you can stay by him."

"That sounds good. But maybe later. I'm fine for now."

Ooby nods at Holly, then kneels by Nicholas and takes his limp hand. "Keep healing, my friend. Sarcastacles and I fear there is a depraved scheme being hatched against the Pyres."

Holly stops mid-sip from her coffee. "So? I fail to see a negative to that." She turns and glares over her shoulder at Sarcastacles, who is waiting in the corner.

"I know you don't trust him, but the debauchery does not fall on him or any of his kind, save Nimrod," says Ooby.

"Yeah, sure," Holly scoffs.

Ooby turns his attention back to Nicholas. "We have to go."

"You're leaving? Now?" Holly is astonished. "He's still critically ill and nowhere near out of the woods!"

"He knows we must stop this threat and I know that you'll take care of him until we return," Ooby replies with confidence.

"Why do you care so much about vampires?" Holly is having a hard time hiding her disdain.

"They're a cousin race to my own. And if something isn't done to stop Nimrod and Doodle, then the Pyres will be wiped off the face of the planet by the Slayers Guild."

"Slayers Guild? Where do I join?"

"They're not a good group," Ooby answers. "They're a team of assassins that were assembled hundreds of years ago when Vam, the last rogue Pyre before Nimrod, wreaked havoc on the humans. They will be activated if it is thought the Pyres are on the offensive again. Sarcastacles and I have to go to Transylvania to meet with the Pyre Elders to figure out what we must do."

Holly leers at Sarcastacles again. "Then go. I'd rather not be around him anyway. He gives me the creeps."

Ooby is wounded by her curt demeanor, but he only nods. Then, he pats Nicholas's hand. "Heal quickly, Nicholas. Rest."

Nicholas's eyes flutter, but he doesn't awaken. Ooby starts away as Sarcastacles approaches the bed to say goodbye to Nicholas, but Ooby places a hand on his arm to stop him. Ooby shakes his head as he glances at Holly. Sarcastacles sees her glaring directly at him and understands why Ooby thinks it best not to approach. He nods, and the two turn and leave.

A short time later, Ooby and Sarcastacles are sitting in a street rickshaw in a deserted alleyway. Dasher, Dancer, Prancer and Vixen are attached to the front of it with ropes and reins. Lupper is standing by them. Sarcastacles's head is covered by his big, floppy hat and he is wearing dark sunglasses. The other four deer are hovering just off the ground nearby.

"It's the best I could come up with on short notice, sir," Lupper says in an apologetic tone.

"And a fine one it is," Ooby praises.

"Excellent work, Lupper," Sarcastacles echoes.

Lupper's head and shoulders are lifted a bit as a smile crosses his face. "Thank you, sirs."

Ooby takes the reins and flicks them as he addresses the deer. "Be swift, boys. We don't have the benefit of the Time Bender and we've a long way to go."

The four deer tug at the rickshaw and in a moment are airborne and flying out of sight over the alley. Lupper gives a salute as the other four deer huddle close to him. He pets them and feeds them cookies from his pocket.

It's late at night when Air Force One lifts off from a Washington D.C. airport with two jet fighters flanking it. Inside the plane's Presidential Suite, President Applebaum sits at the official desk of his office. Van Helsing enters, armed to a ridiculous degree with an arsenal of weapons hanging from holsters around his hips and shoulders and across his back.

"Applebottom! Why are you sitting at my desk?" he admonishes.

"But it's the President's desk and I'm the President," Applebaum stutters, suddenly unsure of why he's sitting at the desk.

"It's the desk of the Commander in Chief! Am I not the commander of this mission?" Van Helsing asks sternly.

Applebaum hangs his head and gets up, relinquishing his seat. "Yessir, you are."

Van Helsing sits down and puts his feet on the desk. It's a power move, but a totally uncomfortable one because all the weapons dangling from him hurt as he sits. He readjusts the arsenal in an effort to get situated. Finally, he settles into the plush chair. "Do what you're good at and fetch me some water!"

Applebaum starts from the room, but is stopped short when there is a knock on a curtained window by the desk. Applebaum goes to the curtain and pulls it back. Outside the jet, the rocket sleigh is there, keeping up with ease. Nimrod is closest to the window. Doodle is driving. He waves at Applebaum.

Applebaum doesn't know how to react. He simply waves back. Doodle holds up a sign, written in colorful ink on cardboard. It reads 'Open the suitcase under your desk!' The exclamation point is drawn like a peppermint stick.

"Who's there?" Van Helsing demands. "Better not be a solicitor at this time of the night!"

President Applebaum tilts his head at him in a questioning gesture, as if Van Helsing's comment on the time is odd and not the fact that they are miles above the surface of the Earth and there is something outside.

Van Helsing catches the expression and agrees it was a peculiar thing to point out. "Or at this altitude!" he adds as if he meant to from the beginning.

Applebaum shrugs. "I don't know who they are, but they're on a convertible rocket sleigh with the top down and the wind isn't even ruffling their hair. They want us to look under the desk."

"Sounds reasonable," Van Helsing says as he does so without hesitation. There is indeed a leather satchel stowed in the leg space. Van Helsing plops it on the desktop and opens it, revealing the big crystal from the base of the Grandfather Clock.

"This better not be some kind of trick or else I'll–" Van Helsing starts, but then Nimrod appears over the crystal on the desk in front of him and grabs him by the throat.

"It's a vampire!" Applebaum bleats.

Doodle appears over the crystal next to Nimrod. He dives on Applebaum, who is making a break for the door.

"Easy big fella!" Doodle says with a devious laugh as he tackles him.

Nimrod slings Van Helsing against a far wall, then leaps over Applebaum and Doodle as they wrestle on the floor. Nimrod snatches up Applebaum by the collar and slings him next to Van Helsing. Then, he barricades them both against the wall. Doodle brushes himself off and walks to them.

"How'd you get your suitcase in here? And what is the meaning of this terrorist attack on my plane?" Applebaum bellows.

Van Helsing looks at him crossly. "It's my plane!"

"We stowed our bag in here before you even lifted off," Doodle states matter-of-factly.

"Impossible! Someone would have seen you!" Applebaum replies.

"I have the ability to be invisible. I also have a rocket ship and a teleportation device, as you have seen," says Doodle, with as much smugness as he's ever shown.

"Who are you? Who do you work for?" Applebaum says, still cowering from Nimrod.

Nimrod answers this time. "We work for ourselves. But you two, you both work for us. Understand?" He finishes with a low, guttural snarl, revealing his short fangs through parted lips.

Van Helsing eyes him and tries to rise up from the floor in defiance. "I don't take orders from vampires!"

With lightning speed, Nimrod clasps Van Helsing's neck again and bares his fangs.

"Oh, I think you'll reconsider that policy," Doodle smirks. "You see, we're forging a new path for ourselves against overbearing taskmasters. We're rebelling against the old ways and you are either part of the rebellion or you are part of the dying regime and, therefore, our enemy."

"Yeah, get it?" Nimrod sneers with seething anger. "We're revolting against our enemies."

Doodle echoes his succinct sentiment with crossed arms. "Exactly. We are absolutely revolting." Van Helsing, still in Nimrod's clutches, glances at Applebaum. They can't help but share a giggle. "What are you laughing at?" Doodle demands.

"Nothing," Van Helsing chokes. "We agree. You're both revolting."

Applebaum bursts out in a hard laugh. Nimrod grabs his throat with his free hand, but Applebaum doesn't lose his smile. "What's so funny?"

"We're trying to tell you, you're right," Applebaum gurgles through Nimrod's tight grip. "You're revolting."

"I know!" Doodle asserts firmly. "That's what we said."

Van Helsing tries not to chuckle, but does. "You're the most revolting characters we've ever met."

Applebaum guffaws, forcing Nimrod to hold him tighter.

"Yes, we are!" Nimrod roars. "Revolting is precisely what we are!"

Van Helsing's and Applebaum's eyes tear up from laughing so hard.

"That's well established," Van Helsing chortles. "You're revolting."

"We said that already," Doodle roars. "Revolting, revolting, revolting!"

And that went on for quite a while and much longer than it ever should have.

Nicholas opens his eyes and tries to lift his head. Holly is by his bed, but her attention is on the TV, which is still covering the rash of attacks around the globe. On the screen, a News Anchor reports on the protests that are breaking out as the public demands action.

"Huge crowds have gathered in the population centers of every country around the world, demanding that their respective governments do something to stop the alleged crimes by vampires against humans," the New Anchor says on the TV.

Nicholas looks at the nearby screen, his eyes glazed and disoriented. Holly notices that he is awake and throws her hand behind his neck, easing his head back to his pillow.

"Easy now, Nicholas. You have to go slow at first so you don't get lightheaded."

Nicholas rests his head. In a hoarse, barely audible whisper, he says, "Ooby. Conclave?"

Holly is surprised that he knows. "Yes. He went to the conclave or something with his creepy friend."

Nicholas shakes his head. "Van Helsing and the Slayers Guild activated?"

Holly dabs his forehead with a damp cloth, mopping away newly formed sweat. "I don't know, but it sounds like a good idea. We need to do something about vampires once and for all."

"No," Nicholas moans.

Holly points at the TV. "Look at what they're doing. There are innocent victims all over the world. Somebody has to stop them and I'm a little astonished that you and Ooby are protecting them."

"They don't do that to humans."

"Of course, they do. They're vampires. You of all people should know the terrible myths and legends surrounding them. History doesn't view them kindly."

"History is wrong. Half-truths and fabrications." Nicholas closes his eyes out of exhaustion. His voice fades. "Like me."

"They're not like you. None of them. That much I know." Holly shakes her head stubbornly.

Nicholas reaches into his pocket with his remaining strength. He withdraws his small, handheld computer device. Without opening his eyes, his fingers run over the buttons until a document pulls up. Before he loses consciousness again, he puts the computer in Holly's hand. She looks at the small screen. It's a manuscript on the shared history of the Pyres and the Saints.

Obviously, Nicholas wants her to read it, so she does.

CHAPTER 23

The History of Saints and Pyres

The Full and Mostly Complete Chronicle of Saints and Pyres: As told by Sarcastacles, a writer and member of the Pyre Council, and the Pyre Consul to the Aegean region - circa 1945 AD

Pyres and Saints were enchanted beings who predated the current age. They were always biologically symbiotic races, meaning they long depended on each other to survive in a hostile world. At least that was the case before the Crystal Comet cataclysm that reversed the Earth's poles and brought the rise of the humans.

Prior to the humans' elevation to the top of the hierarchy of all living things, the two races were engaged in a necessary alliance. The Pyres, for reasons unbeknownst to the scientists of that time, could not produce their own blood within their bodies. The Saints, being of a sweet and innocent nature, could not protect themselves against predatory forces. They did, however, have an innate ability to replace the precious elixir of life within their bodies at a rapid rate.

The Pyres needed the strength and vitality that blood offers every living thing. The Saints needed a proper defense against harm. They found the balance between their needs from each other and that balance lasted for millennia.

Imagine for a moment, a prehistoric landscape. There are active volcanoes in the distance and plant-eating dinosaurs feeding on a grassy savanna. A group of ten Pyres, tall and strong and dressed in animal skins, stand outside of huts, sharpening stakes and spears. It is immediately clear that they are a warrior clan.

Imagine also, a group of twenty Saints, small and meek, dressed in leaf-based clothing, creating a meal of gourds and assorted vegetables outside of huts that are near those of the Pyres. The largest of the Pyres hears a screech in the distance. He motions to the others. Most of the Saints retreat into their domiciles, but two of the Saints hurry to the large Pyre. They extend their arms to him. He nods respectfully and reveals his fangs at full length.

The symbiosis about to be revealed in this scenario, a very true and accurate diegesis, is necessary because the entire race of Pyres have a defect in their long bones. Since blood, like all living organisms, dies over the course of time, the Pyres couldn't produce enough of their own blood to sustain their strength or, over the long term, their lives. However, where they had a physical anomaly in one area, they were blessed in another. They had incisor teeth that were hollow with a complex system of valves deep inside their roots. These teeth were connected directly to their circulatory system.

In the prehistoric landscape, the Pyre bites one Saint's arm. The Saint yelps in pain. This is a demonstration, a very true and accurate one at that, of the Saints part in this dynamic relationship. The Saints overproduced blood, or more precisely, quickly produced whatever blood may have been lost through natural means.

So, on occasion, the Pyres extracted what they needed, such as when a dire physical threat was near. The Saints had strong and vital blood that made the Pyres strong and vital, too. In return for the donations, the Pyres protected the Saints.

In the prehistoric setting, the other Saints emerge from their huts to follow the lead of the first two and offer their arms to the other Pyres. As the large Pyre removes his fangs from the first Saint and then bites into the arm of the second, the other Pyres find partners among the Saints and do the same. Their weaknesses as single races of beings were strengthened when they were together. One race made the other race whole. As if by design, they made each other better.

The prehistoric Pyres finish quickly and grow stronger than they already were. A pack of four Tyrannosaurus Rexes burst from the forests around the savanna and run toward the Saints' huts. The Pyres leap into action and encircle the Saints, stakes and spears at the ready. They battle the T-Rexes with amazing skill and aerial acrobatics. And they win the battle that would have otherwise ended very poorly for both races of beings had they not worked together.

Scenarios exactly like the one described played out over and over through the course of history. However, when the Crystal Comet struck the Earth, it ended the Enchanted Age and sent the Earth into a great upheaval. A new era was born. The humans rose to dominance, and when that happened, the cherished alliance between the Saints and the Pyres had to be broken.

Humans had it all. They were the full realization of the Creator's image of a self-sustaining race. They didn't need a partner race to survive. The thing they lacked, though, was the need for help. And beings who are completely independent have a tendency to turn on all others.

The humans saw the Pyres extracting blood from the Saints and thought it was an act of aggression. Fearing they would be threatened also, and not recognizing the need the Saints and Pyres had for one another, they attacked the Pyres. Since they were stronger than the Pyres and their population grew so fast, the Pyres went into hiding. Eventually, the humans saw the Saints as the weaker race and, predictably, turned on them as well.

Humans, as blessed as they are, have never had a great history with things they don't understand. Where the Pyres and Saints turned what could be perceived as curses upon their races into blessings, the humans unfortunately did the opposite. They turned their blessing of self-sustainability as a race into a curse. Since they didn't require assistance from any other creatures, they crushed the other creatures under their feet in their march of progress toward a civilization greater than the world had ever seen.

In response to the human threat, the Saints' leader at the time moved his kind to Antarctica, where they live to this day. The Pyres, due to being blood poor, elected to stay in warmer climates and tried to find their place in the new order of the world by segregating themselves from the humans. The human population grew too great and too fast, though. Their races were bound to interact. Terrible legends about the Pyres began in ancient times due to their dependency on other beings' blood, but they were relegated to whispers in Black Forests and Swamp Shires. The unflattering tales never reached the greater public psyche at large.

All remained fairly peaceful between the reclusive Pyres and the Humans for many, many millennia. Then, like a lightning strike on a bright, beautiful summer afternoon, the Great Pyre Uprising in the early 15th Century brought the name and legend of vampires to the forefront of society.

The Uprising was led by Vam, a disgruntled Pyre who, empowered as the senior Pyre Council member and the Consul to the Southeastern Region of Europe and the Carpathian Mountain Ring, felt he deserved to lead the Pyres from the darkness of hiding and back to a place of dominance on the world stage. It was rumored that he was influenced and assisted by an aberrant Saint, who kept to the shadows and never revealed his or herself to the outside world. Ooby, the leader of the Saints at that time, could not account for a missing Saint from his tribe, so that rumor remains unsubstantiated to this day.

Vam's rhetoric drew a great many Pyres under his banner and he encouraged an all-out attack on the humans. Until then, the Pyres never knew one simple fact about human blood. It was mightier in its essence than Saint blood. It made the Pyres stronger than ever, but it also tended to make them more aggressive and selfish. It quickly became much preferred by the Pyres who had tried it. And the more they consumed, the more they craved.

Vam's years-long campaign of decimation nearly succeeded until the Slayers Guild was formed by the humans as a solution to the growing problem. The Guild hunted down all the Pyres they could find, and they didn't get the name 'The Slayers Guild' because they imprisoned the Pyres. They did much, much worse.

The entire population of Pyres was at risk. In fact, they were nearly hunted to extinction. Fortunately, at this grave time, an honorable human named Nicholas and his Saintly counterpart, the aforementioned Ooby, stepped in and brokered an accord between the Pyre Elders and some of the human rulers at the time. The Pyres would return to obscurity if the humans would let them live in peace.

The Saints of Eno (Eno was the land beneath the ice in Antarctica where the Saints settled) would continue donating their blood to help the Pyres subsist. As medical practices evolved and the value of blood transfusions became evident, the Pyres offered their services as phlebotomists in clinics around the world. They developed the first blood banks and began soliciting humans for voluntary donations. The Pyres would be responsible for drawing the blood of the humans since they could do so effortlessly and without hurting the donors. They then offered ninety percent of the proceeds to hospitals and blood banks through the donative infrastructure that they organized. In return, they got to keep a tithe for their own survival purposes.

However, the ten percent wasn't enough. The Pyre population grew again and humans rarely donated unless there was a critical need due to one disaster or another. In times of desperate need, the Pyres waived their portion and relinquished all of the donated blood back to the humans to help them through whatever crisis had caused the shortage. Nicholas and Ooby continued to offer donations from the Saints, even though the human blood was stronger.

Nicholas and Ooby did what they could to keep the Pyres 'hydrated', so to speak. For hundreds of years, they regularly held donation parties in Eno, where they would accept donations from the Saints, then distribute the product to the Pyres. It worked to a degree, until the Pyre population outgrew that of the Saints and the donations couldn't keep pace with the demand. The ideal and natural population ratio was two Saints to one Pyre, but that was eventually upended due to the separation of their kinds. The result was that there was too little of a supply for much of recent history and the Pyres began to live in a state of chronic anemia. They became lethargic and tired quickly. They got dizzy with exertion. Their skin grew thin and they sunburned easily. They avoided daylight as much as they could, but this action weakened their eyes until, after many years, sunlight practically blinded them.

The negative legends about the Pyres grew from there. They became pariahs among the humans. The Saints, also weakened from their separation from their cousin beings, and tucked safely away under a glacier in Antarctica, slipped into oblivion as far as the humans were concerned.

Names, quite horrible names, became associated with the Pyres and their peculiar practice of blood acquisition. Vlad Dracula of Transylvania was one. Giure Grando was another. Both were human. From those two unfortunate souls, the names of Pyres everywhere were ruthlessly besmirched. Life for all three kinds were forever altered. At the time, it seemed the relationships between the humans, Pyres, and Saints could never be reconciled.

Though there is more, Holly stops reading Sarcastacles's historical account and breathes deeply. She hangs her head in quiet shame.

"Oh my. Those poor Pyres," she whispers. "I was so mean to Sarcastacles." Nicholas's eyes flutter open again. He's disoriented at first, but quickly focuses on her. She puts her hand on his forehead and continues. "Sarcastacles wrote that the Saints and Pyres existed at the time of the dinosaurs. Have they really been around that long?"

It's hard for Nicholas to speak and he quickly gets short of breath. "Maybe not quite that long. In reality, saber tooth tigers and mastodons were likely the main antagonists of the time instead of T-rexes, but the dynamic between the Saints and Pyres is true."

"Should he take such liberties with history? Fudging some of the facts puts him at risk of discrediting the whole document."

"Sarcastacles may not be human, but he shares our flair for the dramatic," Nicholas chuckles listlessly. "As most reporters of history, he isn't above a bit of poetic license."

Nicholas tries to sit up, but Holly grabs his shoulders and eases him back down. "No. Not yet. Sleep. You still have much healing to do."

"No time," Nicholas mutters. "Peace hangs in the balance. We'll need Lupper and the reindeer. But first," he says as he holds out his hand for the handheld computer. Holly gives it back to him. "Let's see if we have any friends in the area." Nicholas fumbles with the buttons for a moment, then gives a weak smile at something on the screen. "We may be in luck," he says. He tries to sit up again. This time Holly helps him to the side of the bed.

"I'm sure you have friends everywhere," she smiles, holding him under his arms to steady him.

"This guy might help us, but he isn't exactly a friend," he rasps. "I'm sure I'm the last person he'll want to see again."

In central Greece, a picturesque, 800-year-old building is perched on the summit of a rocky precipice 1300 feet above the plains of Meteora. Named the Monastery of the Holy Trinity, it's atop one of numerous sandstone columns and cliffs that overlooks the Peneas Valley. The monastery's cruciform church and the other small buildings of the complex are all constructed of red and brown brick.

Above the monastery, four reindeer fly in a square formation with Nicholas's bed from the clinic hanging between them in the center. Nicholas is flat on the bed and Holly is on her knees, looking over the front edge, as if she were riding a magic carpet. A folded wheelchair is on the back of the bed.

Inside the monastery, there is a beautiful room covered with elaborate, post-Byzantine frescoes on the walls. Saki Crocodile, the Japanese mobster who reluctantly assisted Nicholas the previous Christmas, is standing in front of an open window overlooking the valley. He holds a dish of green ice cream as he takes in the view.

Behind him, a large Japanese henchman named Wallaby sits in a chair, reading a Japanese newspaper's comics pages. The comics are typical American cartoons (i.e., Peanuts, Hagar the Horrible, Calvin and Hobbes) redone anime-style. Since the over-sized Wallaby wishes he were Australian, he wears an Aussie-style jacket and hat and talks with a horribly fake Aussie accent.

Saki asks Wallaby, "Want some of my Mama's ice cream?"

"No thanks, mate," Wallaby answers. "Trying to keep meself lean and mean."

Saki turns and looks at him, as if amused. "Lean and mean, uh?"

"Too right."

Saki turns to the window and savors his ice cream and the view. "I can't imagine a better vacation than this," he muses until the door opens and Nicholas, in the wheelchair, rolls in with Holly pushing him. Saki instantly recognizes him and sighs heavily. "Not you again."

He looks Nicholas over, and quickly notices his casts and bandages. Wallaby drops his paper and jumps up, ready to attack. Saki motions for him to stand down. "Relax, Wallaby. I know him," Saki mutters.

Four big, beefy henchmen slink in behind Nicholas and Holly. They are wrapped in bandages and are all holding ice-packs to various body parts.

Saki, at the sight of his four men and Nicholas's wheelchair, cracks a big grin. "At least my boys did their share of damage to you this time," he says to Nicholas.

"I came here in this," Nicholas says with a glance at his chair.

Saki motions to his injured henchmen. "Then who did that?"

Nicholas nods to Holly behind him, who cracks her knuckles. Saki shakes his head and glares at his henchmen, who all look at the floor or ceiling or walls or anywhere else so as not to meet his stern gaze.

"Okay, Mister Super-Spy, you've started following me even when I'm on holiday. Well, bad news for you, I've no rockets to strap you to this year."

"I don't need your rocket, but its cargo may be of help."

Saki steps toward him. "Yes. I remember you indicated that you knew what was inside my rocket." He runs his hands through his hair and sighs. "I was never able to figure out how you knew."

"I told you, it's my job to know things," Nicholas says. The tone of his voice is still weaker than usual, even though he's trying to project strength. "And I know you're not the ruthless mobster you pretend to be."

Saki shushes Nicholas, then motions his henchmen out the door. They turn and leave. Holly closes the door behind them. Nicholas waits until they're gone before continuing. "Not everyone knows that! Nor should they," Saki steams.

"Your satellite is intended to allow the farmers of Japan to work their fields into the night. With greater light and a longer growing season, their crops will grow faster and yield more. All thanks to you."

"No one can know I'm responsible for that! It'd ruin my highly cultivated, bad reputation!" Saki retreats from Nicholas and goes back to look out the window.

"There are worse things than being known as one who helps others," Nicholas says as he tries to wheel himself toward Saki, but it's an obvious struggle. Holly takes over quickly and pushes him.

"Not in my business," Saki grouses.

"Perhaps, Mister Crocodile, it's time to consider a career change. One that you wouldn't be ashamed to tell your mother about," Nicholas says lowly as his voice begins to fail him.

Saki looks at his dish of ice cream. "Her homemade Wasabi ice cream is my favorite." He shakes his head. "She thinks I'm a legitimate business owner who helps the masses, but she hears the rumors about me. Until now, she refused to believe them. I guess my satellite was meant to reward her faith in me. It was supposed to give me something to prove her belief in me was warranted." He takes a bite of ice cream. "Unfortunately, we've had trouble getting the satellite on-line. I haven't even been able to turn it on yet."

"I have friends who can help with that," Nicholas says. "They can even repair it remotely if you allow them access to your system."

Saki sighs heavily again. "Perhaps," he starts before he's cut short by a loud roar.

The sound of the rocket sleigh drowns him out. It flies by the window in a flash, then veers up toward the roof. On top of the monastery, Doodle lands the sleigh near the four reindeer. Nimrod is beside him, covered head to toe in sun-shielding garments. Both of them wear filtered gas masks. Two of the Vanhelsingers, Garlic Scallopini and Big League, leap out of the back. Doodle gives a smarmy salute to the deer when they see him. The four narrow their eyes because they recognize him and know of his recent betrayals.

Doodle turns to the vampire hunters. "Can you two nincompoops handle this?" His voice is muffled by the mask.

Garlic Scallopini answers with a heavy exhale of a green, stinky fog. "No pppproblem!"

The foul cloud of his breath hits Doodle. Despite the mask, he nearly faints from the stench. "Good gracious, even with the mask," he gags.

Big League and Garlic Scallopini turn away and go through the monastery's rooftop door. Doodle collects himself and tears off his mask. He sneers at the deer and manipulates the joystick, which turns the sleigh toward them, still tied to the bed.

"Dumb deer," Doodle grumps as he punches the gas. The sleigh takes off out of sight as the fire from the engine roars toward the deer. They scatter in different directions, snapping their ties to the bed. The bed ignites and burns in the heat of the flare.

Back in the Fresco Room, Holly and Nicholas are by the window with Saki between them.

"Was that Nimrod and Doodle?" Holly asks.

"Yes, and Big League and Garlic Scallopini were with them," Nicholas answers, his tone low and foreboding.

"Who are they?" she continues.

"Members of the Slayers Guild."

"Slayers Guild? That sounds bad!" Saki pipes in. "And, now, thanks to you two, I have no men to defend me!"

"It is bad," Nicholas returns. "They're both highly skilled fighters. Even at full strength, all of your men would have a hard time with them." Pressing hard on the armrests of the wheelchair, Nicholas struggles to stand on uneasy legs. He loses his strength and plops back down into the seat. Then, he sees a cooler under the chair where Wallaby had been sitting.

"Your ice cream was in that cooler?" he asks Saki.

"Though it is delicious, I don't believe now is the time!" Saki fusses. "How do you keep it frozen?"

Both Saki and Holly reply in unison. "What? Why?"

Holly shakes her head in disbelief. "They're almost here! You can't be worried about his cooler!"

Regardless, Nicholas wheels himself toward it. "Bar the door. If they get in, you all take care of Big League. I'll handle Garlic Scallopini."

Holly balls her fists. "I can take them both!"

"Big League will keep you busy enough, trust me. Send Garlic Scallopini to me, okay? Promise me you won't engage him," Nicholas implores.

"It's just two guys. I'm more powerful than them and Saki's men are here too, so I can't see how–" Holly starts, but Nicholas interrupts.

"You don't want to tangle with Garlic Scallopini. Promise me you won't try."

"Okay, okay," Holly says, a little too curt. "Fine."

In the hall outside the Fresco Room, Big League steps up to the closed door with Garlic Scallopini behind him. He knocks with the end of his bat. "Knock, knock, little piggies!" he says with a chuckle. Garlic Scallopini puts his ear to the door.

In the Fresco Room, Holly has her ear to her side of the door. Saki and Wallaby and the other henchmen, injured though they are, stand behind her. "Who is it?" Holly asks through the door.

From the other side, Big League says, "Let's us in or else."

Saki nudges Holly out of the way and leans against the door. "Or else what?" he barks. He directs his men to be ready. The group strike fighting stances right behind him.

Outside the room, Garlic Scallopini kneels down and puts his mouth to the crack under the door. "Or I'll hhhhuff and I'll ppppuff," Garlic Scallopini says with heavy emphasis on the H and the P.

Inside the room, a thick, green fog seeps from under the door and rises to Saki's face. He gives a horrid expression before falling over backwards. The fog reaches the henchmen, too. They all pass out, side by side. Holly and Wallaby scamper from the door and escape the creeping tendrils of the fog.

"What the heck is that?" Holly groans.

Outside the door, Big League draws back his bat. "And I'll bash your door down!" he bloviates. "Like this!" He pounds the door mightily, blasting it to bits. Big League darts into the Fresco Room and leaps over the unconscious bodies of Saki and his henchmen. He goes right after Wallaby. Garlic Scallopini runs in and looks at Holly.

"Where's the Wonderworker?" he says, holding back, careful not to breathe out his wretched stink. Holly backs up against the wall and points to another door. Garlic takes the cue and runs through it as Big League engages Wallaby, bat reared back.

"Batter up!" Big League screeches.

Wallaby, mimicking Mick Dundee from a famous movie in the 1980s, says, "That's not a bat." He pulls a big, wide bat from behind him. "That's a bat."

He swings at Big League, who ducks. Big League jabs Wallaby in his soft belly with the tip of his weapon. Wallaby wails as he drops his bat, grabs his stomach with both hands, and falls. Big League turns to Holly, who is still against a far wall.

"He was too easy. Wanna step up to the plate, little lady?"

Holly smiles, inviting his charge. Big League runs toward her, bat over his head. When he swings, Holly dodges the blow and pivots around behind him. She grabs the bat on his follow through, and as he swings it around to rear it back again, she hangs on and swings with it.

Big League pulls the bat over his head. He's so strong that he doesn't even notice Holly's extra weight clinging to it. He searches for Holly, who is no longer right in front of him, but over his head, clutching the bat like a Koala Bear on a tree limb.

She leaps off the bat and onto Big League's back, reaching around his neck with a tight headlock. Big League swings the bat maniacally, but Holly holds on, seemingly enjoying the fight. He bucks like a bull, then turns his back to the wall. He slams Holly into it several times, which loosens her grip. He reaches over his shoulder and grabs her head and flips her. She lands on the floor in front of him, but she scrambles from under him before he can deliver a downward blow with the bat. She leaps to her feet and engages him with a flurry of high kicks and punches. He blocks her, but she kicks his bat away, sending it flying across the room.

"You like to play the chin music, do ya, lady? Well, how do you like cheese at the knees?" Big League spins low and deftly foot sweeps Holly, a spectacular feat for a man of his immense size. "That's some mighty fine low cheddar!"

She goes flat to her back. He tries to bring a heel-kick down on her, but she moves her head just in time. She rolls to her feet and executes a perfect jump-spinning back kick that connects right in the middle of his chest. He staggers back a few feet, hurt and breathless.

She swarms him with a new flurry of kicks and punches. Big League weathers the storm with sharp blocks, but a few of her blows get through and wallop him in the face. She has him on the retreat until he gathers his strength and pours it all into a single haymaker. It collides with her cheek and spins her across the room.

"You got moxie, missy, but it's back to the dugout with you!" Big League brags. "Spend a little more time in the batting cages and maybe you can try again later."

While Holly is reeling, Big League retrieves his bat from the floor. He runs at Holly and swings it hard, slamming her in the back. She yelps and staggers all the way across the room.

Garlic Scallopini enters the colorful, golden space known as the Nativity Room. It has high ceilings and ornate paintings and murals on the walls, many of which are of Mary and Baby Jesus. There's a podium with candelabras on each side. Potted Poinsettias are placed throughout the room. He looks around until he sees Nicholas in his wheelchair near the podium, head hanging as if he's asleep. A smoking, corncob pipe rests in his hand. Garlic Scallopini walks toward him, chuckling.

"I entered this room expecting a great warrior and an opponent worthy of my skill set. Instead, I find you, brokedown and dilapidated. Not such a worker of wonders today, eh?" he says, his boisterous voice echoing in the room.

Nicholas lifts his head, weary and listless. "Garlic Scallopini, I presume."

Garlic Scallopini nods with pride. "'Tis I indeed. I see you've heard of me?"

Nicholas looks at him, but his eyelids are heavy, as if they may fall closed at any moment. "Your name is feared by even the mightiest of fighters. I hoped I would never meet you in combat." Garlic Scallopini grins wide, revealing black and rancid teeth. He gets closer, only a few feet from Nicholas now. When Nicholas speaks again, his voice is feeble. "You know chronic halitosis is a sign of tooth decay and gum disease, both of which can be indicative of other, more serious health problems."

"Flattery won't help you, I'm afraid," Garlic Scallopini says. "And your infirmed state won't win you any mercy."

"I don't want mercy. I want your finest effort. I've always wondered if I could withstand you at your best." Nicholas puts the pipe in his mouth. The smoke boils forth from the bowl.

Garlic Scallopini draws in a deep breath, then lets it out in a prolonged, horrid exhale, right in Nicholas's face as he says, "With ppppleasure." Garlic Scallopini's breath is a green fog and it encircles Nicholas's face and head like a cloud. Nicholas closes his eyes.

When the fog dissipates, Nicholas looks at Garlic Scallopini and grins around the pipe.

Garlic Scallopini is taken aback that his breath had no effect on Nicholas whatsoever. "What? How?" he stammers.

"Did you have gingerbread lately? I'm getting a hint of gingerbread in there." Nicholas puffs the pipe, sending white smoke upwards in a cloud as thick as Garlic Scallopini's breath.

Garlic Scallopini is incensed. "Absolutely not!" He whips off his chef's hat. He pulls a spoon and a covered dish from the hat. Inside the dish is a slurry of blended grossness. Nicholas peeks inside the bowl, but Garlic Scallopini turns so he can't see it.

"Go ahead and reload. I'll wait," Nicholas whispers.

Garlic Scallopini digs into the bowl with the spoon and takes several heaping bites. He turns back to Nicholas, smiling again. "Now you get my special blend. Cat food, cigarette ash, vinegar, anchovies, coffee grounds, all mixed together in a hearty caper pesto."

Nicholas waves him in. Garlic Scallopini belches a big one, holds it in his mouth, swishes it around for a moment, then blows it at Nicholas. The fog, more gray than green this time, swarms Nicholas's face. Again, he smiles.

"Have you chewed on eucalyptus leaves? Or eaten a menthol cough drop? A warm buttery cinnamon roll, perhaps?" Nicholas says in a slightly teasing tone. Garlic Scallopini stomps his foot. He digs another bowl from his hat. "Maybe you need to hydrate." Nicholas reaches by his side in the wheelchair and retrieves a bottle of water. "The extra moisture will really make the stink stick."

Garlic Scallopini rips the bottle from Nicholas's hands and drinks it down in a single slug. He pitches the empty bottle over his shoulder, then stirs the bowl. "No one can withstand my secret weapon. A minced fish head, cream of tartar, pepperoni, Limburger cheese, and black licorice!"

He stirs the new bowl violently, then takes a huge bite, rolls the mess around in his mouth, then does a few stomach undulations. Finally, he rumbles up a burp from way down deep, and blows it at Nicholas, who wafts the cloud to him, as if sniffing a fine perfume.

"Pumpkin spice. That's what it is. I love pumpkin spice this time of year."

Garlic Scallopini is astounded. He pulls out a third bowl. "My international blend then. Not even the most olfactory-impaired can withstand it. Kim-chi, Muenster cheese, squid sashimi, sauerkraut, Turkish espresso, and a Cuban cigar!"

He takes a bite, then frowns, hardly able to stand it himself. He smacks his lips bitterly. "Oh darn. It seems I've forgotten the Cuban cigar. It's not the same without it," he complains.

Nicholas offers him his pipe, which pours forth with smoke. "Please, help yourself. It isn't Cuban tobacco, but this might do in a pinch."

Garlic Scallopini snatches it from him. "It surely makes a hearty smog so it must be good."

"Smoke all you want. As I said, I want your best effort," Nicholas says.

Garlic Scallopini draws deep on the pipe, not only taking in the smoke that is boiling from it, but also all that has escaped the bowl and is floating within a foot of it. He holds it in. His eyes widen and his face turns blue.

"Smoking is terrible for you, by the way," Nicholas says. "Especially if it's dried ice. Just another reason why you shouldn't inhale." Nicholas gives him a sympathetic smile.

Inhaling wasn't a problem, but exhaling absolutely is. Garlic Scallopini's mouth is frozen by the boiling dry ice, as is his throat all the way to his lungs, thanks to the water he so recently slugged. When he finally does manage to breath out, it's a solid plume of brown-tinted frost.

Nicholas leans forward in his chair, breaks the breathsicle from Garlic Scallopini's lips, and pokes him in the chest with a single finger. Garlic Scallopini falls like a board to his back, his eyes crossed.

Nicholas snorts out through his nose and a small, round peppermint shoots out of each nostril. He drops them in Garlic Scallopini's chef's hat. Garlic Scallopini moans enough to show that he is alive.

"You need to start flossing every day, Garlic." Nicholas says as he wheels himself toward the door. "And be very liberal with the toothpaste when brushing."

He grabs a potted Poinsettia and puts it in his lap as he exits the room.

In the Fresco Room, Holly holds Big League in a side headlock and rams his head into the wall. Big League rebounds and swings his bat. She ducks under it and gives him a stiff uppercut that sends him plopping ungracefully to the floor. Holly dives for Wallaby's large, discarded bat. She comes up with it just in time to block an attack by Big League. She quickly leaps over him.

Big League turns around to follow her, but Holly dives and slides between his legs, coming up behind him again. She swings the bat over her head and brings it down with all her might toward the back of Big League's head. He raises his bat over his head, an end in each hand, and blocks the blow just in time. He spins toward her yet again.

"Nice try," he sneers. "You almost had yourself a dinger, sweetheart,"

She brings the bat back down low, then upward, hitting him squarely between the legs.

"There's your dinger," she quips back. "Sweetheart."

Big League drops his bat, holds his hands to the area of impact, and falls over in agony. Nicholas enters from the back door that leads to the Nativity Room. He raises an inquiring eyebrow at Holly, who shrugs.

Saki Crocodile and his men finally regain consciousness and slowly get to their feet. Saki shakes himself to full alertness. He points at Big League, still wallowing on the floor, clutching his groin.

To his groggy men, he says, "Tie him up."

"The other one is in the next room," Nicholas says listlessly, fully exhausted.

"This Slayers Guild of which these two are a part? There are more?" Saki asks, as his men swarm Big League. Nicholas nods. "And my satellite will help you defeat them?"

With another nod, Nicholas says, "It just might save the world."

"Saving the world is good Bushido," Saki muses. "It would please my mother and undo much of my bad Karma from my actions in years past."

"You have access to heavy construction equipment, don't you?" Nicholas asks.

"I have access to anything I need to get a job done," Saki says with a dismissive wave of his hand. "What do you want? Bulldozer? Backhoe?"

"Well, I was thinking of something on a little larger scale than that," Nicholas returns. Holly steps by his side and puts her hand on his shoulder.

"You name it, I'll get it," Saki says. Then, he looks at Holly. "You're a pretty solid asset in a fight. Do you work for the same agency as Nicholas?"

"No," she shrugs. "I'm a free agent. Though, if he'd like to consider this as my audition, I might break down and join him."

Nicholas pats her hand and looks up at her. "Saki Crocodile, this is Miss Siltoe."

"You can call me Holly," she says as she extends a hand to Saki. They shake, then she returns her attention to Nicholas with a special eye on the Poinsettia. "So, do you always roll around with a potted plant in your lap?"

Nicholas, as if he'd forgotten, grabs it and thrusts it up toward her. "Sorry, but roses were in short supply."

She takes the plant with a grateful smile. "They're beautiful. Thank you so much." Holly leans over and kisses the top of Nicholas's head. He blushes in a way that Saki and his henchmen cannot miss.

Nestled in the foothills of the Carpathian Mountains, Vam Castle is built of the Gothic-style with Renaissance elements, but recent neglect has allowed the building to show its age of over 600 years. Despite falling into some cosmetic disrepair, it still has tall and strong defense towers, a wide, interior courtyard, and a sturdy bridge which traverses a deep moat encircling the fortress. The castle is a large, imposing structure with tall and colorful roofs, ramparts, and parapets. It looks down on an ancient, rundown village which has also suffered from ages of deterioration.

Vam Castle's myriad roofs and white brick walls reflect the sun's fading light as if it were a theater on Broadway. Sarcastacles and Ooby, wearing white robes with the hoods over their heads, enter the castle's inner courtyard, hands folded solemnly in front of them. Another group of tall, robed Pyre Elders, heads down, enter the courtyard from the other side. The group of ten meets Ooby and Sarcastacles in the center.

The leader of the Pyre Elders, Idiotis, pale and thin like Sarcastacles, looks up so that his grim face is barely visible. Next to him, Dorkamemnon does the same. Other notable Elders are Jerkus McGerkis and Moronicon. Sarcastacles meets their reverent gaze with one of his own.

"Idiotis," he says with a nod. "Dorkamemnon."

The duo answer in unison. "Sarcastacles."

Dorkamemnon continues. "You have summoned us?"

"Yes. We have a grave matter to discuss," Sarcastacles answers.

"Your request for a Pyre Summit has been approved," Idiotis advises. "You may call the meeting to order."

"Thank you," Sarcastacles says with a respectful half-bow. He raises his head and claps once. "Let the conclave begin!"

The eight Elders behind Idiotis and Dorkamemnon cheer as they all drop their robes. Jerkus McGerkis, holding an accordion and wearing lederhosen beneath his covering, launches into a lively Polka tune. They all begin dancing about with high kicks and claps, including Ooby, who has clearly been through a conclave or two in his time.

After a moment of unfettered fun from everyone in the group, Ooby throws up his hands to stop the festivities. "Whoa! Whoa!"

The group pauses as the music halts. The Pyre Elders and Sarcastacles look at him as if he popped a child's balloon. "Guys, I'm sorry to break conclave protocol, but we have a serious matter on our hands! There is trouble on the horizon!"

As if synchronized, night darkens the sky completely. A heavy fog rolls in across the village and sweeps over and around the castle. The twelve look up at the sudden change.

"Your words still hold power with the mists, Ooby," Dorkamemnon says, in awe.

"Not my words, I'm afraid. A Transylvanian coincidence," Ooby says, looking overhead.

Idiotis muses, "The fine Romanian evenings, known for sudden fog and eerie ambiance." He looks at the Elders around him and speaks again in an intentionally ominous and spooky voice, like a grandfather telling ghost stories around a fire. "What lurks in the fog? The creepy, creepy fog?"

The other nine Elders laugh off his joke, even though a few of them can't help but take a quick look behind them.

Sarcastacles snaps back to business. "Ooby is right. There is much to report. A plot is afoot that threatens our alliance with the humans. If a bit of fog scares you, imagine a world where the humans turn on us again."

They all grab hands and form a circle as Jerkus's accordion moans a sad melody.

"We know of your concerns," Dorkamemnon laments. "Young Nimrod has betrayed us."

"As has one of my Saints," Ooby adds. "We must seek an immediate resolution before an unjust attack on the Pyres is perpetrated by the Slayer's Guild."

From the top of a turret overlooking the courtyard, Nimrod's laugh rings out. They all turn. He is squatting on the steep roof of the turret, also wearing a ceremonial robe.

"The attack already happened, my Elders," Nimrod yells down to them. "Five hundred years ago when my Uncle Vam was vilified and all the Pyres were forced into the servitude of the humans!"

Ooby steps to the front of the group toward Nimrod. "Vam was hurting innocents in his quest for absolute power! He didn't care about the Pyres! He only cared about becoming their king!"

"He was showing us the truth!" Nimrod bellows as he crawls around the roof of the turret like a spider. "We are the most powerful beings ever created, but we have submitted to the humans and we have been forced to live in their shadows!" Nimrod stops and stands on the edge of the turret's roof. He is taller than he's ever been. He drops his hood. His pinkish eyes are now a glistening red, and his pale skin has lost much of its pallor. He drops his robe. He's shirtless and bursting with strong, powerful muscles. When he smiles widely, his fangs are at full length, making him a frightful sight.

Sarcastacles gasps at Nimrod's metamorphosis, but then steps forward by Ooby. "It was the Creator's will that we take our place where we are!"

Nimrod is not swayed. "You are the creator, Sarcastacles, along with Nicholas and Ooby! The three of you are the creators of Pyre enslavement!"

Behind him, the rocket sleigh rises slowly from behind the turret with Doodle driving. He pulls to Nimrod's side. "A bit of a crisis and you all gather in the same spot like you have for hundreds of years," he laughs. "A place that once belonged to you and your kind, but was stripped from you by Vam and now bears his name! Every human map calls this Vam Castle! How does that feel, having your ancestral home named after him?" He throws his head back in a defiant guffaw. "And let me guess! You started with a Polka dance!" He laughs again with such arrogance it makes Ooby wince. "I told you, Ooby, predictability is your downfall."

Ooby grows irate. "That is quite enough, Doodle! You stop this madness right now, young Saint!"

Doodle rockets the sleigh halfway into the courtyard and hovers ten feet over Ooby. He looks past him, as if ignoring him, to address the ten Elders. "The Saints and Pyres can reclaim what is rightfully ours! Join us and we'll take you to the heights of power!"

The Elders all look at each other. Sarcastacles notices that they don't immediately refute Doodle. *Are they seriously considering it*, he wonders. He interrupts quickly before they think too long about it. "Vam was wrong and so are these two!"

The Elders are jolted from their momentary stupor. Dorkamemnon voices his strong agreement. "Sarcastacles is right, gang. Vam was deranged. We were nearly wiped out because of him."

Nimrod seethes as he leaps from the turret to the front of the rocket sleigh hovering over the courtyard. It dips under his weight, but he jumps again and lands right in front of Sarcastacles in a low squat. He comes up fast and backhands Sarcastacles in the chin. The blow sends him flying across the courtyard and into a side wall of the castle.

Ooby makes a quick move for Nimrod, but Doodle steers the sleigh down and plows into him from the side, sending him flying as well. Ooby lands against the wall next to Sarcastacles. Both are unconscious.

"Doodle and I can return the Pyres to the top of the food chain," Nimrod growls. "Refuse us and..." He motions to the unconscious pair against the far wall. "Well, don't refuse us."

There isn't a moment of hesitation this time. The Elders line up and assume fighting stances. "Though we're weakened and you're at full strength, we still outnumber you ten to one," Idiotis says to Nimrod.

Doodle squares the sleigh next to Nimrod and hovers there. "You're assuming I don't count?"

Dorkamemnon says, "Not in this fight, little fiend."

Behind them, Van Helsing walks through a courtyard entrance. He totes a Gatlin-style gun, loaded with wooden stakes. "Stake through the heart. Stake through the heart," he sings in a childish tune. "All my life, I've heard the only way to end one of you pests is with a stake through the heart."

Idiotis turns to Nimrod. "You brought a Slayer?"

Van Helsing keeps on. "But Nimrod tells me a stake through the stomach, back, or big toe will do the job just fine." Van Helsing levels the gun on Idiotis.

Up on the ramparts surrounding the courtyard, the remaining Van-helsingers (Rip Tide, Tumbleweed, Tiddlywink, and Powder Keg) stand up, each with a stake gun. President Applebaum is also there. He's dressed in a Marine uniform and a red beret and he's holding a stake gun too, but his is smaller than the other Vanhelsingers' guns.

Ooby, still against the wall, but stirring from unconsciousness, shakes his head. When he sees the President, he can't believe his eyes, perhaps hoping he is suffering from delirium due to a concussion. "President Applebaum?" he mutters before passing out again.

From the rampart, the President nods his head. "Nope. Not anymore. My name is Applebottom. General Applebottom." He cocks his weapon for dramatic purposes.

Van Helsing turns and looks up at him with a raised eyebrow. "General?"

Applebaum shrugs. "Sargent?" Van Helsing shakes his head. "Corporal?" he continues sheepishly, but gets a negative response from Van Helsing again. "Private? Can I at least be a Private?" Van Helsing thinks for a moment, then gives him a slight nod. "My name is Applebottom," says Applebaum, now with growing confidence. "Private Applebottom!" He cocks the weapon again for more dramatic effect, but the already loaded stake pops from the chamber and clatters across the walkway.

Van Helsing rolls his eyes and turns back to the Elders. "He's a trainee. Don't let his ineptitude allow you to think the rest of us aren't highly capable." Over his shoulder, he shouts to his team. "Vanhelsingers, show 'em we mean business!"

The Vanhelsingers aim their weapons and shoot. The wooden tent stakes stick into the grooves of the stones around the Elders' feet, forming a circle of spikes. The Elders immediately raise their hands in surrender.

Vam Castle's dungeon is made of stone and is as damp and dank as any self-respecting dungeon should be. The cell holding the ten Elders, Sarcastacles, and Ooby is small and dark. The only light flickers from a single torch outside the heavy steel door, which has a small, barred window.

Sarcastacles slowly awakens. Out of reflex, he reaches up and holds his aching chin. Next to him, Ooby, more awake, but also holding his head, leans heavily against the wall. Dorkamemnon, Idiotis, and the other Elders are standing over them, looking down at them anxiously.

Idiotis is the first to speak. "Oh, goody, you're awake. Any ideas on what we should do now?"

Ooby, still dazed, stirs slowly, then sits bolt upright when he realizes they're in a jail cell. "We're in a dungeon?" he laments. Sarcastacles takes a bit longer to orient himself.

Jerkus McGerkis plays a few bars of a sad, pathetic song on his accordion. Ooby stands and feels along the stone wall for a way out.

"How did this happen?" Sarcastacles whispers, the sound of his own voice hurting his head even more. "Surely the ten of you could defeat one Pyre and one Saint."

"They brought Slayers," Dorkamemnon whines. "And they brought fancy guns that shoot wooden stakes!" His suddenly loud voice echoes in the small cell.

Sarcastacles winces at the noise. "So? Stakes don't hurt us any more than anything else."

Idiotis is quick to rebuke him. "They were rough and shoddy made stakes, though, sure to leave plenty of splinters! Trust me, you don't want one of them in your big toe!"

"Yeah!" Dorkamemnon agrees. "And that's not us just spouting off. They literally threatened to shoot us in the big toes! Who does that except crazed maniacs?"

Ooby, with growing urgency, pushes against the steel door. "Help me push. If we all work together, we might be able to get through."

In the small, barred window, Nimrod appears. "You're wasting your time. This door is reinforced and as strong as a bank vault. You're not going anywhere."

"Nimrod," Sarcastacles gripes from the floor. "Just what do you think you're doing? Truly, what's the meaning of this whole ordeal?"

Nimrod finds Sarcastacles in the darkness and peers at him sharply. "Fifty or more Pyres are coming to this castle as we speak in response to a distress signal from the conclave. When they get here, they'll be told of the unfortunate termination of their Elders at the hands of the Slayers Guild. They'll be so angry, they'll demand a king who will lead them into righteous battle against the humans."

Ooby peers up through the bars at Nimrod. "You attacked people so they'd retaliate against the Pyres so the Pyres would turn on the humans?"

Nimrod adds extra snide to his reply. "It's called a black flag operation and world governments use them all the time to sway public opinion!"

From somewhere beyond the door, Doodle's voice chimes in. "False flag, you numbskull! It was a false flag operation!" The top of Doodle's head appears in the window and is barely visible. "Look what the humans have done to the Pyres. Your names, once heralded among your kind as symbols of great strength and intelligence..." He jumps midsentence so that his face is beside Nimrod's but only for a split second. "Have been reduced to derogatory epithets in the human lexicon."

Nimrod nods. "Yeah. They've made mockeries of our names."

"Nimrod, I can't see," Doodle says from below the window. "A little help."

Nimrod looks down, then squats out of sight of the captives in the dungeon. The Elders and Sarcastacles and Ooby can hear their conversation below the window.

"You want on my shoulders?" Nimrod whispers.

"No. Just get down on all fours. I'll stand on your back," Doodle says.

"But I'll get my pants dirty," Nimrod argues.

"Seriously? You can get other pants."

"No, I can't," Nimrod says as he continues his hushed protest. "Nicholas's blood made me outgrow my old ones. Now, I'm in a bigger size and bigger sizes are way more expensive."

Ooby and Sarcastacles look at each other and shake their heads at the two youngsters' silly and superficial argument. After a prolonged moment of quiet, they hear the sound of a sweeping broom.

"Jeez. How's that? Happy?" Doodle whispers.

"Much better," Nimrod returns. "Was that so hard?"

Doodle's face finally appears fully in the barred window. He acts as if no time has passed since he was addressing his captives nearly a whole minute before. "I read the ancient texts of the mighty Pyre heroes! Idiotis, you're named after your great grandfather, a thinker of the highest order. Jerkus McGerkis and Moronicon are both descendants of the very Pyre who led your kind out of the caves at the beginning of the Enchanted Age. Dorkamemnon the Original was the first to map the stars." Each Elder nods and swells with pride as Doodle names him. "Even Nimrod was the name of a fierce hunter of the thunder rhinos!" Doodle continues. "Do the humans think of glory when they hear any of your names now?" The Elders slump because they know what Doodle says is true. "No! They mock you! Jerk, moron, dork, idiot! Your family names are shamed!"

From under the window, Nimrod's voice is heard again. "Don't forget Arisnotle and Boogermedes."

Doodle shakes his head slowly as he looks from one Elder to the next. "Who could forget Arisnotle and Boogermedes?"

Sarcastacles runs to the window and grabs the bars right in front of Doodle's face. The sudden action startles Doodle, and he nearly falls off of Nimrod's back, but he catches his balance and leans toward the bars to meet Sarcastacles eye to eye.

"Vam did that! He demonized us and our names to the humans in his effort to overtake us!" rebukes Sarcastacles.

"Sarcastacles, I guess your name escaped unfazed," Doodle says with such heavy sarcasm that it's clear he's pointing out that 'sarcastic' has come to mean something less than flattering in the English language.

Ooby runs to Sarcastacles's side and points up at the window, his finger just inches from Doodle's face. "It isn't even Nimrod doing this, is it, Doodle? It's you! It's all you!"

Doodle has to get close to the bars to see him well below the window, but he acts like he can't. "What? Who said that? Whose finger is this?" He laughs as he mocks Ooby. "Again, I am above you, Ooby."

Ooby pats Sarcastacles shoulder. "Do you mind?"

Sarcastacles follows Ooby's eyes as he looks down. Sarcastacles doesn't get it. Ooby then nods his head toward the floor.

"What?" Sarcastacles says, finally getting what Ooby is suggesting. "Really? On the floor?"

"Yes," Ooby whispers. "Just for a second."

"I would, but, you know, the floor on this side of the door is no cleaner than what is on their side, so..."

"Sarcastacles!" Ooby shouts. Sarcastacles drops to all fours and Ooby leaps on his back. Only the bars in the window separate his and Doodle's faces.

"You're the one who wants to take over the world! You've erred, young Saint, and you will pay dearly for orchestrating this!"

"Says the twerp in a jail cell!" Doodle yells in his face.

Nine of the Pyre Elders gasp and turn quickly to the last Elder, the sole female of the group. Her face falls. "Pay no attention to him, Twerpitina," Moronicon soothes. "He's just being mean."

"Look me in the eye, Doodle, so I can see into the depths of your sullied soul!" Ooby commands, his face still inches from Doodle's, but deep red with fury.

"Look me in the eye and see what you have made!" Doodle yells back. Just then, a bat zips by Doodle's head and through the barred window. Doodle panics and drops below the window with a yelp.

"Bug!" he screeches. "Big bug!"

The bat flutters about the cell, over the heads of the Elders. Moronicon sticks out a finger and the bat lands on it. It has Nicholas's crystal necklace in its mouth. Ooby leaps from Sarcastacles's back and goes to it. The bat drops the necklace into his palm. Ooby puts his finger to his lips to signal the others to keep quiet.

Outside the window in the door, Doodle and Nimrod are arguing again.

"Was it a humbug?" Nimrod asks.

"I don't know, but it was big and fast! Get back down on your hands and knees," Doodle says.

"With a humbug on the loose? I don't think so!"

"I said I didn't know if it was a humbug! Get back down!"

Ooby puts the necklace over his head as the Elders form a tight circle, hands together. Ooby touches the crystal and they all disappear. Doodle's face reappears in the window when he climbs back up on Nimrod's back.

"I've told you before, Ooby, I'm smarter than you and I can do anything you–" Doodle sees the cell is empty. His face contorts with rage as he grips the bars in angry fists. "Nicholas!"

From below, Nimrod says, "The humbug's name is Nicholas?"

Doodle rolls his eyes. "No! The humbug's name isn't...." He leaps off Nimrod's back. "Never mind. It's pointless to try to explain!" Doodle storms away. "How did I ever encumber myself with you anyway?"

CHAPTER 30

How Resplendent Doodle Met Daft Nimrod

(And subsequently became encumbered with him)

All stories have a beginning. Just as the stories of the Pyres and Saints and Nicholas and Holly had starting points, so too did Doodle's and Nimrod's. It didn't begin with Doodle making cold calls from a radio aboard a Pirate Ship and Nimrod coincidentally hearing him and responding though. No, their story went back much further than that.

In fact, Doodle had fixed Captain Dagger's radio with the solitary intent of contacting Nimrod. The two were of like mind about authority figures. They had known that much since their initial introduction, not that their earliest conversation with each other had been any kind of indicator of such a thing.

Nimrod had spoken first. "I'm a ham radio enthusiast. Do you like ham radios?"

Doodle had looked at Nimrod like he had a screw loose and Doodle could see it. "No. I don't think I could care one iota less about ham radios," Doodle had replied. He knew right away he was older than Nimrod, even though Nimrod was taller.

"They're not really made of ham, you know," Nimrod had kept on. "Which was disappointing at first, but it turns out, I liked them anyway.

You can communicate really long distances with people you don't even know. And without wires and stuff."

It really wasn't a conversation that Doodle had engaged in, but it would come back to him all those years later when he was on the Pirate Ship and needed an ally to help him hatch his nefarious plot to pit the Pyres against the humans and upset an unfair peace. Truthfully, he found Nimrod to be a bit of a bore at the start. Doodle was, after all, over two hundred years old at that time, which roughly equals middle teens in human years, which is to say, he knew a lot. However, Nimrod was under a hundred, maybe eight or nine in human equivalency, and was a bit on the doltish side. A better mental fit, in Doodle's opinion, for that much younger suck-up Lupper, who was a mere one hundred and ten and still a gibbering fool (not that he still wasn't a fool now, just not as gibbery).

Nimrod and Lupper would have hit it off just fine, Doodle surmised, had they met. But Lupper hadn't gone to Europe with Nicholas and Ooby on that trip. Doodle had. And that's because Ooby had recognized Doodle's inherent brilliance and burgeoning genius at an early age and sought to encourage his growth, or at least that's what Ooby always claimed. Doodle figured it was the opposite. Yes, Ooby recognized Doodle's intelligence maybe, but Ooby was threatened by it more than anything. Ooby would take Doodle on missions and whatnot with the sole purpose of proving that he, Ooby, was the supreme boss in charge.

Fine, Doodle thought back then when the idea was rolling over in his mind and Nimrod was going on and on about pork-product radios or some such childish nonsense. *You're the big, almighty, super-important leader, Ooby. For now.*

It's important to know the reason they went on that particular trip to Europe. It was Krakow or Bruges, if Doodle remembered correctly. Sometime in the 1940s. Going to Europe wasn't a big deal, even then, with the Time Bender and the wormhole-creating crystals (Ooby insisted on calling them space-time conduits, but everyone knew they were wormholes). The trio had gone there for a summit of sorts. Not quite a conclave, but close. Ooby and Nicholas had to meet with Sarcastacles, Twerpitina, and Moronicon to discuss a rather pressing matter (weren't they always?). The humans were at war or something along those lines and, like a bunch of Idiotises, the group insisted on meeting right in the middle of the wreckage of whatever bombed out city they were in.

Nimrod had come with Sarcastacles, because (for some ridiculous reason that wasn't readily apparent to Doodle), he was considered a smart and up-and-coming Pyre. *Sure. Whatever.* It was more likely that Sarcastacles, like Ooby, just wanted to show off in front of Nimrod.

Doodle and Nimrod had sat in on the proceedings at first, but were excused after a while when things got heated. It was Nicholas who got so mad. It seemed he wanted to do something to stop the war or whatever. He was proposing some kind of drastic intervention, but it was, of course, dismissed by Ooby.

"You know we can't interfere with the humans in something like this!" Ooby had preached in his bolstering way. "They must be left to navigate these waters on their own. Things such as this are a plague to every group of beings on their path to the destiny the Creator has set for them. He has ordained it and we must let it take its course as He sees fit, no matter how painful it is to watch." *The Creator.* Doodle noticed Ooby brought Him up every time he was trying to force Nicholas (and the Saints for that matter) to think a certain way. "It's outside our mission."

"Our mission is to save the innocents!" Nicholas had said with great and fiery passion. "And innocents are suffering!"

Doodle liked Nicholas's intensity, but he didn't show it near enough. If he was a little more ardent in his rare disagreements with Ooby, he might have had things go his way more often. Or so Doodle figured. *He could certainly beat Ooby up if he wanted. So why didn't he?*

That's when Moronicon weighed in. "We agree with Ooby, Nicholas. I know it pains you to stand by when everything in you demands action, but we can't give in to the temptation of steering humankind's fate." He probably only agreed with Ooby because of the guilt Ooby garnered with the Creator comment. *He really does go to that well a little too much.*

Nicholas really went off on a tirade then. "It's no one's will that children suffer!" *Go, Nicholas. Give it to them good.*

The Pyres and Ooby should have cowered at Nicholas's frightful outburst, but they didn't. They just ganged up on him. Sarcastacles started it.

"It's how we've done these things since the beginning," he had said, sounding a bit too much like Ooby to be likeable. "We only fight the small fights."

"To small effect, but we stand by and watch the big fights when the cost is insurmountable!" Nicholas could really be angry when he wanted to be. Being around Ooby all the time could do that.

"That is a fight for the humans to work through, Nicholas," Twerpitina weighed in. As the lone female Pyre amongst the Elders, one would have thought she would have been the most empathetic and might have sided with Nicholas on the subject of suffering children. Alas, she was proving to be as calloused as the others. "And they have a One Horn as we all do," she added. "If he wanted to act, now would be the time."

Oh, yes. The One Horns. It would take volumes of books to tell their tales, or so Ooby had always said. Doodle knew enough about them to know it really wasn't all that hard to figure. The One Horns, or unicorns or whatever, were guides or sorts, meant to be stewards of their given beings. In essence, they were overseers, installed by the Creator (Ooby's words, Doodle would be sure to point out if he were ever asked) to guide their entrusted beings over the tortuous terrain of existence.

Enlitas was the One Horn for the Saints. Excitas was for the Pyres. Their magic (if one wanted to call it that) was that they could influence the hearts of their beings or, as Ooby claimed, influence the subconscious that permeated their beings as a whole. They were meant to guide their beings to their fullest, brightest existence. The Sea Beasts had their own One Horn. So did the Sky Creatures, the Forest Dwellers, Jungle Inhabitants, the Reptiles, and the Desert and Mountain Animals. On and on it went, for every conceivable kind of life. Insects supposedly had a guiding One Horn full of magic and Creator-imbued power, too. Maybe the tiny germs did, as well. For all Doodle knew, even the skitter skunks, booger bears, mud ducks, and swamp monkeys had a One Horn, but Doodle didn't know if they shared one or had their own. Who knew? And, really, who cared? That was one area of life that Ooby didn't over explain ad nauseam.

Doodle heard a rumor about the One Horns that did interest him, but of course Ooby would never confirm it. Supposedly, the One Horns of any extinct species or kind (or however they were categorized) were still around, roaming the Earth with no souls left to guide. One Horns were eternal and sometimes way outlived their reason for existing, so Doodle figured there were untold numbers of One Horns aimlessly banging around without purpose, like ancient ghosts. Those rumors interested Doodle for some reason. He really wanted to meet one of those discarded One Horns, but he knew, if they were even real, they would never cross his path.

The One Horns are great and mighty... and blather, blather, blather and on and on, according to Ooby, but Doodle, really, wasn't all that impressed with what they did. Enlitas just watched Ooby run amok among the Saints. Excitas wasn't much better. After all, he let the Pyres stow him away down in Eno. *For his protection* (Ooby's words again, of course). As far as Doodle could tell, Excitas and Enlitas didn't do much except laze around and get in the way of poor, overworked Saints like him.

"And where is the human One-Horn?" Nicholas fumed. "He's been absent for longer than I've been around and his kind suffers and he does nothing!"

Now would be a good time to punch Ooby in the maw, Doodle thought as he watched. He giggled to himself at that mental image even though he was sure it wouldn't happen. *Still. It would be hilarious.*

That's about the time Nimrod and Doodle were ushered to another room by Moronicon. Like the bombed and battered walls of that *Schloss* in the middle of No Man's Land would keep them from hearing the rest. The walls couldn't, but Nimrod's incessant droning about radios and frequencies and electromagnetic radiation sure did.

"What's the deal with Sarcastacles?" Doodle had asked when Nimrod's dissertation had a merciful lapse. "He's a bit..."

"Sarcastic?" Nimrod had said, like a true nimrod. "That particular characteristic is named for his, um, characteristic."

"No. I was gonna say he's a lot like Ooby." Evidently, Doodle was going to have to spell this out for him. Slowly, to be sure.

"Like how? Sarcastacles is much taller. And paler. And balder."

"He's oppressive. I bet he always bosses you around like Ooby does me."

"Sometimes, I guess, but he says it's because he has to teach me the ways of the Pyres and of our place in the world. He says I'm smarter than most of my brethren and I might be an Elder someday so it's important that he teaches me things."

Poor oblivious Nimrod. "Really? He said that you're smarter than other Pyres your age?" Nimrod had nodded dumbly, so ready to buy into that obviously manipulative narrative. "Same with me." Doodle meant it about himself, though. He knew he was smarter than the others. "You ever think they're just saying that to us to keep us from learning the truth?"

"What truth?" Nimrod's cluelessness had no end.

"Of our own power. Of what we can accomplish if we do what we want and not listen to them. Maybe they're scared of our potential and our ability to steer our kind differently from the way things have always been done."

Nimrod's light came on at that point. Doodle could almost see it. "They're squashing our dreams?"

"Feels good to finally be awake, eh?" Doodle loved pulling back the curtain for others. At that moment, he realized it might even be his purpose.

"Yeah!" Nimrod echoed, fully on board. "They're just keeping us down, man!"

They would have talked more, but Nicholas stormed out of the adjacent room right then. He didn't stop there. He just kept on bounding out of the castle and into the ruins of what probably used to be a nice city. Ooby and Sarcastacles and Moronicon and Twerpitina followed him out. They paused in the room with Nimrod and Doodle.

"Will he be all right?" Twerpitina asked, finally showing some of that missing empathy. *Too late. He's right chaffed about something.*

Ooby nodded. "He just needs to blow off a little steam."

"And how will he do that?" Moronicon asked.

"Well," Sarcastacles started... or maybe it was Ooby because what followed sounded irritating like something Ooby would say. "That's why we wanted to meet in a city already in ruin."

They continued outside so Doodle and Nimrod followed them (not that the Schloss wasn't already nearly outside with its burned-out ceiling and all). Several buildings over, Nicholas was pounding a half-crumbled brick wall with heavy punches. A piece of the wall gave away with each powerful blow. Single bricks flew hither and yon, but Nicholas kept pounding. When one part of the wall completely crumbled, he'd just move down a bit and start again. He made pitiful, miserable sobs as he punched. While Ooby and the Elders shed tears over the display, Doodle found it to be a bit trifling of Nicholas. Maybe a little embarrassing.

For the first time, he had an inkling that maybe Nicholas wasn't so great either. There were better places he could focus his energies (like on Ooby's aforementioned maw). Doodle found that thought as funny as the last time and he couldn't help it when he let out a loud gush of laughter. Everyone looked at him, even silly Nimrod, as if he was out of line. Doodle didn't care though. They were out of line with their oppressive ways, not him. Doodle knew he was right. Doodle, in fact, was always right.

And someday they'll all know it and beg me for forgiveness.

Nicholas knocked down three walls with his bare fists before he came back to the silent group, emotionally spent from his shameful crying. He didn't say anything to anyone except Ooby. "Let's go." It wasn't a request. He walked by the Elders, but he crossed closest to Nimrod on his way to the waiting sleigh and two deer.

Doodle saw Nimrod's nose flare and his eyes blast wide open. It took Doodle a moment to realize what had caused his reaction to Nicholas's passing presence. Nimrod wasn't just watching Nicholas. He was watching his hands. Nicholas had hit the brick walls so hard and for so long that his fists were battered and bloody. Doodle grinned when Nimrod licked his lips.

Ooby nodded to his Pyre comrades and followed Nicholas. *Not so tough now, huh, Ooby? All quiet and cowering.*

Doodle just stood there and watched. Were the Elders looking at Nicholas's fists, too, he wondered. Were they secretly craving his life source? That enchanted stuff coursing through his veins that had to be ten times better than what the strongest humans offered?

Good to know. Doodle grinned again. This trip had unexpectedly brought him lots of good cheer. *Everyone has their weakness.* He waved at Nimrod as he followed Nicholas and Ooby to the sleigh. They were already in it, but not talking. "If I ever find a spam radio, I'll call you and we can hang out and get into some trouble."

The Elders didn't even hear him. They were still nonchalantly sniffing the air where Nicholas and his bludgeoned knuckles had passed. They were trying, and failing by the way, to act like it wasn't driving them absolutely crazy.

"Ham," Nimrod had returned, but he was still in a daze like the Elders. "It's a ham radio."

"Sure, buddy," Doodle giggled. "That. If I ever use one, I'll call you." Right then, Doodle never could have guessed that the time would be eighty some years later and would come on a Pirate Ship in the weeks leading up to Black Friday.

Doodle leapt in the sleigh behind Nicholas and Ooby and they lifted off and headed home. All the way back to Eno, they didn't talk. That was good, though. Doodle needed quiet. He had a lot to think about.

And while he thought, he shifted his glance from Ooby to Nicholas and back again. Both looked a lot meeker and a lot weaker than on the trip to the city. At least to Doodle, they did.

Why did I ever look up to you two? He glared at the old, pitiful Saint who thought he was so smart and the sad excuse for a human who let himself be diverted from doing what was right for his people.

One day, he assured himself with certainty, *I'll show you what a real leader looks like. Then, you'll be sorry you ever tried to rule over me.*

And, just like that, one day came.

Part Three

Outside the dungeon, night has fallen. Ooby, Sarcastacles, and the ten Pyre Elders appear on the deck of Captain Dagger's ship, huddled in a tight circle. A loud hum comes from overhead. Ooby is shocked that he's on the ship again. The heavy fog obscures anything around or above them.

"The Pirate Ship." He nudges Sarcastacles as he retrieves the other small crystal from the deck at his feet. "We're on the Pirate Ship." He puts the necklace crystal over his head.

"What Pirate Ship?" Sarcastacles asks.

From up on the bow deck above them, Ooby hears a hearty laugh. It's Captain Dagger, at the wheel, hands on his hips. Around the ship, the Girls and Boys work steadily and gleefully with their Pirate mentors, raising sails and tying ropes.

"'Tis a Pirate Ship no more, my fine Saintly fellow!" Captain Dagger boasts loud enough to be heard over the strange, constant hum. "We're Freedom Fighters now, aye mates?"

The Girls and Boys and the Pirates (now Freedom Fighters) give a hearty and synchronized "Aye, Cap'n!"

Ooby goes toward the bow deck. "No offense, Captain Dagger, but the sea is miles from Vam Castle! We have to go back where we were! Fifty Pyres are coming for the verdict of the conclave, but all they'll get is a team of Slayers waiting to ambush them!"

Sarcastacles looks over the side as Ooby speaks, just as the ship emerges from the thick, soupy fog bank. Sarcastacles sees that the ship is a thousand feet in the air. He looks up. The fog above is also dissipating. It's now clear that a heavy construction tandem-rotor helicopter

(CH-47 Chinook) is carrying the ship via heavy chains. It is the drone of the Chinook's engine that is causing the loud hum. The eight reindeer fly freely around the chopper. They all nod to Sarcastacles. He smiles and waves back at them.

"I believe we're closer than we think, Ooby," Sarcastacles says over his shoulder.

Captain Dagger nods to Ooby with a smile. He gives the wheel a spin, which does nothing for the course of the ship. A lone figure shimmies down one of the chains connecting the ship to the chopper. The figure leaps from the chain while still halfway between the chopper and the ship. It's Holly. She lands gracefully on the deck by Ooby.

"Who said youth is wasted on the young?" she says with a wink.

Ooby is finally starting to piece together what is happening. When he finally has everything straight in his mind, he says, "Well, you sure know how to make an entrance. How's Nicholas?"

Holly points upward. Ooby looks up to see Saki Crocodile in the open door of the chopper's cargo bay, wearing a headset. He gives a thumbs up to those below. At the controls, also wearing a headset, is Nicholas. He looks down at Holly, smiles, then gives Ooby a nod.

"Is there anything he can't fly?" Holly asks with admiration, still looking up.

Ooby sees the expression on her face and would have to be blind not to know what it means. He shrugs. "Flying a boat is fairly new. Even for him."

"We're storming a castle, folks!" Captain Dagger roars over the noise. "Where's my battle drums?"

Jerkus McGerkis throws off his robe and plays his accordion with delight. It's an upbeat polka version of "The Little Drummer Boy". Captain Dagger hears the accordion's tune and bobs his head for a moment. He looks at Jerkus with a grin.

"Close enough! I like it!"

Sarcastacles feels a sudden surge of invigoration and runs to the front of the bow. He points forward. "Charge!"

Everyone on the ship, Freedom Fighters and Children alike, repeat the command as Jerkus McGerkis plays and the Elders begin to dance like they did at the outset of the conclave.

A group of about fifty robed Pyres cross the long bridge over the moat as the gate into Vam's Castle creaks opens. The Pyres walk three by three through the entrance. A gatekeeper, also wearing a hooded robe, nods as they walk by him into the courtyard. The gatekeeper lifts his head. It's Van Helsing.

The group of Pyres walk like a herd of sheep into the contained area and meander to the middle of the yard. When the last one enters from the bridge, Van Helsing closes the gate with a deafening slam.

The Pyres turn and look at him in unison. One of the Pyres, Dipstickio, drops his hood. "Have the Elders reached a decision about the humans?"

"No, but the humans have reached a decision about the Elders." Van Helsing whips his stake gun from under his robe as Tiddlywink, Tumbleweed, Rip Tide, and Powder Keg step out of the recessed shadows of the castle walls. The platoon of a hundred well-armed Slayers Guild Recruits follows them out and encircles the Pyres in the courtyard. Van Helsing finally drops his hood to reveal that he's human.

"What's going on here?" Dipstickio demands.

"Let's call it a 'stake out'," Van Helsing smirks. The named Vanhelsingers and all the Recruits chuckle together while they raise their weapons. "Vanhelsingers, on my command," he continues.

There is a cacophony of weapons being cocked. The Pyres, suddenly fearful of the sheer number of sworn enemies surrounding them, huddle together in a defensive maneuver.

Van Helsing raises his hand. "Ready! Aim!" he barks, but before he can give the command to 'Fire', the sound of a helicopter draws his attention to the far side of the castle. The wall is topped by an even higher wall of fog, which is roiling above and around the ramparts and roof. Van Helsing looks for the sound, then drops his hand. "Fire!" he yells.

Before anyone does, the airborne Pirate Ship bursts forth from the fog bank. The Pyres all crouch as the Vanhelsingers and their Recruits watch overhead, stunned. The helicopter is nearly obscured in a higher layer of thick fog, so the ship looks like it's crashing through tumultuous waves as it plows into the airspace above the courtyard.

Onboard, Captain Dagger sits in his foam noodle throne. "Prepare the cannons!" Cannons emerge from the sides of the ship as it glides over the courtyard, dragging blankets of fog with it. The sides of the ship drop level with the top of the castle.

Tiddlywink sees the cannons pop from the side of the ship. He runs in circles, searching desperately for cover. "The Pirates have cannons!" he screeches.

Captain Dagger hears Tiddlywink's cry and rolls his eyes. "We're not Pirates! We're Fishermen!"

One of the children on the deck below Dagger looks back at him. "I thought we were Freedom Fighters," she yells.

"Yes, we are! Freedom Fighting Fishermen!" he replies.

The girl, still looking up at him, tilts her head in a questioning gesture. Captain Dagger sees and corrects himself. "Freedom Fighting Fisherpeople!"

The girl nods and raises her hand high, then drops it back down as she roars, "Fire the cannons!"

The cannons blast at the befuddled Vanhelsingers and their Recruits. Fish nets shoot from each one, covering and entangling multiple Slayers at a time.

Sarcastacles leans over the ship's rail and yells down. "Fight, my Pyres, fight!"

Behind him, Holly calls to the Freedom Fighting Fisherpeople. "Go, Freedom Fighters, go!" As she throws a rope over the rail, she adds a caveat. "Adult Freedom Fighters only! Children, stay on the ship with Sister Abby!" Then, she dives over the side.

Sister Abby, frazzled again, is more than pleased that she isn't expected to follow Holly and she motions for the children to stay behind. "All children remain here with me!" None of the children disembark, but more than a few are dejected that they can't shadow their mentors.

Sarcastacles and Ooby follow Holly down the rope as rope ladders drop from the sides of the ship. The adult Freedom Fighters scurry down to the ground in the courtyard. All the while, the Slayers wrestle with the nets over them.

The Pyres and Freedom Fighters spread out in the courtyard. A mega-fight ensues as they engage the Vanhelsingers and their one hundred Recruits. Van Helsing punches a passing adult Freedom Fighter and takes his sword. He starts swinging, meeting with several swords of other Freedom Fighters. He does a fine job of clearing a path in the melee until he sees Captain Dagger awaiting him, also armed with a sword.

"My quarrel is with the vampires," Van Helsing growls. "Take your men and leave us to our business."

"Today, we're Vam-Pirates, so your fight is with all of us."

From the ship, the same little girl who had just corrected Dagger yells out again. "I thought we were Freedom Fighting..."

As if he expected it, Captain Dagger looks up at the girl, leaning over the side of the ship, and runs his fingers across his lips. "Zip it, Emily! It was too good to pass up!"

The girl shrugs, as if to say he's right and she'll allow it, but just this once.

"Very well, Vam-Pirate!" Van Helsing says as he charges Captain Dagger. "Let's play!" They clash swords and begin a fantastic duel in the crowded courtyard.

At the controls of the Chinook, Nicholas sees the battle igniting in the courtyard below and pulls up on the joystick, lifting the chopper up and away. Behind him, Saki leans into the cockpit. They talk through their headsets.

"Where are we going?" Saki asks.

"We have to get the children a safe distance away," Nicholas replies. "We never should have brought them."

"We couldn't leave them in Greece without chaperones," Saki returns.

"True," says Nicholas. "Now that we've dropped off the Freedom Fighters, they'll team up with the Pyres and the battle will be over in no time. They don't need us anymore."

"Then get us out of here," Saki says, a little too eager to put distance between himself and the battle below.

In the courtyard, Ooby and Sarcastacles are in the middle of the melee, fighting back-to-back and fending off charging Slayers. Ooby uses kicks and punches while Sarcastacles dispatches his attackers with perfectly timed Aikido moves.

In the close hand-to-hand fighting, the Slayers reveal a coordinated battle effort. The Recruits slug it out face to face and toe-to-toe with the Pyres and Freedom Fighters, but the named Vanhelsingers move quickly through the yard. They don't allow themselves to be bogged down by single combat. They are able to run freely through the fight. Though the two sides are nearly equal in their numbers, the Slayers get off to a better start thanks to the expertise of the four Vanhelsingers.

Tiddlywink's speed and agility enables him to maneuver around quickly and throw his discs, which prove to be formidable weapons. He targets a Freedom Fighter and hits him in the head, but the disc doesn't stop. It ricochets off him and hits several more of his comrades, knocking them all out in succession. Tiddlywink does this same thing over and over again, rendering many Freedom Fighters unconscious in a short amount of time.

Meanwhile, Rip Tide rides a skateboard through the courtyard, performing his fly-flying trick-jumps that send the board into the stomachs and heads of Pyres, rendering them immediately out of commission. He leaves many injured Pyres in his wake as he makes laps around the court-yard.

Tumbleweed balls up and somersaults through the crowd and bowls both Pyres and Freedom Fighters completely off their feet. Powder Keg, who blocks incoming punches with his hard hat, throws small concussion charges here and there, sending everyone flying when the little bombs detonate.

President Applebaum is also in the fray, using his ample rump to bounce Pyres and Freedom Fighters this way and that. With the Recruits keeping the Pyres and Freedom Fighters occupied with fisticuffs and the Vanhelsingers running rampant with their specialized attacks, the start of the fight doesn't look too promising for the good guys.

However, it isn't a lost cause by any means. The good guys have their own weapon cutting through the crowd with ease, causing formidable damage to the Slayers Guild. Holly runs about like a Tasmanian Devil, punching and kicking the Recruits with such power and precision that she is thinning the opposing army considerably with each frenetic lap through the yard. Holly's courage inspires her comrades and the tide of the battle gradually begins to turn.

Van Helsing and Captain Dagger, who are still dueling, try to one up each other with extravagant swordplay. Dagger is diverted from his fight with Van Helsing when a mob of fighting Pyres and Slayer Recruits get between them. Dagger begins fighting several Recruits at once while Van Helsing turns his attention to nearby Pyres.

Not too far away in the mob, the monstrous Achilles engages the swift and nimble Tumbleweed. Achilles swings his sledge hammer at him in broad, sweeping arcs, but Tumbleweed keeps balling up and rolling under the blows.

"Stand still, ya landlubbin' hornswaggler!" Achilles commands in full attack mode. Tumbleweed keeps laughing as he evades his onslaught.

"What's a matter?" Captain Dagger yells to Achilles.

"He scuttles like a sand crab!" Achilles exclaims, exasperated. He's clearly stumped by Tumbleweed's tactics, who rolls under his hammer swings. Tumbleweed kicks Achilles's legs hard with every pass and the blows are adding up. Achilles is starting to wilt with the accumulating damage.

"Have you tried to either maul his mizzen or mizzen his muzzle?" Dagger asks.

"Of course, I've tried to maul his mizzen in addition to mizzening his muzzle! What self-respecting former-Pirate wouldn't do those two things straight away?" Achilles barks back.

"Okay, sheesh! I was just spitballing some ideas!" Dagger remarks defensively.

From nowhere, Spitball Spalding runs in front of Tumbleweed, straw already in his mouth. Achilles sees his approach and waves him off. "Shiver me timbers, Spalding, it's just a figure of speech!"

Despite Achilles's objections, Spalding lets loose a gigantic wad of wet paper, which zips from his straw at lightning speed. It splashes into Tumbleweed while he's mid-somersault and knocks him flat in a dripping, sticky heap. Achilles's jaw drops at the surprise result. Dagger, still fighting his opponents, is shocked too. Spitball Spalding just nods, withdraws the straw from his mouth, and blows the end of it, like a cowboy blowing the smoke from his pistol barrel after a good shot.

"Spitballin' is all about simple math," Spitball Spalding says in a weak, sheepish voice. "Velocity times Voluminous Viscosity squared equals Victory."

Achilles peers down at Tumbleweed, who is writhing in agony and holding a hand to his rear, right where the wadded paper is still stuck in a mushy, drippy mass. "Simple math all right. You got him right in the hypotenuse!"

A few feet away, Rip Tide skates toward the rampaging Holly's back as she fights several Recruits at once. Jerkus McGerkis and Moronicon see the impending sneak attack, so they grip hands and clothes-line him before he can get to her. They leap on him and pummel him into submission. She gives them a 'thumbs up' of appreciation and keeps going toward Tiddlywink, who is whipping his discs at her.

Holly deftly ducks and dodges the flurry of dangerous discs, rushes Tiddlywink, and slugs him. He stumbles against the wall where Idiotis and Dorkamemnon corner him. Dorkamemnon wrestles Tiddlywink while Idiotis steals his disc bandolier from behind, effectively disarming him. The two then swarm him together and take him out of the fight.

Holly is about to storm through the dwindling crowd again, but she hears a voice from somewhere above her and she stops.

"Your fragrance? Is that Eau de Nicholas?" Nimrod leans on the wall of the rampart over her, watching the battle in the courtyard below, but not engaging in it.

"Come on down and get a whiff," she says as she waves him down to the courtyard.

"Is that anyway to talk to a blood-brother?" he asks with a confident smirk.

Holly grits her teeth. "Never mind." She squats low and leaps upward with all of her superhuman might. "I'll come to you." She lands next to Nimrod on the rampart.

He immediately leaps to his feet, grabs her by the throat and lifts her up. "You may have his blood, but you lack his skill," Nimrod grins, bearing his fangs. "You don't deserve such power. Why don't you give it to me?"

As he opens his mouth wide and goes for her neck, Holly kicks him in the stomach, then grabs his wrist and twists, forcing him to release his grip. She continues until he bends at the waist in front of her.

"Talk or fight. You can't do both," she says, then knees him in the face. He flies onto his back, but immediately springs up, angry. He charges her, leaping into kicks and punches that she blocks, but just barely.

Above them, Doodle flies over the battle in the sleigh and swoops in low, just over the combatants' heads in the courtyard. He drops one of the large crystals in the corner of the yard, hovers, and whistles to Powder Keg, who is now trading punches with Wallaby.

Powder Keg looks as Doodle points at the crystal before he flies off in a streak. Many combatants battle between him and the crystal, so he abandons his fight with Wallaby and makes a break for it. He throws punches on his way through the crowd, but he also takes some. He realizes he isn't getting closer to the crystal, so he reaches into his bag and withdraws a huge bundle of dynamite with an attached timer.

"Gotta go, folks, but you just keep having fun without me! In fact, have a blast!" He tosses the dynamite in the crowd.

The timer counts down from twenty seconds. The crowd, seeing the dynamite, scatters, clearing a path to the crystal. Powder Keg runs and dives on it and disappears. Ooby, still back-to-back with Sarcastacles and fighting off two large Recruits, sees the crowd disperse. Then, he sees the dynamite.

"That bomb is big enough to blow up the courtyard and everyone in it!" he yells over his shoulder to Sarcastacles.

"Do something!" Sarcastacles replies. Ooby sprints toward it. Sarcastacles turns to watch Ooby. That's when the two Recruits rush him. Without looking, he knocks both out with a right cross. He then follows Ooby. By the time they get to the dynamite, only ten seconds remain on the timer.

"I'll go to the dungeon! Send it to me!" Ooby says as he tosses one of the small crystals to Sarcastacles, who stands over the dynamite to keep anyone else from coming near it. Ooby sprints inside the castle. Sarcastacles motions for everyone to fall back, which they do, Pyres, Freedom Fighting Fisherpeople, Recruits, and Vanhelsingers alike.

The timer on the bomb counts down to three seconds when Sarcastacles taps it with the crystal. It disappears, just as Ooby appears where the bomb had just been.

"Done!" Ooby shouts.

"Let's go!" Sarcastacles says as he darts away from the wall. Ooby, though, elects a different escape. In full-on action-movie tough-guy mode, Ooby walks away in a slow-motion stroll, eyes squinting bravely and his arms swinging slowly to match his pace.

The section of the castle with the dungeon explodes behind him in a fiery plume, spewing smoke and debris like a volcano. Ooby doesn't even seem to notice, still calm and taking his time, sauntering away from the danger. He doesn't look back or blink. He doesn't quicken his steps. And, quite honestly, he looks absolutely awesome compared to the others who are fleeing the scene without a care of how cowardly they may appear.

Ooby stands alone as the only hero in the castle, his demeanor too cool for the chaos. As the explosion dies down, he starts to draw attention for his intrepidly smooth withdrawal, which stands in high contrast to everyone else's shameful-in-comparison retreat. The others gawk at him, thoroughly impressed, until a single brick flies up from the fading explosion, arcs high, and drops right on top of his head. Ooby collapses upon impact. Rubble rains down on him. When the firebomb subsides completely, Sarcastacles runs back to him, kneels by him, and cradles him.

"Ooby, are you alright?" Sarcastacles yells.

"I got hit in the head with a brick," Ooby moans. "What do you think?"

"Of course, you did. It was a massive explosion with pieces of stone and all manner of detritus flying everywhere! You just strolled away like you were window shopping. What were you thinking?"

"Did it look cool?" Ooby asks sheepishly.

"If something big is about to blow up, I think it would be cool, and fairly intelligent, to flee the requisite shrapnel as fast as possible."

"Bah. You're giving me a headache," Ooby groans.

"I think that would probably be the brick," Sarcastacles says, unable to hold back his smile.

Ooby rolls from Sarcastacles's embrace and, still dazed, searches the rubble for the crystal. He finds it among pieces of glass from an exploded window, which are similar in shape and size to the crystal, but the crystal is clear and diamond-like. He grabs it as Sarcastacles helps him stand.

The combatants all start fighting again, soon filling in the empty space around Ooby and Sarcastacles that was momentarily vacated by the explosion.

From the cockpit of the Chinook helicopter, which is now a safe distance up and away from the walls of Vam's Castle, Nicholas sees the massive explosion. He gazes down with concern and brings the chopper around enough to survey the damage.

Luckily, Nicholas surmises, no one is hurt except Ooby who, for some inexplicable reason, took a carefree dawdle from the fiery blast before receiving an errand brick on the crown of his head. Though Nicholas admits to himself it did look awesome for the briefest of moments, he doubts that is reason enough to be so nonchalant in the face of grave danger. After all, he himself had fled many explosions over the years and he was always in quite a hurry when doing so.

Nicholas sees Sarcastacles rush to Ooby's side and is quickly assured his friend is well-cared for and uninjured in any serious way. He watches the large fight resume in the center of the courtyard, so he swings the chopper up and around the walls of the castle, eager to gain more distance from the mayhem.

Then, he sees the clash between Holly and Nimrod. They're on a rampart above the courtyard on the far side of the castle. They are so locked in on their fight with each other, Nicholas doubts they even know the bomb went off. Though Holly is battling fiercely and seems an equal to Nimrod in every way, Nicholas is aghast.

"No, Holly," he whispers. "Get away from him."

From the cargo bay behind, Saki follows Nicholas's gaze down to the castle and spots the reason for his sudden worry. "She can handle herself, Nicholas. Need I remind you of the number she pulled on my guys?" Saki says into the microphone on his headset.

"This is different," Nicholas replies into his own headset. "He's not human."

"She looks to be doing just fine so far," Saki returns.

"He's toying with her," comes Nicholas's answer, fast and anxious.

Suddenly, the sleigh streaks by with Doodle at the controls and makes a fast circle around them.

"Do you see what I see?" Saki blurts as the sleigh zips very close at near supersonic speed. The chopper rattles with the flyby and they hear Doodle's high-pitched laugh. "Do you hear what I hear?" Saki chatters nervously, frightened by the aggressive action of the sleigh.

Nicholas strains to track the sleigh in its path around the chopper. Suddenly, it stops next to Nicholas's side and hovers there. Doodle's laugh is loud and clearly mocking. He is staring into the cockpit, right at Nicholas, trying his best to appear intimidating.

"A child?" Saki says into his headset, then he chuckles, not at all buying Doodle as a force to be feared. "A child!"

Nicholas cuts him off quickly. "That's not a child! That's a Doodle! Come up here and take the controls!"

"Why? I can handle this little stinker!" Saki says. He throws open the bay door on Nicholas's side and is about to leap over onto Doodle, but Powder Keg pops his head out of the back of the sleigh by the large crystal. Saki is shocked when Powder Keg jumps into the bay beside him. Saki tries to push him back out, but Powder Keg gives him a stiff arm that floors him.

"I used my grand finale down below," Powder Keg shouts at Nicholas over the engine noise. "But I got a little something here I think you'll like!" He holds up a grenade, pulls the pin, and shoves it deep into the exposed mechanics in the ceiling of the cargo bay.

Upon seeing the grenade, Saki dives into the sleigh in a quick retreat. Powder Keg follows him. Powder Keg shoves past Saki and is about to jump on the crystal, but Doodle jams the joystick, rocketing the sleigh away from the chopper. Both Powder Keg and Saki are pitched to the far back of the sleigh and Powder Keg tumbles over the side. His ammunition bag catches on the sleigh's runner and he dangles there, shrieking.

Nicholas opens the window in his cockpit door and looks to the ship below and the children on its deck. "Hold on to something, children!" he yells.

On the deck of the Freedom Fighter Ship, Sister Abbey repeats his command and the Children grab tight to the nearest rails and handholds.

In the Chinook's cargo bay, the grenade explodes. Though it isn't too big, it's enough to send critical internal mechanisms flying. In the cockpit, Nicholas leans away from the explosion. Hydraulic fluid spews from a new gouge in the ceiling of the chopper, which gives out a sharp and cataclysmic crack. The chopper's back rotor sparks and the blade gives a sputter. The back end drops when the rotor dies. Nicholas fights the controls as the cockpit fills with smoke. Down below, the children are thrown about as the ship rocks violently with the instability of the chopper overhead.

In the sleigh, well away from the chopper now, Ooby appears over the crystal in the back, pushes past Saki, and leaps forward into the seat next to Doodle. Doodle has the joystick jammed forward, speeding the sleigh into the night's sky when Ooby tackles him. They tussle for a moment, each trying to gain control of the joystick. Ooby kicks an obscure button on the dashboard with his foot. It glows red for a second.

Doodle sees Ooby's action. "What's that do? I don't remember ever seeing–" His seat ejects him out of the sleigh.

"Minor upgrade after last year," Ooby says as he takes command of the joystick and turns the sleigh back toward the chopper. He sees the eight reindeer flying around the Freedom Fighter Ship. In a concerted but failing effort to steady the vessel, they are right next to the back end of the hull and leaning heavily into it. Ooby whistles through his fingers, catching Cupid's attention. He points at Doodle. Cupid understands the command and darts downward.

Doodle yelps helplessly as he free-falls toward the small village beneath the castle. Cupid swoops and catches him just ten feet from the cold, icy ground. Doodle, furious, shows no gratitude to the deer. Instead, he straddles Cupid's back and grabs his antlers. He steers him by pulling his antlers left and right.

"You'll pay Ooby! You'll pay right now!" He turns the helpless deer back toward the chopper.

The Chinook is angled sharply, tail down and nose up. The front rotor can't support the total weight of the chopper and the Freedom Fighter Ship, so the chopper starts sliding back in the air like a ball on a tilted table.

In the cockpit, Nicholas fights the controls, but knows he's losing. Below, on the deck of the Ship, the Children hold tight to the railings. They are still high in the air, but losing altitude fast.

Ooby steers the sleigh beneath the chopper, positioning it vertically under the back. The sleigh is straight up and down and pushing the rear of the chopper upward just below the back rotor. Ooby forces the joystick forward, giving it full thrust.

Behind him, Saki hangs on in the bed of the sleigh, screaming with all of his terrified might. Powder Keg still clings to the end of the runner under the sleigh, but his ammo bag is slipping. Saki sees Powder Kegs struggling to hold on and, still screaming, reaches out for him. His hand misses and Powder Keg slides off the runner and falls to the deck of the ship fifty feet below.

In the cockpit, Nicholas looks out the window and back at Ooby in the sleigh.

Ooby yells up to him. "This can't hold!"

An alarm sounds on the control panel and the front rotor pops and begins to sputter. The entire chopper quakes. Nicholas scans the night horizon. In the darkness, he can see a lake a half a mile ahead. "There isn't much time! To the lake!" Nicholas yells back to Ooby. "We'll get the ship to the lake!"

Ooby gives a thumbs up from the sleigh. As Nicholas powers the chopper forward, the cargo bay's ceiling behind him continues to fizzle and spark until it finally catches fire. On top of the chopper, the front rotor slows even more, which causes it to now dip forward into a slow nosedive. The sleigh is still positioned at the back end, thrusting upward. The ship, sleigh, and chopper begin moving forward from their hovering position and in a steep downward trajectory.

"We'll never make it!" Ooby shouts as he fights the sleigh's joystick.

On the Ship below, the Children surround Powder Keg, who has landed on the deck on all fours. A brave boy named Trevor steps forward.

"We're gonna crash thanks to you!" Trevor yells accusingly.

"Yeah, well, what're you gonna do about it?" Powder Keg snarks as he draws another grenade and pulls the pin, but loses it when he's rocked about by the ship's turbulence.

Trevor begins to wonder that himself.

Flames engulf the ceiling of the Chinook's cargo bay as Nicholas pulls out his seat-belt as far as it will go. He ties off the control stick with the loose belt, locking it in an up-steering position. Then, he moves himself from the pilot's seat into the wheelchair beside him.

In the cargo bay, with little room to maneuver, he wheels himself under the flames and to the open doors and rolls directly out of them. Nicholas free-falls toward the Pirate Ship below. Ooby, still using the sleigh to push up the back of the chopper, watches in shock, but can't do a thing to help his friend.

On the deck of the ship, Nicholas hits hard, chair-first. His wheelchair tires splay out, but they don't break. He rolls quickly down the steep decline of the surface, carrying the momentum from his free-fall, and plows right into the unsuspecting Powder Keg. Powder Keg tumbles forward. Nicholas grabs the grenade as he rolls by and flips it over the side. It explodes just beyond the railing. The Children cheer upon seeing Nicholas's triumphant arrival, but he is too hurried to acknowledge them one by one. He looks to Trevor, the obvious leader of the group.

"Are you the acting Captain of this ship, Trevor?"

Trevor looks around, sees no other options, shrugs, then salutes. "Aye, sir! Give your order and I'll see that it's done!"

"Captain Trevor, kindly drop the anchor."

Trevor runs to the helm. Nicholas pushes himself up from the chair, but he's clumsy and unsteady under his own weight and the shimmying tilt of the ship. Trevor yells loud enough for all the Children to hear. "Anchors aweigh!" Then, he punches a lever with an Anchor symbol.

Inside the Ship's hull, a huge winch turns and unreels a large chain. Outside the hull, a monstrous anchor descends into mid-air. On the Ship's deck, Nicholas stumbles to the railing. He looks over the side, then back at the Children, who have locked their attention on him. He smiles, nods, and pitches himself over the side. The Children give a collective gasp.

Several of the kids run to the side and look over the railing. They let out a sigh of relief when they see that Nicholas is standing on top of the anchor and holding onto the chain as it descends from its recessed housing on the side of the ship's bow.

The anchor drops quickly toward the castle below as the chain unrolls. Nicholas climbs down on the anchor and stands upon one fluke. He is wavering, but holds the long shank tightly. The anchor drops toward a corner turret of the castle. Nicholas rocks back and forth to swing the anchor toward the turret. The ship continues losing altitude despite Ooby's best efforts to keep it airborne.

Nicholas guides the opposite fluke of the anchor into a window of the stone turret. Just before impact, Nicholas leaps onto the rampart's adjacent walkway. The anchor breaks through the glass and snags in the window's sturdy frame for a second until the chain fully tightens. The turret explodes in stony debris as the anchor and chain finally tear through. The anchor drags forward through the floor of the rampart.

Nicholas limps on weak legs ahead of the anchor as it grinds a long seam in one side of the castle's perimeter wall, right up the middle of the walkway. At the far end, Nimrod and Holly are locked in tremendous combat. They see Nicholas stumbling toward them and the anchor tearing its way behind him. He waves them off the walkway.

Nimrod leaps down to the courtyard. Holly, though, is stunned by Nicholas's approach and even more stunned by the ship roaring closer overhead. She's momentarily paralyzed as she tries to make sense of what she's seeing. Nicholas tackles Holly and they fall to the courtyard below. They land on the ground, Nicholas hitting first to cushion Holly, who is on top of him. Above them, the anchor finally starts to catch in the castle's reinforced rampart and its advance through the wall slows.

"You can walk?" Holly says with a deep gaze into Nicholas's eyes.

Nicholas grins back up at her. "Not wanting a flying Pirate Ship to crash on top of your date is a great motivator."

Holly smiles widely, completely flattered. "Aww, this is a date?"

Over her shoulder, Nicholas can't help but see the ship still dropping toward them. He eases Holly from over him and sits up fast. Holly leaps to her feet and looks up, too. The Children have all rushed to the side of the ship and are looking over the railing. They see that the anchor has rooted itself deep in the wall of the castle, but the chopper is still being supported by the sleigh and both are failing in their effort to keep the ship airborne.

Trevor, holding tight to the wheel at the helm of the descending ship, searches the courtyard until he finds Nicholas, who signals for him to raise the anchor. Trevor flips the lever with the anchor symbol the other way. In the ship's hull, the winch reverses course and quickly tightens the chain.

The ship is caught in mid-air between the castle, where the anchor takes hold, and the sky over the village, where the chopper and sleigh fight to keep it from falling. The anchor draws the ship to the castle as the chain pulls into the hull.

Nicholas grabs Holly's hand for a moment, then hobbles toward the large crystal, still in the corner. "Please get outside where it's safe, Holly!" he says, letting go of her hand.

"Where are you going?" she asks as she starts for the gate that leads outside.

"The children," is all he says as he steps on the crystal and disappears. Holly stops her run to the gate and looks about at the courtyard, where the two opposing mobs are battling it out again.

Nimrod steps from a hidden recess and glares at Holly. "Looking for the way out like Nicholas told you?" he asks.

Holly gives him a confident grin. "Nope. I was looking for you."

He waves her to him, so she rushes him and gives him a hard right cross to the chin. Nimrod rocks backwards but rebounds, smiling. They start fighting again.

In the sleigh, which is still straight up and down, Ooby fights the joystick, trying to keep the chopper airborne. The futility of it is becoming painfully obvious. Saki hangs on behind him.

The fusion device beneath the sleigh gives loud and jarring snaps, indicating impending failure. Nicholas appears over the crystal behind them and has to grab hold of the sides immediately to keep from falling out of the back. Saki grabs his hands to help him. He pulls Nicholas up and helps him climb into the seat next to Ooby.

"The low energy nuclear propulsion apparatus is failing!" Ooby shouts to Nicholas when he gets beside him. "I told Doodle it wouldn't work when bearing too much weight!"

Just then, Doodle laughs maniacally as he makes a sweeping approach, steering Cupid by tugging his antlers left and right. Nicholas takes over the joystick from Ooby. "I got this," he says as he nods toward Doodle. "You get that."

Ooby's face turns to a stern grimace. "Gladly."

As Doodle steers the deer in close, intent on attacking the sleigh, Ooby leaps out and tackles him, nearly knocking him off of Cupid's back. Doodle holds on though and elbows Ooby hard. Ooby falls.

Nicholas whistles loudly to alert the other seven free-flying deer around the ship.

Ooby is in a free-fall, but he still has the small crystals, so he throws one upward. He touches the necklace, and appears a bit higher in midair. He does this several times, seeming as though he is suspended in one spot, 50 feet below the sleigh, but the laws of physics will be denied for only so long.

Doodle makes another sweep around to attack Ooby. He is a few feet away when Comet, responding to Nicholas's whistle, flies in and broadsides Doodle. Ooby grabs his antlers and pulls onto his back, like a cowboy leaping on a galloping horse.

Cupid and Doodle swing close to Ooby and Comet and Doodle punches Ooby as hard as he can, nearly knocking him from his mount again. Ooby holds on though and steers Comet away from the castle's airspace.

On the sleigh, Nicholas motions Saki toward the large crystal. "Go! Go!" Saki doesn't hesitate to slap the crystal and disappear.

The Chinook's one sputtering rotor can't compensate for the loss of the second rotor and the entire chopper threatens to spin out of control. Nicholas steers the sleigh more directly under the center of the chopper to keep it, and the Freedom Fighter Ship under it, from crashing.

In the corner of the courtyard, Saki rolls from the crystal. He crawls on all fours through the melee that continues on and finds refuge in a recess in the wall. Over him, the ship is still being reeled by its chain toward the anchor buried deep inside the castle. The sleigh keeps it suspended in air until the anchor pulls it all the way to a corner turret of the castle. The ship sets down hard on the turret, which pierces the bottom of the ship like a rocky outcrop might puncture a shore bound ship on the water. In fact, as the dense fog settles around the hull of the ship, that's exactly what it looks like.

The Children and Sister Abby brace for the hard landing and are rocked about upon impact. Thankfully, no one is hurt and they all cheer when the ship settles safely. The impact was much better than if the sleigh hadn't kept the upward pressure on the Chinook to prevent it from spinning out of control and if the anchor had not brought the ship to the castle in a controlled and steady descent.

Nicholas steers the sleigh in a spin beneath the chopper with the rocket on full power. Its flames burn through the chains holding the ship to the chopper. Free of the weight of the ship, he rockets the sleigh and chopper straight up. Under the sleigh, the cold fusion device blasts sparks out of its side, on the verge of exploding.

The sleigh pushes the Chinook upward until both are over two thousand feet high. The sleigh and chopper veer over the lake, well away from both the castle and the village. Then, they explode in a huge fireball. Molten debris rains down on the lake.

CHAPTER 36

Holly and Nimrod are like two rams locked at the horns. Each one takes as many blows as they deliver. Holly fights with a ferocity that Nimrod matches with skill and strength. Both use high kicks and flurries of punches to back the other up. The fight goes through ebbs and flows. No matter which fighter a bystander might be rooting for, they'd have reason to cheer. One second, Nimrod has the upper hand. The next, Holly fights her way to the top.

When the explosion rocks the sky a short distance from the castle, Holly glances up with worry for Nicholas, knowing that he was on or near the Chinook. Nimrod throws a sucker-punch while her head is turned, hoping to take advantage of her distraction. Unfortunately for Nimrod, Holly anticipates his move and catches his arm at the wrist.

"I knew you'd try that," she says as she twists his arm under him, which forces Nimrod to turn his back to her. She pulls his wrist up, torquing his arm behind him and between his shoulder blades. Then, she grabs him in a vicious rear headlock. She clenches the hold tightly and Nimrod gasps for breath. Suddenly helpless, Nimrod claws over his head at her face with his free hand to no avail. Holly is too strong and simply will not let go with victory so close.

Nimrod closes his eyes as his arms go limp. Holly stays tight to his back while she lets him fall to a seated position on the ground. As she does, there's only a momentary separation between his throat and her arm, which allows him to slip his chin into the space.

She tries to re-tighten her clench, but Nimrod keeps his chin between her arm and his neck. That's when panic sets in on Holly. She lets go of her hold, hoping to separate completely and re-engage Nimrod from another angle, but he grasps her arm firmly with both hands and holds it by his mouth. She bucks wildly, but can't get free of his clutches.

"Trap set and trap taken," Nimrod chuckles in a low whisper. "I knew you wouldn't pass up a chance at a chokehold."

Holly realizes that Nimrod's sucker punch while she wasn't looking was indeed a ruse to get her into the very position she is in now. And she also knows what's next. Nimrod's fangs extend and sink into her forearm. She tries to pull away again, but can't.

Nimrod slurps deeply from her arm. As he does, Holly ages rapidly and she quickly loses her strength. Her hair turns white again and her wrinkles return. Within moments, she looks as old and emaciated as she did on the Pirate Ship. After a minute of this, Nimrod pulls away from Holly's arm and wipes a trickle of red from his lips. He breathes in heavy gulps. More veins pop out in the muscles of his arms and neck. He grabs her by the throat and lifts her completely off the ground. Her suddenly frail body hangs from his grip like kelp hanging from a fisherman's hook. A new strength surges through him and he laughs maniacally.

CHAPTER 37

In the sky over the Carpathian Mountains, Ooby and Doodle steer their reindeer through the air side by side at full speed as they exchange punches, each trying to dismount the other. Far behind them, the explosion can be seen. Comet and Cupid seem oblivious to the fight occurring on their backs. They smile when they get near each other and frown when they are steered apart.

Doodle seems to be winning the high-flying fight since Ooby's punches are losing power the longer they go at it. He misses his target nearly every time he throws a punch while Doodle's blows become more precise and painful. Veering in close, Doodle grabs Ooby and they wrestle from their mounts. Ooby grabs the small crystal from his pocket and seems like he might use it when Doodle successfully tears it from his hand. Then, he rips the crystal necklace from Ooby's neck. Ooby is able to swipe Doodle's refashioned Time Bender watch from his wrist in the meantime and Doodle is so intent on procuring the pair of small crystals that he doesn't even notice. They steer away from each other, but Doodle zips back in and resumes pummeling Ooby with haymakers.

Ooby veers Comet away. Doodle pursues, but Ooby stays ahead. He leans forward and whispers something in Comet's ear. A few yards behind, Doodle sees Ooby put something in Comet's mouth, as if feeding him. Doodle heel-kicks Cupid harshly to make him accelerate and they catch up.

"I have the crystals, Ooby! There is no way to beat me now!" Doodle yells.

As they pull alongside, Ooby turns and leaps on Doodle, tackling him and driving him off Cupid's back. They fall to a mountain peak below, wrestling the whole way down. Comet continues on, not looking back. Cupid tries to follow him, but Comet streaks out of sight at superspeed under the effect of the Time Bender. Cupid slows and circles back around toward Doodle and Ooby.

On one spire of rock out of many in the high peaks, Doodle has worn down Ooby's defenses and is slugging him at will.

"You think I never listened to you, but when you and Nicholas practiced martial arts, I listened!" Doodle yells as he throws a mighty right cross that connects hard. Ooby crumbles at his feet, helpless. Doodle picks him up as if to body slam him, but he pitches Ooby like a limp doll, across a deep crevice, to another spire.

Down and away, in the castle courtyard, Nicholas crawls from the large crystal, his clothes blackened and charred by his narrow escape from the chopper's explosion. He looks up in time to see Nimrod carrying the defeated and aged Holly toward the gate to the drawbridge.

Through the combatants still battling in the yard, Nimrod turns and sees Nicholas. He drops Holly to the ground like litter, watching Nicholas the whole time. He continues through the gate alone. Nicholas hobbles through the melee, where Captain Dagger and Van Helsing are dueling again. Van Helsing wallops Dagger, who falls at Nicholas's feet. Nicholas keeps on to Holly, unfazed by the events around him. He drops to his knees beside her and cradles her. Lupper comes up behind Nicholas.

"Nicholas, sir. I will see to her," Lupper says with grave concern.

Nicholas lifts Holly's frail body as he glares at Nimrod through the gate, who is now on the drawbridge, staring back with a callous smile.

"Protect her, please," Nicholas says.

"With my life, sir," Lupper returns.

Nicholas gives her over to Lupper, who handles her gently. Nicholas turns and exits the castle through the gate.

On the drawbridge over the moat, Nimrod waits in the middle. He's a frightful specimen, veins and muscles popping out everywhere and rage emanating from him in a dark aura. The heavy steel gate descends behind Nicholas. Not only does that block a path for any kind of retreat back into the castle Nicholas might make, but it also blocks out most of the light from the castle. Only indirect light from the village makes it possible for Nicholas to see Nimrod in the darkness.

"Thanks to your girlfriend, I have more of your blood than you do," Nimrod snipes. He charges Nicholas, who retreats, circling to the side on the narrow bridge. Nimrod charges again, but Nicholas retreats once more. "You are right to be scared of me! I am now what all Pyres will soon be again!" Nimrod taunts, squaring himself with Nicholas's new position.

"Doodle lied to you," Nicholas rasps, his voice weak.

Nimrod advances toward Nicholas a few steps. "No. He's right. You want to oppress us. You and Ooby and Sarcastacles and all the humans. You want to keep us under foot!"

"Sarcastacles and Ooby and I only want to protect your kind. All the Pyres know that but you," Nicholas says.

"We don't have to be protected! We are mighty!" Nimrod pounds his chest with balled-up fists.

"Not against Men. Not when they decide you are a threat to them."

"Untrue! Did you see what my Pyres are doing to the Slayers Guild in there?"

Nicholas holds up his hands in surrender. "Have you forgotten whose side you were on in this fight? You brought the Slayers Guild, re-member? The Pyres are in there fighting against you right now."

"Yes, but the Pyres. My Pyres... they..." Nimrod shakes his head as if to clear it. He points at Nicholas. "Doodle said you would confuse me with talk!"

He puts his fists up and steps rapidly after Nicholas in pursuit again. Nicholas circles away. "A fight will solve nothing," Nicholas implores.

"Fights solve everything! That's how you and Ooby deal with hu-man criminals, isn't it?"

Nicholas stops. "Only to protect children and only when there's no other option."

Nimrod laughs. "You know as well as anybody that fighting is nature's way of separating the strong from the weak! So put up your dukes!"

Nicholas charges Nimrod and leaps with surprising agility and strength. He punches Nimrod in the face, knocking him back several yards to the edge of the drawbridge. Nimrod takes the blow, but quickly recovers.

"Your blood rebuilds in you," Nimrod says, a bit shocked by Nicholas's power. "I shall help myself to that, too."

"You have plenty of blood, Nimrod," Nicholas responds. "It's heart you lack."

Nimrod charges, head down like a linebacker. Nicholas kicks him, flipping him over to his back. Nicholas leaps on him, attempting a quick finish, but Nimrod scrambles out from under him. They wrestle until Nimrod shrugs him off. They stand and square off again. Nimrod attacks with a flurry of mighty punches. Nicholas dodges the blows.

In the courtyard, the Pyres, Freedom Fighters, and the Vanhelsingers gradually realize Nicholas and Nimrod are fighting on the drawbridge outside the closed gate. The skirmishes cease as the fighters go up on the ramparts to watch.

The Pyres and Vanhelsingers line the castle walls overlooking the bridge. Nicholas is genuinely struggling to keep clear of Nimrod's furious attacks. Finally, Nimrod connects with a punch, sending Nicholas reeling across the bridge. Nicholas tries to regroup, but Nimrod is on him, his rage reaching a crescendo again. He kicks Nicholas, then uppercuts him. Nicholas goes down. Nimrod straddles him and rains down blows.

"Succumb and the rest will, too! You can save yourself and countless others if you just give up!" Nimrod commands. Nicholas fights to his stomach under Nimrod, but Nimrod sinks a deep headlock. Blood streams down from Nicholas's nose. Nimrod sees it and smiles. His fangs extend and he is about to sink them in Nicholas's neck, but Nicholas pounds an elbow to the side of Nimrod's head. He grabs Nimrod in a side headlock and flips him to the ground. The fight begins anew.

"Saki!" Nicholas yells out. "Now, Saki!"

Nimrod escapes and leaps to his feet. He peppers Nicholas with body blows. Nicholas goes to both knees, breathless. In a barely audible whisper, Nicholas repeats, "Saki."

In the now vacant courtyard, Saki, still hiding, hears Nicholas's first call for him. He digs his cell phone from his pocket. The screen has an image of a red button on it with a series of coordinates below it. He moves to press the button when he is grabbed and dragged from his hiding spot. It's Van Helsing. He pitches Saki across the yard. Saki hits the cobblestone floor hard and his cell phone clatters away. Van Helsing steadies his stake gun on him.

"It'd be a good idea not to move," Van Helsing says, but Saki does. He leaps for the phone. Van Helsing stomps on him with his foot, right in the middle of his back, flattening him on his stomach. Saki yelps. Van Helsing puts the barrel of the gun between Saki's shoulder blades. "I've waited a long time to put a stake in somebody's heart and it's gonna happen tonight. Vampire or not!"

Just then, a bat flits around Van Helsing's head. He waves it away just as Sarcastacles steps out of the shadows. He rushes Van Helsing, but Van Helsing turns and fires, striking Sarcastacles right in his chest with the stake. Sarcastacles falls backwards.

Van Helsing turns to Saki, who is going for his phone again. "I thought I told you not to move!" He re-cocks the stake gun and Saki freezes. Behind him, Sarcastacles rises up, his body perfectly straight, his arms crossed like a frightful vampire rising out of a coffin in so many old movies. The stake protrudes from between his hands as if it is stuck in his chest. Van Helsing looks at him with shock.

"It's right in your heart! How could you survive that?" Van Helsing barks, indignant.

Sarcastacles pulls the stake away from his chest. It never penetrated his skin. Its tip is broken, practically sawdust. "Your tent poles have termites. Too long in the warehouse perhaps?" Sarcastacles says in his most sardonic tone. He upper-cuts Van Helsing, rocketing him five feet in the air before he falls flat on his back, instantly knocked out.

Saki finally gets his phone. He presses the button on the screen and the coordinates light up. "Please finally work!" Saki implores.

Far away in Eno, a group of Saints are sitting at new computer consoles, rebuilt by Ooby after the previous year's events. They are tapping feverishly on their keyboards. On the large screen over them, a schematic diagram of a satellite with big, mirrored plates is outlined in red lights. One Saint crosses her fingers on one hand and presses the ENTER key with the other. The satellite's diagram turns green.

"That's it!" she chirps happily. "It's on! We fixed it!" All the Saints cheer.

In the courtyard in Vam's Castle, there is a loud beep on Saki's phone and the coordinates begin changing at a rapid rate. A blinking box fills the screen. It reads, *Satellite Re-Targeting in Progress.*

In Earth's orbit, a Satellite that looks like the schematic on the computer screen in Eno repositions its plates against the Earth's curved horizon. The reflected sunlight gleams and dances in the mirrors.

On a large farm in Okinawa, Japan, bright daylight illuminates the fields for an instant. Suddenly, the sunlight retreats to the West, like a spotlight that has been pulled away. Night falls again on the fields with the withdrawal of the reflected light from the sun on the other side of the planet.

In the South China Sea, the half mile wide beam streaks across the water. Then, it bolts over the mountains of China and Tibet. The light flits over two Sherpas by a fire. It's gone before they even look up. The light continues over the countryside of Afghanistan, a momentary, fleeting brilliance in the darkness. The waters of the Caspian and Black Seas come and go in the blink of an eye, as well as the Georgian and Turkish lands that lie between them.

On the castle drawbridge, Nimrod plows Nicholas against the fortified gate. Nicholas can't offer any more resistance. He's much too weak now. Much too injured. Nimrod grasps his throat and extends his fangs again as he holds Nicholas against the gate.

"Good to the last drop," Nimrod growls. He sinks his fangs into Nicholas's neck. As he does, he gains even more strength and Nicholas begins aging at a rapid rate like Holly did.

The Satellite's light beam flits across Romania until it stops abruptly on the castle and lights the dark drawbridge as if high noon has come in a split second. Nimrod, feasting on Nicholas's neck, is blinded by the light. Though his body has grown strong with so many blood infusions, his eyes haven't. He throws up his arm to shield them. Nicholas, near death and as old and frail as he appeared so long ago when Ooby found him in the Turkish chapel's courtyard, grabs Nimrod in a bear hug. Nimrod, eyes squeezed shut, tries to pull away, but Nicholas presses Nimrod's chest with all of his remaining might. Under the pressure, the blood that had been leaving Nicholas and going into Nimrod through his fangs reverses course and begins flowing back into Nicholas.

Nicholas opens his eyes with a spark of renewed strength. Nimrod tries to pull away again and retract his fangs, but Nicholas holds Nimrod's face to his neck. With his other hand, he continues to compress Nimrod's chest. Nimrod's skin goes pale and his muscles deflate. Nicholas keeps on squeezing him until he shrinks considerably. Soon, he is as puny as he was on the Pirate Ship.

Nicholas, totally revitalized and young again, finally lets Nimrod fall to his back on the bridge. Nimrod's fangs retract and he appears to pass out. Nicholas stands over him in the bright daylight for a moment. The group of Pyres have shielded themselves from the sunlight by pulling up the hoods of their robes and donning sunglasses. They, and the Freedom Fighters beside them on the ramparts above, cheer Nicholas's victory. He gives them a quick wave as he turns to the gate. He tears through it with his bare hands, bending the steel bars wide enough to step through.

Before Nicholas can re-enter the castle, Nimrod leaps on his back from behind and throws his arms around his shoulders. He makes a desperate attempt to bite into Nicholas's neck again, but Nicholas reaches up and grabs Nimrod by the top of his head, palming his skull with one hand like it's a basketball. He pulls Nimrod completely over his shoulder, sending his feet flailing in the air in a high arc. He smacks Nimrod against the drawbridge, as casually as if he were slapping a wet towel against a pool deck.

Nimrod had pretended to be unconscious seconds before. He wasn't pretending now.

Nicholas looks up at the rampart and makes eye contact with Twerpitina, still cheering his victory. "See to him, please." He then hurries into the castle.

President Applebaum is among the group of Vanhelsingers who have watched the fight from the rampart. Once Nimrod is down for the count, he turns to the others nearby.

"Find Van Helsing and let's get out of here," he says to the others in a low whisper.

Tiddlywink points to the far end of the courtyard. "Found him." Van Helsing is still out cold on his back from Sarcastacles's punch.

Applebaum shakes his head. "Follow me back to the plane. We'll be stateside in no time."

Dimwiticus and Dipstickio lead a band of twenty Pyres to the rampart on one side of the Vanhelsingers, blocking their escape. "Don't think so," Dipstickio says.

Applebaum and the others turn and start the other way, but Captain Dagger, Achilles, Wallaby, and Spitball Spalding, straw at the ready, file onto the rampart, blocking their escape in that direction, too. President Applebaum stops, as do the others, knowing they are totally surrounded.

"Do you know who I am?" he demands.

The Pyres all nod. "You were the President of the United States," Dimwiticus says. "But that is no more."

"Hah!" Applebaum clucks. "I'll be back in my office in Washington by morning!"

Idiotis flies in close to the rampart on Dasher's back. He's holding a cell phone in his hand, the light on top shining in President Applebaum's eyes. "Smile for the camera, former-Prez. We're live-streaming to the Senate and House of Representatives," Idiotis says.

President Applebaum is indignant. "Turn that off! I've a re-election to think about!"

Idiotis keeps the phone on Applebaum as Dasher hovers steadily. "I believe the new impeachment proceedings currently underway may hurt your re-election chances," he quips.

President Applebaum slumps, knowing his political career is over.

CHAPTER 38

Deep in the dark, icy Carpathian Mountains, on the two spires separated by a deep, narrow crevice, Doodle stands facing the beaten Ooby. The wind whips snow around them in a torrent. Ooby is beside a steep drop-off. He is exhausted, on his hands and knees, breathing heavily. Doodle wears the crystal necklace and has the second crystal in hand.

"I've won, Ooby! Admit it!" Doodle says in triumph. "For once in your miserable life, admit you've been beaten!"

Ooby just shakes his head. "You can beat me, but you'll never win the hearts of the Saints by demanding their allegiance."

"I don't care about them!" Doodle declares.

Ooby looks at him crossly. "I thought they were the reason you were so adamant about rebelling against me. I thought it was all for them."

Doodle dismisses the idea with a big, sweeping wave of his arm. "You and me! That's all that matters! Not the Saints! Not the Pyres! I don't care about any of them! It's always been about you and me! I want you to acknowledge that I'm smarter than you!"

"You're the smartest Saint I know," Ooby says with resignation.

That's not enough for Doodle. He demands more. "Admit I'm smarter than you!"

"Doodle," Ooby starts, but Doodle interrupts him.

"You're predictable and I'm not! If all else is equal between us, then that alone makes me better!"

Ooby fights to stand up on weary legs. He looks across the deep divide at Doodle and shakes his head with disappointment, then he limps along the edge of the crevice. Doodle prowls after him on his side. As they walk several feet along the edges, the gap between them quickly widens.

Finally, Doodle scoffs. "Even in abject defeat, you can't see the truth! So, now, I will finish our little standoff once and for all." He reaches for his watch, but it's not there. He raises his sleeve, looks for it for a second longer, then glares back at Ooby. "Where is it? Where is my Time Bender?"

"If I'm so predictable, you should know," Ooby says. He keeps shuffling on his side of the chasm, growing bolder and standing taller as the distance between them gets wider. Doodle keeps walking opposite him. It doesn't take long for them to be fifteen feet apart. Ooby finally stops and stares across the crevice. It's now too far to step across or even leap.

"Enough of this!" Doodle says as he makes circular waves with his arms and the faint fog around him coalesces into a thick cloud. He shoots the mist bank at Ooby so that it shrouds him completely. "Enough blathering! Welcome to Doodle's world of pain, Bub!" He yells the last words in earnest. He wasn't ironically or sarcastically mimicking Ooby's similar exclamations to bad guys he'd heard hundreds of times before. He was yelling at them because it was the first thing that came to mind. Had he given it much thought, he would have picked something else. Something far and away from anything Ooby would have ever said. He tries something new. "I meant 'Welcome to Doodle's universe of...'" His mind races to find another word for pain, but comes up lacking. "Nagging discomfort!"

Frustrated with himself, Doodle shakes his head, yells "Bah!" and pitches the crystal over the crevice at the misty cloud enveloping Ooby. Ooby makes no move to avoid it. Following it, Doodle runs to the edge of the crevice and leaps into the air in a side kick, roaring out all of his three hundred years of built-up angst and anger. He would never make it across the deep and wide expanse normally, but he has the power of the crystals and he uses it. He touches the necklace just as the other crystal is about to hit Ooby's face. Doodle disappears over the gouge in the mountain, but never reappears.

The crystal clunks off Ooby's forehead and falls to the icy rock beneath his feet. He bends down, out of the dissipating mist cloud around him, and picks it up. It isn't the crystal, but a chunk of glass from the earlier explosion. He tosses it into the ravine as a sad expression crosses his face. Doodle is gone again, out into a world that will not heal him, but make him meaner and more bitter. It breaks Ooby's heart.

Cupid swoops in over Ooby and hovers by him. Ooby climbs on Cupid's back and off they go, both dejected.

CHAPTER 39

Somewhere in a faraway desert, Doodle appears from oblivion, still in his perfect sidekick. He lands in the sand and is immediately disoriented as he looks around.

From above, Comet dives down and bites the necklace from Doodle's neck, then he swoops down and snatches the second crystal from the sand at Doodle's feet that he had dropped there just moments before Doodle's arrival. Before Doodle can react, Comet is high over him. It's then that Doodle sees his Time Bender watch around Comet's ankle. He futilely jumps for it, but isn't even close to reaching it.

"Come back here, dumb beast!" he commands, but Comet just looks down at him with something close to the same dejection Cupid and Ooby had shown. After a moment, Comet taps the watch with his nose and blurs in a time warp.

"Don't leave me out here!" Doodle cries. "I'll be good from now on! Honest!"

In an instant, Comet is gone. Doodle looks around and sees nothing but sand dunes and cacti. He turns his gaze back to the bright, cloudless sky. He stares upward, hopeful that Comet will return. When it is clear that he has been abandoned, Doodle gives in to his inherent rage once more. He clenches his fists and screams into the clear blue heavens.

"Ooby!"

CHAPTER 40

In the cavernous dining hall of Vam's Castle, Lupper tends to the frail and unresponsive Holly on one of several long tables. She appears older than ever with thin white hair and wrinkled, hanging skin. Nicholas rushes to Holly's side. Sarcastacles arrives right behind him. A small crowd of Pyres, Freedom Fighters, and Children from the ship begin to filter in.

"Holly, no! Holly!" Nicholas weeps as he runs his hands over her beaten and battered body. He kisses her forehead. "Don't leave me. Not yet."

Sarcastacles leans by Nicholas, puts his ear to Holly's chest, and listens. "She's very close, Nicholas. I'm so sorry."

"Give her my blood. Give her all she needs," Nicholas says as he rolls up his sleeve and thrusts his arm at Sarcastacles.

"It's too late for a simple blood transfusion, even if it's yours. In her state, it won't work." Sarcastacles lifts his head from Holly's chest and puts a sympathetic hand on Nicholas's shoulder.

Big tears flow down Nicholas's face. He drops his head beside Holly's face. Ooby flies through the open doors on Cupid's back. He leaps off and runs to Holly's side by Sarcastacles.

"I love you, Holly. I love you," Nicholas whispers.

Holly's eyes flutter halfway open. Her lips give a weak smile. Nicholas is ecstatic to see her slight movement. Ooby is behind Nicholas and sees Holly's weak and fading response. He then looks at Sarcastacles, who shakes his head slowly.

Nicholas stays focused on Holly. Her last moments are upon her and he wants to spend them looking into her hazy eyes. He smiles at her. His voice is soft and sincere when he says, "Holly, will you marry me?" She tries to focus on him. "Will you marry me? I want to be your husband."

A tear forms in her eye. She gives a slight nod.

Sarcastacles hears Nicholas's quiet proposal. He nudges Ooby. "Can you perform a marriage?"

"Can I? As the first ever Justice of the Peace appointed by Richard the Lionheart in 1195, I'd say I can," Ooby pipes. Then, his eyes light up and he looks at Sarcastacles hopefully. "If they're married…"

"No," Sarcastacles mutters. "We can't. Don't even think about it."

"Why not? Comet has the Time Bender! We can use it to find the large crystals, get one of them to Eno, and then we can bring Enlitas and Excitas back here! We can do it!"

"Time is too short, even with the Time Bender," Sarcastacles retorts. "There's nothing we can do. I'm very, very sorry, but there is absolutely nothing we can do. The thing you're asking me is very uncertain under normal circumstances, much less dire ones such as these. It can't happen like this and it can't happen so quickly."

Nicholas turns to Ooby, his expression pleading. "Please Ooby. Perform the marriage." Ooby pushes by Sarcastacles to get closer to Holly and Nicholas.

Ooby puts one hand on Holly's shoulder and the other on Nicholas's. Everyone in the room falls quiet. There is absolute silence. No one moves. No one breathes. Ooby stares into Nicholas's face, who won't look away from Holly.

"Are you sure about this, Nicholas? Marriage is forever. This isn't just because of her grave condition, is it? You have to be sure it's for the right reason."

"Ooby, I'm sure!" Nicholas asserts urgently.

"Nicholas, you're acknowledging before the Creator that she, Holly Siltoe, is the only person, in your long years, that you would consider marrying, and if it were possible, you would live with her for the next thousand years and beyond?" Ooby recites quickly.

"I do acknowledge. Absolutely, I do." Nicholas says.

Ooby turns to Holly, who is on the closest edge of her eternal night. "Holly, is Nicholas the only man for you? The only Earthly man with whom you would live out your days, whether it be seconds or eons?"

Holly uses all of her strength to answer with her last bit of breath. "He always... has... been." The exertion is too much. Her eyes close and her chest stops its ever so shallow rise and fall. Ooby grips Nicholas's and Holly's shoulders.

"Then it is done," Ooby says.

Nicholas bends over to kiss Holly's lips. It is a gentle kiss. A kiss of true love.

"Do it, Sarcastacles," Ooby whispers. "They're married. I'll take all the blame if it goes bad, but we must try. Please, my friend. Do it."

"I make no promises," Sarcastacles returns. While Nicholas kisses Holly's lips, Ooby steps away and Sarcastacles moves in. "I'm sorry, Nicholas, but this is going to hurt more than anything you've ever felt," he says lowly.

Sarcastacles opens his mouth wide, his fangs, this time, are long and frightful. He bites into the back of Nicholas's neck, who is focused on Holly and not expecting it. Nicholas rears up and howls in great pain. Sarcastacles stays on him as he pushes away from Holly and tries to shake Sarcastacles off. In seconds, Nicholas ages rapidly again and his skin withers. He roars until the night that threatens Holly finds him too.

CHAPTER 41

The brink of a black place. The edge of eternal darkness. The final journey that begins at such a stepping-off place is not completely foreign to Nicholas. After all, he had been there before, so long ago. He'd heard those words from Sarcastacles then. He heard him speak to them before he'd ever even met him.

"I'm sorry, Nicholas, but this is going to hurt more than anything you've ever felt," he'd said in that same low whisper. But that wasn't right, was it? He'd said something close to that, but not exactly. Nicholas searched his memory, fading as it was. Something was off.

Ooby. Sarcastacles had been talking to Ooby instead of Nicholas. That's what was wrong.

"I'm sorry, Ooby, but this is going to hurt more than anything you've ever felt."

Nicholas had heard Ooby's deep, painful cry after that as he himself was crying out now. Somewhere. Back in the light, Nicholas howled, but not here. On the precipice of eternity, he was silent.

The odyssey that nearly began the first time he was in this place ended when dawn's rosy fingers reached out and pushed the darkness back. He awoke then, not in the snowy courtyard of the modest Turkish chapel, but in Eno. It was the place he would come to call home. The small man that had approached him on that long ago Christmas Eve had told him a grand story of immortality and offered him an opportunity to continue his life's work. That small man was beside him then.

Ooby.

Like Nicholas had been, Ooby was comatose and on a precipice all his own. He was so very old and frail at that moment when Nicholas awoke. Much more so than he had appeared in the courtyard. Something had been sacrificed. Whatever it was that had been taken from Ooby had been, in turn, given to Nicholas.

He had sat up that day, young and vibrant and alive, when he had been awaiting death in the snow by the statue of Baby Jesus just, what felt like, a few moments before. He looked beside him. Sarcastacles was there then, his tall, pale appearance, so strange and disorienting. Then, he saw the unicorns. Excitas and Enlitas. What a revelation they had been with their single horns softly illuminating the darkened room. Nicholas gasped at the sight of the mythical beasts and nearly passed out, but Sarcastacles rushed to him and steadied him.

"It worked," Nicholas heard Sarcastacles say over him. "He's pulled through. Great job, Excitas and Enlitas. Your enchantment worked. He's alive. And look at him. He's so young and strong."

It was the first time such a thing was ever attempted.

Nicholas looked at the small, now frail being next to him, the Saint who would lead him on the greatest adventure a man had ever lived. Sarcastacles read his expression of concern.

"It's only temporary. He will heal and replenish himself in a day or two. An hour ago, he was much worse. A mere fig left in the sun to dry. It was necessary to take him to the same brink as you in order to save you. I transfused his Saintly blood into your long bones and it was blessed by the One Horns. Now your body produces the Saintly blood, too."

"Why would he do that?" Nicholas asked, his voice hoarse, but deep. He felt the booming resonance down in his chest in a way he hadn't felt in many, many years. "He barely knew me."

"Because he felt you were worth it. He says the two of you will be guardians for human children and Eno Saints for thousands of years to come." Sarcastacles helped Nicholas to the side of his cot. Then, Nicholas stood on his own. An inexplicable power surged through him.

"Why say 'human' children as if they are separate from you? And what are Eno Saints?" Nicholas stretched to his full height and felt the muscle fibers activate and fire throughout his body, like a new hot rod revving its engine for the first time.

"I'm not human," Sarcastacles said. He looked at Ooby. "He's not human." He looks back at Nicholas and smiles, just barely showing his blunt fangs. "You're not entirely human anymore either." He motions to the unicorns. "They're the most human souls in this room."

Was that sarcasm? Wondering, Nicholas tilted his head at Sarcastacles, his question clear in his expression.

"Of course, I'm being sarcastic," Sarcastacles answered without being asked, as if he somehow read Nicholas's mind. "They're unicorns, obviously. And sarcasm is totally my thing."

Sarcastacles patted Nicholas's arm and pointed to a door. "Let's get you something to eat. As soon as your stomach realizes you're awake, you're going to be starving. It's part of the process." He paused, then shrugged. "Or so I would assume. Actually, I can't really say what the process is. You're the first." He walked to the door.

Nicholas shivered a bit, suddenly very chilled. He grabbed his blanket from the cot behind him and wrapped it around his shoulders. "Is being cold part of the process, do you suppose?"

Sarcastacles threw open the door and Nicholas got his first glimpse of the icy world of Eno. "Oh, I'd say there's a good reason for that," he said. "Come. We have much to discuss."

Nicholas left that room that day with one more glance back at the small Saint who had given him new life. *Was he already younger than just a moment before? He certainly appeared to be. Is he really healing that rapidly?*

"What is this place," Nicholas asked Sarcastacles as he stepped into the glorious wonder of Eno, the city under the glacial ice-dome in Antarctica, with water lapping at his ankles. "Who am I now?"

But something wasn't right. Nicholas heard ripples and Eno didn't have a lake or a body of water of any sort. The memory began to fade as Eno darkened around him and Nicholas felt himself drift back to a supine position on the ground.

Cultures throughout history told of a black river between the world of the living and the world of what comes after. Was that where he was now? The fights with Nimrod, in both Athens and at Vam's Castle, were brutal and the damage he suffered both times was severe. Had it been too much? Perhaps, he had finally succumbed to his injuries that used to heal so easily.

Nicholas searched the darkness with new eyes as his agonizing howl from the living world still echoed in his ears. He was doing something back there. Giving something up. A thought crossed his mind. Did Ooby suffer a mortal injury at Doodle's hand? Had he demanded back the gift he had given Nicholas so long ago?

From his confusion and fogginess came another name. Not Ooby.

Holly.

It was his turn to sacrifice something so she could live. It would come at great cost to himself, just as it had Ooby. In the other place, Nicholas was paying that price. Something in him told him it was necessary. It was worth it. But here, in the deepening darkness, he was oblivious. There was just the sound of the water. Moving. Babbling. Its sound grew as everything else just faded away.

I can hear the river flowing...

CHAPTER 42

From the deep place of endless darkness, the sound of water persists. Not of a black river, though. No. It's the sound of the sea and the ebb and flow of gentle, lapping waves.

I am Nicholas, he thinks as he opens his eyes. *I am the Wonderworker. The defender of innocents. The Giver of gifts. I am alive.*

Nicholas awakens on a cot, the bright sunlight shining through every crack in the wooden hut. The hut is small and he is alone. He sits up slowly, appearing his young, vibrant self again. He has a distinct scar on his neck from Sarcastacles's bite.

And I am in love. Holly!

On shaking legs, he rushes out of the bamboo door and finds himself on a boardwalk over the water. He instantly recognizes the fifty huts on stilts that are linked by walkways over the sea. He is at a resort in Bora Bora. Nicholas looks up to the sunshine, which momentarily blinds him. A pitter patter of little feet on the boardwalk draws his attention. Twenty Saints, led by Lupper, run to him and surround him. They cheer happily at the sight of him.

"My friends!" Nicholas says, so glad to see them all. Lupper hugs his waist. From behind, he hears Ooby's voice.

"Doodle was right about one thing. Bora Bora is warm," Ooby trumpets. Nicholas turns. Ooby is coming from the next hut over. Sarcastacles, in sunglasses and a straw, wide-brimmed hat, must stoop to exit his hut next to Ooby's. Nicholas smiles wide as he and Ooby embrace, then Sarcastacles grabs them both in a tight hug.

"How is Holly? Is she here?" Nicholas asks with urgency as he breaks the embrace and looks from Ooby to Sarcastacles.

Sarcastacles is the one to answer. "I had to go deep into your vertebral bones, Nicholas. Deep into the marrow of your cervical spine and into your brain stem. It was the same for Ooby so long ago when he brought you to me. My apologies for the scars."

Ooby turns and pulls down his shirt's collar to reveal a two-dot scar high on the back of his neck. "Now we match," Ooby says.

"Did it work?" Nicholas begs, as he subconsciously reaches back and feels his own raised scar at the base of his skull.

"Comet came back with the large crystal in time for us to get you both back to Eno," Ooby states. "Sarcastacles did the transfusion and the One Horns gave the sacred enchantment for only the second time ever."

The unicorns, Enlitas and Excitas, emerge from another hut down the boardwalk and skip toward the growing crowd around Nicholas.

"Did it work?" Nicholas persists.

"She was taken so close to the edge, Nicholas. So very close..." Ooby starts.

"Ooby, did it work?" Nicholas nearly shouts the question.

Sarcastacles jumps in. "What Ooby is trying to say is that Bora Bora is a great place for a vacation, but a better place for a honeymoon."

Finally, Holly steps out of a hut, dressed in a white sundress and a flowery headband. She is young, appearing about 30 years old again, and she is absolutely beaming. The Saints cheer loudly again and clear a path as Sarcastacles and Ooby withdraw. Holly runs to Nicholas and leaps into his arms. He holds her and gazes into her eyes with deep love.

"Do you feel okay?" Nicholas asks.

Holly gushes her answer. "I feel married. Very, very married. To the only man I've ever loved!"

Nicholas smiles and he and Holly continue to stare into each other's eyes. "Mistletoe," he whispers.

She looks at him oddly. "Aren't you listening? We're married. I'm not Miss Siltoe anymore."

Nicholas shakes his head. He glances up. She follows his eyes and sees that Lupper is using a fishing pole to dangle a twig of mistletoe over their heads.

"Aah," she says. "Mistletoe."

They kiss, long and wonderful. The Saints explode in laughter. Out in the lagoon around the huts, Captain Dagger's patched up Freedom Fighting Fishing Ship sails into view as Excitas and Enlitas touch horns, sending a huge colorful blast of fireworks into the bright sky.

On the deck of the ship, Captain Dagger and Achilles, all the Freedom Fighters, and Sister Abby and the Children, and all the Pyres applaud at the sight of the fireworks over the lagoon. Jerkus McGerkis plays a fast-paced "I Saw Three Ships Come Sailing" on his accordion. The eight tiny reindeer frolic in the air over the ship.

On the boardwalk, Ooby, ever the pragmatist, folds his arms. He's smiling at the spectacle around him, but when he leans into Sarcastacles, his hushed whisper carries a concerned urgency. "It would have been better to postpone this merrymaking until after Christmas. The next three weeks are the busiest of the year for us."

Sarcastacles isn't going to let Ooby's hyper-active sense of worry bring down the gaiety. "Worry not, Ooby! The Pyres will visit Eno to help you catch up with your work!" He claps Ooby on the shoulder with unrestrained glee. "It's a great time for an extended family reunion!"

"Well," Ooby says. "I'm all for it, but you may want to bring some heated blankets."

Sarcastacles whips out his phone and shows Ooby something on the screen. "Already placed an order for something better."

Ooby squints at the picture on the screen, then laughs. "Yeah," he chuckles. "That will do, too."

Sarcastacles looks at his phone with a grin. "Love me some Black Friday deals on hot tubs."

Saki Crocodile emerges from a hut. Wallaby and several henchmen are behind him, carrying a platter with a red, multi-tiered cake.

"Who wants some Sriracha Wedding cake?" Saki exclaims to the crowd of Saints. "My mother's special recipe! It goes great with her Wasabi ice cream!"

Ooby, now clearly at ease, and Sarcastacles raise their hands as all the Saints break into dance to the tune coming from the ship.

And in the middle of all that, Nicholas and Holly still kiss.

Epilogue

In a faraway desert, Doodle shuffles through the sand, sunburned and weary. His shirt covers his head to protect him from the sun and his lips are chapped and peeling. In the distance, he sees a band of nine horses and riders across the plain, coming his way, with a scattering cloud of dust behind them. Nearby, he sees a cactus with a sun-faded and weather-worn sign pinned to it, which reads, "Wanted: Ornery Cuss and his Rootin' Tootin' Outlaws". There is a hand-drawn portrait of a big, mean cowboy.

Doodle eyes it as the riders pull their horses up to him, smothering him in the dust plume. The face from the poster is staring back at Doodle in real life when the dust settles. Ornery Cuss, big and grisly, with a tobacco-stained beard and tattered cowboy hat, stares down at him. Behind him, his Outlaws, equally hard and coarse, position their horses in a wall of meanness.

"Howdy, fellas," Doodle says with a sheepish wave. Ornery Cuss leans forward and spits a gooey black wad at Doodle's feet. The Outlaws burst into laughter, but Cuss just stares. "You must be Ornery Cuss," Doodle continues.

Ornery Cuss answers in a raspy, harsh voice. "Maybe I am. And maybe you run with the Sheriff who's been putting up them there 'Wanted' posters everywhere."

The Outlaws all draw their pistols and aim them at Doodle, who throws up his hands in surrender. When he speaks again, he does so with an adopted drawl of a cowboy. "I'm just passin' through! I don't run with no cotton-pickin' Sheriff!"

Ornery Cuss unsaddles and steps in front of Doodle, towering over him.

"In these parts, we take a man's word only if he makes a sacred vow." Ornery Cuss sneers at Doodle and spits another humdinger in his palm, making a black oozy puddle. Then, he offers his hand to Doodle.

"Spit shake, little man." There's a gross squish between them when they clench their hands. Ornery Cuss glares down at him for a moment. Finally, he nods with approval. "You check out." He looks around at his crew. "He checks out."

The Rootin' Tootin' Outlaws put away their weapons and relax a bit.

"How can we be of service, young buck?" Ornery Cuss continues. "Do you need a ride into town? A plug of chaw? Can of beans?"

"Actually, I was hoping to be of service to you, Pard'ner," Doodle replies. He shakes the grossness off his hand, then his eyes narrow into a glowering scowl as he glances from one Outlaw to the next until he is back on Ornery Cuss.

"How would you fellas like to make a world of money?"

THE END

Jeff Malphurs is a Respiratory Therapist from New Smyrna Beach, Florida. When he isn't writing or working, he enjoys spending time with his wife, Angie, and their two daughters, Zoe & Jillian. Besides *Santa Claus Rebooted & Revamped*, Jeff has also written a novel titled *The Finger of God*.